ADVANCE PRAISE FOR *SPEAKER*

Peter Wallace has written an unforgettable novel about communication, trust, faith, and the power of embracing our individuality. Entertaining, thought-provoking and beautifully written, *Speaker* is tough-minded magical realism for the 21st century. Trust me, you'll never talk to your pets the same way again.

> — **Karen Karbo, *New York Times* best-selling author of *Yeah, No. Not Happening.***

Part fable and part adventure story, *Speaker* is that rare piece of beautifully written fiction that both enchants and compels. Peter Wallace exalts in the hope and wonder of a child coming of age while exploring the deeper, more adult meanings of language. On the pages of *Speaker* is an imagined, stunning world where the animals have more wisdom and humor than adult humans could ever hope for.

> — **Ann Garvin, *USA Today* best-selling author of *I Like You Just Fine When You're Not Around***

In his highly original debut novel, Peter Wallace creates a cast of diverse urban characters in Brooklyn revolving around a recently transplanted 14-year-old boy, Hamish Taylor, who finds that he can talk with animals. A gift he barely fathoms, he must use it to protect the community he gradually builds around himself. Somewhat like in Phillip Pullman's trilogy, His Dark Materials, Wallace combines magic realism and moral clarity in a riveting story with an intellectual undertone. It is also a love song to Brooklyn. I recommend the audiobook version because the author's reading of his own poetic text is astonishing, as he finesses the mix of character and animal voices so perfectly.

> — **Laurie Taylor, author of *Said the Fly***

Hamish is an endearing and unforgettable character. This teenage boy, gifted as a Speaker to the animal kingdom, discovers he has a sophisticated mission and an array of surprising allies that puts him on par with yet deeper than Mowgli, Pi, or even snake-whispering Harry Potter. *Speaker* is a poignant book about the power of words and love and devotion to a higher purpose.

> — **Jeffrey Davis, author of *Tracking Wonder: The Surprising Path to Effortless Mastery***

D1502531

Set in a contemporary Brooklyn filled with stressed-out parents, Russian mobsters, eccentric chess players, streetwise cops, and a panther who hunts her prey in Prospect Park, *Speaker* is the story of a real teenager with real problems who learns he has uncanny powers that can change the world. A supernatural adventure and a journey through grief and coming-of-age, *Speaker* is one of those rare novels that resonates with readers of all ages.

— **Arthur Goldwag, author of *Cults, Conspiracies and Secret Societies* and *The New Hate***

In *Speaker*, Peter Wallace has fulfilled the ancient promise of storytelling as medicine: an immersive event from which we emerge inexorably changed. Masterfully weaving the polarities of the magical (yet utterly believable) voices of the animals with an unflinching navigation of the horrors human beings can perpetrate against one another and nature, Wallace transmits a potent message that we would not believe without the horror and we could not bear without the magic. Every sentence of *Speaker* is a surprise: an utterly original use of language and thought, yet resonating some primordial knowledge inscribed in our cells. When you close the book and walk out your door, you will find the world transformed, opened. Every living creature— the sparrow, the cat, the coyote, even the human—will be recognized as part of an intimate yet symphonic conversation that was always alive beyond your awareness. *Speaker* is an essential contribution to the tapestry of wisdom working to dissolve the illusory walls human minds erect against the natural world, walls that must go if we are to succeed in changing the vector of the real-life story of destruction coming to climax on our planet today.

— **Kim Rosen, author of *Saved by a Poem: The Transformative Power of Words***

SPEAKER

A NOVEL

Peter Wol

SPEAKER

A NOVEL

Peter Wallace

PARTICLE + WAVE PUBLISHING
Portland, Oregon

Speaker
© 2020 Peter Wallace

ISBN13: 978-1-7351552-0-3

This book is a work of fiction. Any references to historical events, real people, or real places are used fictitiously. Other names, characters, places, and events are products of the author's imagination, and any resemblance to actual events, places or persons, living or dead, is entirely coincidental.

First Particle + Wave edition 2020.
Ebook and audiobook versions available.

Particle + Wave Publishing
1715 SE 46th Avenue
Portland, OR 97215
info@particleandwavepublishing.com

Cover Design and Photograph by Alec Boehm
Interior Design by Stephanie Argy

Colophon
The body text was set in Adobe Garamond Pro, designed by Robert Slimbach and released in 1989. It was based on types by the French printer Claude Garamond (1480–1561). The font is considered one of the most eco-friendly types to print. The headers were set in Futura, designed by Paul Renner and released in 1927.

To the animals. All of us.

PART 1

LEARNING TO SPEAK

CHAPTER 1

By the time Hamish found out he was a Speaker, he'd been through two of the three telling traumas of a young life: the death of a loved one and the uprooting of his home. Divorce, the third, of course became impossible once his father had passed.

Nobody could understand how a Speaker could appear so young. Usually, the skill of understanding all different animal speech comes with maturity. Hamish was many things, but at fourteen he was certainly not mature.

I suspect his father knew his true nature.

This is what Hamish tells about the moment he knew his father was going to die:

Hamish was just beginning to forget about the unfinished cancer. Ed, the main stable hand at Mohegan, had called and asked Hamish to grab his bike and get to the stables.

"It'd only take you a minute," Ed said. "Your daddy's asking. Got a problem with Aching Thunder—you know, that mare, stubborn as a goat in July?—she having some issues with her foal. Your daddy think you maybe got the touch to get her going, get this little one outta her. You game?"

Hamish had been a help to his father as Henry moved away from his disease and back into his veterinary work, and not in the way a child is let in on adult activities, not like a boy gathering sticks instead of real firewood. His father had said he'd never seen anyone who attracted animals to him the way Hamish did, which makes it seem as though he knew something of his son's future. Songbirds landed within reach of Hamish's hand when he was outside. A chipmunk would occasionally zip through his legs as the shortest route home. Late one spring night, his family came home to find a bear leaning against the front door where they lived in the Pennsylvania hills. It ambled over to the car as they drove up and tapped on Hamish's window as though it had an appointment. And the horses in their stalls always walked over to him, snuffling in his hair and gently shoving at his chest with their muzzles.

Hamish arrived at the track stables sweaty, tossing his bike to the ground and running down the row of stalls. Henry, on his knees, looked up from the supine horse.

"Oh, good! Let's see what—"

But Aching Thunder, her belly round as a giant's potato, suddenly lurched herself around and up to her feet, leaning back and forth to get her balance. She moved towards Hamish, opening her mouth as though to bite him. Henry reached to grab the halter, but Hamish raised his hand to her neck.

"I got her," he said to his dad, and his dad let go. Hamish could feel the hot quivers of the mare's skin, smell the stinky paste of fear in her blood. The pain registered as huge—night broken by hollow streaks of lightning. Hamish leaned his face into Aching Thunder's cheek.

"Hurts, hunh?" he whispered.

The foal started coming out with a gush of fluids, its front legs under its head as though it were praying. Henry eased it to the ground, and Aching Thunder turned to look. She pushed at Hamish's head to get him out of the way, and she stood still, her flanks shivering a bit.

Sometimes you just need the right witness.

Henry threw the towel he'd been using to wipe down the foal out of the stall. He yanked a stethoscope out of his bag in the corner and shouldered the ends into his ears, placing the diaphragm on the foal's body as though putting pins in a map. He flung the stethoscope over his right shoulder, the curve of the ear pieces hanging on his neck, and he pushed and pushed on the foal's ribs. Then he suddenly grabbed the foal's head, holding the mouth tightly closed, and sucked mucus out of the nose. He turned and spat gobs into the hay. Then he put his mouth back on the small horse's nose, and breathed in.

"Ed," he said between breaths. "Massage the chest. Right there."

"Got it." Ed, with the hands of a craftsman, moved the new muscles and bones, trying to help the air get into the lungs, while Henry Taylor breathed into a new-born horse's nose.

Hamish's hand rested on Aching Thunder's neck as they watched, sure the foal would cough and rise.

But it was Henry who coughed. The fit consumed him. Hamish could see blood on his chin, and he was hoping it belonged to the foal, but knew it came from deep inside his father, magma bellowing up from under surfaces not meant to be breached. His father was choking, and Ed turned all his attention to him.

Hamish couldn't get his hand off Aching Thunder, not until the ambulance came, and Ed removed his hand gently, like a prop that was going to be used again. He never knew whether the foal lived or died.

∞

Sarah Taylor got a day shift, and Henry Taylor's doctor's appointments started anew. Then there was the hospital again. After they took out Henry Taylor's voice box in the fall and they started radiation and chemo again, Hamish and his dad exchanged notes on a steno pad, "The Mute Pad." Hamish wrote back on the same page as his father. Sometimes he drew. He started not talking just as a game since his dad couldn't talk yet. His mother wasn't worried because he still talked, on occasion, with her and with kids in his school. So he wasn't acting out, even though he seemed young for fourteen. But it became a point of pride, and a new way of communicating with his dad that no one else could share.

One note started as Hamish drawing a boy falling down an endless hole with a winged elephant's trunk acting as a bungee cord that the boy's outstretched hand held onto. Henry Taylor had written,

You know you're crazy, right?
Hamish had written back, *Not as crazy as you!!!*
Why? Cuz I got this cancer craziness going on?
Oh that and so much more!!!
What more???
I could tell you, but then I'd have to kill you.

Or:
You want to become a vet like your old man?
SOOOOO old!!!
You have a gift with animals.
I don't know. Maybe.
It may be more than a gift.
What are you talking about?
More soon. Too tired....
Or sober, on one little sheet:
Your mom?
6:00.
Eat.
Are you going to die?
Squiggly pen marks crossed out a couple of lines, then:
I will die. I will not want to, but I will. It will seem like the hardest thing in the world for you, but it won't be. It
That note never finished.

Hamish kept all the notes in an army green box that held, among other treasures, a fossil shell collected on the Maine coast when he was younger, a nearly whole robin's egg, pale blue-green in its nest of Kleenex, one of his baby teeth, a small wedding photo of his parents, and a postcard from Bali that his aunt Shirley had sent him when he was five.

And then, with a suddenness that was inexplicable, his dad was in a hospice facility forty minutes from their house.

And then he was gone.

Hamish forgot even the most mundane things, like whether he had brushed his teeth. There were vacuumed gaps in his days and nights which frightened and numbed him. There was such a rush and Hamish couldn't get his bearings, a sailor suddenly on impenetrable land after months on a rocking and frothy sea.

Everyone always said it was going to be OK.

There was a movable gathering – first in a funeral home, then at a graveyard, and finally in his house. He knew it was the funeral but he could only watch as though covered with plastic. His rich Uncle Colin, Henry's brother, held him for an eternity in an inarticulate hug and then put him out to arm's length.

"I'll make sure you guys are looked after when you come to Brooklyn," he said, nodding at his own thoughts. "Aunt Cammy and the kids, well, you know we all love you."

"Brooklyn?"

"How dare you tell him!" It was Hamish's Aunt Shirley, in from the West Coast. Ten years younger than her sister, she was a fierce free-spirit – at least that's what Sarah called her. "That's not your job. You fucking rich people." Shirley smacked Colin's arm hard. She was a little drunk.

"I just wanted to—" Uncle Colin backed away.

"Well, don't!" Shirley pushed him.

Sarah moved in. "Shirley Weg, stop that!"

"But he –"

"What do you mean, Brooklyn?" Hamish tried.

"Don't—"

Hamish yelled, "What do you mean, Brooklyn!"

His mother turned to him, nervous and abrupt. She confirmed it: they were moving to Brooklyn, a place he'd visited once when he was six, a place that just seemed like movement and cousins who knew more than he did in a country where he didn't even speak the language. Before he could recover from the horror, they were packing and eighth grade was over and he didn't really have a chance to say goodbye to anyone. They moved.

∞

Brooklyn.

A strange place for the emergence of a Speaker. It sounded to Hamish like a place out of old movies with harsh, fast people who had been to war, or who lived above bars and walked the streets with swagger and fear. It seemed like a sentimental place, with one tree growing in it, where children get sick and die hopeless deaths surrounded by poor family members and neighbors who can do nothing. It looked like a gray and rusty place, all asphalt and crumbling edges, with crowds of odd-looking characters in washed-out colors and cars lining every street as though waiting for the junkyard. Hamish could not imagine being cursed to a worse hell.

Back towards the end of May, Sarah Taylor had gone to New York City for a few days, leaving Hamish with Saba and Bubbe Weg, Sarah's parents who'd come up from Florida to stay for a while after Henry's death. She instructed them all to pack up the house. When she'd come back, it was like his mother had turned into a different person, infected by that city with wide-eyed urgency and a forced, winner-take-all enthusiasm. She'd laid it all out for him, like a surgeon explaining a complicated double-amputation to the patient.

"They call it a railroad apartment because it's laid out like a railroad car, you know, long and narrow. We were so lucky to get it, especially in Park Slope. Uncle Colin has this connection, this guy in real estate, who knew the owner of the building and someone had just moved out, so he put in our name and we got it. No fees. The rent's OK. You get your own room. Look—" and she pulled over a piece of paper and a pen and started drawing a long rectangle.

"Mom— "

Drawing. "Here's the living room. You can see out across the street to the park. Here's your room. The window only goes onto an airshaft, but it's something. I know it's not like you've got here, but we're on the top floor so you get some light."

"Mom. Mom!"

"Honey…"

"Why do we have to move?"

"What do you mean? We talked about this."

"You talked about it. I never said anything. I just don't get why we have to go."

"Hamish, I got a job there."

"You had a job here!"

"It's a better job. And we've got a lot more family around there than here. We've got no one here."

"You've got no one. I've got someone. I've got my friends. This is where I grew up. Besides, you don't even like that family. You think Cammy is a phony and you've always hated Colin for how he treats Dad. How he treated Dad."

Sarah bowed her head. She crumpled the paper. When she looked up at Hamish, there were tears starting in her eyes which she sniffed back.

"I've got to go," she said, "And you're going with me. We're going to try something different."

"There is no reason to go to Brooklyn." He stood up, knocking over the chair behind him.

His grandfather Saba Weg came to the doorway. "Everything OK?" he asked.

Hamish tried to drill holes with his eyes. "You can't make me," he said to his mother. "I am already—I have plans—high school, here. Just because dad died doesn't give you the right to ruin my life."

Sarah's eyes were streaming tears as she tried to peer into the refrigerator.

Hamish screamed and stamped from the kitchen, backhanding a coffee cup on his way out that smashed through the backdoor window that he knew someone would have to clean up.

They moved to Brooklyn.

∞

Hamish called his best friend Charlie O'Keefe back in Plains. They made up schemes for his escape. He could get a bus from Port Authority to Wilkes Barre, and then hide out over the summer. At the end of August, he could just arrive at school the first day as though they'd never moved. How would the school know? He'd get most of his food from the school, and Charlie would help. He knew of places he could homestead—barns and abandoned cabins he and Charlie had scouted as kids. He could even break into summer houses, staying quiet all fall and winter, until spring would bring new hope and new solutions.

The day after they got to Brooklyn, Sarah's shift started early. Hamish waited until she'd had a chance to get on the subway before he began to pack his bag with care, taking good boots and a jacket for a different winter, his entire savings of $473 in cash, some pens and paper to keep himself from going crazy, his treasure box, a sleeping bag and some of the family's camping equipment. By 4:00 that afternoon he was in Pennsylvania, on the street, heading towards his rendezvous with Charlie.

They were going to meet at the new Starbucks that had opened just before Henry Taylor had died, where Charlie and Hamish used to meet to have coffee and grown-up conversations. Hamish went into the coffee and spicy smells and wash of air-conditioning, looking around for Charlie. Charlie was at the back and looked like he'd just been arrested. Sitting with him was Mrs. O'Keefe, who turned and looked at Hamish wearily.

As she drove him back to New York, Mrs. O'Keefe droned about the times she moved, how she thought it was the end of the world but it wasn't, how when people died they went to a better place, how time healed. Hamish wanted to reach over the seat and throttle her, crashing the car and feeling his flesh burn in the gasoline fire and hear her and Charlie screaming in pain before ambulances and fire trucks roared up to the hopeless cause. But he sat in the back looking at the darkening landscape slide by, pulling his lower lip out and letting it go.

When he got to the apartment in Brooklyn, his mother tried to embrace him at the door, but he shouldered his way past and into his room. He heard the two mothers talking, expressions of sympathy and support and gratitude and commiseration, all out of the playbook on mothers of adolescents in crisis.

∞

I know Sarah Taylor felt a desperation for Hamish and herself that only movement could fill. She couldn't get anything out of him. The conscious concrete of his adolescent silent treatment squatted in a sludge of violence; the pediatric oncology ward where Sarah worked was a haven compared to this.

Sarah determined Hamish was going to be occupied, and with the help of her sister-in-law Cammy Taylor in Queens, she signed Hamish up for a chess class and something called Junior Rangers in Prospect Park, in the hope that his brain and his urge to escape to nature would be mollified. His uncle Colin had also promised to give him some part-time work at his real estate development company, just so all his time would be taken up.

"Honey," she said at his door. "You can't go out while I'm at work."

From the bottom of his room, "You're grounding me?"

"You ran away."

"I ran home," he said through the door.

"You can't do that and not tell me."

The door suddenly flung open. Hamish was tall enough to look her in the eye, and that shocked her.

"You decided we were moving to Brooklyn without telling me."

She held his eye. She could see him, restless as a caged monkey.

"Fuck you," He said. He grabbed his keys and headed out the door as though it were his job.

CHAPTER 2

Hamish knew his life was ruined completely. Movement seemed to be the only thing that calmed him. He spent every free moment walking, walking in as straight a line as he could until his calves were numb. His walks ranged for miles around Brooklyn. He found himself in industrial cul-de-sacs, on crowded blocks where there wasn't one other white face, in neighborhoods where clothing seemed more like costumes, on tree-lined streets with noisy clouds of green parrots instead of pigeons, on postcard beaches, movie-set row houses, bucolic schools, and strip malls in Chinese. He went from apocalyptic desertion to circus fecundity in the space of a couple of streets. Wide, crazy avenues with wild, crazy trucks and town cars driven by Italians and Nigerians and Ukrainians and Pakistanis and Hungarians and Ecuadorians and Jordanians. Or tiny streets, with small decorations on the quiet houses, a pot with a plant in front, maybe, with a small chained dog barking, or a motorcycle being repaired and smelling of oil on a tiny square of cement next to the brown plastic garbage cans. At any given moment on his travels, he found he could be in almost any given spot in the world if he blurred out his peripheral vision and sucked in his breath to silence the adulterating noises. He could be in the forest, he could touch the soil that breathed a darkness into his nostrils, that made him feel strong, that made him feel like the crumbs of black earth on his fingers digging through fallen leaves and loam were connected to his heart and his legs, and that when things got buried, they seeded and grew and you could come back and see them whole and giant and waving in the crackling winds, ready to walk with you over the mountains and into the white, white snow.

The chess club his mother had enrolled him in—a kind of leash, Hamish thought—met three times a week at a small storefront down on 4th Avenue, a mad-dash place furious with buses and trucks trying to beat the elevated highway traffic and taxis crowding out from and returning to their garages like desperate geese finding a landing spot in the pond. Then two days a week he was expected to show up at a "Junior Ranger" program in Prospect Park where they learned about flora and fauna even in the middle of the largest city in the nation. It only made him despise the city more. He couldn't believe there were people who didn't know where milk came from.

His first day at chess, his mother came with him, opaque to his distress at being left in a small room crowded with tables and mixed metal chairs and one young kid with a buzz-cut next to the wall playing a game of speed chess by himself, clicking the clock and banging pieces down on the files and ranks with childlike precision. Sarah Taylor had a low conversation with Kaphiri Shenouda, the teacher. Hamish, paying no attention, caught the words "summer" and "quiet" and "father" and "talented" and "lost."

"Not to worry, Mrs. Taylor," Kaphiri Shenouda said, taking her check and guiding her to the door. "We will not falter."

Sarah Taylor looked at him for a shocked second, trying to parse his peculiar phrase. She called to Hamish, "I'll see you at home," and then left with a bell tinkling on the door and a sucking of traffic that muffled under the doorjamb.

Kaphiri Shenouda turned like an elephant in a circus ring, his dark Egyptian eyes glittering from under brows that sprouted black hedges, only making sense because all the features of his face were way too big by themselves.

"Hamish Taylor. A strong name. A humble name. Good. Let's see your chess chops. Come."

Hamish was suddenly sitting at one of the tables with this large man who seemed as though he was actually sitting at four or five of the tables and occasionally dusting the walls with his voluminous clothing, even though the heat outside was enough to soften concrete and the air-conditioner over the door complained like a randy cat. His sausage fingers delicately placed the pawns.

"I place the men at their starting gate. You, the pieces. Give them homes."

Hamish reluctantly set up both the black and the white sides.

"Well done," said Mr. Shenouda with one clap of his hands. "But let us reverse the King and the Queen so the Queen is on her own color. This way she can recognize herself."

Hamish flushed deeply, ready to stammer an excuse for forgetting even the most basic thing. But the Egyptian moved forward like a flood.

"And now we begin. And this is the beginning." He reached his hand across the board. "My name is Kaphiri Shenouda, from Alexandria in Egypt. I am pleased to be your opponent."

Hamish looked at the hand in front of him as though it had appeared out of a cloud. He could not but put his hand into it, like putting his hand into a building made out of bread. It was strangely comfortable.

"Hamish Taylor."

"From?"

"Up on Prospect Park West."

"I thought you were from a place in Pennsylvania, the forest of the Quakers."

"I was. But we had to move."

"But that is still where you feel the presence of home, no?"

"I guess."

"Then. Until Prospect Park West is your refuge, your nest, where you are from will have to be elsewhere. And that is…?"

"Plains, Pennsylvania."

"Ah. Superb. You're white. It is your move first."

Hamish was not ashamed of his play. He knew that Mr. Shenouda was not bringing his full force to bear on the game, but his attention was generous and unwavering. When Mr. Shenouda moved a piece, always with a warm "Ah!" or calculating "Hmm," the round and crinkly scent of curry or flax urged itself across the chess set with the movement of his garments.

To close the brief endgame, Mr. Shenouda announced, "And now we finish with a: Check. Mate." He moved his remaining black rook gently next to Hamish's white king, and once again he extended his hand, into which Hamish's hand became folded. His smile was serious and inevitable.

"We have much wonderful work ahead of us." Little did either of them know, yet.

The small bell above the door broke into the room like a thief and four young teenagers crowded in out of the heat.

They were all boys, and so much like a miniature council of races it was comical. Mr. Shenouda made sweeping introductions.

"We have a new student with us, starting today. This is Hamish Taylor, newly from Plains, Pennsylvania, but his people come from here, and from Europe previously, Ireland and Russia many years ago. Hamish plays a very thoughtful game. Be careful of letting him relax.

"This is Daniel Zhao. His family is most recently from Hong Kong—"

"Mr. Shenouda! One hundred years is not recently. We're more American than you are."

"Of course you are. Daniel plays a reckless game and is therefore to be considered a dangerous and unpredictable player.

"Abraham Shelley. His people were brought here from West Africa 180 years ago. They have been in Brooklyn since the Civil War."

"Hey, man." Abraham shook Hamish's hand loosely.

"Abraham's game is very fast. He likes scorched earth. Do not play his game."

Abraham snickered and rolled his eyes as he threw his backpack on a chair.

"That is Steve Mondolfi. Jews from Italy who came early on the swelling tide of fascism—"

Steve looked up from adjusting pieces on a board, his jaw tighter than a strung bow, his blue eyes stretched with angst. "Oh, Jeeezus, Mr. Shenouda, can we just play?"

"Watch him, Hamish. He plays two games at once." Kaphiri Shenouda rotated his bulk easily to take a diminutive dark-eyed boy under his gaze. "And this is Pradeep Rao. His people hail from—"

"Yeah, yeah, India, we know, we know." Pradeep played up his annoyance.

"Not just India, but Tamil Nadu in the south, home of one of the oldest civilizations in the world."

"Why you have to do that?"

"Tell our newest where you are from?"

"Yeah," Pradeep turned on him. "What difference does it make?"

"Our past and our ancestry are a part of us here. It gives us a head start to know what that is."

"I still don't get why you do that all the time," Pradeep grumbled his way into his chair.

"Hamish, you will play Pradeep," Mr. Shenouda announced.

The rest of the afternoon was spent playing two games and watching Mr. Shenouda go through an endgame in which Abraham and Daniel were engaged. Steve played the kid with the buzz-cut who had been sitting by the wall when Hamish first came in. After a while, Hamish realized the kid was a girl. He kept on looking at her as she played, trying to figure out how old she was. She did not look up from her game. She moved her pieces confidently but disinterestedly, hitting the clock button with pieces that she captured. She won, and then ignored everyone, writing in a notebook for a while, then going to the back of the room and lifting a polka-dotted sheet that was over a bird cage and peeking under, mumbling in a falsetto.

Suddenly there was a piercing scream. Mr. Shenouda glanced back.

"Madonna!" he called to the jungle voice under the sheet. "You know we can't have that."

"Can I take off the cover, Kaphiri?" asked the girl.

"All right, my dear. But remember: do not put your finger near her."

The girl dragged the sheet down to reveal a cage with a large car-paint blue parrot bobbing its head and screaming its guttural scream again. The scream was cut off, and the parrot blinked, twisting its head as though to get a better perspective on the scene.

"Whoa," said Hamish. "Time out." And he went between the chairs to get closer to the parrot.

"She'll bite off your finger," whispered the girl. The parrot gave a chirrup in agreement.

Despite the warning, Hamish came close to the cage. She was a panoply of blues, with yellow rings around her black eyes, and yellow cheek flaps at the smiling point of her ivory black beak. She turned her head completely upside-down to look at Hamish, then whipped upright and came closer to him, shuffling along a wooden bar.

"Can she talk?"

"She has never said anything I can understand," said Mr. Shenouda, coming behind them. "Oh! Hamish, how remiss of me. This young person is my friend Polly."

Polly rubbed her buzz-cut hair and looked at Hamish with mysterious self-satisfaction.

"I thought you could teach parrots to talk," said Hamish.

"She is a hyacinth macaw, a jewel of her species. She was left in my care by a famous dancer when I was not all that much older than you are today. These creatures live an astonishingly durable time. But she cannot live in the wild; it has been too many years. She should be in the Amazon. But, alas, she is here, with me. I call her Madonna, don't I, yes." Mr. Shenouda handed Madonna a grape, which she took from his fingers with a delicacy suggesting connoisseurship. She walked the rest of the way on the wooden bar until she was as close to Hamish as she could get. Then she reached up to her beak with her foot, gently grasping the grape and handing it out between the bars in Hamish's direction.

"This is impossible!" gasped Mr. Shenouda. "You must take it. Carefully!"

Hamish lifted his hand slowly and took the grape. He sensed only momentarily the scaliness of the foot and the smoothness of the claw. For reasons unknown to him, he bit the grape in half with his teeth, chewing his half, and handing the other back to the bird. As she leaned her head to take it, Mr. Shenouda's breath sucked itself to a stop. She took the grape in her beak, and nibbled it, turning it with her foot, and watching Hamish the entire time.

The boys had all gathered around, and now asked if they could try it. Clearly, feeding Madonna had never been allowed. But Mr. Shenouda denied them their turns. He said quietly to Hamish, "You now have a friendship. And a responsibility." He patted Hamish's shoulder gently. "And there's someone you should meet." As impossible as Shenouda thought it was, he was already thinking of Thaddeus Knox.

Hamish nodded without hearing, watching the hyacinth macaw watch him.

CHAPTER 3

The shower could barely keep Hamish awake, even with only cold water stinging the top of his head. His body throbbed with heat. His skin was icy and hard and sticky with clean. He rubbed his hands quickly over its film of running water, ready to slap his hands on his stomach or thighs.

Sarah knocked and opened the bathroom door.

"Mom!"

"I'm sorry, honey." He could hear her slurp coffee. "You remember this is the weird week with my shifts all over the place. I have to be at the hospital in an hour. That silly Sunday dinner at your Uncle Colin's made me change my whole schedule. Oh! Dammit. I'm going to be late. Honey, I've got to go." She started out the bathroom door, her voice fading as she closed it. "You remember about Junior Rangers."

Hamish grabbed the shower curtain to get his head out. "Mom, that is so fucking stupid."

She stopped closing the door. "Well, you've 'fucking' got to go."

"Why can't I just stay here?"

"It's either that or you go to Queens to your aunt and uncle's. You want to spend every day with little cousin Drew?" Hamish said nothing. "Unh huh, I didn't think so. Today, it's Junior Rangers. Next week, you work with your uncle. There's directions about the Rangers thing—" she pointed to the kitchen table "—and a note from me if you need it. And I love you." She left the bathroom door open, and Hamish heard her leave the apartment.

Hamish and his mother had gone to his uncle's landed-gentry house in Queens the day before for an official welcome-to-New-York Sunday dinner. His Aunt Cammy served them soft-shelled crab, flown in every day from Chesapeake Bay to a shop in Manhattan and expensive as gold. His relatives were among the very wealthy. Hamish's father used to grouse that Cammy's mother, being old money, hated the peons who worked. She was only slightly mollified that Colin had money of his own, he having shepherded some of the largest real estate deals in the city. Hamish's three cousins were aliens, even though 17-year-old Samantha and her older boyfriend with his prosthetic leg intrigued and attracted Hamish so that he actually thought he would like to stay and become friends. They sang a duet together for Hamish up in the attic "music room," and Hamish felt he was in the presence of movie stars. He asked Samantha's boyfriend David how he had lost his leg, and David laughed a full and long laugh, saying no one had ever had the balls to ask him like that, straight out. His older cousin, Jeremy, was away at college, and eleven-year-old Drew stayed in his room with his guinea pig playing computer games.

Hamish's Uncle Colin, a plumper and buttoned-down version of Hamish's father, admonished him to appreciate the opportunity he was being handed by being able to intern in real estate, and cuffed Hamish's cheek as they said goodbye.

∞

The very idea of Brooklyn Junior Rangers made Hamish feel like a warrior who'd been handed a squirt gun. He felt accustomed to wilderness. The summer before Henry Taylor's testicles swelled and hospitals became a part of the family routine, Hamish and his parents went up to Maine to camp. It was the first time they had been able to get away together since Sarah had gotten her job at Geisinger Hospital about an hour away in Danville. They packed the car full of gear and tied the canoe on the roof. Hamish was awestruck at the firm swiftness of his dad's knots, and his confident shaking of the boat and car to make sure winds wouldn't launch the craft somewhere in New York or Massachusetts. As they were locking the front door, Henry stooped down to the eight-year-old Hamish.

"I've got something for you for this trip."

Hamish knew this was a grownup moment because Sarah said, "Henry, are you sure this is such a good idea?"

"We'll teach him. OK?"

Sarah sighed, clearly understanding this was going to happen. "OK."

Henry took a small red box out of his pocket.

"This is something you have to be careful with. You have to use it with great respect. For this summer, you can only use it when me or Mommy are around. OK?"

Hamish was mystified and already grateful. "OK."

Henry opened the box and extracted a Swiss Army knife from under its elastic. He handed its smooth lipstick-red and stunning mirror-chrome body to Hamish. It felt weighty and alive in his hand. He opened the main blade, pulling against oiled resistance until it clicked into place, ready to cut.

"It's very sharp," Henry pointed. "You can open all these other things when you like, but this one and this other smaller blade, only with us there. See that one?"

"Uh-huh," Hamish acknowledged.

"OK. Let's go."

Maine was a blur of compact adventures and isolated moments of practical wisdom, lodged like charged and life-altering photographs in his mind. His father teaching him how to make a fire with nothing but his new knife and three matches. A moose swimming in the lake, its rack of antlers dripping and oddly clumsy. Fresh-water mussels on the bottom of the cold water, seen through a mask that opened up a door to a vast and closeted world. Smoking out mosquitoes from the tent flaps in the rain. Tracking a black bear through a bog, and seeing it drift into trees up ahead. Paddling into the wind, knowing his father in the stern could steer them straight. Pulling foil-wrapped potatoes out of the fire with sticks, brushing off the ash and stabbing into the hot and soft flesh and watching butter melt into it. Landing a lake trout from deep in the cold, dark waters and splitting it open from anus to throat, spilling its innards back into the water and sloshing its body clean.

The second to last day, Hamish woke very early. His mom and dad were dark rumpled shapes in their sleeping bags. Hamish slid under the tent flap without zipping it open, avoiding that sharp cold sound. The air was moist and chilly in his nose. He put his jacket over his pajamas, planted his bare feet on the path that led further into the woods. He could feel pine needles and remnants of fallen branches on the soles of his feet that pushed slightly into the loam as he walked. He could hear the breeze on the lake, feel it as the air arrived through the trees. The sky was not even blue yet, it was so early.

The first wolf appeared in front of him about ten yards away. He could see about seven of them in a loose semi-circle between the trunks and undergrowth. The first wolf was gray—pure gray with black on his ears and tail and white cheeks and belly. The others seemed more mottled, one almost solid white and beige. The gray wolf walked slowly to him, his liquid yellow eyes never wavering. His head only had to lean up until his black, cold, wet nose touched Hamish's, and he licked Hamish's chin and mouth once. Then all the wolves turned and trotted away through the trees.

As though it were a dream of flying in which he knew he actually flew, young Hamish knew he would never tell anyone of the visitation of the wolves until he told me so many years later. He walked back to the campsite and made a fire for the first time by himself. As the flames started a satisfying crackle, he turned to see his father watching him. His father barely smiled and gave one nod of his head as though in confirmation, as though he knew what had happened, as though he knew everything that would ever happen.

The small, memorable disaster of the trip happened at the end, when they were canoeing off the lake. Hamish was in the middle of the boat with the rolled-up tent and packs, using the knife's little magnifying glass to pin-point the sun on a leaf he'd brought along, when—in some kind of mysterious and sudden magic trick—he lost the knife over the side and it disappeared. His father stopped paddling, and the silence spread out into the world.

"Damn," Henry breathed. Sarah turned, questioning. "Hamish's knife. Gone."

"Oh…"

Hamish felt the tears start.

"That's too bad," said his father. And he started paddling again.

Often, in times to come, Hamish would imagine going back to that lake and somehow retrieving that knife from the depths.

He didn't need this little Brooklyn Junior Ranger educational experience. He knew the difference between deciduous and evergreen, between insects and arachnids, between magnetic north and true north. He would survive, not perish like a helpless child in the forest. But his mother had decided this was how he was going to spend two mornings a week, traipsing around Prospect Park with children, learning about plants and animals and gardening. Juvenile detention would have been a better choice.

∞

The kids met at the Picnic House, a brick building that looked like it didn't know the difference between a picnic and dumpster-diving for pizza. Upstairs was an open room that was used for functions and wedding receptions. Downstairs were some offices and bathrooms with sheet-metal urinals and large closets with equipment and cardboard boxes of supplies. Ranger Sally greeted parents and sitters while focusing her loud cheeriness on the children, stooping slightly even when the child was her height. Her blond ponytail hung out the back of her hat, and it wiggled as she effervesced. She was like a puppy about to get long-anticipated kibble. She leaned down to Hamish.

"And what's your name, young man?"

"Hamish Taylor."

"Where's your mom?"

Hamish looked at that dimpled face. "At work."

"Oh," Ranger Sally said, momentarily defeated. "Well, I wish she'd been able to drop you off, don't you? But here you are —" she checked him off on her clipboard "—and I'm sure it'll be just fine. You're one of our older ones, I see. I'm sure you'll be a big help. You can wait over there until we get started."

The morning was a blur of resentment. There were about fifteen kids in the group. The two oldest were fifteen-year-old girls who smoked cigarettes behind trees when Sally and the other Ranger were wrangling the fifth and sixth graders. The other Ranger was a skinny, laconic college student named Hurley. His hair fell almost to his shoulders and had the look of stringy vegetables about to turn. He guided children with his large hands, saying nothing and looking off into the distance. Hamish decided he was on drugs.

Their task that first day was to clean up the Fallkill Falls and pool, the beginning of the watercourse in the park. Water traveled some hundred miles from the Catskills and was pushed to the highest point in the park just off Quaker Hill, then it spilled down over rocks placed more than a century ago in an attempt to recreate a babbling mountain brook and ravine. The water could be turned on and off like a kitchen faucet. Thousands of wandering Brooklynites had, over the decades, left tons of litter, and, as Ranger Sally giddily announced, it was their awesome job to help restore the park to its original beauty and glory.

Everyone spread out with black plastic bags and gloves and sticks with metal spears out the end for poking at garbage. Smaller kids squealed and splashed, and huddled in an intense little group as Sally picked up a beetle or small amphibian or worm in her hand and expounded in a disquisitional chat on its place in the cosmos.

They were allowed to go over the fencing that kept people on the paths that wound around the ponds. It gave everyone a sense of seriousness and entitlement. Hamish did his best to separate himself from the others. He climbed around the side of Fallkill Falls and up to the top where the water came out of a grated hole. He could see Shauna and Vivian, the old girls, lighting up down the hill towards the playing fields and spitting out sudden streams of smoke. On the other side most of the kids had gathered around Sally, their crushes obvious in their eagerness to comment on the turtle in her hand. Hamish jabbed the ground with his litter-stick, his cloak of loneliness gaining weight with each breath and each spark of metal against rock. The white noise of the waterfall made the edges of him seep into the heat, and the hot smell of powdered bark crawled into his sweaty pores.

The crying sounded like it was coming from his brain at first. But it was such a snotty crying that he looked around to spot the culprit. It slowed, and he heard a girl's voice muffled by the waterfall, "You stupid stupid Mongol. Why are you so stupid?" He leaned over the edge of the rocks and there at the bottom of the falls was a plump girl, her shoulders quaking which she would then control with an angry and despairing "Oh, so stupid stupid stupid."

Hamish called down, "Are you OK?"

The girl tilted her tightly braided head up, her black skin darker than anyone's Hamish had ever seen, and then Hamish could see the wide set eyes of Down syndrome.

"I lost my glasses."

"You need some help?"

"I'm older than I look."

"Oh. OK." Hamish was at a loss. "Congratulations."

"My mom's going to kill me if I lose my glasses."

"Do you want some help?"

"I can't find them."

"Hold on a second, I'll come down."

Hamish scrambled down and skirted a couple of large boulders to find the girl sitting on a rock with her shoes submerged and her pants and lower part of her shirt soaked. Cool drops splashed up from the rocks behind her as the water dribbled from above. She had clearly spent some time looking.

"How did you get back here?"

"I was getting that." She pointed to an empty Nestea bottle with the label half worn off.

"So where'd you lose your glasses?"

"They were just here."

Hamish could see them in the water next to her foot. "Let me look around." Hamish splashed here and there, turning over rocks and grabbing at leaves dramatically, until he finally came nearer the girl.

"Oh, here they are! Hiding. Glasses always do that."

The girl shrieked. "There they are! You found them! Wow, man, you found them." She held them religiously for a moment before suddenly sticking them on her face.

Hamish was surprised at how thick they were, distorting her dark eyes small and making it impossible to know where she was looking.

"I love you," she said. "What's your name?"

"Uh, I'm Hamish."

"I'm Clothilde White." She said her name with a near-lisp that, oddly, revealed a sense of pride. "I'm very pleased to meet you." And she stuck out her hand.

Hamish took the proffered hand, and Clothilde shook his violently as her smile opened on her dark face.

"You are my hero. You saved my life. My mom would really kill me if I lost these glasses. They cost a fortune, and we can't just go around spending fortunes on glasses, you know."

"That's OK. I'm glad I could help."

Clothilde stood in the water and wrapped her arms around Hamish in an enthusiastic embrace. Hamish looked up to look away, and there at the top of the falls, leaning over the boulders, was a man—maybe 30, maybe 50, maybe even older—inexplicably in this heat wearing a full-length duster and a wide-brimmed hat. He tipped his hat to Hamish, turned and disappeared. This was the first time Thaddeus Knox had ever seen Hamish. Of course, it wouldn't be the last.

Hamish felt witnessed.

Extricating himself from Clothilde, Hamish suggested that they find everyone else.

"Good idea!" exhaled Clothilde, as though Einstein had just walked into her life.

Hamish turned. There, on the other side of the pool was a red fox. His black nose was polished, and the white and black tip of his tail preened to a point. His white bib was a bit dirty, and his legs were that black of having just escaped the tar pit. He watched Hamish steadily, as though he had an expectation of him.

Hamish stopped Clothilde with his arm. "Look! It's a fox."

Clothilde surveyed the scene and whispered, "Wow." Then she asked, "Where?"

"Right there."

The fox moved quickly away, up and over the hill.

"No, he's gone."

"Oh, shoot."

Hamish thought, A fox in the middle of Brooklyn? A man fresh from the old West or the Outback? Chess prison? Do I really hate my life so much, or am I just going crazy?

"Come on, we should find the others."

∞

They had to walk all around the ponds to find the group. Clothilde stabbed leaves on the way with little cries of triumph—a fencing match with the earth. A couple in their twenties jogged along the path, red faced and gleaming sweat. The man stumbled when he saw Clothilde, and he turned to jog backwards for a few steps, his face playing with pity and disgust. Hamish felt himself move closer to Clothilde, who was shouting at a duck on the pond, "Come over here so I can see you! Don't be afraid of me!" He stared the man down, and the couple faded around the bend.

"Clothilde!" Hamish touched her shoulder. "I don't think the ducks like being shouted at."

Clothilde's eyes widened at this new idea. "Oh," she breathed. "OK. Shhhhh!" She took Hamish's hand as though he had walked her through the woods since the beginning of time.

Vivian and Shauna, the smokers, came up behind them.

"Who's your girlfriend?" They giggled as they trotted faster and left them behind.

Clothilde leaned towards Hamish and said in a stage whisper, "That girl's jealous of her friend."

"What are you talking about?"

Still in a stage whisper, she continued dramatically. "She's in loooove with her. But she won't tell her 'cause of the boyfriend."

Exasperated, Hamish insisted, "Come on. Let's go."

As soon as they found the group on the edges of the lower pond, Clothilde ran up to Ranger Sally.

"We saw a fox! We saw a fox!"

"Oh, Clothilde." Ranger Sally looked her over, shaking her head at the mud and the wetness. "What happened to you?"

"We saw a fox. Tell her, Hamish."

Sally put her hand on Clothilde's shoulder. "There are no foxes in the park. Maybe you saw a dog."

"But Hamish said—"

"It must have been a dog."

Hamish breathed deeply. "It was a fox. A red fox."

Everyone looked to Sally. Even Hurley paused, wondering which way the wind would blow. Sally's voice was lower.

"There are no foxes in Prospect Park. There are feral dogs, and you have to watch out for them. It's easy to mistake a dog for a fox."

"This was not a mistake. This was definitely a fox. I've seen them before. At home."

"Well," said Sally, breaking the bubble. "Why don't you take Clothilde back to the Picnic House to help her clean up. Thank you!"

∞

Pick-up happened just before lunch, when everyone turned cranky. Hamish realized that Vivian and Shauna had already absconded, returning to the home turf of the streets. So Hamish headed towards Prospect Park West from the Picnic House. But suddenly Clothilde grabbed his hand and yanked on it.

"This is him! This is him! He found my glasses. See? They're here. I've still got them."

Hamish saw a girl catching up to Clothilde. She was clearly her sister, older, slimmer, even darker skinned, and with straightened bangs over her oval face. It occurred to Hamish how very few conversations he'd ever had with a black person.

"See?" said Clothilde. "This is Hamish."

The girl took Clothilde's hand possessively. "Thanks for helping Clothilde."

"It's OK. No problem."

"I'm Lilly."

Hamish cocked his head; he couldn't help himself. "Lilly White?"

"Don't even…"

"Sorry."

"My parents were really stupid."

"No, it's—"

"You in ninth-grade?"

"Yeah."

"Where?"

"We just moved here. I'm going to Herman Melville High."

"All right! So'm I."

It slipped out. "You're fourteen?"

Clothilde tugged. "Lilly. We gotta go. You can fall in love later."

"Clothilde! Stop that." She turned back to Hamish. She smiled. "Why, how old are you?" She laughed at his silence. She indicated Clothilde pulling on her. "Really. Thanks for taking care."

Hamish just lifted his fingers, embarrassed. He wanted to touch her shoulder.

CHAPTER 4

He didn't want to be alone in the apartment. He had a little time before he had to go to downtown Manhattan for the job his uncle had arranged, so, as usual, he walked. When he realized he was getting near the chess shop, he did an abrupt turn from 4th Avenue up 9th Street.

After a dreary post office was a McDonald's, and he thought maybe he would go in. His mother never went in. It wasn't that she didn't allow him to go, it was just that she held it a moral failing to succumb to the hype and sugar and salt and fat of a conglomerate that claimed to serve "billions and billions." "Of what?" Sarah would ask. "Dead cows from the Brazilian rain forest and poisoned potatoes from the fields of Idaho?" It was when Hamish had caught her smoking a cigarette outside their house in Plains the week before they moved to Brooklyn that he realized there was sway to everything. Nothing was hard and fast.

As Hamish reached for the glass door, some girls came pushing out. There were five of them, wearing mixtures of pajamas, lace, and high fashion. The first one, an Asian girl about Hamish's age, bumped into him and looked at him as though she had stepped in dog-poo. She laughed too hard at her friends following her, another Asian girl and three white girls. They were nervous and stunning, like young horses, and their laughter was a cartoon of itself. The last girl touched Hamish as they came through, and she muttered, "Sorry," as she left. Hamish's jaw burned where she had brushed him with her fingers, and he watched her get into a long black limousine with the other girls. A man with a fedora and wearing a light leather jacket and rings on each finger followed. He caught Hamish's eye and pointed a blunt finger at him, looking down it as though measuring Hamish with a knife.

"I know you, faggot. Don't get any ideas." The man laughed with a personal glee. He almost skipped to the limo and got in with the girls. The limo drove away.

∞

His stop was Park Place, and he thought he should be playing Monopoly. He hadn't realized that the properties in Monopoly were real places—even though the places were in Atlantic City—until he'd moved to Brooklyn. He'd been told to meet a woman named Fiona McKenzie at a new building that his uncle's firm was developing. Hamish was to help make the model apartments ready for viewing that weekend.

As the subway screeched into the station, Hamish felt his peripheral vision contract, as though he got up too fast and the blood was rushing out of his head. He left the car and held onto one of the painted I-beam posts as the train left the station, rumbling loudly down the tunnel. As the train receded, the noise did not, but changed into a charged hubbub, demanding attention. Hamish looked around as though he would place the sound, but there was nothing but the stuffy station with a few bored people waiting for trains. Hamish found the stairs, but the noise, which seemed now to be coming from just out of his sight in all directions, pressed him.

He was pulled south and west, stumbling past the wrought-iron fence surrounding Trinity Church—such a tiny place amidst all the skyscrapers. He knew it was the wrong direction—he was supposed to be going east—but he felt an irrefutable compulsion to follow his feet which seemed caught in this river of sound no one else could hear. He didn't know it, but he was headed towards the World Trade Center, still a fenced off construction zone after the burning pile had been taken away cinder by cinder over the course of a year.

Suddenly a seagull landed on the sidewalk in front of him. The seagull flapped his wings wide and cried that seagull cry, somewhere between a scream and a call. His wings lifted him inches, and he did a clumsy crash landing. Another gull imitated a hummingbird two feet above

Hamish's face, his beak spread wide as he called down. Very soon, gull after gull was zooming from one side of Hamish's vision to the other, as though pushing him back. People pulled themselves up as though dodging spray from a tire through a puddle. The first gull advanced on the sidewalk, another gull joined him and ran forward, leaning out to peck at Hamish. Between the sounds in his head and the squawking at his feet and above, he turned and walked quickly away, over City Hall Park, and onto the Brooklyn Bridge.

As Hamish headed up the long ramp of the bridge, he could feel its cables directing all sight and sound into a vanishing point way ahead, as its designers the Roeblings, crisscrossed as they were with their own disappointments and loss, had intended. His breathing slowed as the sounds of a thousand voices quieted in the breeze at the crest of the bridge. At the end, he veered left and walked up the chaos of Flatbush Avenue, past Junior's and Fulton Street, past the no-man's land of the Atlantic Yards and up the slope to Grand Army Plaza. He knew he should find a way to call his uncle, but he couldn't. That chore was like a small memory from another year. Something else was going on.

The end of the afternoon was hot. As Hamish entered Prospect Park, dust hung in the air, and each breath brought turmoil to the lungs. All the color of the park was leached and putrid, and the shade of the trees that Hamish crossed under only wavered the temperature, like ripples in old glass. Someone was setting up some small electric-orange cones on the great lawn, marking out a field for soccer later that evening. No one else was out in the sun except people walking through it, a kid on a bicycle, a man with a dog pulling him along. And then he saw it, just out of the corner of his eye.

The squirrel fell spinning, bringing a few leaves and twigs down from what must have been forty or fifty feet. Hamish heard it scream, and he didn't know squirrels did that. It hurt the inside of his head. Hamish was stunned, thinking to himself that squirrels never fall out of trees. That's like a bird suddenly falling out of flight. Like a cloud in a blue sky turning into a bucket of water and splashing down. Like a huge boulder powdering into a handful of dust. Like a man becoming an infant in an instant.

He kept the place where the squirrel landed in his eyeline. He tried to hold his breath, but it escaped with a cry. There were some early evening dog-walkers in the distance, a dehydrated runner down West Drive going away. He could even hear a kid's skateboard grinding the asphalt at the Bandshell. The heat wanted to suppress all sound, and only pinpricks of wavelength touched his ears, like strong stars in a misty night sky. He nearly expected ambulance sirens, blue and white police cars emblazoned with "Courtesy Professionalism Respect" on the back doors, SWAT teams in black, K-9 units, at least three cherry or lime fire trucks and men with long sloping helmets, big boots, and yellow axes in their hands. But there was nothing. It was as though the heat had become a blanket of thick snow, softening all edges and muffling all vibrations.

There was a scream of delight from up in the trees.

We got one! Over here!

There wasn't anyone in the tree that Hamish could see. He peered up, searching for some high-school kid who'd climbed up and was using his perch as a terrorizing look-out, and he looked around for other kids to appear from behind bushes, wearing threatening T-shirts and chains dangling from their belt-loops. But there was only a crow that leaned forward off its branch and dipped towards the ground where Hamish had seen the squirrel disappear. Its wings curved, scooping itself to a stop, hopping and looking around as it landed.

Hamish heard, *Come on, guys! But remember, I got here first.* But still he couldn't see anyone.

Hamish ran towards the squirrel. He heard little shrieks of *Look out!* and *Down!* and *Off!* and *Away!* as he slapped through foliage to arrive near the base of the tree from which the squirrel fell. The crow glided up into a small elm with what seemed like a *Whoa, fellas. We got a live one here.*

Ridiculous. Fourteen years old, and I'm insane, thought Hamish. He decided to ignore whoever was being so obnoxious.

The squirrel was on the ground, its hind legs useless, its feather-duster tail crimped and mangled. Blood was seeping from its wet nostrils.

Hamish's ears thundered.

It happened very easily, like cool water spilling gracefully into a parched throat.

Kill me? Be quick.

It was the squirrel. And Hamish knew he was answering.

I'm not going to kill you.

The squirrel's eyes were hard. *I'm not a plaything.*
No.
Hamish realized there were no birds singing, but that the stuffy breeze carried voices as though he were on a crowded street full of conversations and families and vendors and cops. It was difficult to narrow in on any one.

He was at the center of a horror movie.

Leave him alone!

Hamish looked up to see another squirrel upside down on the bark of the tree about ten feet up, her tail stiff against the trunk, her head angled out as though to stare him down.

From further up in the tree, another squirrel cried out, *Get away, you idiot! Get away!*

Hamish looked down at the dying squirrel. The squirrel on the tree launched into a diatribe against Hamish, touching on everything from his lineage to his ugliness and stupidity, as she scooted fast inches up the tree.

The squirrel on the ground was breathing fast and shallow. His eyes hadn't left Hamish. Hamish knelt. Language came from inside his head, inside his sinuses, the tilt of his head.

What can I do to help?

For a minute, Hamish thought perhaps his insanity was complete and true. But the squirrel responded.

You're speaking to me.

Yes.

I've heard of you.

How?

All have heard of you. You exist. You speak.

I don't understand. Hamish was near tears with his confusion.

Don't kill me. The squirrel was begging.

I don't kill.

This is so strange.

Hamish looked up from the ground. The other squirrel had come silently down the trunk until it was only a few feet away from Hamish's head. It stared at him as though looking into a hopeful abyss.

What are you?

I'm a boy.

Yes. No.

The squirrel on the ground coughed. A ruby of blood surged out of its mouth. There was almost no breath left.

It was the softest whisper. It didn't even come in Hamish's ears, but through his skin.

It's the Speaker.

And the squirrel was no more.

The other squirrel zipped up the tree, screaming, *Speaker! It's the Speaker. Watch out! It's here!*

Hamish was empty. This felt more like a dream than any dream he'd ever had, but with a tangible and connected clarity to it, fog dissipating to reveal the solid ground he'd been walking on all along.

He felt rather than saw the crow land on the grass a few feet away.

You gonna share?

Hamish looked at him. His whole body and mind morphed as he said to the crow, *What the hell are you talking about?*

This took the crow three feet off the ground, and straight back down.

Whoa! He crept closer, leaning. *Do that again.*

Do what? Hamish was suddenly impatient. His body, his musculature, the positioning of his eyes, the air inside his nose felt like they were transforming. Only later would he be able to explore how each language changed his being. This language was harsh and comical.

Oh, wow! This is amazing. Guys! Guys! Come here! We got a—I don't know what we got.

Hamish heard yelling in all directions from different trees and from the sky itself. It was like a gang of boisterous bikers, circling and collecting. A few crows landed outside the first crow's domain. Questions started.

Has it got food?

Get back, idiot.

Did it kill the squirrel?

Did you say it spoke?

This is stupid dangerous.

Is it going to leave the squirrel?

Who said it spoke?

Hamish didn't know how, but from deep in his gut came a geyser. *QUIET!*

Like a shaken sheet, all the crows at once jumped back a few feet. They turned their heads and maybe moved one judicious foot.

Someone whispered, *It spoke.*

The first crow said, *I've heard of this.*

Hamish looked at him, pinning him with some sound that came from the back of his throat. *What have you heard?*

Of you. I've heard of you.

A crow above Hamish's head said, *Are they talking to each other?* And a few responded,

Yes.

Yes they are.

Don't know how, but they are.

Careful. Those humans can kill.

When can we get the squirrel?

Keep distance.

Can it say anything else?

The first crow hopped around in front of Hamish. *That's what you are! You're the Speaker.*

This started a loud argument among the crows, which stopped suddenly when Hamish said, *That's what the squirrel said.*

All the crows were silent and that felt dangerous.

The first crow stepped on a stick, its black feet curling around it. *You spoke with the squirrel?*

Yes. He said I was "The Speaker."

The crow was careful. *And the squirrel said this to you?*

Hamish looked at the crow steadily. *Yes.*

Wow.

The crow jumped into the air. *Let's go!*

Hamish felt the instant impulse to follow the crow's directive and he would have, had he wings. As one, all the crows were in the air, banking out over the park, collecting in an oval of ragged black points above the trees, and heading east.

Everyone had left him with death. The white of the squirrel's belly was pristine. Hamish picked some leaf-dirt off. There was still heat coming from the small body, residents abandoning a ruined city in a steady stream, leaving all their homes and belongings and taking nothing but themselves. Hamish settled in his mind, a ship slipping down from its cradle into the sea. He knew it was time to go.

∞

The middle of the night is always private. The circles of privacy can enlarge to include many people and passions and destitutions, but mostly it's one person in a place whose edge is hard to fathom and felt as an orbit or magnetic field. Hamish stared into the dark. There were red glowing numbers from his clock. A tiny green dot of light came from something plugged in. He could sense a change in the density of the blackness where his window onto the airshaft was. Shapes of the things of his room had no substance, just looming solidities with soft boundaries and sharp threats.

His dad was still dead and the world had changed.

He had barely talked since the crows took off. He played the whole scene over and over—the squirrel's fall, the whoosh of wings, the small and fatal bit of blood, the anger of his mate, the sideways eye of the first crow. Sarah had had dinner ready when he'd come back, and Jim Lehrer was almost over.

"What happened? Where have you been?"

"Sorry." Hamish sat with the food.

"What happened?"

Hamish hadn't looked at her. "Nothing."

"You said you'd be home by the news. And it's almost over."

"Sorry, OK?"

"And you didn't go to your internship."

Sarah stewed, picking her battles. "There's orange juice in the fridge. And you've got to call Uncle Colin in the morning."

Hamish picked at his food, and then slugged his way to the cupboard for a glass.

"You want to watch 'West Wing' with me before I go to the night shift? It's a rerun, but I don't think we saw it."

Hamish shrugged and hid his mouth in the juice. He sat down, listening to the slightly Texan drawl of Jim Lehrer thanking him and bidding him good night.

By the time his mother had gotten out the door at 10:00, he had been holed up in his room staring at a blank sheet of paper with one mark slicing diagonally down its face. She had admonished him to turn out the lights and go to sleep. He'd said he would.

The night kept on going.

He got up, turning on a light. His fear was beginning to make him angry, and his loneliness was making him fed up. His dad had once said to him, "You gotta have someone you can call in the middle of the night, and they won't hang up on you no matter what. You can always call me."

Right, thought Hamish, and where the hell are you now?

Hamish went down the hall to the kitchen. He opened the refrigerator and looked in for a long time. Milk. Juice. Bowls with Saran Wrap—leftovers. Weak celery. Butter. A jar of dill spears. A half-drunk bottle of wine.

Nothing.

Hamish went into his mother's bedroom to get out onto the fire-escape. The air was cooler. The city gave off a huge hum as he ducked his head to the outside. A constant buzzing of millions of the tiniest machines ever crafted, with the occasional minuscule honk or shout or slam. He sat, feeling the flat metal struts through his PJs, and the bars felt almost cold on his bare back. The black sky had an ochre cast to it, lights from below hanging their waste on the wind.

The railing of the fire-escape clunked and then reverberated as though someone had dropped a knife into it and it stuck. An owl had appeared out of the night and landed suddenly. He ruffled his wings together and stretched his tail, letting the feathers snap back into place. His gaze was on Hamish.

So it's true! The owl's manner was pragmatic.

"What the hell?" Hamish heard himself murmur. Could he understand everyone?

The owl stared. Hamish could feel what to do to speak. It was as though his brain became a different color, his throat changed shape, his muscles could all operate individually, his nasal passages deepened. This was completely different than talking with a squirrel, but not so different from a crow. The part of Hamish that could speak with an owl did not have any interest in human concerns. He had an awareness of weather, of night, of sounds that were for the moment his entire world.

What the hell is going on?

The owl fluffed. *I think you're supposed to tell me that.*

But I can't believe it's real. I can't believe this is really happening.

The owl was not put off. *A Speaker comes. Change comes.*

It's not me. How could it be me?

It seemed like the owl was laughing, although Hamish couldn't be sure. Nothing that Hamish understood from any animal, then or now, translated into Hamish's native tongue cleanly. It is, at best, as Hamish has told me repeatedly, a pale representation of the experience of comprehension.

You are you, said the owl. *You are a change.*

Silence. The city hummed. The breeze was good on Hamish's skin. Hamish was filled with the idea—as we all must be—of what "change" is, what it fundamentally must be from the perspective of something other than himself.

Suddenly Hamish found himself asking, *Can you really see in the dark?*

Now the owl was laughing. *Of course. I can see in the daylight, too.*

Hamish felt sheepish. *Sorry.*

You'll let me know what the change is? If I should look out for anything?

Hamish shrugged, Sure. *How do I get a hold of you?* He felt sarcastic.

Call. I'll bring you something.

What? How do I call? Bring me what?

A nice mouse.

The owl fell from the railing and blended mutely with the night air.

CHAPTER 5

The night was especially hot. Hamish slept on top of his sheet, waking to adjust the fan which either cooled his sweaty skin too much, or left him pulsing in the heat. The sounds of the night were different and confusing. He realized at one point he was eavesdropping on a conversation of mice. It was humdrum, the way a conversation about groceries could be, but the scale was both mysterious and jarring, as though he'd grown into a giant and could hear whispers from across the sea.

When he next knew he was awake, humid morning had come. He put on shorts and a T-shirt, watered his face, and rinsed his mouth with orange juice. He couldn't imagine talking with his mother, and he wanted to get away before she woke for lunch. When he went outside, there was hardly any traffic on an early Tuesday morning. The people who were out were taking care of themselves, joggers and dog walkers and dads with strollers.

It was almost impossible for him to focus. He felt like the rest of his life he would be off-balance, unless he could prove to himself that he really was crazy and he'd wake from this strange illusion soon. He could sense the clamor of life everywhere, especially from the trees. He passed a dog—a little terrier—who was narrating her guidance of her owner, a man in his thirties with a nascent potbelly and a ponytail. She looked up at Hamish as they passed and she barked, *Get out of the way! This is our way! Our way!*

Hamish bowed, sweeping his arm out, *Of course, your majesty.*

The terrier stopped. *What the hell...* Her owner tugged at the leash, giving Hamish a look reserved for the crazy, and Hamish walked on.

He felt mischievous and powerful, but as though he was headed into a really big storm.

He wanted to return to the park like wanting to return to the scene of an accident. As he passed the bronze statues of the cougars guarding an entrance, he could see the fenced-off stage they were building for the Met opera concert on the lawn later in the week. Loudspeakers were going to go up on poles and a black backdrop held the platform away from the trees. Scaffolding of stage lights framed the area. One lone worker with an orange vest was stooping over equipment inside the fence.

Under one of the benches that lined the path along the Great Lawn was a sparrow hopping at invisible crumbs and glancing up quickly after each peck. Suddenly another sparrow landed in the same space and in a whirr of wings, took the first sparrow's place. He lunged at the ground twice in quick succession.

Little twat.

At least, that's what Hamish heard.

The first sparrow, two feet away: *I'm coming.*

Second sparrow, eating another crumb and fluffing his black throat: *Try it, piece of shit.*

Hamish could see the second sparrow did have a bigger black bib, and he could see this gave the first sparrow pause.

Shut up and eat, said the first sparrow.

Shut up and I'll eat you!

Suddenly a name came into Hamish's head, as he would find would happen with most animals he came to relate to. The name was Ralph, after Jackie Gleason's character in the "Honeymooners," one of the old TV shows he and his father used to watch in the hospital. Hamish approached the bench and sat on the very end.

Shit!

Both sparrows took off in different directions.

Hey! Hamish called out. *I'm not going to eat you!*

Hamish saw Ralph hop on a holly-bush to get a better look back. His wings suddenly took him on a dip through the still air to land on the back of the bench.

Say that again.

Hamish turned slowly. *I'm not going to eat you.*

You couldn't eat me, you moron. You couldn't even catch me. I'm too fast for the likes of you.

How about a cat?

You're not a cat.

What were you two fighting about?

We weren't fighting. We were chatting.

Suddenly three other sparrows landed on the bench. Ralph did a quick flying turn that threw them momentarily off balance, shouting, *I'm first!* The three came back, almost nonchalantly, and talked amongst themselves.

Listen up, losers! said Ralph. *I'm going to take this ancient broken pinfeather to my nest so he can really see some quality craftsmanship.* To Hamish: *Come.* Ralph fluttered a second in front of Hamish's face and sloped off to the other side of a tiny park playground and sandbox. There was one toddler keeping himself up by holding onto a bar, looking around at his mom, letting go and plopping down onto his diapers. Then he would look at the ground as though trying to determine how to get away from it. His mom was reading a book and would glance over the top of it with an automatic smile. Off to the side a girl was sitting by herself. She was wearing pajamas.

Ralph suddenly pinned himself to Hamish's shoulder. *Now you're going to see how to build a nest. You can't get a mate unless you can build a nest. Mine is perfect. You'll never get one like mine.*

I don't want a mate!

You've got to have a mate. There's one right there. Ralph was indicating the girl in pajamas, who was now looking in Hamish's direction.

Show me your nest, Hamish deflected.

Follow! Ralph flew just a few feet into a small blue spruce. Hamish separated a couple of branches, and there, near the narrow trunk, was a lovely woven nest about the size of a flat coffee cup. Another sparrow landed on Hamish's head. He felt little needles extending harmlessly through his hair to his scalp.

Is this him? she asked of Ralph. Hamish instantly thought of her as Alice, Ralph Kramden's TV wife.

Yep.

Humph. It wasn't exactly a "humph," but Hamish knew the mixture of skepticism and disdain, hesitation and dismissal. She took a hair out of his head and flew to the nest.

I can use this.

Hamish's eyes welled a brief second and he rubbed his head. *You're welcome!*

There was a laugh behind him, and he turned to see the girl laughing at him. She was wiping her eyes—she'd been crying—and her distraught blond hair came away from her face. Her feet were bare.

Hamish laughed, too, unable to explain the sparrows.

"They are your pets?" the girl asked. Hamish heard a faint Eastern European accent in the girl's speech.

"No," he said. "They just picked me."

"You are lucky."

Ralph landed on Hamish again. *Did you see? Pretty good, isn't it? What's wrong with this one? You got any food?*

No, I don't have any food. And I just met this one. She's not mine, not for me. I'm not—

"What are you doing?" asked the girl, amused.

Hamish felt himself withdraw from sparrow-speak. He understood Ralph to say, *I can help. You know where.* And then, with a tiny push off Hamish's shirt, Ralph was lost in the trees lining Prospect Park West. Hamish still didn't have a concept of what he looked like when he talked with other animals, what kind of things his body did, which kinds of sounds emanated from him, or what he could do to hide that. He did a quick inventory of the gestures and squeaks he might have made.

The girl sighed. "I've never seen anything like that."

"Honestly, I haven't either. But it's so cool, isn't it? It's—"

"Helena. My name is Helena. My name is Helena Padar." She held out her hand which Hamish took to shake, but it was soft as an unconscious rabbit.

"My name's Hamish. Hamish Taylor."

"Hello, Hamish Taylor." The girl didn't look at him, but smiled at the ground. Only then did Hamish wonder why she was barefoot in her pajamas. Why she'd been crying. And then he realized he'd seen her before. She was the one who had touched his cheek as she and four other girls came out of McDonald's.

"Well, if you ever need anything, I just live over there with my mom. Number 97."

Helena looked over her shoulder as though she could see through the trees and down a few blocks to Hamish's house.

"With your mom?"

"Yeah. It's OK. She's pretty cool."

"She's your mom."

"Yeah."

"And you tell me, stranger, this?"

Hamish shrugged. "You looked like maybe. I don't know. You needed—"

"OK," said the girl. "It's OK."

They lapsed into silence, watching the toddler's determined struggles and the warm morning breeze smoothing things out like making a bed.

Helena looked up the walkway. She sat up, preparing. Her eyes narrowed into a forced smile.

"Number 97?"

"Yeah, that's where we live."

"Maybe I see you again."

A man was suddenly in front of them, and he sat heavily on the bench on the other side of Helena, squeezing her towards Hamish. He wore a fedora, and had the charm of a reptile. He was the man from the limousine.

"Fancy meeting you here! Who's your boyfriend?"

"I don't know," said Helena, looking down at her hands.

"You don't know your own boyfriend's name?"

Helena didn't say anything.

Hamish said, "I'm not anyone's boyfriend. I'm just sitting here."

The man leaned forward to look across Helena at Hamish. "Sit someplace else."

Hamish was still.

"I said, find someplace else to sit."

He reached across the girl and whacked the side of Hamish's head, stunning his ear. Hamish stood thinking he was ready to fight. The man shook his head at Hamish with vicious patience. But then he flicked his hand in front of his face as though slapping away an insect. It was the sparrow Alice. She chirruped and scratched the man's nose as she hovered back and forth in front of his face. Hamish, scared for her, cried out, *It's OK! I'm OK!*

Alice banked away. The man grabbed Helena's hand and pulled her to her feet, whispering gutturally into Helena's ear, his mouth almost pushing her head, his eyes above her hair looking at Hamish. He pulled her along beside him, out of the playground. The mother with the book had watched these events with a fear that almost paralyzed her, but she'd pulled out her cell phone to call 911. The man leaned towards her suddenly as he passed, jerking Helena, grabbing the cell phone out of the woman's hand and throwing it out of the playground into the bushes. He towed Helena away.

Hamish's and the woman's eyes met.

"Call the police!" The words barely came out of her throat.

"I don't have a phone." Hamish turned to leave, but stopped. "You OK?"

The woman looked at her child and nodded.

CHAPTER 6

Pradeep and Daniel were already at chess when Hamish clanked open the door. It had rained while Hamish had walked there. The dampness rising off the asphalt of Fourth Avenue and the sticky sound of tires pulling long lines of wet tape from the pavement muffled as the door closed. Daniel had dumped his backpack in the improvised aisle, and Hamish kicked it aside, aiming for the back of the room.

Mr. Shenouda looked up from the game Pradeep and Daniel were on. "Ah, Hamish. You may set up the board for you and Abraham. He is on his way, assuredly. I will be playing Polly in just a minute. Steve is away this week."

"Do you mind if I say hello to Madonna?"

As soon as Hamish spoke, there was a scream from the covered cage at the back. Mr. Shenouda smiled and said, "Your new lady friend awaits. I have a feeling you may have something for her, no?" He raised his eyebrows in expectation of a response. Hamish gave none.

Hamish heard the scream as, *There you are! Where the hell have you been?* He was soon to learn that parrots have an exquisite way with cursing that he could understand, but that was beyond his linguistic abilities to fully translate.

He lifted the sheet off the cage. The hyacinth macaw's brilliant blues felt drawn into space by artist pastels. It was almost comforting to see the edges where there was evidence of worn or dirtied feathers, where the coloring became real. Her hooked beak seemed tough as ox horn, and Hamish could see her black tongue when she screamed or reached, a little blunted Q-tip of flesh. She turned her head so she could track him with her left eye.

How long have you known, you cretinous limping cat sludge? How long have you known and not come to me? Madonna's feathers arched at the back of her neck and top of her head.

I'm sorry, said Hamish. *But it's only been a day.*

Sorry doesn't crack the nuts, fella. Madonna grabbed an upright with her beak and pulled herself up a few inches. *Come here. Come here. Closer.*

Hamish leaned over putting his head near the cage.

The parrot nibbled her words affectionately. *How's it feel to be the Speaker, Speaker?*

What is that, a Speaker? Everyone assumes I know.

You really are fledgling poop. Everyone's yakking.

You understand other birds?

Some things get understood. But only you can understand everyone, you pus river.

How? asked Hamish. He was beginning to feel like he'd stumbled into a foreign country with a sign on his back that everyone could read but him, and everyone read it a bit differently.

Uh oh. Here comes the food guy who smells like shells. What a neck crease. Madonna reached down to the bar with her beak and levered herself onto it, settled her blueness with a puff and drew her head down like a turtle going into its home, blinking sleepily.

"Is everything all right, Hamish?" Mr. Shenouda strode over towards the back of the room. "Abraham is here. Your contest awaits."

"OK."

Polly had left her chess game with Shenouda to watch Hamish with Madonna more closely.

We haven't finished, Speaker. Unless you insist on being the reptilian half-wit you appear to be. Madonna rocked from one foot to the other, and stretched out the toes on the right, shaking a bit.

"I wonder what this beautiful creature is thinking." Mr. Shenouda leaned down to the cage next to Hamish, tapping the sunflower seed container to make it settle. Kaphiri Shenouda was already planning the connections Hamish needed. He, being a Keeper, had seen Speaker behavior before.

"Who knows?" said Hamish, turning away.

The macaw squawked, *We're not done!*

I'll be back. Give me a little bit. Hamish scratched his ear and stretched his neck in an effort to be subtle.

"Who indeed?" Mr. Shenouda replaced the flowered sheet over the cage.

It better be quick, sneaker Speaker.

Mr. Shenouda made a decision. During the chess games, he placed two phone calls. The Keeper called Rabbi Etan Adams, a lawyer and a friend on the inner circle. He also called Thaddeus Knox, a Witness. Witnesses are action people. They know what to do and when to do it. They have a light footprint and stay in motion. Keepers like Shenouda are intuitives and persuaders. They connect people in common pursuits. They care.

Abraham creamed Hamish in the first game. It only took fifteen moves.

"Shit, Hamish." Abraham's long fingers delicately placed the pieces for starting again. "You usually better than this. What's up?"

"Sorry," Hamish fumbled the queen to the floor. He picked it up. "I just got some news."

"Good news?"

"It changes everything."

They contemplated the board. Abraham turned it so Hamish was white to give him the advantage.

"Give me a game this time."

Hamish's concentration was screeching to be diverted. Talking with animals was magic. Chess was laundry lists. Hamish started with the Ruy Lopez opening, taking control of the center of the board. Abraham's scorched earth play meant a lot of trading, but Hamish managed by the fifteenth move to be up a pawn and was positioned to take a rook in two moves. Kaphiri Shenouda passed the table and whistled low, perching on the adjacent table to watch. Abraham accepted the knight trade, and Hamish could feel Shenouda smile.

"Aw, man! I did not see that one," Abraham leaned his length back in the chair, his head falling backwards until he whipped it forward and hunched over the board.

Hamish took the rook.

Shenouda clapped his hands three times. "And now you have mate in seven moves. See if you can find it."

The three of them hovered, eyes running up and down the ranks and files, possibilities clouding predictions. Hamish could feel Shenouda's smiling gaze and wanted to scream at his own blindness.

"Now," said Shenouda. "Breathe deeply three times."

Hamish looked at him as though he'd asked him to strip.

"Man, this is more of The Shenouda Shit," grumbled Abraham. 'The Shenouda Shit' was what the boys had discovered in the advice from Kaphiri Shenouda that always worked. Whatever it was made them feel like idiots to start, and then they always succeeded. "You got to do it," Abraham directed. "Like he said: Breathe."

Hamish breathed in deeply. Then two more times. He looked at the board.

He could see the first move. It made sense, and went with the logic, the inevitability of the second move, and the necessary response from his opponent, and on to the third. The best Abraham could hope for was a stalemate, a way to lose without really losing. But it would be difficult.

Pradeep stood over Hamish's shoulder. Daniel sat cross-legged on a table watching. Polly's attention on Hamish was openmouthed and hypnotized. Daniel slapped Pradeep's shoulder lightly and with a tip of his chin called attention to Polly's incipient crush. Pradeep smiled with his eyebrows. Hamish made his moves deliberately, calmly, not rushing to push the clock, but pressing the plunger just enough to switch the time. Abraham matched him, and four moves in, saw what the inevitable ending would be.

"Nice, man. Very sweet."

When checkmate came, Abraham extended his hand and said, "Now you're back."

Kaphiri Shenouda applauded them both with quick claps.

∞

The bell at the front door rang and street noise swelled inside. The man who came in had a body that touched both sides of the door as he entered. Turning sideways a bit didn't help. He had a gray beard, shaggy gray hair, a black yarmulke and a shaggy black suit. A second, taller man suddenly appeared behind the first, holding the door. The rabbi looked up at the man and smiled. They were in the middle of a debate.

"Ah, Thaddeus," the fat rabbi intoned with delight. "This still won't get you what you so mistakenly want. We must still talk to him as an adult."

The taller man opened the door wide so the fat rabbi could squeeze through.

"Not so, Etan," he said severely. "There are things we must know first."

Hamish recognized him. It was the man at the top of the falls in Prospect Park.

"Mr. Knox, Mr. Adams," said Mr. Shenouda. "I'll be right with you." He turned to his young prodigies. "Extremely well done, boys. Hamish, coolly done. And Abraham, you could not possibly have done better; an honorable, honorable game." He leaned to speak softly in Hamish's ear. "I would like you to meet my friends here, who have just entered. One I believe you have seen before? Give me just a minute. Please, attend to Madonna, and I'll be right with you." Before Hamish could respond, Shenouda called, "That's all for today, boys! Go, into the world, do good and tend to your families." His arms were spread, ushering them out the door. "And Daniel, please remember your backpack this time."

Hamish looked at the men. The rabbi peered at Hamish over his wire-rimmed spectacles as he sat, nearly collapsing a chair and waving at Shenouda in good humor and small talk.

The other man was in a long duster and a wide-brimmed leather hat. He stayed near the entrance. His face was old but solid, as though time hadn't really found a purchase on the surfaces of his features. His eyes were that blue that movie stars envy, visible as deep water even at a distance. He didn't seem sweaty, despite having come from the humidity of the outside. His expression was one of perpetual curiosity, like a biologist in a jungle.

Hamish felt the pull of Madonna, so he went back to the cage.

You think you're the greatest nest-builder nut-cracker jaguar-killer eagle-flyer shit-eating limp-dicking ugly-assed naked monkey who can't seem to get it into his eyeballs what he owes certain blue creatures who explain even the dumbest facts of life to him without complaints and expecting only an occasional strawberry, which doesn't appear forthcoming, you gummy-snot idiot.

I love you, too, said Hamish gently. *Sorry about the strawberry. I'll remember next time.*

That's better, preened Madonna. *So what's the job?*

I don't know.

You're here for a reason!

I don't know!

Damn! You really aren't much use. Madonna strummed her beak on the cage uprights like a pianist. *I'd always thought you Speakers were supposed to be smart.*

I'm just—

Hamish felt a hand on his shoulder. It was Mr. Knox.

"I am thinking that perhaps it was you I saw the other day in the park. At the falls. With the girl." The voice was slightly accented with German, and like warm sandpaper.

Hamish looked up. Mr. Knox's face had some deep lines around the mouth and two cutting down between his eyebrows, like fissures in the earth. The light blue of his eyes was almost scary.

"Yeah," said Hamish coolly. "I think I saw you, too."

"Kaphiri tells me you are only recently come to New York."

Hamish was stunned that he'd been the topic of any conversation. "Yeah."

"And you like the park, I think."

"It's better than nothing."

Madonna screamed, *Why are you talking to that vacant hole?! Turn around! Turn around!! To me!!!*

Mr. Knox laughed. "Your friend is very demanding."

Hamish quickly glared at Madonna. *Shut it, you cat diarrhea.* He turned back to Mr. Knox.

Madonna was admiring. *Wow! That was good, even for you.*

"She's taken a liking to me," said Hamish.

"It's more than that, isn't it?"

Hamish knew he knew. "She called you something like a 'vacant hole'. Only, it's worse, I think."

Mr. Knox burst into long laughter, so that he had to wipe his eyes.

Get this slime channel to swallow his own anus and pay attention here! Madonna's scream was rapid fire.

He knows something! Hamish screamed back.

We all know something. Get me a fucking strawberry.

Mr. Adams chuckled, stroking his gray beard and making his bulk shake with merriment. "It is always so amazing to me to see. And yet it seems normal, doesn't it?"

"Yes," said Mr. Shenouda, "it does. Always."

"Kaphiri recommends we talk about what is happening with you," said Mr. Adams. "With you and animals, like this parrot in front of us."

"Hamish, my dear boy," beckoned Shenouda. "Please meet my friend, Mr. Adams. Mr. Adams, this is Hamish, one of my students."

Mr. Adams continued to look at Hamish as Hamish walked over to their table. He extended his hand.

"I'm very pleased to meet you, young man." Mr. Adams' accent was British, high class, university educated. It did not go with the body or face in front of Hamish. Hamish shook his hand.

"And this, of course, is Mr. Knox."

Mr. Knox formalized their encounter with a handshake.

"So what is going on?" asked Hamish.

"Well," said Mr. Adams, "I know becoming a Speaker can be somewhat of a shock."

"You know what a Speaker is?"

The three men looked at each other as though debating who was going to lead the next dance. Mr. Adams started.

"A Speaker is a person who can, of course, as you know, speak with all manner of animals, even when they can't understand each other. It seems to have something to do with tapping into the animal—the living!—impulse to communicate. It is quite mysterious how it works—I'm sure even you would have a difficult time telling me how you speak with this parrot, and then go on the street and speak with a passing dog. You know there seems a kinship with telepathy, but you also know smells and gestures and the minutest motions figure into the discourse. I would love to talk with you further on this."

"Etan..." said Knox warningly, as though they had a deadline.

"But how do you know this?" Hamish asked.

"Oh, I have met a number of Speakers around the world."

"There are others?"

"Oh yes, there have been—well since before we can know. But since the turn of the century, Thaddeus has felt that there are Speakers appearing more regularly, and that that is of concern because they usually appear in times of trouble." Here Adams laughed a laugh that made Hamish suddenly enjoy his company, making his old beard and religious costume something approachable and not a shield. "He used to think there are thirty-six of you in the world, like the old tale of the righteous ones. That you are one of the Tzadikim Nistarim. The ones who keep the world from ending."

"Now...." Knox was exasperated.

Hamish laughed in spite of himself. "Am I?"

Adams' eyes twinkled. "I have no idea. You could be, if there is such a thing. There's a tribe in the mountains of Colombia that thinks it is caring for the world, and if they stop, the world will end. Maybe. But what matters, it seems to me, is that you can do what you can do, and that you learn more about what you can do, and that you use that for good. Don't you think?"

"I guess so." Hamish knew they were expecting something. "Everyone says I'm here for a reason, like the animals say I have to fix or that there's some kind of trouble I'm supposed to make right. But nobody knows what that is."

"Nobody?" asked Mr. Adams.

"The owl, the crows, the dogs—well, they're kind of into their own thing anyway —different birds, and this parrot here, they all keep asking me what I'm here for. What do I tell them?"

They were silent. Madonna broke in:

Are you done with those jerks yet?

Hamish decided to try a different tactic with Madonna. *Listen you beautiful arrangement of blue, you who can fly true and stay steady and knows more about all things than I will ever, I must talk with these worthless pieces of beetle dung because they are older than old and have only until sunset to tell me the secret of where they hid the treasure, so I will get that and return to you soon so you can teach me the meaning of wonder and delight.* Hamish had no idea if that would work.

But it did. *Well, I should say... Go, speak with them, nestling,* Madonna almost purred.

Mr. Shenouda said, "And that was...?"

"We came to an understanding," said Hamish.

Mr. Knox considered, as he did about most things. "I think you should come to my place and I'll make us tea."

"Thaddeus."

"Wait a minute," protested Hamish. "Who are you guys? You've got to tell me what the 'trouble' is that you're talking about, that everyone's talking about. What the hell is going on?"

"I will tell you," said Rabbi Adams, leaning forward.

Knox stirred uncomfortably.

"Too little information too late shows lack of trust," Adams said to him.

"But he's too young, younger than anyone has ever been. And in this country! You know how unusual that is. It must be that there's something we have to prepare him for. We must protect him, keep him anonymous, until he comes of age."

"Thaddeus," said Mr. Adams in that British tone that seemed to apologize and brook no opposition at the same time, "the levels are myriad, and we have no way of knowing, do we?" He turned to Hamish. "Young man, you are the first Speaker born on this continent since Kai Pearson, and she's in her eighties and doesn't like talking to anyone. We don't know why this continent has been so bereft. Around the world they are spread fairly evenly, aren't they? With maybe five on each continent. But not here. You are also the first Speaker to develop abilities before maturity—not that you aren't very mature for your age—but no one has ever appeared before they were in their mid-twenties. So with you, there seems to manifest a sense of urgency and precipitation. We are determined to help. Thaddeus is correct about protection and anonymity—that is true of all Speakers around the world. People fear what they don't understand."

"But who are you guys?" asked Hamish.

Mr. Adams laughed. "I am just an old rabbi who has a degree in the law and came to this country years ago at the behest of Thaddeus to organize some things here in New York. I have no special talents. Kaphiri here, however, is a Keeper. A Keeper has an incredibly deep understanding of human-centered energy. I've seen Kaphiri stop a frightened murderer from running away. And then he talked him into giving himself up."

Hamish saw Mr. Shenouda smile at the memory.

"And then there are Witnesses, like Thaddeus Knox—prodigious memories, astonishing organizational skills, profound understanding of human endeavors. There are many more Keepers and Witnesses than Speakers. You Speakers are rare and, even after centuries of wondering why, inexplicable. As far as the trouble that seems to have called your talent into being— ”

"Etan," interrupted Mr. Knox. "I will finish the telling him of these things. But not here."

Mr. Shenouda stepped in. "Ah, Thaddeus, you are correct to use such caution. But you can see with what you're being called to attend, and with Alicia in the state she's in, with what's been occurring in the Middle East and in Congo, there are a plethora of things that call out loudly to those who could use his company and—”

"But we don't know what's a distraction, do we?" retorted Mr. Knox, his duster nearly knocking over his little metal chair as he stood.

Frustrated, Mr. Adams leaned his enormity back, addressing Hamish. "Mr. Knox likes to extend a little authority here. He and a Mr. Smith from the subcontinent are the ones, after all, who, just after the war in '45, started finding people around the globe who felt as they did, that care needed to be taken. That we must on a very grand scale care for each other, watch out for each other, help each other along. He's gathered a loose group, a few hundred of us, all over the world, because Speakers are evenly spread all over the world, except here. We involve ourselves in projects, sometimes just by ourselves, sometimes in concert. But always with the idea, if this were the thing to save the entire world from absolute destruction, how would I go about it? What would I do? What love would I not give to this enterprise?"

"What 'enterprise'?" asked Hamish.

"My young friend," Mr. Adams leaned forward, straining the little chair he was on, "that is the mystery we are devoting ourselves to, don't you see?"

"That's enough, I think." Mr. Knox stood. "Kaphiri, thank you for this. Etan, always good to see you. Come," Knox directed Hamish. "Let us go, let us converse about the things that have been happening to you. I have things that might be of interest to you. I will give you tea." Mr. Knox smiled and extended his hand to Kaphiri Shenouda as though this were the end of a business meeting. Adams brought himself to his feet and kissed Knox on both cheeks. He then grasped Hamish's hand as though he were an adult.

"Chess on Wednesday!" reminded Kaphiri Shenouda with a twinkle.

CHAPTER 7

Knox and Hamish walked up the slope to the park. Hamish suddenly remembered he had to be at his Uncle Colin's real estate office that afternoon.

"I have to make a phone call," said Hamish. "I have to call my uncle. There's a pay phone up on 7th Avenue there."

Mr. Knox reached into his pocket and pulled out one of the newest flip phones that reminded Hamish of the old Star Trek TV show communicators. "Use this."

Hamish had actually never held one of these phones. It felt small and seductive in his hand. When he opened it, it softly clicked into the proper angle, waiting for him to touch the rounded space ship buttons. "You just press 'send' after you've put in the numbers," instructed Knox.

Hamish's uncle's secretary connected him. "Where are you?" Uncle Colin demanded.

"I'm sorry, really. Look, something's come up and it doesn't look like I can make it—"

"What's 'come up'? What is so goddam important that you can't get here?" His uncle's voice on the little phone was surprisingly strong and present.

"I just—"

"You call in sick yesterday, your first day, and then you do the same thing the second day. This is no good, Hamish, your father would not like this—even Henry would want you to keep your commitments."

"Well," said Hamish, a surge of rage surfacing, "maybe you and Mom can come up with a suitable punishment to go along with this suitable city."

"Young man—"

"I really have to go. Goodbye." Hamish looked at the phone, blinded. "How do you hang up?"

Mr. Knox gently took the phone and pressed the red button.

They walked in silence into the park and across the Great Lawn. There were people all over the park as Knox led Hamish along paths to the Nethermead, and then along the side road as though they were going to leave the park. But Knox turned towards the forest and went up to the Quaker Graveyard gate. The graveyard, Hamish knew from reading the modest signs on his meandering through the park, was privately owned by the Quakers of Brooklyn, and had been here since before the park was created. No one could go in to peruse the simple headstones, or picnic under its elm trees. It was a garden for the dead, except, as it turned out, Mr. Knox.

Mr. Knox was the caretaker of the graveyard, and had been since anyone could remember. It was one of his pleasures after his many journeys as a Witness, to come back here to this sanctuary in the middle of a city and to garden. He tended the few acres, making sure the lawns were kept in check and there was room for the daffodils and irises in the spring. On occasion he would lop off a dead branch that threatened to crash down in the next storm, or repair the chain-link fence that surrounded the hilltop after teenagers bent holes in it to get in and wander at night. When there was a burial, or family members wanted to visit, Mr. Knox would let them in and let the rituals devolve as days wore on.

Mr. Knox unlocked the gate and ushered Hamish through. Down a small road was a building—more like a shack—that Mr. Knox also unlocked and switched on a light. It was a small room, like a cozy den, with books on the walls, a couple of bronze patina colored overstuffed chairs on either side of a rounded coffee table; memorabilia and handy tools were crowded into corners. A small lamp lit a table that served as a desk, and there was a large oval rag rug on the floor. Hamish felt he had stepped into an America of a hundred years ago.

"So. Tea, yes?" Mr. Knox was already busying himself with a hotplate near a small corner sink.

"OK."

"Sit, sit. We have much to talk about."

Hamish sat in one of the big chairs, feeling swallowed, so he scooted to the edge of the seat.

"How did you know?"

"About you talking with birds and other creatures?"

"Yeah."

"Kaphiri told me." He reached for two mugs. "And I suspected when I saw that fox shadowing you, when you helped that girl. But it really was Kaphiri. He saw you."

"What did he see me do?"

"Very distinctive movements and sounds. Small, but noticeable. But he like all Keepers has a sixth sense about these things. I saw it, too, however, with that parrot. And that hawk as we crossed the park just now."

Hamish chuckled. The hawk, swooping overhead, had screeched a warning to others as she came back to her nest, and Hamish had almost instinctively called back that he would stay away. She broke her flight to do a landing turn on an oak limb. She spied him instantly on the ground and had offered him food from the nest she had near 3rd Avenue – a little regurgitated mole. Hamish had almost wanted to say yes just to find out what would happen.

"There's a kind of relief in it, yes? Have you ever seen someone who speaks sign language?"

"Yeah."

"It's how they change when instead of trying to get through to someone who is speaking slowly and loudly, they are talking with someone who understands sign, and language flows out of them. You are like that." Mr. Knox brought over the tea. "And that one crow." Mr. Knox offered some sugar.

"Yeah, Ron." Hamish sprinkled a little in his cup.

"Ron?"

"Well, not really. But I call him Ron." The crow had found Hamish as they walked and followed him a while, trying to engage him in a scheme to get pizza, something Hamish would find out was ambrosia to some crows.

"What's his real name?"

"They don't have names, not like we do. It's like you call them by what they are. It's like nothing smells like banana—you wouldn't mistake it for cheese—but a green banana is totally different from a really ripe one, with that edge of going brown, and if the green banana is on a glass plate in a room where coffee was made that morning and it's sunset now so you can't see the banana the same as earlier, and you can hear a fly landing on the skin while a car drives down the street—that might be someone's name. At least, that's what it feels like," Hamish laughed. "But like, I call that crow Ron. I don't really know why. He just feels like a Ron."

"I wonder."

"What?"

"Well, you know how many traditions talk of the power of knowing someone's name. The difference between someone's given name, and their true name."

"Like in some magic, in, you know, fantasy books."

"Yes, but I was thinking of some Native American lore, or the idea that it is a powerful act to name God."

"Yahweh."

Mr. Knox looked at him. "Precisely." He stirred his tea. "There is an idea that if you are able to truly name something or someone, you then have power over it."

"Or it just pays attention to you," said Hamish.

A light came into Mr. Knox's eye. "Or it pays attention to you. Yes."

Hamish began to get nervous as Mr. Knox watched him and sipped his tea. The silence flowed around them like cool water. Breezes went through from one window to another, out into the graveyard night. Hamish had to break it.

"Where are you from?"

"From?"

"Your accent."

"Oh. I was born in Austria. I'm sure that's what you're hearing. But I haven't spoken German much for a long time. I would like to. There's a wonderful precision to German that is at the same time expansive. German poetry—Ach!—it is so lovely it can break your heart. Do you have any German?"

"No." The silence came again. "Do you speak other languages?"

Mr. Knox smiled. "I get by in a number. Something over twenty."

"Twenty languages?" Hamish couldn't grasp it.

"A little more than that."

"Jeez. How do you keep track?"

"How do you know what to say when you're talking with a hawk or a cat?"

Hamish shrugged. "I just do, I guess."

"Me, too." He chuckled. "Except apparently I maintain a slight German accent in every language."

Hamish pondered. "I wonder if I have an accent."

"We all have an accent. That is something I do know. Even if I can't speak to animals." Mr. Knox stood. "Come. I want to show you something."

Mr. Knox indicated to Hamish to grab an edge of the rug, and they pulled it back, a little swirl of dust coming into the light from the floor. There was a ring embedded in the floor, and the outline of a trap door.

"I want to introduce you to the Under-Hut."

Mr. Knox pulled up the trap door, revealing a stairway going down. He leaned over and flipped on a light. They went down into a small room, that gave way to a large room with a kitchen and a comfortable place to eat and sit, a large roll-top desk and some oak file cabinets. There were a couple of doors. Hamish felt like a hobbit.

"That's the bathroom, if you need it. And that's a bedroom. In the closet is a doorway to the outside, if you should ever need it."

"Did you make all this?"

"Oh, heavens. This was made over a hundred and fifty years ago, part of the Underground Railroad. People waited here until they could get passage to Canada or Europe. Some went to Africa, but not many. They were still capturing people and bringing them here." Mr. Knox touched the wall lightly. "Oh, the pain and the relief that's in these stones. You feel it?"

Hamish realized that he did feel something, as though his blood was moving faster than his heart was beating, as though all the hairs on his body and head were dancing in quarter-inch circles, bobbing and weaving in some tiny ballet. He looked at Mr. Knox and realized he was frightened.

"People have died in here." Hamish wiped away sweat.

"Yes, I think they have."

"They're gone now."

"Yes, I think so." Mr. Knox took Hamish's shoulders. "Breathe, my boy. Deep. Exhale slowly. Again."

Hamish did as he was instructed, and his body calmed, becoming more his.

"Can we go up?"

"Of course."

Upstairs, Hamish drank two glasses of water, choking on the gulps of the second one. He sat with his coughs, and Mr. Knox laughed.

"It is a lot, is it not?"

He laid a photo album on the coffee table between them. It was leather-bound with frayed corners. Knox opened it up to the first page. There was a man in an old black-and-white photograph leaning on an elephant. The man had a push broom, the handle cupped to his chest. Hamish noticed the elephant's trunk was draped over the man's shoulder as a friendly mantle, the tip tickling the man's ear.

"This is my father. In the Tiergarten Schönbrunn. Vienna. The zoo in Vienna."

"When was this?"

"This photograph was taken in—let's see—" Mr. Knox took the photo with its scalloped edges out of the black corner guards and turned it over. Hamish could see written on the back in fountain pen: Der Redner—1938. The "D" and the "R" each had a flowing curl; the "1" looked like a slice of pie.

"Is that your father's name?"

"No. Der Redner means the Speaker."

Hamish felt he was entering a tunnel. Everything was closing in on him, but if he kept moving, and moving fast, he could outrun the constriction and burst out the other end, free and in a new country.

"Your father was a Speaker?"

"This is what he was telling me, yes."

Hamish looked at the photo as though he could will the man there to talk to him. The man was smiling, his eyes beginning to crinkle like the beginning of a sneeze at the elephant's trunk on his earlobe. Hamish could see how the elephant was with the man, how her ears were cocked, the tilt of her head, the steadiness of her legs, the peeking of her old paintbrush tail out from behind. She loved him.

CHAPTER 8

I must say that Thaddeus Knox was one of the great Witnesses I've known and a great friend, but he had a difficult time with Speakers, and a difficult time with young people. The simple explanation is that his father disappeared at a crucial time in his son's development, and Thaddeus had to grow up faster than he should have, with the shadow of a giant in his wake.

He was born with a different name. His given name was Amadeo Gustav Schiller. He changed it to Thaddeus Knox sometime after coming to America in the late '50s. He chose it himself. The first name was after the Polish-American General during the Revolutionary War, Tadeusz Kosciuszko, who had made himself into a newcomer hero of the new country; the second after Fort Knox, because he wanted to be rich. He was a very romantic young man.

His father was the operations director at the Tiergarten Schönbrunn, the oldest zoo in Vienna. It was a convenient hiding place for a Speaker. But with the Anschluss of 1938 when the Germans took over Austria, Herr Schiller decided he had to get his family out of Vienna. The young Amadeo remembered going with his father to the Tiergarten to say good-bye to his father's charges. That is when he learned of his father's talents. The streets were crowded with people moving swiftly, not like a regular working day. One intersection was filled with trucks of men with helmets hurtling past from over the Danube like horses on the track, the black and white Balkenkreuz fluttering on small flags attached to hoods. It was so much noisier than usual, the sky cloudy and cold, even for March.

Amadeo remembered a white colorlessness to the day, as though something important were being leeched out.

It began with a playful otter who wanted Herr Schiller's son to splash water, and he swooped his front legs up like a couple of apostrophes, leaning them onto Amadeo's knee. Herr Schiller explained that he could talk with the otter, as he could with all animals, and that he was a Speaker. This of course mystified and intrigued the ten-year-old Amadeo, who wanted to be a Speaker, too. His father told him then he was probably a Witness, with his penchant for languages and his eidetic mind.

Mr. Knox remembers his father telling him:

—You must see, you must organize, you must tell people what you see, but you must be careful, because there are those who would stop you, even those who would harm you. A Keeper I know calls them the 'one-life people.' They have no interest in the future, so they can hurt things and destroy things without feeling loss.

—We have more than one life?

His father had laughed.

—I do not know the answer to that question, Amadeo! No one does.

As far as I can tell, and what Mr. Knox told Hamish, it has always been like this. There are people from very ancient times—they are even pictured on walls in temples in India and China—they appear in stories all over the world—who have had these skills, conversing with animals, seeing and remembering. There are the Speakers, small in number, who are connected to a vast system of rhythm and impulse; Witnesses who try to point the way; and Keepers who connect us all, who have a kind of love in them that is deep and shiny. They are like seeing the sunlight reflected at the bottom of a cool well.

At the American grizzly bear's cage, the young Amadeo was thrilled because he'd never been so close to such a large animal. The bear stood up, standing nearly five feet taller than his father. He leaned his head back, letting out something between a roar and a crying sob. Schiller took his son's hand and pulled him away from the fencing.

The zoo was laid out like a wheel, with the elephants off from the center. The boy and his father walked up to the octagonal Rococo building at the hub of the zoo, the Kaiserpavilion. This was where the Emperor nearly two hundred years previous could have his breakfast surrounded by wild animals and feel himself king of the jungle.

In the elephant house, the smell of cool, humid hay and pungent digestion hit Amadeo. A few pigeons flapped noisily up to the top of the grand space. Amadeo saw his father move towards the elephant as though to embrace her leg or neck, and she warded him off and pushed him in front of her so her left eye could see him. He tried again, and she pushed him again. His arms hung at his sides as his head swung back and forth, and sounds came out of him that Amadeo had never heard a human being make. He raised his arms high together and looked up, as though seeing a shooting star through the ceiling. And then his arms lowered, with one outstretched, palm down, fingers spread towards the matriarch. She lifted her trunk into his hand, bumping it up gently, and then looped her trunk around his neck and pulled him to her. She breathed out of her mouth on the top of his head and turned her head slightly side to side so her tusks pressed each shoulder, invisible epaulets imprinted on his bones.

For the first and last time, Amadeo saw his father weep.

Mr. Knox was able to quote to Hamish exactly the conversation his father and he had had as they left to zoo:

—Can you speak with all animals? Even those birds up there? Amadeo pointed straight up to some Danube seagulls coasting over the zoo, riding the chilly air.

—Even those, when they are saying something.

They waited for the tram.

—That first day in the zoo, it happened to me. Walter Grün is my best friend. He came here the same day. I came to work here just after the Great War. The destruction was terrible. Thousands of animals had been killed—food, neglect, sport. The ones who were left were shocked, some were going crazy.

—Animals go crazy?

—Just like people, if life is hard enough.

Then he continued:

—I was overtaken, like a fever or an hallucination. Almost too powerful for me. Walter kept me from running off to God-knows-where. Birds came from all over, swirling around my head. I was the center of a cyclone that had a huge pull on it, like gravity pulling on the tide, and I knew I had to move, that I had something to do. I learned that it is in a way like what happens to animals when they are called upon to migrate. The urge is so strong you cannot willingly stop it. I could understand the animals and they me and we were all moving together. The animals in their cages wanted out so they could move with me. And then it became very fantastical. Although, now that I think on it, perhaps for a boy it is not so strange.

—All through the zoo there were animals who were not there. I mean to say, they were, but they had passed. They were—I am saying this badly—they were the spirits or the essences of the animals who had been so suddenly killed. It's as though necromancers have been right all along. Except I knew what I had to do. All the animals following me had been saying, It's the Speaker, there's the Speaker. And I had no idea what they were saying about me. But when I came to these spirits, I knew. And I spoke.

—What did you say?

—You know, Amadeo, I don't really know. I couldn't repeat it to you now. Maybe you could, if you had been there, but I don't think so. I only know that I showed them the way home.

—Home?

—The way home. And they went. And the air cleared and it was as though light could shine on this little piece of earth again.

—Is that what you do, Papa? Talk to dead animals?

—I think a Speaker does more than that.—Schiller was laughing.—I think a Speaker comes during a time when cycles go off balance, and teeter too far over the edge. I think somehow a Speaker must help right the balance.

—How, Papa?

—Do you remember when you were sick last year, when you had pneumonia? And the doctor who came to help, finally?

—Dr. Fu Manchu!

—No, Amadeo.—His father admonished him.—His name was Dr. Zung, and he saved your life. Do you remember how he held your hand and felt your pulse for a very long time? He was listening to your heart. That's something a Speaker can do. I can hear the heart.

—What does it sound like?

—It took me a very long time to learn, just like I imagine it took Dr. Zung a long time to hear people's hearts. But I hear the heart of the earth, the part of the earth that I'm on. When that's out of balance, like your pulse was when you had pneumonia, I learned to call in things to help right the balance, just as Dr. Zung did things for you that helped right the balance in your body.

—What things?

—Living things. Animals. They are part of this, and they will do what they can to achieve balance, even when they don't know that's what they're doing. They need someone to speak to them about it. And sometimes they tell me what needs to be done.

—The Nazis are like monsters among mammals, he continued, and they are not alone. Perhaps they are one-life creatures. There are forces using power that will turn back on itself. Think if the lions killed all the animals around them, even if they couldn't eat them. Then the lions would eat each other, and then they would starve. That's out of kilter.

The tram arrived.

—What did the elephant say to you?

—She told me to take care of my herd.

CHAPTER 9

Mr. Knox sat quietly, then took a last sip of his tea. "I was not much help to him. We went to Switzerland and stayed there, working a dairy farm because my father was so good with animals. But my father was not with us often. I think he told the cows to be good to us." Knox chuckled and grimaced at this. "I do not know really what he did when he was away. I suspect he went into Germany and Italy and Austria—I know once he went to Poland—but he always said it was better we not know. Then in '45 my father heard from a refugee they were eating the animals in the zoo, and he said he had to go back to Vienna. I was fifteen and full of myself, and I insisted on going with him. We got back, and Vienna was in shambles. Mr. Walter Grün and his family were gone, except for his oldest son Alexander, who was a year younger than me. He was still hiding out behind the tiger's cages, even though the tigers had been killed by a soldier a couple years before so he could sell the teeth and skins. Poor Alexander was crazy and thin and freezing. He attached himself to my father like a puppy, which may have been what killed him. I was out scouting for food on only our second day back in Vienna when a bombing hit the zoo. It killed my father and Alexander and hundreds of animals. Hyenas and ostriches and even a wounded orangutan were wandering all over the zoo when I got there. It was horrible. To my shame, I fled. I couldn't get back to my mother, and I never saw her again. I ended up in the Levant, and then India, where I stayed for some time."

The quiet of the hot summer night settled on them like ash flakes from distant fires, barely making an impression yet spacious as time.

Hamish tried to see into Mr. Knox, see what part of his history would help him when he was fumbling around in the dark, even now.

"Do you really remember everything?" asked Hamish.

"It is sometimes unfortunate, but yes, I do. That is one of the things Witnesses do. You, a Speaker, engage with energies I still can only imagine. I, a Witness, remember."

"Mr. Knox, how old are you?"

"You ask because I look only fifty or so?"

"If you were born in 1928, then you are seventy-five. I've never known someone who is seventy-five like you."

Mr. Knox chuckled. "There's no magic. That's your department. I just live a clean life." He laughed loudly and stood, indicating their evening was at an end.

"I will walk you to the edge of the park."

"That's OK. I know my way around." Hamish stood also, feeling awkward with leaving.

"Have you met my friend yet, the one who lives in the park?"

"There are many people—I mean, creatures, uh, animals—lots of them live in the park."

"This one you will know is special. I will be very interested in what you have to tell me about her."

"Mr. Knox," asked Hamish after a moment. "Are there other Speakers around here?"

"Not here, no." Mr. Knox looked up at the summer night sky. "You are both the youngest, and the only one on this continent for quite some time. I think that may have something to do with the plagues and genocide that afflicted this land when Europeans came. There is an older Speaker who is part Navajo somewhere in Arizona, but she keeps to herself."

"Can I meet her?"

"In a few days, I will introduce you to the oldest Speaker I know. She's from Britain, but she's in New York just now, and ill. But she will see us. A dancer, Alicia Markova."

"Here?"

"An astonishing woman. She will like you, I am thinking."

"All the animals think I'm here because there's trouble. But there's trouble everywhere! What do I look at? What should I change?" pleaded Hamish. "I seem to just screw things up."

"Like most skills in life, I think you have to learn." Mr. Knox smiled. "As my father said, it has to do with riding the forces moving against the tides of destruction and entropy."

"What the hell does that mean?" asked Hamish, exasperated. "That doesn't mean anything."

"Of course, of course," said Knox with a note of frustration in his voice. He patted Hamish's shoulder. "Kaphiri Shenouda is a Keeper. Trust him. For now, let the animals teach you. Then, let Kaphiri teach you."

Hamish put out his hand to shake. "OK, thank you, Mr. Knox. And thank you for telling me about your father."

"It is a pleasure to have someone to whom I can tell this story. Someone who can understand."

"You won't tell anyone about me, will you?" Hamish knew as soon as he said it that it was the wrong thing to say, but Mr. Knox put on a show of graciousness.

"Of course not. Your secret is safe. As, I trust, is mine."

Hamish nodded. Mr. Knox let go of his hand, and Hamish turned into the coming night.

∞

On his way home, Hamish detoured the long way through the park. In the evening like now, people bent the rules and a few dogs wandered free. Officially, dogs could be off-leash only before 9:00 in the morning. He was to discover later that Long Meadow was always difficult to cross at off-leash times. All the dogs seemed to know him as soon as he stepped onto the lawn. A few dogs treated Hamish like the discovery of fire, and they wanted to take credit for it. Jealousies developed instantly and fights broke out which brought owners running, desperate to separate the animals and proclaim indignation or abashed guilt.

The first time, when a chocolate lab and a large shepherd-mix were raising hackles and hurling insults, Hamish said, *Your enemy is not your meal. Your friend is.*

The two dogs were immediately still, and looked at Hamish who had surprised himself with his words. The shepherd-mix said, *Again?*

Your enemy is not your meal. Your friend is. Hamish hoped he'd remembered right.

Hunh. Both dogs looked at each other, wagged their tails a bit, saying, *That's interesting,* and then turned to other dogs who had gathered and there was a sudden seminar that quickly dissipated into playing and discoveries. Hamish eventually discovered that the crushing boredom most dogs felt made them oddly stupid, and even though they couldn't hold on to ideas for very long, it was enough to jog them away from social crises to throw a new idea in their midst, which their minds then grabbed like a clumsy but strong robot hand. They would stop nearly mid-stride if he told them something paradoxical, like a Buddhist koan or haiku abstraction.

This evening, the refuge that Prospect Park was becoming was cool and busy, like a dormitory both at bedtime and breakfast. As he headed over towards the boathouse, a group of kids, tall teenagers with do-rags and gold and baggy pants, came rapidly through the paths, their energy full of suppressed violence like a flash flood looking for a way out of the canyon. One of them slapped Hamish on the back of the head, and the hard laughter of the crew dopplered away ahead. Hamish's teeth hurt with the confrontation, and it made him cautious with his moves. He was still in Mr. Knox's story wondering where all this new information put him in the world, and realized he was completely outside himself. He tried "The Shenouda Shit," breathed three times, and realized that if he listened to the animals, he could know where people were.

This was a time of shift change. The daylight animals were bedding down, and the night was being entered into by bats and nightjars and raccoons and rodents. Owls flew softly off branches. Muffled quacking came from duck nests on the island. Cats hurried across open spaces. Hamish thought he saw a coyote, but whatever it was sped away. The zoo was alive with conversation, but Hamish refused to engage. There was something that stirred a huge anxiety in him as he approached the zoo's fences and walls, like someone was demanding something from him and he didn't know what it was. His skin bubbled with goose-bumps and his breathing came from cast iron lungs, taking him back to the panic of passing the pile of the World Trade Center. So he walked towards the Boathouse and let his body come back to itself.

He came down the path along the inlet from the lake. There was splashing in the inlet and Hamish froze. He could only imagine a person making that kind of noise, and wondered if the teenagers were there and would mug him for real. He stepped off the path into the trees, making a circle so he could see who was there. He thought he saw a large dog trying to get something out of the water in the settling darkness, but he couldn't be sure in the mixture of lamplight and late evening haze. He turned to continue.

There in front of him was a black panther. Hamish couldn't believe it, but he couldn't mistake it either. He could see it begin to crouch, its paws firming themselves on the earth.

Whoa! said Hamish in his surprise.

The panther lifted her head quickly. They stared at each other for long seconds.

You were fishing, Hamish realized.

The panther blinked. *You were watching.*

Hamish felt in no danger. On the contrary, he felt oddly protected now. *I have never seen your kind.*

Hmf, said the panther with a hint of pride. *I know of you, Speaker. But it is strange to have food talking.*

I am not food.

You are to somebody.

Hamish realized the panther was laughing at him.

Did you catch a fish? asked Hamish.

You came too soon.

I will leave you, then. Hamish backed up.

The panther approached, her blackness in the dark moving as a supple shadow whose edges cannot be determined. Hamish could smell her, could see light reflected from her eye. She came within a foot, and slowly calmed onto her haunches.

Do you submit?

Hamish looked steadily into the eyes of the panther. He knew it was important not to blink.

I do not submit.

I could kill you.

Yes, said Hamish. *But you won't.*

No, I won't. The panther seemed almost wistful. *Ears.*

Excuse me?

Scratch my ears.

Hamish reached out and touched the panther's ears. Her head was higher than his waist, and she leaned into his fingers. He scratched hard, her short black fur warm and soft, her skull bone hard as steel underneath. He felt her vibrate.

Suddenly she pulled back and took a leap away. Someone was coming. Hamish leaned against a tree, and also became invisible. Bagheera, he thought. That will be your name. And I am in "The Jungle Book." He laughed to himself. He did not see her again that night.

∞

Hamish realized this must be Mr. Knox's "friend" who lives in the park. How was this possible? he wondered. Where did she come from? How did she eat? Did she kill people? Children? Dogs? Why hadn't she been discovered? Surely she must have left paw prints and surely someone must have questioned their size, their shape. Surely someone must have seen her somewhere, slipping behind a dumpster or coming down a tree, lit by streetlights or cars. How did she live through the winter? Where did she come from?

Hamish thought it must have been someone who had her as a pet when she was small, and then let her go when she became too much. Or maybe she just escaped, and no one said anything because it was illegal to have wild cats in the city. In the next days Hamish found time to go to the Brooklyn Library, the imposing art deco building on Grand Army Plaza between the botanic gardens and the park, looking for articles or rumors or trivia that might point him to the historical truth. The panther could have come from the Brooklyn Zoo itself when it was closed for a complete overhaul in the late '80s and early '90s. Changes were motivated in part because of a horrible incident in 1987, where three kids tried to go wading after hours in the moat of the polar bear enclosure. The bears, named Teddy and Lucy, killed one 11-year-old boy named Juan, and then were shot by arriving police officers, who thought the other boys were there, too. The fusillade of shotgun and revolver blasts must have put the zoo into a panic and woken the entire neighborhood. But the other boys had run home, shoeless, pantless, and scared out of their minds after Teddy had taken Juan by the head up the rocks.

Hamish discovered they did have a young panther before the renovation, but he could not discover where she had been moved to. Most of the Brooklyn animals were distributed among the four other New York zoos, and then zoos around the country, but Hamish could find no record of the black panther.

He had talked with a black panther. Brooklyn was suddenly an exciting place to be.

CHAPTER 10

Summer and insomnia seemed to be kissing cousins, heat making sheets cloying and the dark amplifying distant sounds. Hamish turned in his bed. Pale light leaked under his door from the bathroom down the hall, and the airshaft window was a musty salt rectangle in the black of his room, only really visible if he didn't look at it directly. He was bursting with the last few days, his brain full of the messy traffic of questions and fantasies. He had discovered an entire world and he couldn't talk to anyone about it except three old men. No one would understand. Besides, who could he tell in this ugly, depraved city? He was every lonely hero in every lonely fantasy he'd ever read, bursting through a wardrobe or cave or time-warp into a crazy, alien world. Mr. Knox had said, Learn from the animals. They will be your teachers.

Hamish and his father had always talked of going to the Bronx Zoo. It achieved a mythic status in the adventures they were going to have when he got well: the biggest zoo in America. Henry wanted to use the fabled trip to make a point, and he was vocal about the speciousness of zoos' missions to introduce the public to wild animals, to make them more sympathetic to protecting what they see. But Henry thought it made animals more like pets, that people didn't understand the meaning of wild, that they couldn't comprehend the vastness of living space and the power of instinct. He told Hamish about visiting a zoo in Barcelona where they clipped off half the wings of eagles and chained one leg to a log on little square islands in a pond so people could see them without bars interfering. Or the dark cages in Brooklyn—gone now—that held jaguars who paced back and forth in a ten-foot loop like blind autistic children trying to comfort themselves.

Hamish thought he could bring relief to these imprisoned animals. He could find out what they really wanted, and then find ways to alleviate their confined lives. He could find out what he was supposed to do. He could find out if this was real.

∞

The subway to the Bronx Zoo took over an hour and a half on the 2 train. No one knew where he was, and he was grateful. He felt lucky the second he got on the subway car and breathed in the air-conditioning. It made the car crowded but Hamish could feel his skin drinking in the cool. There was an astonishing array of people, nothing like back home in Plains. He saw men with different kinds of headgear, and women completely covered in cloth or seemingly naked in shorts and halter-tops. He couldn't stop looking, and people stared back at him with sudden and vicious neutrality. Even in the air-conditioning he sweat. He could feel his palms grease the handrails, and drops tickling down his ribs. At the Park Place station which was near the disappeared Twin Towers, the anxiety and sensation of thousands of voices crowded his brain again, but he breathed his way through it as the train pulled north. He knew for certain now that the World Trade Center was a place he needed to avoid. At the 96th Street station, all the white people except him left the train as though by a prearranged pact. Hamish had never been the only white person in a room, and he wondered if he should be afraid. But he was ignored, and the train screeched through the tunnels north.

He found the zoo, paid for his admission, and went under the archway.

He had entered an alternate universe. Japanese and German and Spanish-speaking tourists flocked in the heat, chattering in languages he couldn't fathom. And all around him were cries and shouts from animals in languages he'd never heard but could understand in ways that opened his gut and made his head feel like a transparent globe. There was playful and angry and annoyed, ecstatic and joyful and teasing, kind and awful and dangerous. And he hadn't seen anyone yet except a couple of exotic birds full of self-importance.

A lion roared. The experience changed Hamish. It was like hearing the entire Declaration of Independence in five seconds, compacted in all its complexity into the simplest of messages: *This is me, and this is mine.* It was clear that this was not what all roaring was, in the same way not all "ah" sounds meant the same thing. There was a current of power that the hearer could choose to understand or not, but to misunderstand was perilous. This was nothing like talking with a pigeon or a squirrel.

Hamish followed the sound to his left. There was a modest sign for African Plains. Over a fence and through some small trees he could see a field. There were some deer-like animals, heads to the short grass, taking turns lifting their gaze around, tails flickering occasionally like mild bursts of police car lights. A few long-legged birds strode like matrons through the herd. Walking on, Hamish realized there were moats and strategic fences between hills and rocks to keep animals separate. Then suddenly, to his left, there were the lions.

A male was standing apart from two females and another smaller male. He looked at the people on the path as the others lounged in the shade. Hamish noticed a younger lioness draped over a low branch, a loose and tawny mattress. Hamish bellied up to the fence over the moat. His excitement took hold of his stomach and danced an unknown dance with it, and his peripheral vision seeped ink with surprising messages hidden in the stunning blots that he knew he should take a moment to decipher, but what was in front of him was so seductively compelling he couldn't bear to not indulge every sugary ounce of this wild power.

Hello, he said, quietly.

All five of the lions turned to him, the ones lying down standing to face him. The young lioness oozed off the branch and crouched in Hamish's direction, eventually spotting him in the movement of people. Hamish felt their gaze as light, clear and dangerous, the way an armed bomb is dangerous. This was better than flying free, and at the same time Hamish felt he shouldn't be here. He felt it was only a matter of time before he was found out, that his fraud would be discovered even though he didn't know what that fraud was except that his life was so unbelievable. So he decided to fake it, to pretend he knew what he was doing.

An older lioness took a few steps down the rock, nonchalant and careful. She sat, and lifted her head again.

What do you want? she said with infinite patience.

Just to let you know that I'm here, that I'm around. You know, if you need anything.

The Speaker asks if we need anything?

Yeah, you know, if there's anything you want that I can do for you.

The next thing that happened was so fast that Hamish remembered it only as a soldier remembers a sudden firefight.

The male, the leader, streaked down the hill and, gathering himself at the moat, leapt across, his claws extended as they tried to dig into the concrete of the wall that held the fence Hamish was leaning on. People screamed. Hamish could hear the claws furiously try for purchase on the wall, and the wild splashing as the leader fell into the water. The green moat water became black with mud from the bottom and the putrid smell of it exploded up in the heat. He tried twice more to get up the wall, and Hamish was certain he would climb it like a tree and wipe his paw across Hamish's neck and crush Hamish's skull between his teeth. But Hamish was frozen.

With no pause, the leader relinquished the wall and emerged on the other side of the moat. He shook water out his mane, turned to Hamish, and roared.

The roar said: *You are dead. You will never have what is mine. You will never give me anything because you have nothing to give. You are a lie. You do not exist.*

The lion turned and walked up the hill. He started to pass the young lioness who made a small move as though to look at Hamish. He snarled, *You snake.* And he turned on her pinning her throat to the ground with his jaws. She was trying to claw him off with her back feet, scrambling against an impossible landslide of fur and teeth and muscle and claw. Hamish realized there were warning sounds everywhere in the zoo. Calls were loud and panicked and repeated: *Watch out. Defend yourself. Protect the children. Run. Hide.*

The report of an explosion jarred everything into a second of silence. The zookeepers were trying emergency measures. The leader released the young lioness and she pulled herself away from him, lifting herself to a wobbling stand, dark blood coating her neck and side. Zookeepers were yelling. People now crowded to the fence to find out what had happened.

The leader looked back at Hamish, and turned to walk into an enclosure hidden from view.

The older female said to Hamish, *Go. And never return.* She followed her mate.

A zookeeper was ushering people away from the fence. Another had a rifle and was scoping the rock where three lions were left. Hamish was pulled back and told to leave, to go to a different part of the zoo. This area was closed for the day. Already orange traffic cones and yellow caution tape were being placed on the path. He followed the flow of people further into the zoo. He looked back hoping to see the young lioness walk, but as he turned, she toppled to the ground, out of his view.

As he let himself be swept along, he heard reactions from all around as though to an invading army. He knew that he was the invader. But he didn't know what he'd done to bring such fear and rage into the world. He was in front of the bears. A grizzly bear was looking in the direction of the lions. Hamish felt he should know him, as though he were an old friend. Another bear came up to the first.

What is it, can you tell?

Not sure. Feels like ghosts have risen.

Then they need someone to listen.

No, it can't be ghosts. We'd feel it.

Hm.

The bears contemplated the air, their noses quivering through hot breezes.

Nothing different. Just fear. Some blood. And this boy looking at us. He's rich.

As the second bear turned to look at Hamish, Hamish tried to shut down his mind, to even out his breath, to slow the beating of his heart.

He's trying to hide.

You know who he is, right?

Sure. Wonder why he's trying to hide?

Hamish turned away and walked quickly, afraid of the ascendant fearlessness in the grizzly bear's gaze.

There was a building ahead under the trees. They asked for some money and Hamish gave it to them. It was a dark auditorium, and they started a movie about gorillas. Hamish was relieved to have only people around him, and he closed his eyes. But even in the film, he could hear snippets of the animals' language, gorillas talking about humans, asking for food, complaining about each other, teasing. The narrator hoped everyone had enjoyed the film, and then asked them to look at the real thing.

The movie screen lifted, and there was a whole family of gorillas behind glass, carrying on as though this were the most normal event of their day.

Hamish couldn't understand them. The glass kept out sounds and smells. It was like he could get only every fifth word, and since words weren't exactly or exclusively the way language was transmitted, it was only enticing pieces of misunderstanding. Hamish realized that these gorillas did use what he thought of as words more than, say, hawks did. But the idea of one-to-one correspondence was not a useful concept. Even Hamish's nose felt left out of the conversation.

But he could see what was taking place on the other side of the glass. This was love. These creatures knew who they belonged to, and they allowed themselves to belong. It was not some kind of idyll. There was nothing romantic about it. Life still happened, Hamish could tell. The younger male off to the left was bored crazy, ready to scratch himself into oblivion. Two females were in some kind of feud, hunching near each other, assuring the other got nothing they themselves didn't get, angling for favor from an older female who had a baby on her lap. A youngster was quickly chased away, up into a tree, after annoying a graying male. But even the loneliest of them was not alone, and they knew it.

Hamish was lost. Clearly they didn't need him. No one needed him. Here he had this gift, but of what use was a gift so profound and measureless if he could only use it for birthday clown tricks? Useless as a hobby, like collecting ashtrays or license plate sightings.

As he got up to leave, his stomach started vibrating as though a pillow was punching him. The gorillas moved quickly and screamed, and the screams got through the glass. Hamish could understand *She's trying to find someone. Wow, is she pissed! It's OK, kids, it's not us.* The younger ones were moving around fast. The older ones all looked in the same direction, and at each other for reassurance.

Hamish knew he was being summoned. It came to him clearly, out of the earth and straight into his gut: *Speaker, come here.*

CHAPTER 11

He stumbled out of the gorilla house, following the summons that was a trail of sensation heading north. A small sign with an arrow leading ahead said, Elephant House. He passed more tourists beginning to hide from the intense sun of midday. The walkway opened up to lead to a large building that looked to Hamish like a church. On the way was a life-sized bronze rhinoceros standing inside chains on stanchions, patinaed and armored. On either side of the lofting archway were stone elephant heads, their trunks and tusks draping down the marble. The crown keystone of the arch was a limestone rhino's head, looking astonished to be tacked there, as though it had been shot and mounted before it could realize it was dead.

The rumbling was everywhere in Hamish's body as he went under the arch and stood under the cupola of latticed brick and a dozen round windows that opened to the pallid sky. There she was, a large Indian elephant, her tail twitching and her head rocking side to side. The plaque on the side said her name was Happy.

Come here, Speaker.

Hamish could not refuse. He came as close as he could, the railing stopping him.

Oh. You are a young one. No wonder you're such an idiot.

Hamish felt himself flushing with shame rather than fear. *I can't help being young.*

Stay still.

The elephant reached her trunk out and ruffled through his hair. The trunk was amazingly warm and soft, if wet on the end. She snuffled his shirt and down to his pants. She touched his hips and then sniffed and moved his ears. Impossibly, she opened his mouth and gently rubbed his teeth. She cuffed the side of his head with her trunk, a bump from a living medicine ball, which made him feel both admonished and accepted.

Nothing special about you.

Hamish looked up into her wrinkled face. *Except I can talk to you.*

Happy seemed both amused and exasperated. *I met one of you when I was young. She came and moved around here, like she was crazy. But she was beautiful. We danced together. I liked her very much. She must be dead now.*

Hamish wondered who this might have been, and if it was the woman Mr. Knox wanted him to meet. He reached toward the elephant's trunk and touched it with the tips of his fingers. He thought of the photograph of Herr Schiller and his elephant in Austria so many years ago. The elephant pulled away.

What did you do that caused such a ruckus? she asked.

I asked if I could do anything for the lions.

What are you talking to the lions for? Are you a complete baboon baby? They don't like anyone telling them anything they didn't already think they knew. Especially grandfather. He'll slice your face as soon as smile. He's gone insane, you know.

He hurt a young one, a lioness.

Of course he did, you fool, because he couldn't get to you. Asking what you could do for him… What are you going to do for him, a grub like you? You going to get him some nice gazelle meat, all skinned and warm? You going to spread the land before him so he can see herds for miles in all directions? You going to kill all snakes and hyenas to keep them from getting his own babies?

I—

Don't offer what you can't deliver. And don't ask the wrong question. You creatures are so strange. The dancing woman, that other Speaker, said she had to stop people from destroying everything. I think she was playing with my mother a bit. How could you destroy everything? But she was very worried. She came in with my mother so she was telling truth. But it never seemed real. What people do doesn't seem real.

She came in to where you live? Hamish thought for a second this was what he was supposed to do, live with the animals as they lived.

No, something different. Happy tossed some straw on her back. *Did everything get destroyed?*

I don't think so. We're here now.

So either she was a fool like you, or she succeeded. I think she probably succeeded because my mother wouldn't have allowed a fool to come in.

Come into your pen?

Another elephant entered from outside. He was younger than the matriarch, and larger. A male named George. He was her child. He clearly didn't trust Hamish.

You're going to let him come in?

I think he should, said Happy as she waved her ears at him, warning him to keep his distance.

Suddenly Hamish knew exactly what she meant. To enter into another consciousness, another spirit, another being. Not something that can be forced, only shared. Hamish knew he wanted it. Something was waiting for him.

Can I come in?

We'll see.

When?

Now.

A rumble started deep inside the elephant. It was an invitation, as though there were an entrance to a cave and the cave itself beckoned and spread open its hands. It was not an easy step for Hamish to make over the threshold. He felt his hands tightening on the railing around the elephant enclosure, and his legs deciding on their own to hold him in place while he was gone. He moved forward with a kind of satisfying squeeze. And he was with the elephant. As suddenly as that, he had come in.

He was in the enclosure standing there looking out. There were two men, who drifted through. The other elephant, George, came over and gave an inquisitive touch on the head with his trunk.

You good?

Happy and Hamish batted him gently away with an amazingly dexterous and sensitive tube of flesh, and Hamish realized they were moving the trunk. George seemed to smack his lips.

Don't stay too long, he said.

Happy turned as though looking back for Hamish, and Hamish came with her.

As Hamish tells:

It is raining. The sky is white and the land is green, and the hill makes it difficult to see very far.

Teacher. Teaching her. She's just up ahead. Paths weave in between trees. Reach up and strip leaves. You can munch as you walk. The leaves are sweet and bitter. The crunch wets each curl of lip, tongue getting it off of teeth and down the throat. Oops! Mom's gone. Hurry ahead. She's already across the field going towards a man in blue, skin the color of Mom's eye. He smells of things burning, ashy and sugary. His hands are fun rubbing my back. We bump him. He squirts water—not his trunk—like from his hands. Cool. Right in the mouth. Too much!

Dark, bright spots of light on poles, hum of metal like tiny chains turning in the distance. Ashy-and-Sugary has his hand on our cheek and we follow up a ramp that clatters into a square space above the ground. Mom is there. She's Ok. She moves some hay, tells us to let Ashy-and-Sugary attach us to the room. She believes him. We don't want to, but she nudges us. That's it. There's clanking on our legs. The square space—Hamish realizes it's a train car—moves and moves us over the ground until after the sun comes up, light flickering over us. Lots of oily smoke. We're somewhere different.

Hamish can see what she saw through her memory/vision. He can read the signs she can't, know the things she doesn't. He thinks to himself: Cincinnati smells so different from the farm in Georgia where Happy was born. Ashy-and-Sugary, a man with blue overalls, weeps when he has to say goodbye after the train trip north.

Someone else. Sometime else. We don't like him. He's a young bull elephant, and thinks he knows everything. (Hamish is nervous; he knows what this is supposed to be, and he doesn't want to know where it will lead.) The bull has an erection like a second trunk, nearly down to the ground. He tries to push us around, is trying to position us so he can mount. Happy—we—turn and whack him, yell at him to get the fuck off. He's offended.

It's years later. Hamish recognizes the Bronx Zoo building. There's a woman with black hair and wearing old-fashioned clothing literally doing ballet in front of Happy's enclosure. She's maybe 50, completely un-self-conscious. She asks Happy, *Do you do this? Do you dance?*

Of course, we say.

Then let's dance, you and I, before the Russians and the Americans lob their bombs on each other and the world ends, she says. She Speaks. Please. Dance with me.

So we dance.

∞

Hamish remembered the dance seeming to last forever, he and Happy caught up in the rhythm, the back and forth, the hypnotic turnings of the head and whisks of the tail, the clap-flap of the ears that was syncopated to the brush of feet on the cement floor. Every seventh step, a snort and a curl of the trunk, touching both shoulders and swinging down to the ground. It was easy and full and then over because Hamish was back in himself and Happy rocked a little as Hamish reached for the bar in front of him to steady himself. He had felt no transition. It was like waking from a particularly vivid dream, taking a minute to know if the dream was finished, and then wondering if you could just turn around and go back in.

Wow, exhaled Hamish. *What was that?*

I invited you. You came in. Happy was still swaying slightly. George peeked around the corner to see what was going on. Happy snorted at him, *He's just as strange as they all are. But he's young.*

Everyone thinks I'm too young.

Not too young. Just young.

Hamish reached for her trunk. She let him. He rubbed it with an affection that astonished him. *Can I do that with anybody?*

You have to be invited.

But if they invite me, I can?

I don't know! Sheesh, you ask a lot of questions.

Hamish was reveling in and humbled by the difference he felt, and the kinship. *May I come see you again?*

Of course, young Speaker.

Thank you. As he turned, he saw the plaque that said the elephant's name, Happy, again. *What's your name?* He asked her.

The response was so deep it hurt, a vibration through the cement floor and a shimmering in the air. She was angry.

You don't ask. I give if I want. It's too dangerous to give it to just anyone.

I'm sorry, Hamish flushed. *My name is—* He suddenly didn't know how to tell the elephant his name was Hamish because he suddenly realized that was not the name she meant. *What is my Name?*

Ah. The Speaker grows.

Hamish turned to leave, stunned as though he'd looked down at his body and seen feathers and scales and paws and whiskers instead of his small hands and thin knees. He felt like he'd forgotten everything.

Speaker!

Hamish turned.

What did the lion say to you?

Hamish shrugged. *That I wasn't real. That I should be dead. That I should never come back.*

The elephant laughed. *You can come back. Just don't tell the lions. And bring peanuts. I do so love salted peanuts.*

∞

Even with all that had happened, Hamish felt his understanding getting smaller and smaller. The subway from the Bronx was too crowded, so he got off the train at 96th Street. He was going to walk all the way back to Brooklyn. He found himself on Broadway and went south, skipping between cars at crosswalks, daring cabs not to give way, the sweat soaking his back and sticking him to the cloying air. As he crossed Houston Street, he began to smell the remains of the World Trade Center, the chemical, metallic, rotting odor that even nearly two years later hung in the atmosphere like a stain. His skin began to itch and his heart to race. He kept east, as far from the construction site as he could. He ran over towards the Brooklyn Bridge, lungs and legs already burning. He ran and suddenly his father began to overrun him. He went faster, trying to keep the image at bay, holding the inexorable tide back with the cliffs of his heart. But the ocean of his father always seemed to find a low point in the resistance and would flood over, pouring through the landscape of his body. And then Hamish knew that one of two things was coming. Either a choking that was like drowning, the water sharp and harsh in his throat and spewing out his eyes with a suddenness that ended in a surprised and gasping silence. Or a floating, like the moment he watched his father die.

∞

His father had been unconscious for two days. The scars from the operations on his throat were small and pink and hard. His red hair was wispy and caked as though it had old flour in it. His eyes were not completely closed, sometimes moving, dreaming of elsewhere. The oxygen tube looping around his nostrils was a halter on a horse, holding him back despite his vastly superior strength. Everything was quietly hissing and low lighting and over-heating, like a church in midwinter. The hospice staff was spirits, barely there.

His mother rose to go get them something to eat.

"You gonna be OK?"

Hamish nodded at her with a low glance.

"You can go find Aunt Shirley if you need anything."

"I know."

She waited by the door.

"You sure?"

"Mom —"

"OK. I'll get some Doritos, too."

Hamish didn't answer as the door clicked shut. He sat with his back to the bed, his feet on the windowsill. The gum was stale as dry snot in his mouth. He took it out and looked for a trash can. Walking around the bed, he saw his father in the filtered fluorescents. His eyes were open, and they were following Hamish. Deep eyes. Clear eyes. Still yellow in the whites and red as licorice on the rims. But they saw him. They knew he was here. They knew who he was.

"Dad?"

Henry Taylor's expression didn't change. Hamish watched his father watching him as he came the side of the bed. The boy felt his father's hand rise to his son's face, felt his fingers touch the temple and jaw of the boy. Hamish knew the easy liquid in his own eyes was seen by those deep, clear eyes. He felt the warmth of his own hands as they slowly covered the radiating cold of his father's. He felt the young movement of his own breath deep inside him as only small air went into his father's body.

This was OK.

As his father's eyes dulled, there was a trick of light that made Hamish think a lavender spiral of dust motes twirled up from his father's head. And then a pop of white, like a flashbulb going off. But there was no after-image. It was just him and the body of his father, which sank slightly as the breath left him and there was a cough or a gurgle, a couple of gentle jerks, and then a nothing. The hand in his hand was nothing. He knew what had happened, and he was so scared because the world had just changed as though it had reversed the direction of its rotation and no one knew it except him. He was weightless. Fear took him over, filling his mouth with sourness, pouring chalk into his ears, gripping him on the edge of a sneeze that would not come. His joints rubberized, and he flowed to the floor.

It may have been an hour or a couple of days before he breathed when his mother touched his back and then lifted him to her lap. He breathed in her skin and her heat and her crooning and she rocked him with one arm, the other outstretched to touch the dead man on the bed.

CHAPTER 12

Hamish did something he hadn't done in many years. He fell asleep on the couch watching TV with his mother and leaned like a slowly falling tower until his face was on her shoulder. She must have treasured it for as long as she could, wanting to extend her arm around him and let him fall to her lap, nestled there til morning. But American Idol ended and she apparently didn't want to watch the news, so Sarah nudged her son into a standing position and guided him to his room. He slept in his clothes, and when he woke, his mother had already left for her job nursing dying children.

He went to Junior Rangers, just as a way to keep moving.

At the Picnic House, Hamish heard Clothilde's too-loud voice, "There he is! He's the one there! That's Hamish Taylor. You remember him? I introduced you. He's the one you got to ask."

Hamish was smiling in spite of himself as he turned to greet Clothilde. She was with her sister, Lilly, who was still tall and still had dark liquid eyes. Clothilde reached for Hamish's hand and shook it like she did the first time, trying to yank it out of his shoulder and down to the ground.

"Hey, Clothilde. You trying to kill me?"

Clothilde cracked up, literally slapping her thigh. She laughed so much she couldn't catch her breath. She reached out and held onto Lilly's arm to keep from doubling over. "Man! You are so funny!" She came up, her wet mouth open in a snaggle-tooth grin, her eyes opaque behind her thick glasses. "Lilly's got something she's got to ask you." Clothilde pushed her sister in front of her.

Lilly was shy. "Our mom wanted to know—"

"Can you come for dinner?!" Clothilde shouted.

A few kids turned around, and both Lilly and Hamish shrunk with embarrassment.

Lilly said quietly, "Mom wanted to invite you to dinner to thank you about Clothilde. She thought, like, since you were new here and all—"

Clothilde interrupted again, this time in a hoarse whisper. "You going to come, right?"

Even though he was dying of exposure, especially with the smokers Vivian and Shauna looking on planning their next attack, Hamish found himself laughing, as though he found himself naked in a crowded room and there was no place to hide so he gave up trying. "Sure. Thanks. That'd be great."

Lilly's relief was palpable. "Is tomorrow night OK?"

"Yeah," said Hamish. He might need a way out. "I need to ask my mom."

"Sure, yeah. Here's our phone number." Lilly handed him a piece of paper. She had prepared. "We just live over in Prospect Heights, on Prospect Place."

"OK."

Clothilde panted, "Bye, Lilly." She grabbed Hamish's hand and then suddenly pulled him down to her level. "See what I told you?" she hissed. She was pointing at Vivian and Shauna as they left the picnic house. Their fingers were playing with each other casually, intimately, like they were kissing with their hands.

"Boyfriend's gone!" Clothilde waggled her eyebrows.

Hamish looked after Lilly walking away on the path. Her shorts made her pale peach T-shirt move with each stride.

∞

Ranger Sally was talking to them in her first grade voice. "We just found a fantastic thing! You'll never guess what it is."

A couple of young children raised their hands with a desperate "I know, I know!" on their lips.

Ranger Sally humored them. "What do you think it is, Warren?"

"Is it—ah—a elephant?"

"No, it's not an elephant. They live in Africa. That's way on the other side of the world."

Eight-year-old Ashley would not be outdone. "It's a unicorn!"

Hamish was losing the patience he'd lost a couple of weeks ago, like a prisoner coming down to his release date.

"No," said Ranger Sally. "It's very small, but there are very many of them. Thousands of them. And they're all together in a thing called a swarm."

Three hands shot up and one kid called out, "Bees! It's bees!"

"That's right, Nathan! It's a swarm of bees. And we're going to go see them. Now line up, and remember that when we get there, you have to listen to everything I say, because I don't want anyone to get a bee sting. OK, everybody?"

They walked across the empty playing fields and headed up the hill towards the Quaker Graveyard fence. Hamish began to feel exposure coming on, hoping that Mr. Knox would not be anywhere near to see him in this humiliating group. Especially being led around by a bubbly loser like Ranger Sally. He snickered sardonically, wondering if he could feed any of these children to Bagheera.

Hamish saw the swarm long before anyone else, except Ranger Sally who knew where it was. It pulsed at him, like a busy heart. It hung in a maple tree near the fence about ten feet off the ground, like two pointillist pears connected by a thick webbed bridge of moving orange and brown and glints of transparency. It was as though the swarm couldn't decide on which branch to cluster, and had compromised on both, with a few thousand bees making up a connection between the two. Little spots hovered all around as scouts left and returned.

"Don't get any closer!" called Ranger Sally, grabbing Nathan before he could run right underneath the swarm. "We'll stay here and just watch."

The kids clustered around Ranger Sally, the younger they were, the closer they got. Some of the older ones got bored, and turned away to find a way out of sight to smoke. Clothilde let go of Hamish's hand, and approached Ranger Sally, taking her arm as though Sally were going to lead her into a dance.

Hamish went into a daydream, wondering what he was doing there. There was certainly a better place than this. If only he could get his mother to move. Maybe they could get a place really out in the country, where the land is fertile and things grow with abandon. This place is way too crowded, the streets and buildings too sterile for growth. With his new talents, he could get animals to help them, tilling and sowing and harvesting. Birds would be his allies in keeping bugs at bay, foxes would patrol the fields for varmints who wouldn't listen to his own instructions about leaving his crops alone. Fruits and vegetables would ripen and be fresh for his family every day. His mother would meet a man who was just as kind and patient and wise as his real father, and they would get married and have more children for Hamish to help raise, the big brother of a brood of wonderful siblings who someday could form a baseball team or a band.

He was woken by Ranger Sally's squeaky voice, "Hamish! Hamish! Not so close! I told you!"

He was nearly under the swarm, and a few bees had landed on his face. He didn't touch them; he felt in no danger. He felt excitement, weirdly as though he were going on a first date with a beautiful girl who he knew liked him.

"Stand still, Hamish. Stand perfectly still." Ranger Sally was now approaching him, and the other ranger was keeping the kids back.

Hamish realized bees were all over his back, and he felt their movements as little grumbles and gifts through his shirt. The itch and tickle as they got on his neck and arms was electric, static moving through him before a lightning storm. More bees collected on him until he could feel their heat. There was so much joy and anticipation he could barely contain himself. He turned to Ranger Sally and smiled.

She could see his features through the ever-increasing coating of bees. She held his eyes. "Are you OK?"

"I'm fine," he said with wonder.

"Can you hold on a while?"

"Sure." And Hamish laughed quietly, as though to a private joke.

"Hamish!" yelled Clothilde. "Get those bees off! They're going to sting you!"

"It's OK, Clothilde," assured Hamish, surprising even himself. "They just want to know what I'm doing here. They want to know if I know where they should go."

Ranger Sally was on the phone, but listening to Hamish. She hung up with a "Hurry." She came back closer to Hamish.

"I'm not going to leave, Hamish."

"I know."

"They're going to come and get them off you."

"I don't know whether they'd like that."

"The guy's coming with a smoker, and they'll just sleep."

Hamish laughed inside his blob of bees. He looked liked a swollen orangutan whose parts were in constant motion.

"They're all girls," he giggled.

He knew they were talking to him, but he had such a difficult time talking back, like having a name on the tip of his tongue which just would not come out. He was hearing:

What are you going to tell us me me I we look look look for newer the next maybe it's time to choose you go I go into you and I go some out into some in into fields are long there trees are hard there color of desolation to color of sweet and warm Oh! Remember the color of joy and busy mist two thousand eight hundred fifty one pulses with the pull on the right eye always no danger there there are you warning us from a line are you here She is the heart when did She? There there move again move again is the breeze shifting no not yet flying strings of whitish brown landing game might enter the body might land.

He realized Sally had come close and taken his hand. She was quiet. He could see she'd sent everyone about a hundred yards away. Bees landed on her, and crawled under her collar, but she didn't flinch.

"You need to put your ponytail under your hat," said Hamish.

"My ponytail?"

"They like it. But it distracts them."

"How do you -- ?"

"Just do it slowly, not thinking about it, as though it's something you forgot about long ago and don't need to remember."

Ranger Sally looked into Hamish's eyes through all the bees, let go of his hand briefly to casually sweep her yellow ponytail up under her hat. She brushed a few bees out as she did it, and they acted like children in waves at the seashore. She took his hand again.

"This is really interesting, isn't it?"

"You can't imagine."

It came upon him again.

Here she comes! Out of the heart comes the heart cool breezes make them breathe to find out what we have found out why are you here? What do you tell us about next?

Hamish found a way to say, *You know better than all I know, if I find anything I will come to dance before you and all will be busy and sweet.*

A promise going out into no impediments He can follow She has told him She has told him where.

"They're going to go, now," Hamish said. "Can you keep holding my hand?"

She squeezed his hand gently in response.

The density of bees on Hamish seemed to thin and the air became dangerous with flying. Bees landed for a few seconds and took off again, drunk and purposeful. It looked like evaporation, until Ranger Sally could see Hamish's suprasternal notch, that dip at the bottom of the throat between the collar bones, with the queen bee nestled there. Sally watched her dance around in a circle before zooming off of Hamish's neck. And suddenly he was dry of bees. They were in the disappearing air, with stragglers jetting past Sally's ears to catch up.

Holding Hamish's hand was suddenly awkward, and Sally and Hamish let go.

Hamish turned to look where the bees went, knowing he could visit Mr. Knox and find out if they got where they were going. The kids were running over, with Clothilde huffing behind. Sally had to deal with the bee keeper who was coming over with an official park ranger.

The queen had said to him, *Home. Always. Here. Light. Speak. Listen. All. Home. You. Purple. Yellow. Sweetness. Red. Speaking. Always. Home. Protect. Now. Fly. Build. Light. Moonlight. Dance. You.*

It took Hamish a while, but he did get away from Junior Rangers early. Clothilde was gasping about him being alive. The other kids treated him as though he'd suddenly grown up and they didn't know how to talk to him any more. Ranger Sally took him aside.

"I know you don't want to tell me, but something happened out there."

"You saw."

"Yeah, but something else. I'm just saying, if you want to talk about it ever—Just...You were pretty brave."

"I wasn't afraid."

"I know. That's what I'm talking about."

Another kid came taking Sally away.

Hamish walked home, lost and full. He felt like he'd just talked with a city, with everything from the sewers to the air traffic control weighing in. It was a swirl of communication curling down a nautilus shape and then emanating from a center, but changing slightly on its way, a game of telephone that amplified meaning instead of scrambling it, that added thought and image and decision-making along the distances ideas traveled. Hamish began to have an idea what was really meant when he heard on the news "Russia feels that...." or "Brazil wants...." He began to know the power and impossibility of speaking to a collection of people all at once.

The apartment when he got back was quiet as velvet. His mother had left him a note: "I'm back at 10. You home?"

CHAPTER 13

The heat in the apartment was stifling. The sun had spent the morning leaning on the roof, squishing itself through the dense tar and wood and insulation and plaster and paint until it oozed into the still air of the rooms, liquefying any hope of oxygen and making Hamish's temples hurt with hot blood pulsing. Hamish now questioned their stoicism about air-conditioning. Of course his father had been against it, but that had been in the country where it was possible to be against it. Here in the city, it now seemed to be either air-conditioning or death. He crawled over his mother's bed and accordioned back the metal gate on the window, like he was opening his own jail cell. The screen protested its way up, and Hamish scooted out onto the fire escape. Clouds had built up over New Jersey, and breezes presaged change. Hamish could see down to the harbor, the Statue of Liberty a small figure after tiny cranes and distancing water towers and ship super-structures. Manhattan rose like a dragon's back, its snout plunging into the East River, its tail only imagined far to the north.

Hamish climbed up the ladder to the roof. It was a flat, silver slope, glaring in the sun like an old cookie sheet. On each side was a low wall capped with cement blocks or clay roof tiles, held on with tar. Wires were everywhere, connecting antennae and satellite dishes and scurrying over the edge on missions through apartment walls and windows. Some of the roofs had doors into little trapezoidal sheds, like misshapen ice fishing cabins. There were three-foot square caps, like the lid of a trunk that led down into someone's bedroom or closet. Hamish saw one on his own roof, noting that it seemed to lead into his room.

He felt his feet sinking into the hot asphalt, and with a shot of adrenalin got to the wall. It, at least, was solid. He scraped off some black goo from his shoe as he surveyed this world above the world. Places of height gave him a feeling of power—like all boys, he supposed—but now he could talk with eagles who kept watch on the world from an aerie.

Brownstones and apartment buildings lined the entire rectangle of the block. In the center of this rectangle were the small back-yards that people lavished gardenly attention on, each small fenced-in rectangle its own little landscape, from Japanese pristine to English overcompensation, from children's toy battlegrounds to barely disguised landfills. Occasionally enormous and ancient trees, like reminders of the days of the Canarsie and the deer and the yellow fever in the swamp down the slope, loomed above the roofs. There were at least a dozen narrow metal towers with laundry lines attached, clothing pulleyed out of windows to belly in the summer air. A few utility poles attracted spider's nests of wires, some hidden by volunteer trees, spilling onto chain-link fences and improvised property-line separations. Each defined little patch of dirt was a claim of ownership of the earth, like a towel on an endless beach.

Hamish crossed the neighbor's roof, and that was a Rubicon. He started to hurry, pausing at each low wall to scope the next twenty feet of open space. He became vigilant as a deer at the edge of a clearing when there was patio furniture, or a platform with a plant on it. Even discarded pallets and rolls of tarpaper gave him pause. But his confidence grew with the breeze, thinking no one would come out in this heat. A taller building had a ladder lying by its wall. Hamish leaned it upright, and poked his head over the top. There was a cluster of cages, pigeon coops, on tall legs filled with birds resting in the shade. They were cooing to each other. Hamish caught things like *My food* and *Stay away from her or—*. He came over the edge and walked lightly.

But one saw him. *Watch it!*

Hamish was casual. *Hey, guys.*

Oh my oh my oh my oh my...

Did he speak?

Stay away from me!

Maybe he's going to let us out.

Don't touch! He's moving!

Hamish came close. *It's OK, guys. I'm just passing through.*
You're here, aren't you?
I am certainly here.

The coops erupted in a billow of bobbing and prancing, a dozen incomprehensible conversations in the background of a movie.

"Hey, kid, what you doing there?"

Hamish turned to see a man approaching him from the roof door. Another New Yorker. Another person who owned the territory he stood on. He had a sweaty t-shirt and wiped his face with a red bandana. His flip-flops clapped on his feet. Hamish looked for a way out, but found none.

"I was looking at your pigeons."

"How'd you get up here?" The man knew Hamish couldn't get away, so he slowed his approach.

"I live a few buildings over. We just moved here. I was exploring."

"Exploring." The man wiped his face again. Then he laughed. "What kind of dumb are you?"

Hamish was empty of defense. He opened his arms and shrugged.

"Get the fuck out of here. The owner here's a real rompehuevos."

"OK, OK." Hamish headed away from his own house.

"Hey, you little shit." Hamish had never been called a "little shit" in such a laconic and unaggressive way. "What the hell you doing? You gonna explore all around the world?"

"Yeah," smiled Hamish as he stepped over the low wall onto the next roof. "All around the world." He crossed over to the next one.

The man laughed in an attempt at derision and waved his hand dismissively, turning to go back.

Hamish got to the end of the row of buildings. A gigantic elm tree loomed between the corner building and the building that would lead him down the next side of the rectangle. In that way that courage and stupidity are sometimes indistinguishable, Hamish reached up and swung his legs over a branch. He shimmied down towards the rough trunk, finding himself suddenly forty feet up in the air. His mind both numb and aglow with what was in front of his eyes, beneath his skin, going into his lungs, he made rock-climber moves onto another branch that headed over to the next building. Astride the branch as though it were an elongated horse's back, he pried himself forward and up until he could drop lightly onto the next building's roof.

The exhilaration took him all around the block, vaulting walls, using fire escapes and drain-pipes to change levels, balancing on an archway put between two buildings as a portal for a backyard garage. The roofs were littered with things: a flat soccer ball, a kite, a surprising number of stuffed animals, occasional tools and construction materials in ripped bags or white plastic buckets, furniture of various kinds from expensive wicker to mildewing couches. On one roof, just caught under one of the trap door covers, was a pair of pink lace panties that seemed as though they had just been left. He picked them up. It was the first time he'd ever held panties, except for his mom's laundry. They made him feel strange things. He wondered why they were a "they" instead of an "it." The things people think of. Even though it made him feel guilty, he put them in his pocket, justifying it by telling himself he was cleaning up litter.

He got back to his own roof, and for a moment wasn't sure which roof was his. He leaned over the front of the building, looking down to the street, and counted the entrances. The green of the park across the way hid all the pathways and squirrels' graves. He had made it. He looked back, taking in the whole block.

"Around the world," he whispered.

CHAPTER 14

"Hamish Taylor, you are tardy. Quickly now. You are competing with Polly today." Mr. Shenouda nearly swept Hamish towards the back like a broom sweeps leaves, and Hamish landed at the table opposite the little girl with the buzz-cut. She looked at him as though he might be a dolphin who had just nosed his way through the floorboards. Mr. Shenouda whispered casually over Hamish's shoulder, "You and I, Mr. Taylor, might have a chat before you leave, yes? Yes, I think that would be a good idea. I would love to get your impressions of Thaddeus." Polly then paid no attention as she set up her men.

Pradeep and Daniel were hunched over their game, and Abraham and Steve were sprawled at their table, looking in opposite directions as though there were no game between them. They would glance at the game, and then casually move a piece, lazily clicking the clock button. Abe was being true to form; each move resulted in a captured piece, and Steve was reduced to retaliations.

Polly Bissell had her chin on her fists, moving only her eyes as Hamish sat on the black side of the board. She immediately moved her queen pawn, and Hamish just mirrored moves.

"God, boring," Polly sighed, melting her cheek into her hand.

"Excuse me, princess," said Hamish. He felt like an alien. His body hummed with bees and pigeons and pink panties. Every shadow had a panther in it. Every bird seemed to have a message for him. Every step reverberated with deep elephant calls. He kept seeing the young lioness teetering and bloody. He could feel the grating of the lion's claws on the cement of the wall, smell the dry burnt limestone that powdered out from under the algae, pulverized by the lion's violence, the splashing crash as the lion plummeted back into the moat, arising muddy and feculent and attacking the insurmountable wall again. He and the lion were still the center of an appalling stone dropped into a peaceful pond, circle waves of panic spreading out like the shock waves of a bomb over the entire zoo.

And he had no name.

Speaker! Madonna shrieked from under her flower sheet.

Hamish tried to quiet himself. He wanted to sink backwards into the wall.

"It's your move," said Polly, tapping the table impatiently.

"Polly," called Mr. Shenouda. "Are you bothering that parrot? You know the rule."

"Kaphiri, I'm not doing anything," Polly protested.

Speaker! Talk!

"Make sure you don't ruffle her cover." Mr. Shenouda turned back to Daniel, pointing out an alternative piece.

Speaker! I'm waiting!

"Come on. Hamish! Earth to Hamish. Your turn." Polly tapped the table again.

"All right!" Hamish moved a piece. "How come you call Mr. Shenouda 'Kaphiri'?"

"None of your beeswax." Polly looked down at the board. "That move's kind of stupid, even for you."

Hamish leaned forward. "I wish you and Shenouda and that fucking parrot would get off my back," he hissed.

"Don't you dare!" Polly leapt out of her chair. "Come here!" Polly grabbed Hamish's t-shirt sleeve and pulled him out the back door before Shenouda could stop them. Daniel snorted, pointing. In the tiny cement lot out back, little Polly got in Hamish's face.

"Kaphiri is a hero and don't you ever disrespect him, ever ever ever! He saved me and he saved my dad, and I – I -- I –"

"OK, OK, OK," calmed Hamish, his own world dissipating in front of this passionate onslaught. "What happened?"

"None of your business."

"Polly, you just made it my business. Come on." Hamish could almost feel himself alter, adapting himself to this young animal who was both furious and frightened. He could feel her defenses, and the openings in those defenses she wanted breached. He reached out. "Tell me."

In spite of herself, she did. "But if you ever tell anyone else—"

"I won't."

∞

Polly couldn't tell her whole story in the few minutes she had in the back of the chess shop. It is possible she will never be able to tell her own story fully. But she told enough. Some of this came from Hamish, some from Kaphiri, some from her.

Polly told Hamish how Kaphiri Shenouda had come into her life.

Polly's mother left Polly's father nearly two years previous to this. Just left. No note. No word to neighbors. No announcement to her mother or her sister. Nothing to her daughter. Just gone. So Polly's father, who was never a bad guy, but was no prize, drank more, couldn't work for the beer delivery company any more, drank a little more, forgot to take his daughter to school, forgot just about everything except how to find money to drink. A couple of months after being left with this ten-year-old girl and a chaotic affliction, he was coming back to the apartment but he couldn't get his key to turn in the door. He had merely been taking his little girl Polly to the bodega for a cheese sandwich, which was her dinner, which he remembered at 10:00 she hadn't had. But he had remembered and was a little smug about that. The temperature had plummeted that day to twenty-two degrees, and he'd thought they wouldn't have to put on coats because they were only going to the corner bodega after all, but the key snapped off in the lock, and in his alcoholic obsession he wasn't going to do anything else until he got the broken part out of the lock. He told Polly he was going to a bar he knew so he could borrow a couple of tools. He'd be just a minute. He sat his little girl on the stoop in her little red hoodie and leg-warmers and moccasins without socks. She wrapped her arms around herself, trying to sleep in her own cold lap.

She was only dimly aware as a towncar pulled up to the curb in front of her stoop. The window on the passenger side and a man in a hat and with a winning smile leaned way over to call out, "Hey, kid! You OK? Your dad said I should come check on you."

"I'm OK," Polly decided to say.

"Look, it's freezing," the man opened the car door. "You want to wait here until he comes back?"

Polly looked around, not trusting this rescue. "I don't know."

"We could just go find him." The man seemed so reasonable. "He just wanted me to check on you, but it's so cold. You wanna go find him?"

Polly was numb. She felt as though she was watching someone else do the thing you're never supposed to do as she nodded and got in the car.

It was so warm in the car. The man was so friendly and concerned. He had a thermos of cocoa, as though he'd been expecting her, and she held the hot cup, letting the heat soak into the palms of her hands and holding the steam up to her chin. The cold had numbed her so much she couldn't really understand what the man with the hat was saying. It eventually came to her that he was taking her to a friend of his who he said could help her. She wasn't supposed to be out on the street like that, in the cold, and if she didn't want Social Services to take her from her parents, she should talk to this man.

"So who is it who's in your family? Your mom? Is your mom at home?"

The cocoa was so good and sweet. It made her so sleepy.

Polly leaned into his voice that was full of concern and authority. "My mom, she's gone," she finally told him. "Just Dad. Just him, now. I thought you said—? He's—"

"Is he mean to you?"

"No!" Tears came to Polly eyes, trying to find a way to defend her father. "He's fine. He—he just forgets. He can't deal with everything."

"Mm-hm. Well, maybe my friend can help. He's very good at helping people. Especially young people."

"But we gotta find my dad." Polly's face throbbed with thawing and nearly painful exhaustion.

"We will. Let's just see my friend first, just for a little bit."

They drove through dark Brooklyn until Polly had no idea where they were, the warmth of the car fogging her brain. She knew she fell asleep. The man, Fallon, was then ushering her through doors and hallways until they came to a comfortable office. There weren't any windows, but the lights were low and the couch was deep. Fallon had a short conversation with the white-haired man behind the desk, who smiled at Polly, nodding. Polly was overcome with sleepiness on the couch, and she could feel herself drifting into its soft comforts, dreamless.

When she woke, she was in a small room with a bed, a cross between a hospital room and a nun's cell. She was dressed only in a large t-shirt with the name of some radio station on it. Like the office, there was no window. She had to pee, and she got up, looking for her clothes that were nowhere. She tried the door, but it was locked, and Polly tried not to panic. She knocked on the door, timidly at first, and then more insistently. A woman opened it about a foot and stood in the opening. She was an older woman, at least older than her father, thin, with hair tied back in a tight bun. She said nothing.

"I have to pee," said Polly.

"There's a bedpan under the bed." The woman began to close the door.

"I don't understand," said Polly, stopping her.

"You can pee in the bedpan."

"Isn't there a bathroom?"

"Not yet." The woman closed the door.

The little exchange frightened Polly more than she'd ever been frightened in her life, more than seeing her father drunk and howling, more than being lost, more than being hungry and not knowing when her father was coming back, more than realizing her mother had left her forever. She knew she was a prisoner, and she knew she had to escape.

She found the beige plastic bedpan and figured out how to pee in it, and then stuck it back under the bed. The door was a plain wooden door. The bed was blond IKEA, and scratched from many moves. The blanket was polyester pale green with a paler yellowing stain in the corner as though bleach had spilled on it a hundred washings ago. Nothing was on the walls except glossy white paint, so cold it was almost blue. The place smelled of ammonia and wet mops.

Polly knew she was going to cry and she didn't want to, thinking she wouldn't be able to see the opening for escape when it came if she was crying. She yelled at herself inside, saying "Shut up! Just shut up! You're so stupid, you should never have gotten in the car, you should have just waited for Daddy, you stupid stupid idiot. Swallow and just shut up. Swallow." She wiped her eyes with the T-shirt and realized that she first had to get back her clothes.

She knocked on the door for about three full minutes before the woman came back.

"What?"

"I peed. What do I do with it?" She held out the bedpan for inspection.

"What the hell do I care?"

"Can I have my clothes back, please?"

"You just have to wait."

Polly moved into the doorway. "Please?" She tipped the bedpan and lurched forward. The bedpan spilled over the woman's front and she screeched, her hands avoiding the splash of urine. Polly dodged underneath her upraised arm and down the hall, her feet slapping on the painted cement. A gray door led to some stairs down, and Polly's hand skimmed down the pipe banister, holding at the turns, until she got to the bottom. But the door down there was locked, and she had to turn back up. There was the man with the hat. Fallon.

"Hey, pretty baby. You looking for something?" He came down the stairs easily, as though they'd agreed to meet there. "Come on, let's go meet the man who's going to help you." He held out his hand.

"I just want my clothes," Polly said in a small voice.

"We'll get them to you as soon as they come out of the laundry. They were a mess." Fallon smiled widely at how messed up her clothes must have been to warrant laundering. He reached down and took her stiff hand. "Come on, now, pretty baby."

He practically lifted her up the stairs to the next floor, and they went down the hall to the same comfortable office with a couch and a desk. Her hand hurt with his squeezing.

This time the white-haired man was in the room with three girls a little older than Polly. Two were sitting on the couch, and one – an Asian girl – was sitting in the white-haired man's lap as though he were her uncle. The Asian girl was laughing at some joke the man had just told her, a long laugh, her mouth held wide open as though there weren't quite enough room to express how loud and long the laugh needed to be. The man's left hand was on the girl's hip.

The girls all turned to look at Polly as Fallon ushered her in.

"Ooo! How cute you are," said a girl on the couch. She immediately stood up and came over to give Polly a hug. Polly could smell the makeup on her. All three girls had makeup, extensive and tasteful, making them seem like grownups to Polly. The girl finished her quick hug and then turned Polly around for observation. "You need some clothes, baby."

This cracked the other girls up.

Heigo Kuusk smiled. "You think you girls can set her up?"

"We told you, Mr. Kuusk, we can do this," said the Asian girl, hopping down from his lap. He gave her a double tap on her bottom, which made her jump.

Polly spoke up. "I just want to go home. Can I just have my clothes back?"

"Oh, dear. Polly. That's your name, right? Oh, Polly. I'm afraid you can't go home." Heigo Kuusk looked as though he were saddened beyond measure about something so profound and distant that Polly couldn't imagine how truly awful it was.

Polly was silent.

"There's no home to go home to. Your father last night, well, with drinking—you know—there was a fight, he fought the wrong person, one who had a knife, and, well—" Kuusk spread his hands. "Your father's gone."

The sea filled Polly's ears.

"I just want to go home."

"Your home will be here, now. We'll take care of you."

Polly turned to make a run for it, but Fallon caught her arm.

Polly spent that night in a dorm-like room with the other three girls. B.B., the Asian girl, was the unspoken leader. She had made the other two try clothes on Polly as though Polly were some kind of inert mannequin. They finally settled on a plaid pleated skirt, white blouse and sparkling vest, so she looked like some fantastical Catholic school girl. She had white socks and patent leather shoes. B.B. put a bow in her hair that was the same plaid as the skirt.

Polly had tried to resist at the beginning, but one of the white girls had pinched her arm so hard it left a bruise, and she let them dress her. When she asked them what they were doing this for, they waggled their eyebrows and said that she would see, that it would be fun, that she would get rich, that people would like her. When Polly said she had to go to school, they laughed and said, No, that was over. Wasn't that fun?

Everything floated, as though time itself had lifted her and everything around her—all she saw, all she felt, all people and objects and backgrounds and sensations—drifted slightly swollen through a clear, honey-like ether. She simply didn't believe any of it was really happening. She didn't believe her father was dead, she didn't believe any one here was trying to help her, she didn't even believe she was in danger although she knew everything around her was dangerous.

The older woman came around and told them to go to bed, that there would be work the next day. She held out two pills to B.B. and a glass of water. B.B. swallowed them down. Mandy, the cruel one with the strong grip, also got pills. The woman came over to Polly.

"Here, take these. It'll help you sleep." Her gaze was steady and bored as she offered the pills and water.

Polly saw behind her the third girl shake her head slightly, fear in her attention on Polly.

"Take them," ordered the woman.

Polly took the pills from her, and tongued them between her teeth and lip. She almost choked on the water.

"Sleep. No talking." The woman clicked off the light and closed the door. Polly heard it lock, and she spit out the pills into her hand, looking for some place to put them. She pushed them under the radiator next to her bed.

The third girl whispered, "Good job." She got out of bed and took Polly's hand. "Come on."

They went into the bathroom, a sterile place that even the three brightly colored toothbrushes and the debris of makeup and hair products couldn't humanize. The third girl was a foot taller than Polly. She held Polly's shoulders, leaned down, and said calmly and urgently, "You have to get out of here."

"What do you mean?"

"You do not want 'start work' tomorrow."

"But how—? What's the work?"

The third girl hissed, "You no want some guy fuck you tomorrow!"

Polly looked down, ashamed. She had no idea what that meant. "But my dad—"

"They lie. They always lie."

"We're locked in."

"You go out window." The third girl stood on the toilet, reaching for a small window. It was no bigger than Polly's head. The girl unhooked it and let it open top down into the room. It was held by a chain.

"How am I going to fit through that?"

"You fit."

"Why don't you come?"

"I don't fit." The girl lifted Polly up onto the back of the toilet. "You get head, arm out window, over to your left. There: fire escape, you grab. OK?"

Polly stuck her head through and saw the fire escape in the dark. "OK." She looked back at the girl. "Then?"

"Then home. You just go home."

The journey seemed one to the other side of the world.

"'R' train, two blocks. You go there. No police. Kuusk kill me if police come."

"OK."

"Promise? No police."

"Promise." Polly started crying. "Thank you."

"No crying. You just go. Come on. Up you are. You light as feather. Up."

With the girl's hands and arms and then her shoulders even guiding, Polly got through the window. She went down the fire escape, figuring out the last drop to the ground. She was freezing in just a t-shirt and underpants, and she was afraid of cutting her bare feet on street glass. She found the subway, and it was one she recognized. She got on the train with no one stopping her, hardly anyone even looking at her. She felt momentum, as though if she stopped the world would come to an end.

CHAPTER 15

She perched on the seat on the subway. Opposite her was a large man who smiled at her. She had a shot of terror that someone else was going to take her, but she saw the man knew what she was thinking as he shook his head and spread his palms as though to demonstrate his open heart.

A woman on the other side said to him, to the train in general, "Someone should call the police. That little girl shouldn't be here like that."

The large man stood. "Oh! Madame, you are absolutely correct in your assessment of the situation. She is indeed in great need, and here she is in a world that is harsh and cold and completely ignorant of what she's been through in the last few hours, much less the last lifetime." The man's accent was mysterious and compelling, like a foreign movie star. He removed his fur-collared coat, one of those old overcoats with yellow silk lining that moved like air and was warm like an adored pet. "This is yours," he said to Polly, holding it for her to put on. In a dream, she stood and let the man help her on with the coat as though they were going to the opera. The tails of the coat puddled at her feet and her hands were lost in the sleeves. The man turned to the woman and the concern on her face vanished as he said, "Look how your help has put soothing oils on the waters of distress. You should look back on this moment with satisfaction, as I will also." He sat next to Polly, careful not to touch her. "And now, my dear, I think you had better tell me your address so that we can get you home, don't you?"

In spite of everything, she told him.

When they got to her stop, he pointed out she had no shoes, and suggested he carry her. She nodded, anticipating a shift in her world, as though she were about to get on the back of a very large horse for the first time.

She must have fallen asleep, cradled in the warm coat in Kaphiri Shenouda's arms, for she woke the next day in a child's bedroom that had two beds. She did not know that Kaphiri Shenouda had taken her to her apartment and found her father wailing in drunkenness about his lost child. He had admonished her father as only a Keeper can, spurring him into the action of following him to his house, where he lay Polly on his son's former bed, and made Polly's father shower and drink strong tea and then put him to bed also in clean sheets and quiet.

Polly was not sure she was done with her nightmare, and she started planning another escape, even though she didn't want to escape this beautiful place. She wandered through the house and found the man with the accent from the night before, who smiled broadly and said his name was Kaphiri Shenouda, and he got her to say it a couple of times, finally determining that it would be best if she called him Kaphiri only. He took her to another room to see that her father was there, asleep, sleeping deeper than sound can go, and they tip-toed back to the kitchen and had breakfast. Before her father woke, Kaphiri asked her her age, and when she told him, he declared that ten years old was exactly the right time to learn to play chess. So they went to the living room where there was a beautiful set with a marble board and pieces carved from stone. The game made sense to her, and she felt like she was on an adventure. And then her father was standing there, unkempt and embarrassed and saying it was time to go. But Kaphiri set her up with toys, and insisted that Mr. Bissell indulge in some coffee and croissants and discuss what they were going to discuss. The toys were all boys' toys, but they were enough to keep her entertained.

It was as though Kaphiri had performed magic on her father. Kaphiri came back into the living room to explain the new rules to Polly, and her father was there nodding. Kaphiri would come to walk her to school every day after having breakfast at Daisy's Diner on Fifth Avenue, and then she would come to his chess shop every day to help him. He would deliver her home at dinner. The new rules worked. Her dad cried a lot, but he wasn't drinking. He talked about meetings but she knew they didn't have so many meetings in the delivery trade. She went to Kaphiri's sometimes on weekends also, and went to his mosque and played with other kids while Kaphiri did worship things with the men. And now her dad is a quiet man but works and has meetings and helps his daughter with homework sometimes and always has dinner with her and she didn't freeze to death in Brooklyn because Kaphiri Shenouda decided to be her friend.

She was sure Shenouda had saved her from death. But she had saved herself from worse.

∞

They sat in silence. Polly's jaw jutted a bit: she wasn't going to show herself anymore. She hadn't told him everything, but Hamish was a smart boy. Coming in with Happy the elephant had taught him a thing or two.

He leaned forward, making sure he'd caught her eye well and openly. "You are the bravest girl I think I have ever met."

She smiled, and then leaned in also. "You can't tell Kaphiri I told you any of this, OK?"

"Promise."

"And don't you ever disrespect him again," she warned.

"Promise."

As they came back inside, Madonna hurled shrill epithets from under her cage cover.

Mr. Shenouda came back to their table, edging his bulk towards the cage stand. "Are you sure you're not intruding on her?"

Polly was indignant. "Kaphiri," she demonstrated the distance. "Look!"

Mr. Shenouda took off the cover, tsk-ing to calm the macaw. She squawked loudly, pumping her head up and down.

Get over here, you worthless piece of maggot bait! Get over here!

Mr. Shenouda was annoyed. "She's impatient for her new love. Hamish? Can you do something with this recalcitrant piece of blue poultry?"

Hamish went to the cage too fast. Madonna had grabbed the upright wires of the cage and pulled herself up towards the front as Hamish laid his hand on the wires. She bit his ring finger, hard. So hard that drops of blood spurted out. The pain was extremely sudden and slow, like something that gathered speed as it hit him. He shouted and yanked his hand away just as Madonna let go.

What the hell did you do that for?

Don't ignore me, retorted Madonna calmly.

Mr. Shenouda was over to Hamish in a second. "My boy! Are you all right?"

Hamish was quick. "It's all right, it's all right." Mr. Shenouda looked at the small gushes of blood coming out. "It's just a mistake. It's OK."

Mr. Shenouda took him by the hand, keeping it elevated, back to the bathroom and with one hand extricated first aid supplies. He sat Hamish on the toilet seat as he prepared his pharmaceutics. Hamish was surprised Mr. Shenouda was humming.

"Thaddeus tells me you will be meeting Alicia Markova on Friday." Mr. Shenouda beamed as he tore open bandaging.

"What?" said Hamish, offended. "He hasn't told me."

"Oh," Mr. Shenouda was nonplussed. "I'm sure he will."

"She's really another Speaker?"

"My boy!" exclaimed Mr. Shenouda. "Miss Alicia Markova. She's been a Speaker since well before even your mother was born. Elegant. I think you will agree." He smoothed the sticky side of the bandage onto Hamish's thumb and winked at him. "And you and I must begin a process of sharing information. We will learn from each other."

CHAPTER 16

The Whites lived on the long block of Prospect Place above Flatbush. Hamish walked up the shady stoop, the brownstone emitting a coolness in the evening air. He didn't even get a chance to ring the doorbell when Clothilde opened the door, smiling and holding herself back like a princess at her first ball. She ushered him in, offering to take his coat, and then immediately sinking into the floor. "Oh, you got no coat. It's summer."

"That's OK. Thanks for asking."

To the left was a large living room, towards the back a dining room, and then a kitchen off that. A polished wooden stairway led up to the next floors. There was woodwork everywhere. The mantel in the living room was black marble and wood, and there were plaster acanthus leaves on the ceiling.

Clothilde took him back to the kitchen where Mrs. White was cooking dinner. She was wearing a gray long-sleeved T-shirt and jeans, and was barefoot. Her hair was just a suggestion on her skull with smatterings of gray. Her skin was lighter than Lilly's, but this was certainly where Lilly got her smile.

She reached her hand for Hamish's. "I'm so pleased to meet you, Hamish. Clothilde has told us so much about you I'd recognize you in a dark alley."

Hamish laughed with guilt. "I don't know what I'd be doing in a dark alley—"

"No, I—" Mrs. White was exasperated with herself. "I meant, I know I'd have a friend there."

"Oh." Relief.

"Seriously, thank you for rescuing Clothilde's glasses. She's lost without them." Mrs. White enfolded her plump, short daughter, who leaned against her mother, unable to control her smiling. "Rescue Clothilde's glasses, you rescue her." She kissed Clothilde's head.

"It was no problem."

"No problem?" gasped Clothilde. "I had looked everywhere!"

"Well, at least we found them, right?" Hamish couldn't help himself. He liked this beaming, awkward girl whose heart sat on the outside of her chest and beat for all to see.

"Clothilde, why don't you take Hamish upstairs, so the young people can say hello."

"Ma-ahm," said Clothilde, warning.

"Wait a minute. Did you pretend you were a youngster again?"

"Don't tell," begged Clothilde playfully.

"Don't tell that you're 19, and you're trying to pick up a younger man?" Mrs. White winked at Hamish.

He didn't know what to do.

"Ah, you ruined it. You ruined the surprise." Clothilde took Hamish by the hand to lead him out of the kitchen and upstairs. "Come on."

The house was huge, if narrow. Lilly's room was two flights up. Clothilde whipped open the door with a loud, "He's here!" She shoved Hamish inside.

Lilly was sitting at a little desk with earphones on, writing in a notebook. She was wearing shorts and a tank-top, and she turned to see Hamish. Hamish felt himself blush all the way down his neck, his ears beginning to close. But then he suddenly realized his overwhelming sensation was one of relief, as though the chaos of the last few days was more distant, and he could rest here with Lilly in the room.

Lilly said, "What's happening?"

Hamish smiled, flummoxed. "Uh, I don't know."

Clothilde snorted from the bed.

Lilly searched for topics like a cat doing a taste test. "You into music?"

"Yeah." Hamish looked at the posters on the wall of Beyoncé and 50 Cent and Eminem, and knew he was not in his world.

Lilly unplugged her earphones and the music came over loudspeakers, a rap beat with a high female vocal line in the background.

"So where you from?" Lilly's inquisition had begun.

"Pennsylvania."

"Why'd you come here?"

"My dad died, and Mom got a job here, so we moved."

"Oh," said Lilly. "I'm sorry. I didn't know."

"No, it's OK. I mean, it's not OK, but—"

"Yeah."

They let the music be the silence. Clothilde watched them as though she were watching an exciting chess match.

"You like it?" asked Lilly.

Hamish had no idea. "Like what?"

"Brooklyn. New York. Being here."

He told her the truth. "I hated it. I never wanted to come here. And most of it sucks. But stuff has happened. I mean, things are different now."

"I can't imagine having my father die."

"I couldn't until it happened."

Clothilde suddenly spoke loudly, "That's why he thinks he's special."

"Clothilde!" Lilly, furious. "Shut –"

"But he is special. That's not the reason, though." She giggled.

"Girl, you got to stop talking like that." The warning in Lilly's voice was palpable.

"OK," Clothilde was quickly meek. "But he is. You'll find out."

Neither Lilly nor Hamish could think of anything to say. The music took center stage again, thrumming the space where they didn't have to look at each other because the music was filling out and moving through. Clothilde started squealing from the bed, and held a pillow up to her face.

"What are you doing now, Clothilde?" Lilly said, shaking the covers from where she sat.

"He thought I was young." She unplugged a laugh and let it go, a balloon suddenly released.

Hamish laughed, too. "I thought she was your younger sister. But she was fooling me. She's an old lady!"

Clothilde screamed, "I am not an old lady! I'm nineteen!" She rocked back on the bed, screaming her laughing scream into her pillow.

Lilly and Hamish smiled at each other. Ice had been broken.

∞

Mr. White was coming in the front door as they sat down for dinner, the wind of his entrance like a movie director entering a set. "Thank God it's not like it was yesterday," putting his backpack down on the living room coffee table. "I would have melted. So maybe global warming is a fiction, right?" He spied Clothilde and bent over, arms wide, rushing at her. "There she is!" Kissing her fatly on the cheek. "Hamish," extending his hand. "Welcome." A touch on Lilly's head, "Hey, honey." Kissing his wife on the lips, "Sorry."

"Just shut up and pour the wine," Mrs. White set down the salad.

"I humbly obey all that the great mother directs. But let me wash up." And he disappeared into the kitchen.

When Mr. White swept into a room, all heads turned; he was short and dark skinned and had a little goatee on his rounded chin, not like Hamish's idea of a head-turner. Here was someone exciting because he was excited, and Hamish watched him not knowing if he was predator or prey, or if it even mattered.

"I enjoyed talking with your mother, Hamish," said Mr. White between bites.

Hamish was nonplussed. He'd no idea they had spoken.

"Her work is fascinating. Have you been there yet?"

Hamish shook his head. "Not in New York, not yet."

"Working with these children with these amazing conditions. It is very courageous work, I must say."

Clothilde waved her spoon. "What conditions, Daddy? Are they like me?"

Mr. White leaned forward. "No, honey. I used the wrong word. The children Hamish's mom works with are sick. They have different diseases, and we haven't figured out how to cure those diseases yet. And Hamish's mom is helping to find out, and helping those kids while they are sick."

"I'm not sick, right?"

"No, honey. You're not sick."

Clothilde turned to Hamish and glowed. Mrs. White laughed and Lilly rolled her eyes. Lilly turned to Hamish.

"My mom's work is in the same world as your mom's."

"Lilly, I don't work with sick children."

"No," her eyes on her mother, "You save them."

"What do you do?" asked Hamish.

"Oh, I work with an agency that gets kids out of rough home situations. I'm just a glorified social worker." Mrs. White didn't like talking about herself, it seemed. "We have to take care of each other, you know."

Hamish found himself in these strangers' house talking as though someone else were directing him.

"Back in Plains, I used the think my mother was just a nurse, you know, like those women when my dad was sick—I mean, they were kind and everything, but you know it was like they were just holding back the flood. But sometimes I used to see my mother at her work—she'd have to take me because my dad, well, he wasn't home—and there would be some little kid who was bald and had tubes and was kind of gross, and she would hold him like he was my baby brother, you know?" He touched a chicken bone on his plate with his fork. "It's like on my walks here, in Brooklyn. You see in someone's window at night—not like a peeping Tom, not—it's just—it's a picture of a perfect world, a perfect moment, and you want to stop everything right there. It's—you know?"

Hamish looked up. They were all gazing at him, suspended, listening.

Clothilde saved them by breaking the spell. "Ooooo! I love this man!" She banged her fists on the table and the silverware rattled. Mr. White chuckled and settled her by putting his hand on her arm.

When Hamish caught Lilly's eye, he knew something had changed.

Mrs. White handed Hamish more of a vegetable dish she'd made, which he took gratefully. He had no idea what was in it, but it was something his body clearly craved. This was the best meal he'd had in weeks. He felt more welcome at this table than anywhere he'd been in his life.

Mr. White said, "Your dad was a veterinarian, right?"

Hamish nodded.

Mrs. White said, "We don't have to talk about that."

"It's OK. I don't mind."

But a quick silence went around the table like a whisper through leaves.

Clothilde broke through. "Hamish is really good with animals. He saw a fox at Junior Rangers."

"In the park?" asked Mrs. White.

Hamish nodded. Hamish didn't say that he'd since talked with this fox, who was kind of nasty and, true to stereotype, tried to play tricks on Hamish.

"And he got covered in bees!" Clothilde gloated with the strange news.

Mrs. White said, "I heard about that. I'm glad you're OK."

"It was OK," Hamish fumbled for something to say. "It tickled."

"I've seen pictures of beekeepers like that." Mrs. White asked, "You been to that little zoo in Brooklyn, in the park?"

Hamish flushed for the second time down to his roots. He felt like all his secrets were going to get exposed in this house. He had avoided the Brooklyn Zoo, the edges of which gave him the feeling he was on the verge of an agonizing natural disaster. He had wanted to go in before the calamity of the Bronx Zoo. But he couldn't get himself past some horrible barrier that seemed to surround the place, even though there was the enticement of intriguing animals like seals and spider monkeys. "Yeah. I didn't, I don't know, I didn't like it that much. I mean, no, I haven't gone in yet."

"Oh?" Mrs. White was curious. "You didn't see the meerkats?"

Hamish shook his head. "My dad said zoos were excuses for destroying animal habitats. They're never going to feel at home, no matter what you do."

"Your dad," said Mr. White, "sounds like he was a wise man."

Hamish shrugged, sorry he'd brought his dad into it. He felt like he'd invaded his own privacy.

"Did you know," continued Mr. White, "they once put some people on display in New York, just like in a zoo? At the Natural History Museum. Robert Peary brought I-can't-remember-how-many, five or six, Inuits back from Greenland and let people come gawk at them in the basement of the Natural History Museum. They all died of tuberculosis or something, some disease that white people bring with them everywhere, except this boy, Minik I think his name was. He stayed in the U.S. until he died in the influenza epidemic. Was that it? I can't remember."

"Delightful story, Dad," said Lilly, throwing her napkin.

"I just mean," he said, defending himself, "we do it to each other, not just animals. Queen Elizabeth's court, Chicago World's Fair, the Smithsonian, they even did it in ancient Greece."

"But everyone was a slave in ancient Greece," pointed out Lilly, "except you guys."

"You guys who?"

"Men. Rich men."

"All right, you two," intervened Mrs. White. "Hamish didn't come here to be in the middle of one of your arguments."

"It's a discussion, Ann," said Mr. White in his most professorial tone.

"Well you can discuss those plates right off the table and into the kitchen." She got up, taking left-over food away.

Lilly and her father stood, reaching for plates.

"Isn't Peary the guy who said he got to the North Pole first, but it was really a black guy?" asked Lilly.

"Matthew Henson. First man on the top of the world." Mr. White backed into the kitchen.

Hamish and Clothilde were left alone. Clothilde bubbled gently, like a soup on simmer. Her smile was a mile wide, and she couldn't bring herself to look at Hamish through her thick glasses.

∞

Lilly was delegated to walk Hamish to Grand Army Plaza. Hamish protested that he was fine, but Mrs. White insisted, saying that Lilly hadn't been out all day and needed the air. Clothilde gave Hamish another one of her baseball bat handshakes, and went upstairs to bed.

They got up on Plaza Street, trying to talk about impending high school. They competed in their complaints about school, how boring it could be, how relentless it was in grinding them down each day, how fraught it was socially. It was very strange to them that conversation wasn't easy, but it wasn't uncomfortable, like they had an understanding about the value of things like Clothilde and a summer's evening. As they turned the corner and Lilly hesitated because she was going to turn around, a dog—a terrier with a stiff tail—started barking.

Hamish understood:

Sit down! You've got to sit down now! You're going to fall any second. Can't you smell it? Now! Listen to me!!

He was jumping around a man, his owner, who was in his 50s and looked like he'd just gotten back from work and was finally giving his dog a walk.

Lilly said, "There's something wrong with that man. Something's happening."

Hamish got the dog's attention. *What's the trouble?*

This idiot's going to keel over any second. He reeks of it. It's driving me crazy. If he doesn't sit down, he's going to fall and then I'll never get him home. He'll do all that frothing, drooly stuff, shaking like a hind leg.

Hamish realized what it was. "What's that disease," he asked Lilly quietly, "where you shake, where you have to stop someone from swallowing their tongue?"

"Epilepsy?"

"That's it!" Hamish approached the man. "Excuse me, sir. I know this is, like, weird, but with your dog barking—"

The man growled at Hamish in some other language, maybe French. He was clearly furious. He roughly nudged the dog out of his way with his foot, as though to demonstrate he would punish the dog for being a pest, and waved Hamish and Lilly back.

Lilly talked to the man in the language he had used. She was clearly mollifying him, apologizing for her friend interfering in the man's walk. Hamish was suddenly on the outside. The man said quieter things, but his speech was a bit slurry. He weaved.

It's happening now! The dog's voice was piercing as he bounced on his front legs.

The man just stared at Lilly. "Fout tonère," he whispered as his body started to buckle. Hamish and Lilly guided him down to a bench. His eyes turned up, and his head went back and forth. The seizure took hold.

Lilly said, "I'll go call 911." She ran to the pay phone only a few feet away.

Hamish kept the man from slipping off the bench.

The dog put his paws on Hamish, licking the man's hand. *You got him to sit down. That was so cool. He's not falling. He's not dying.*

You were amazing yourself, said Hamish. *That's such a good trick, knowing when it's coming.*

You just feel it. You smell it. It makes you crazy.

But not everyone can do it. You're special.

The dog licked Hamish. *Speaker, saving my man. Love it.*

Lilly was back. The dog licked her, too. Lilly pet the dog and they waited until the ambulance came. The seizure had calmed some, and the man apologized to Lilly through a sloppy, novocain mouth. They talked like old friends, Lilly translating for Hamish. The man was worried about the dog. Before they could get the address, the ambulance doors closed.

"What are we going to do with you?" Lilly scrunched down and cupped the dog's ears.

"I think I saw where they came out of. Maybe the dog can lead us." Hamish already knew from the dog it was only two apartment buildings down. "What language was that?"

"Oh, yeah. Creole. It's so close to French, you know."

"But you speak it? And French?"

"Yeah, I guess."

"That's impressive."

"Anyone can learn. It's the ones with the other alphabets that are harder. Russian's hard. And I haven't tried Greek, or those ideogram languages."

"You're learning Russian?" Hamish wanted to know more about this girl every minute he was with her.

The man's wife was both grateful and annoyed. Seizures happened frequently, and she was drowning in worry and fed-up with repetition. She took the dog in and closed the door.

"How'd you know where they lived?" asked Lilly.

"Oh, you know," said Hamish innocently. "The dog found his way. He was pretty clear."

"Hunh."

"Thanks," said Hamish. "An exciting end to an exciting evening!"

"Yeah. You did good with that man. I knew something was wrong, I just couldn't put my finger on it."

"I saw a documentary or something about dogs who help people."

Lilly smiled. "You're one strange little white boy."

Hamish smiled back.

"We should hang out sometime."

"That'd be cool," said Hamish. "There's something I could show you." He thought of Around the World.

"What?"

"I'll show you. When we get there."

"OK. Later." Lilly wiggled her fingers in a wave and turned around.

Hamish waved, but she was already walking away.

CHAPTER 17

It was deep dusk as Hamish walked down Prospect Park West, the park on his left busy with closing night. He could see someone sitting on the second stair at his apartment building, feet in running shoes, legs bare, thready Capri pants. As she leaned forward, Hamish recognized Helena, the girl from the park. She saw him half a block away, and waved a small smile, almost shy.

"You are remembering me?" She wore a maroon tank top, and the bra under it was obvious and green. Her hair was in a ponytail. She was slightly wild, like she'd been caught two seconds before doing something vaguely illegal.

"Sure," said Hamish. "Come on in."

They walked up the stairs, and the girl walked through the apartment, looking at everything, poking her head into his mother's room and his room where he hoped he hadn't left his underwear on the floor, and back into the kitchen, as though she were inspecting real estate.

"Can I get you something?" Hamish offered. "We got juice, water. I could make you some tea. My mom doesn't believe in soda, so we don't have any of that."

"What doesn't she believe in soda?" Helena looked perplexed and amused.

"She thinks it makes you fat and rots your teeth, so she doesn't allow it in the house."

Helena nodded. "She is a good mother."

"Yeah, she's OK." Hamish waited while Helena looked out the back window. "So, do you?"

"What?"

"Want something."

"Oh, yes. Tea. Make me some tea." Helena sat on the kitchen stool.

Hamish ran water and filled the kettle. While he was getting out two cups, he asked, "So how did you find me?"

"You gave me your address. Don't you remember? When you played with the little bird. One morning in the park."

"Oh, sure." Hamish put teabags in the cups. He hesitated to ask. "Did that guy leave you alone?"

"Oh," she laughed. "He guards me. Like a big brother."

Hamish looked at her. "He didn't seem like a brother."

"He's not really my brother." Helena seemed slightly disgusted.

Looking at Helena was like looking at a picture. Every movement she made, every expression she had, was a kind of surprise because his eyes had completely accepted her as she was with no notion that what he saw would not be perpetual. It wasn't just that she was a very pretty girl to Hamish—she was—it was that she held something indisputably powerful in her that compelled Hamish. She reminded him of the lioness warning him to leave the zoo, but chaotic, like one of the younger hawks in the park, and full, like a young elephant.

"Did you want something?" Hamish didn't know how not to be rude. "Is there something I can help you with?"

Helena smiled, as though making a decision. "Oh, no. I just drop by, like this, you know?"

"Oh, OK." Now what? "You live around here?"

"OK, sometimes. Around the corner. Strange, same block. Well," Helena corrected herself. "That's where I stay sometime. Mostly, I come through park. My mother, my little sister, they live out Coney Island, around there. I have address." She fished in her pocket and took out a folded and torn piece of paper. She put it on the kitchen table.

Hamish looked at it. "Oh, I've been around there. That's where my school is going to be."

"You go to school?"

"I'll be going to Herman Melville. It's out there."

"That's nice. That's very good." Helena nodded her head at the kettle which was beginning to boil.

Hamish poured water in the cups.

"Oh," said Helena, girlishly casual. "I have something. You keep for me, yes?"

"Uh, sure."

Helena pulled a CD out of her Capri pants. It had been hidden under her underwear, way below her open belly-button. She handed it to him. As he took the CD, it felt alive. Its label had a sexy cover of Britney Spears being coy.

"You keep this, like you keep music, OK?" Then she whispered. "It's not Britney Spears."

"OK." Hamish hesitated. "What is it?"

"If I need to know, if I need it, you bring it me. Or, you know."

"I'm not sure…"

"Music. I don't think you like it, but I think my sister like it, maybe. Maybe just fun. Who knows?" She laughed a little laugh and pretended to swallow tea, her laughter going dead.

Hamish put the CD on a shelf above the toaster.

"You have girlfriend?"

"No, I—" Hamish suddenly didn't know how to answer.

She drew her finger slowly down Hamish's chest. "You want a girlfriend?"

"No, I—" Desperation set in.

Helena patted his cheek. "You are cute." She pulled on his earlobe, pulling his face close to hers. "You stay cute."

"Uh, sure."

Helena swung her feet to the floor.

"Where are you going to school?" Hamish asked.

"Oh, I don't go to school." She was studying the apartment, studying a drawing of Hamish's his mother had framed.

"Wait a minute. Why not?"

"Maybe I do home-school. I don't know." She smiled secretly. "I go to school of Heigo Kuusk."

This was the second time Hamish heard that name. It sounded familiar and crass. It was his father's first name, he would someday find out, only in Estonian.

This was the oddest visit he'd ever had, including with animals. He could not grasp the sense of it. "Do you need help?" he repeated.

Helena surveyed the apartment one last time, picking up a vase that had fresh flowers in it. "You have good mother." She put it down. "You maybe check on my mother, my sister. I don't want her to go to school of Kuusk. Maybe you check." She looked meaningfully at Hamish. "I am not here. OK? OK."

She was gone, leaving a CD, a piece of paper with an address in Coney Island, and a full cup of tea.

∞

That night, Hamish and his mother had the most terrifying fight they had ever had. Neither of them knew they were capable of such verbal violence towards each other. Hamish had blown off his uncle and the job at the real estate company again. Sarah, at her wits end with the opacity of her son, had threatened him with Florida, to stay with her parents for a month.

She: I can't have Colin calling me at the hospital and yelling at me for what you aren't doing.

He: I never wanted it. You and he arranged it without asking me, without even talking to me.

She: You ran away.

He: You ran away! You ran away from our home, our lives, your job, my school, my friends, my life, just because Dad dies. He's dead! It doesn't mean you have to disappear.

She: Shit. We've got to get on with our lives, and that means taking some responsibility.

He: I've got enough responsibility.

She: Oh, right! What responsibilities do you have?

He: You make me go to fucking chess, you make me go to fucking real estate shit, you make me go to fucking Junior Rangers, you make me go to fucking Brooklyn!

She: And do you actually do any of that? Any of it? You don't tell me anything. I know you go out who-knows-where for who-knows-how-long and you don't tell me anything.

He: Why would I tell you anything? You just make shit up, make me do things that are no part of my life. You lie to me.

She: I never lie to you.

He: Not telling is lying! And you said he was going to get better. You said it would all be all right!

She: Then tell me. Tell me what's going on.

He: Leave me the fuck alone.

Neither of them knew how long this all went on. They left it, finally, late, when Sarah said that Hamish would spend off-hours with his cousin Sam and her boyfriend David, and they'd see how that went.

Trust is a difficult thing to build, especially when it is difficult to trust life.

CHAPTER 18

Hamish was miffed that Mr. Knox had decided to send Mr. Shenouda on this meeting with the aging dancer-Speaker.

"At the moment I believe he is in Turkey. The country, not the poultry!" Shenouda burst out laughing at his joke as though it had never been heard.

Hamish was so taken aback he was almost charmed by the naïveté. Of course, what Hamish thought was important was still bound in by the strict borders of the fourteen-year-old mind. Annoying, I know. Hamish didn't realize the Iraq War was in full swing, and the seeds of Syrian destruction were being planted.

As they traveled on the subway into Manhattan, Shenouda made them play with a little magnetic chess set a number of rapid-fire games, which served to settle Hamish's nervous system. Shenouda made mistake after mistake, crying aloud and slapping his forehead in wonder at his own stupidity. He leaned over to whisper after losing a bishop, "I have never done well in enclosed spaces. Even with all these people—" his arm swept around the subway car "—it's too much a reminder of prison." He shook his head without elaborating, setting his mind once again on his losing game.

As far as Sarah was concerned, Hamish was simply at chess.

They walked far east from the subway to the hospital. Hamish could see an occasional ambulance and a number of lab coats as they approached the glass building with its sweeping entrance rising above the hot New York asphalt. Hamish felt his breathing shallow. He had not been in this kind of setting since his father died. He did not like it.

The elevator was slow, like all hospital elevators, and the air conditioning was too much. The chemical smells of cleaners covering human activities and the small quiet sounds of beds and monitors hung in the air under a blanket of fluorescent light. Kaphiri Shenouda seemed to understand Hamish's slowness, his hesitation, as they went down the hall where Alicia Markova's room was. He seemed to know it had nothing to do with meeting another Speaker. He peeked in the door, and gently guided Hamish in.

Alicia Markova had her eyes closed when they came into her hospital room. She was diminutive, with white hair pulled back and an oxygen loop under her nose. She had an elegant face, even with the parchment skin of age and the sag of partial paralysis. Hamish held back from the dangerous place he knew a hospital room to be, expecting at any second a thump of surprise and alarm. Shenouda went forward and took her hand.

"Miss Markova. Alicia," he said in his quiet voice that could be heard down hallways. "Someone has come to see you. Someone I believe you may have been expecting for a long time."

Her eyes opened, befuddled and dark. As she gazed up at Shenouda, she came into the room. "Kaphiri, you came again. Did you—?" Her head turned, and she saw Hamish.

"Ah," she breathed. "You're here."

Hamish took a step, nodding.

"Sit."

He sat on the bed.

She smiled. "Lovely." She closed her eyes and then opened them. "Who have you met?"

Hamish was befuddled. Then it dawned on him. "Oh! I've met Happy."

"She must be all grown now."

"She taught me a lot."

"Oh yes, I imagine she would. Elephants are kind of bossy, don't you find?"

Hamish hadn't, but he didn't say so.

"And Ida? Did you meet her yet?"

"No."

"She's the polar bear in Central Park. Absolutely charming. Had a very hard time coming up, though." She reached for Shenouda to help her sit more upright. Her struggle reminded Hamish so much of his father's time in bed he could feel the pressure of tears behind his eyes. As she gripped Shenouda's hand to pull herself up, she asked, "Darling, how is my sweet Madonna?"

"As sweet as ever." They both laughed softly.

She took Hamish's hand. "I suppose you have questions for me."

Hamish was momentarily stumped. But she went on without waiting.

"I wish I could tell you. I wish I could tell you all the wonderful things... Don't be as afraid as I was. Learn your name."

"I—"

"Trust the Keepers. They are your lifeline. You know about the Keepers, yes?" She was nearly coquettish, something Hamish couldn't fathom in a ninety-three year old woman.

"I think I get it."

"If you think you do, you don't." She patted Mr. Shenouda's arm. "This one's a Keeper. Have you noticed how he seems to put everyone at ease, how he never makes anyone feel left out? Keepers have a knack for understanding the heart. Most of the time they can figure out the thing that needs to be said or done to make it beat more regularly. How they do it, I don't know, but they do and I adore them for that." She pulled Mr. Shenouda's hand towards her and kissed it. He kissed her back. She leaned in to Hamish as though to whisper a secret. "One of my teachers was an absolutely gorgeous Keeper, the accompanist at Ballet Russe – Oh! His hands! I must tell you, his hands...!" She patted Hamish's hand as though trying to summon that pianist's hand from long ago.

"Then there's the Witnesses. Oh! I will never understand them, but they are certainly amazing, like grouchy magicians. They are able to organize because they remember everything. It's absolutely incredible. I'm so glad I can't. It would drive me bonkers, totally bonkers.

"Hamish, my dear, dear boy," she reached for him and he took her hand. "You will recognize each other. I know it takes time, but you will. Thaddeus tells me he knew the moment he saw you. Tell me: did you see something in him?"

Hamish thought back to the moment of seeing the stranger in the hat and the duster at the top of the fall in Prospect Park. He knew now that he knew then, even though he didn't know what he knew.

"Yes."

"Good. That's very good. And you will become more adept."

"But what about Speakers? Mr. Knox told me about his father, and there's you." Hamish wanted the answer to be simple.

"We're more rare, it seems," she smiled at him resignedly. "Mr. Smith – I'm sure you'll meet him some day – he has this grand theory that there are an average of thirty six of us in the world, the magic number!" – she spread her fingers as though to flick fairy dust – "of the Tzadikim Nistarim. The ones who keep the world from ending." She laughed, and her laughter, even from her tiny lungs and half frozen face, was clear and full of delight. "Wouldn't that be wonderful if it were true? But I believe we are the only ones in America at the moment, isn't that so, Kaphiri?"

"I believe Kai Pearson is still in Arizona, but that's all," acknowledged Mr. Shenouda.

"Oh, yes. Of course. I always leave her out because she wants to be left out." Alicia Markova was frustrated. "I'm sure more will come."

"They haven't yet," said Shenouda.

"How are we supposed to save the world?" Hamish was suddenly overwhelmed.

"Oh, we're not. We're just supposed to do the best we can. But we—you—have a special connection to an energy that is like birth and death and love—the impulse and instinct to migrate or procreate or even eat. We tap into that. That's why we speak with animals. They feed us that energy."

"But I don't get—I don't have—when I talk with them, I change, like I change into them. They don't give me anything."

Mr. Shenouda interrupted, "Perhaps it would be better to wait on this. He's just beginning, after all—"

"Oh, Kaphiri, stop that." Alicia Markova was suddenly angry, and Hamish could feel it like a small stiletto being pulled out. "Of course he's just beginning, and of course it's going to take years for him to understand, to accomplish, to—" she erupted into coughing and she could barely get her breath.

Hamish wanted to freeze with fear – it was his father coughing blood again. But he looked at his hand, and he told his hand, Move. Move to her. His hand obeyed, and rested gently on her leg. He could feel himself pour into her, as though water flowed from his heart and head down his arm and out his hand. Her breath came back, and when she could talk again, the clarity was gone from her voice.

"Thank you," she rasped. "Oh! Well done you! I'm terribly sorry. I had so much-"

"It's alright, Alicia," interrupted Mr. Shenouda again, deep concern lining his face.

Alicia Markova ignored him. "You know what you just did, don't you?"

Hamish was so glad she noticed.

"Of course you do. It's not quite healing, but a close relative. It usually comes unbidden, as it just did. You will be quite tired the rest of the day."

"Alicia?" Kaphiri Shenouda wanted to know what they were talking about.

"Oh, hush, Kaphiri. Let us be." She turned to Hamish. "Hamish, You know you are sensitive to the energy of death, don't you?"

Hamish nodded.

"And you will someday find out what it is to Speak someone home. That is a lovely thing, lovely and terrifying. It is sometimes necessary with animals – and children, strong as they are – need to be Spoken home. I've only heard about it happening with adults. I've never done it. Something too stubborn, stuck, with them. Not many Speakers actually Speak, but I think you will." She smiled in some personal remembrance, still clearing her throat. "But mostly this:" -- she took both his hands and looked deeply into his eyes – "Go slowly. Each Speaker can do slightly different things. Maximo, my friend from long ago, he could get crocodiles to do him favors out of the goodness of their hearts. I could never get anyone to do anything for me – they always wanted to do things for someone else. You'll find the things you can do. Over time. Boring, I know, but there it is. But I say go slowly, because you will become dangerous, like a gun is dangerous, and you have to be careful when you pick it up. You understand me, sweetheart?"

Hamish nodded.

"Kaphiri will be your teacher, won't you, Kaphiri?" She reached for him.

"I will do my best, Alicia," he assured her.

"Oh!" she said, brightening with energy. "That is something I can do for you, if you're willing. You did it with Happy, didn't you? Are you willing?" She touched Shenouda's arm. "Steady, Kaphiri." She turned to Hamish and her dark eyes became all Hamish ever wanted to see. "Come."

It was the invitation. Hamish came in. It felt similar to coming in with Happy – the pressure, the squeeze, the coming into new territory – but the landscape was far more complicated.

They were swimming in Greece. Hamish quickly surrendered his confusion and let his mind go into a distance that was planetary, where even light took time to reach. All he was left with was sensation, emotion, presence. He understood that Alicia – a ballerina of twenty five at the peak of her physical abilities – had herself gone into a dolphin she was swimming with she'd named Forrest. Two other dolphins were with her physical self, keeping her floating gently on the surface of the sea. Hamish was giddy, joyous, full. The dolphin Forrest told her his true name, a name that took what seemed like a symphonic span of time to say, although that couldn't have been so. And in telling his name, he opened a crack for Alicia to see and hear her own, like light being spilled into a shadowy room. Hamish could feel Alicia coming in to herself.

Then the most peculiar thing happened, something that Hamish at the time would have thought impossible. Alicia Markova in the warm blue waters off Greece sometime in the mid-1930s entwined with a dolphin she'd dubbed Forrest turned and looked at Hamish and said:

Now: Speak your name.

Hamish couldn't help it. He did.

What came out of his mouth was insignificant compared to what came out of him, his whole self. It was music and dance and singing and rhythm. It lasted a second, but was so deep and so wide it felt like it could go on forever. He said his true name.

He could feel so many things falling into place like dominos falling in an orderly line, but it went faster and faster so that he couldn't keep up. The dolphins, the beautiful young woman in the blue blue sea. He tried to reach —

He was looking at an old lady on a bed. The dream was pulsing around his ears, not fading, but not clear, a sound he couldn't quite make out, a dark shape in darkness he had to look at indirectly in order to see.

Alicia Markova's eyes were closed. She put her hand on Hamish's. "You did very well. It's all very risky, you know." She began a small laugh and tears ran out of the corners of her eyes. "I don't know why you're so young."

She was asleep.

Hamish felt more exposed and filled than he'd ever felt. He wanted to tell Lilly.

Shenouda put his hand on Hamish's shoulder and they silently left the room.

∞

At the glass doors leaving the hospital a young woman in a business skirt and with hair done up with a chopstick caught up with them.

"Excuse me! You are Hamish Taylor?" She was looking at Shenouda. He gestured to Hamish. "Ah," she said. "I'm Miss Markova's assistant. Her grandniece, actually. But. Here. Miss Markova meant to give you this, uh, these. This package. It's some of her diaries. It's from the 1960s, I think. Some things before that. Early stuff. 1940s. At least that's what she said."

She handed over the package, simply wrapped in brown paper and not even taped.

"She said there would be more, when —" she choked and put her hand to the bridge of her nose to keep from crying. Shenouda's hand started towards her to steady, but stopped. "I'm alright. Really." She turned to go back inside. "Oh, and read the note. Yellow paper. I made it legible." She hurried inside.

Hamish opened the brown paper and almost lost the note on torn yellow legal pad paper in the breeze. The handwriting was wiggly and thin, with some letters rounded out or their intentions made clear with bolder blue ink. Hamish read:

> For Mr. Taylor—This might give you some insight. At least I
> hope so. I've marked where it's useful to read the journal. Much
> of the rest just has to do with teaching and traveling. It was
> disconcerting for me at the beginning, as I'm sure it is for you.
> I wasn't able to meet another Speaker until I was nearly thirty,

and I'd begun at twenty-five. As a young man, Mr. Smith
helped me to arrange that. And the Keeper Alison Caldwell,
she kept me from going off the rails. It's a shame you'll never
meet her. I'll be going back to the U.K. as soon as some strength
returns. Feel free to call. I am yours—A.M.

The rest of the package was the journal, green, leather-bound and puffy, like a jewelry box, about the size of a church bible. There were pieces of paper sticking out, different colors—post-its, ribbons and taped cardstock.

Hamish was delirious with exhaustion all the way home until Shenouda opened his apartment door and handed him the keys. But he thought he would never sleep again.

CHAPTER 19

He read and re-read until long after his mother had come home and tapped on his door tentatively. He came out, hugged her silently, said goodnight, and went back to reading. She couldn't know their fight was the farthest thing from his mind.

In Alicia Markova's diaries, Hamish tumbled into a world that would have seemed impossible before—Alicia with wolves near a Japanese internment camp, with whales in the Atlantic trying to thwart Russian and American nuclear submarines, with birds and rats preventing mayhem in Jerusalem—and he realized that everything he did for the rest of his life would remain unacknowledged by all but the very few who really knew him.

One passage from 1942 stood out. In the middle of the night, he read it four times:

"Maximo, the older Speaker from Cuba, met me in Los Angeles after the concert. We drove for hours. He said he was taking me to a place called Bandelier in the high mesa country of New Mexico, and that he wanted me to meet another young speaker from here. Her name is Kai Pearson, and she is ever so difficult and feisty! She wore a cowboy outfit that I think she's worn since she was a child. He took us walking along cliffs where ancient people had lived. Maximo warned us that something was going to happen to us. Kai laughed at him, but then she was struck first, as we passed some empty dwellings and what they call pictograms. She was nearly somnambulant. Maximo made her sit on a low wall, and took me on.

"We went over the high edge onto the red top of the mesa. The fall wind was cool, the blue sky as deep as time. A golden eagle, almost a speck above us, hurtled down to circle just over our heads, calling out, *You see it, don't you?* Maximo called back, *That's why I brought her.* And he pointed to the north, directing me to see where there was a tiny tower being built."

Penciled in with a caret was the short sentence, "This was the beginning of the atomic city, Los Alamos." The passage continued,

"Nothing was different, but everything had changed. Something was there in my being that hadn't been before. It was like a birth, but also like a discovery, where something's been there all along and your finding it doesn't make it new, but it is new to you, and you are now different. A thunderclap in the pit of your stomach and the center of your brain. I knew what had happened to Kai. I needed to sit, and Maximo lowered me to a rock.

"Maximo kept asking both of us what we had experienced. Neither of us talked much. The next day in Santa Fe, Kai and I embraced in silence. I didn't know if I would ever see her again.

"The only thing I could say to Maximo as we drove back to Los Angeles was all I knew: They are making something that can kill everything, and my task is to make sure they don't. I don't know how I knew that, but I knew it with a surety beyond measure. It was my purpose in being a Speaker."

∞

Hamish sat for a while staring at the page. He felt light-headed and immersed, being in kinship with a woman he'd only met when she'd had a different body, almost a different identity. This woman was involved in schemes and events on scales Hamish considered cinematic, and therefore not real. He had been inside her in a way that had nothing to do with social or physical intercourse. It was an extreme intimacy that had no correlation to the world Hamish knew. The coming in, the journal, the touch on her thigh as she struggled for breath—he had been with her. It had nothing to do with him. And yet it was him. He could never be the same.

CHAPTER 20

Part of the truce Hamish and his mother had come to was that his cousin Samantha and her boyfriend David would spend time with him. Hamish snarled that he didn't need a babysitter, Sarah snarled back that he needed company. They had agreed that Lilly could be company, that his chess-mates could be company, but this Sunday during the day, it would be Sam and David.

They picked Hamish up in David's old light blue Datsun pickup that he had gotten and lavished love on when he was seventeen. They were going to go out to Jones Beach for the middle of the day, eat lunch, jump in the water. They were all on one seat, David driving.

Hamish found himself relentless. "Can you even go in the water with your leg?"

"Mishmash," protested Sam using her nickname for him.

"Oh yeah," said David. "I've got a cover for it. Waterproof. I even went diving once."

"So you were going to tell me how you lost it."

Sam turned toward Hamish, blocking David. "You are incredible."

David cracked up. As though recounting the funniest thing, he said to Hamish, "That's cool. People don't just ask like that." He laughed some more. "I gave myself a tattoo when I was 15, and I gave myself gangrene. How stupid can you be, right?"

Now Samantha couldn't suppress a laugh.

"It was really bad," said Sam. "I was only eleven, and I thought he was out of a movie, one of those strung-out characters the cops step over when they bust up a drug pad."

"My parents kicked me out, Sam's folks let me stay, you know, cause I was friends with her brother Jeremy, and they came to see me in the hospital. They got some benefactor—this rich guy named Heigo Kuusk—to take care of all the expenses 'cause I didn't have any insurance. Whew! Talk about your good times. They did the whole thing after, when I was gimping around, being an asshole sorry for himself. They saw me through walking again." He chuckled. "Thanks for asking. Really. That was good." He still laughed.

"Heigo Kuusk?" asked Hamish.

"Yeah," said David. "He's some mysterious real estate guy that Colin knows. He takes on hard cases, like he's some kind of charity. I have to write him every year, a little thank-you note, let him know what I'm doing."

"Weird," said Hamish.

"Not so weird, really. Maybe it's just his guilt money, and I'm assuaging his guilt."

Hamish said nothing. That Kuusk could throw such a wide net over such a disparate array of young people—a little girl in a chess shop, a young woman in a park, his own cousin's boyfriend—made Hamish begin to see conspiracies.

It is one of the troubling things about the vacuous and negative forces of the world. When is the proper time to confront them? Too early, and they turn your suspicions into a weapon against you. Too late, and it's, well, too late.

∞

The beach, as is the case on a Sunday in summer, was crowded. The sand stretched a couple of miles straight in either direction. They set up camp just east of the water tower, the huge Italianate finger that allowed Robert Moses, the designer of all things New York-ish, to imagine he was in Venice, and that you can see from anywhere on the long, straight coast.

The three had a normal day at the beach, if you don't count the seal who couldn't believe Hamish was in the water and kept on trying to do flips over him in his enthusiasm, and accidentally dunked him a couple of times. The lifeguard whistled and then yelled from the shore that Hamish had to get out of the water so he wouldn't get bitten.

Sam was charmed by the seagull who came and simply sat on the sand next to their towels and umbrella.

What are you doing here? Hamish had asked.

I can be here. The seagull was petulant.

But do you want anything?

I'm watching you.

I need watching?

That's what I heard. The seagull ruffled. *And if that girl touches me, I'm going to slice her.* The seagull eyed Samantha's movements.

She did reach out to touch it, but Hamish told her she'd better not. The bird was, after all, a wild animal.

Samantha was acting like a goofy big sister, even if she was stunning Hamish in her bikini. David was the most intriguing man near his age Hamish had ever been around, as though David had fought in some ferocious war, lost, realized it didn't mean anything, but didn't think it was a waste of time. Like a man with no secrets. Hamish became convinced David had no idea who Heigo Kuusk really was.

CHAPTER 21

Lilly came over late that afternoon.

The first time a boy or a girl comes over to the house of a member of the opposite sex there is always a series of sinking feelings, the host sure of the negative judgments of the guest, every knickknack, every parental obsession or purchase, every piece of clothing left out of drawers and closets, even the size and arrangement of the rooms providing fodder for humiliation and embarrassment. But it had taken a turn for the better.

They were looking into his mother's bedroom, across the bed to the window and the fire escape. Hamish had taken all of his heart and spread it out in front of Lilly by telling her about "Around the World."

"And here I thought you were just this quiet nerdy little white boy." Lilly sat back in what passed for admiration. "Your Mom doesn't mind?"

"Mom doesn't know. And what she doesn't know...."

"Yeah yeah. Well. I'm not sure it's such a good idea."

But then Hamish realized he might have an ally. Lilly had come over to his place, first of all. And then, to have someone to show his world to was like the first rush of a drug, the roar in your ears when you stop running hard, the continuous thud of the heart in your tonsils at a precipice. He saw the hint of a smile in her eye, like the shift of light in the night sky an hour before dawn.

"Can those clothes get dirty?" He eyed her jeans and lavender pull-over.

"Do they have to?"

"They will."

Suspicion set in. "Are we going to get in trouble?" Lilly said, her voice going harsh.

"We could."

Now Lilly's smile became real and full, and Hamish knew they were going.

They clambered over the bed, each of them awkward both because they had shoes on a bed and because they were on a bed together. Hamish opened the window and they ducked out onto the fire-escape. Bits of black paint chips stuck to their hands and the railings felt like bark. As they climbed around and up the ladders to the roof, the fire-escape sounded like a huge primitive musical instrument, somewhere between a low xylophone and an open kettledrum. They pulled themselves over the top onto the silver painted roof that felt like the rough side of used aluminum foil. They turned to look west.

"Wow." Lilly became still.

Hamish thought he had never had a more rewarding moment.

The sun was low, nearing the Statue of Liberty, a small figure in the harbor. There were ships strung out towards the Verazanno Bridge, a crane of the neck to the left. Just to the right, the foot of Manhattan was beginning to checker into fine tall sheets of lights against a dark northern blue. Clouds had completely broken apart from the earlier rain, and marched up from the south-west, casting colored shadows against each other and up into the sky. The breeze felt truly fresh for the first time.

"So can you show me 'around the world'?" she asked, still looking at the immensity in front of them.

"It's all the way around. On the roofs."

Lilly surveyed the route. Much of it couldn't be seen, but she knew it in principle. Hamish sensed her fearlessness, and he had the idea that this is what someone looking out over a new mountain range or uncrossed ocean must look like, a Leif Erikson or a Sacajawea.

"But what about there?"

Lilly pointed to the corner of the block. There was a gap the size of a narrow driveway.

"I'll show you."

They vaulted the low walls separating roofs, dodging shallow puddles and seeking paths free of wires and leftovers. They felt they were running on the back of a very large animal who could at any moment wake and demand they explain themselves. Whatever answer they came up with they knew wouldn't satisfy the monster, so they had to hurry before they were noticed. They created a team, feeling, like any good team, as though they could anticipate each other's thoughts.

Hamish was clear in his choices from his explorations before. Sometimes he knew they had to get very close to the cornice and slip low over the wall. Sometimes it was necessary to step up on an abandoned wooden palette or roll of asphalt. There were a few white plastic chairs that they skirted, or used to help get over an unevenness between buildings. When they came to a roof with a series of wooden huts on stilts, Lilly balked.

"It's OK," urged Hamish. "It's this guy's pigeon coop."

As they came close to the cages, the cooing crescendoed and they could see gray puffed chests pumping around in little patterns as the pigeons' beaks searched first high, then low, for the source of their threatened pride. Lilly saw all the pigeons stop when Hamish put his face near the chicken wire. She laughed.

"What, you talking to them?"

Hamish gave her a look, and then chuckled. "Yeah, and they think you're weird."

"Not as weird as you, Hambone."

"OK, OK. Come on."

They went up a ladder that was leaning against the side of an apartment building that rose just a bit too high to reach onto the roof, and crossed its rippley gray surface, the bitumen giving way before softly crunching like humid graham crackers beneath their feet. At a sound of banging, Hamish froze. Someone was pounding on the roof access door from inside, but it was stuck.

"Move! Move!" Hamish grabbed Lilly's hand and rushed her to the far side of the flat roof. They turned over the edge and dropped down a few feet to the next building. Then they shushed each other, waiting. But nothing happened. And they started giggling.

"Come on," said Hamish. "This is where it starts getting interesting."

They got to the corner. They could see a dog walker heading down Fifth Street. Lilly was sure that the dogs were all looking up at them. One of the trees came over the roof they were on.

"So how—?"

But Hamish reached out, pulling a branch to him, and he swung a leg over, straddling it. Lilly felt her tummy twist.

"You got to be kidding."

Hamish smiled and backed down the branch towards the trunk. When he reached it, he delicately turned, and climbed carefully up another branch, which put him a couple of feet above the roof of the next side of the block. And he dropped lightly down.

"T'es rien qu'un petit connard," muttered Lilly – who felt better swearing in other languages – not knowing whether she was aiming at him or herself. But she followed. Lilly had never declined a dare except once last year when a boy dared her to take off her top. She'd told him he wouldn't have any idea what he was seeing, so it wasn't worth it. It would be like showing a golden crown to a slug.

Lilly hooked her leg over the branch, and slid down backwards until she felt the trunk secure against her back. Forty feet down seemed like a very long way, and she had a brief encounter with the fantasy of crashing onto garbage cans. But she found the handholds and secure footing to bring her over to the other branch, and scooted out until she was over the next roof. Hamish had his hands out to help her, but she ignored them and swung herself down.

She grinned. "You didn't tell me we were going to die."

Hamish laughed with relief. "We're not dead yet."

∞

They turned to cross the next set of roofs, regularly spaced smooth silver surfaces separated by small brick walls with concrete caps and slanted away from the street so rain fell off the back. Since it was early evening, the heat was coming up at them from what the roof had absorbed, and the tar below the paint was still soft, so if they rested too long in one place, the roof took on the imprint of their shoes.

There were voices up ahead, and a stifled scream.

"Down!" hissed Hamish. "Down!"

They crouched at a low wall, not daring to move, holding their breath and knowing if they looked at each other, they would giggle. Lilly put her finger to her lips, and then slowly lifted her head above the wall. No one. She gestured Hamish up. He looked over.

On the next roof was only a trap door cap, and a tennis ball that was down by the edge where the rain water drained out. The cap was askew; the voices they heard emanated from that triangle of soft darkness. Hamish realized with a sudden blush that this was the place he'd found the pink panties his first time around, panties he'd eventually thrown out in a neighbor's garbage since he was too ashamed to have them in his possession, and he didn't have any idea what he'd do with them.

Lilly cautioned him again against noise, and crept over the wall, keeping low as though they could be seen through the roof, and knelt by the opening. Hamish followed, dizzy with fears. They heard the voices of two women and a man.

One woman was screaming, "You can't, you can't! We had a deal." Her accent was hard to place. Not Chinese.

The man said, as though washing his hands, "Look, Daisy, Kuusk is on his way. So just shut up. Can't you get this bitch to shut up?"

The second woman was trying, "Come on, honey. Let's go back to your room. I'll see if we can't cancel your appointments for tonight."

The man said, "She's only got one and she's not canceling it. It's Franco. She's not canceling it."

"Well," said the second woman in a comforting alto, "we'll figure something out. Give you a break."

"I don't want break!" yelled the first woman. "I want out. Kuusk promised me, he have promised."

There was the sound of a door.

"He's here," said the man. "Come on."

"Get hand off! Off!"

"I'll help her, Fallon," said the second woman.

There were movements and clunks of furniture that faded.

Lilly started to lift the trap door cap to move it aside.

Hamish whispered, "What are you doing?"

"We have to go see." Lilly's face was the picture of evenness.

"What the hell are you talking about?"

"We have to find out what's going on." Lilly dropped her legs over the lip, and found the ladder below. She whispered with an elfish smile at Hamish, her teeth shining prettily out of her dark-skinned face, "Come on." And she ducked her head down.

Hamish looked around as though someone might save him from leaping off the bridge, but all the roofs were empty. He was so angry he could spit. He followed.

The ladder down from the roof was in a closet, and they pushed aside dresses and winter coats to find the door. Lilly peeked out the open door slowly. The room was small, what had a hundred years ago been a maid's room at the top of the brownstone. But it was now a modest office with one filing cabinet, a phone on a little wooden desk and a couple of red leather chairs. The door out of the room was closed. Hamish couldn't believe it when Lilly put both hands on the door and, with her head down as though listening to a lock on a safe, she opened the door a crack.

"You promised!" they heard the first voice say.

"Daisy, my dear," a man's voice said. "I keep my promises to people who keep their promises to me."

"I keep my promise. I keep my promise."

"Well, let's see." The man's voice was almost comforting, as though here was the authority who could solve this problem. He had just enough of a European accent to make his education and understanding seem worldly. The cracks and gaps in this treacherous path would be filled and sanded smooth. "Numbers don't lie, do they? And you started with quite a debt. Your mother and little brother have not been cheap, and then there are all those expenses you keep on incurring—I don't know why you do that, but you do. I've even been very tolerant of you spending money on some recreation I don't think the INS would approve of. I'm afraid they would have no choice but to send you back to Bangkok, and what would become of you there? Your mother and little brother here, not knowing where to find you, people in Bangkok knowing what they would know about you, and being in debt to them. Oh! It is not a pleasant idea. Standing around in alleys, subjected to all sorts of indignities. Your uncle might sell you again. Up-country with some toothless ruby smuggler, I shouldn't think you'd want that. But if you just pay off what you owe to me…."

"You said three years." The woman's voice was pleading. "You said debt over in three years."

"You clearly need to work a little harder."

"I work very very hard, Mr. Kuusk. I work very hard for you, Mr. Kuusk."

"I know, and I want to let you go. But I have to get my investment back."

"Mr. Kuusk, let me live with my mother. I come here every day, every night."

"Now, you know I can't do that. I have to make sure of my investment, don't I? Surely you don't want your mother to take on what you owe, do you?"

There was a silence. Lilly and Hamish held their breaths. A sobbing came out of the silence.

Kuusk's voice, with more harshness and more hurry, said, "Amanda, take care of this, will you?"

Lilly and Hamish heard the women leaving the adjoining room. With jolts of adrenaline, they realized someone could come in any second. They did long tiptoes to the closet. As they left, they heard Kuusk, all honey gone from his voice.

"Fallon, if you can't handle one hysterical girl—" And then all sound was muffled by the coats and their flight up the ladder.

"Jesus," breathed Hamish.

"Oh my God," whispered Lilly. She gestured frantically to Hamish, and they ever-so-gently placed the cap square on the trap door hole. They snuck over to the next roof, and sat out of breath, back to the small wall.

"Oh my God oh my God oh my God." Lilly let her composure disappear. "What are we going to do?"

"We have to call the police," said Hamish, relieved that there was something they could do.

"Yes yes. Good good." Lilly patted Hamish's arm. "What do we tell them?"

Hamish looked at her like she was crazy, and then realized some of the problems. "We tell them what we heard. What they said."

"OK, good. What did we hear?"

"Lilly, you heard it. That guy is threatening her."

"I know, I know. She's a prostitute, he's a pimp."

Hamish tried to get her further. "It's more than that."

"Hamish, we don't even know what they look like. We don't even know what the address is here."

Hamish gave her shoulder a brief tug as he got up. "Come on." He led up the slope of the roof, and they lay prone, peeking their heads over the cornice, getting momentary vertigo as they stared down at the sidewalk forty feet below.

On the street, they could see a limousine through the leaves of the tree-lined street double parked and waiting in front of the building. The front door opened just then. Out came two men, one with white flowing hair and a dark blue suit, one with a fedora. The acoustics of the street made their voices bounce up the walls to Lilly and Hamish's ears.

"This is sloppy, Fallon. This is not what I pay you for, I don't care whose cousin you are. And Helena getting out without you? She's too valuable for this kind of carelessness."

"Mr. Kuusk, she just—"

"Shut up. Nothing. Take care of my business."

Mr. Kuusk swept a hand through his white hair and moved off the stoop to the car. The driver hopped out to open the door, and they drove downhill. Fallon lit a cigarette, and walked uphill towards the park, swiping a hand at a branch and stripping it of its leaves.

It finally dawned on Hamish. "I know those guys!"

"How?"

"The guy with the hat. I saw him in the park. He had a girl in pajamas."

"Slow down. What are you talking about?"

"And Kuusk! That's the name—Helena, that girl, that's the name she said—I don't know—she was—her brother or something. No, not the white haired guy, the other one, with the hat. And not her brother. And my cousin's boyfriend, his—I don't know—friend." Hamish's mind seethed. "We've got to call the police."

"It's just," said Lilly almost in tears, "we don't have anything. And we broke into someone's house. We don't really know."

They sat side by side, hugging their knees. The sun was beginning to set over New Jersey, and the evening sky took on color after color, saturating slowly.

"I know what," said Lilly. "We'll call anonymously. We'll say we think a woman, an Asian woman, is being held against her will for prostitution. We can name this guy Kuusk, and—what's his name?"

"Fallon."

"Yeah, Fallon." Lilly's body let go slowly. "What you think?"

"I think so," said Hamish, relieved. "And we better go. It's going to get dark."

CHAPTER 22

It took them a while to get back to Hamish's roof. They did have to go all the way Around the World, but the excitement had faded. The present was no longer fun, and their weak plans loomed in front of them. The owl who had visited Hamish that first night alighted quietly on a TV antenna as they approached Hamish's, startling Lilly with wonder and incongruity.

Speaker. Is this one yours?

No, she's her own.

"Is that thing tame?" asked Lilly with a bit of horror in her voice.

"I don't know," said Hamish. "I've seen it a couple of times up here."

"That is so weird. That's an owl, right? I've never seen one before."

"He's pretty, isn't he?"

Lilly gave him a look. "Damn, Hamish. You sure know how to show a girl a good time." And they both laughed at last.

∞

Lilly made the call when they got back to the apartment. In her most grown-up way, she explained their "suspicions." The operator spent a short while trying to ascertain how Lilly got this information, and Lilly was not direct. The operator gave her an ID number in case she wanted to call the cops back and follow up. Lilly hung up.

"She thinks I'm a crank."

"Maybe we'll have to find out more," suggested Hamish.

"How?"

"I don't know yet. I don't know." Over the tea that he made for her, Hamish told Lilly about Helena, and also about David, and how Kuusk's name kept on coming up. The world of their fear grew. He still kept Polly's secret.

"Oh, damn! What time is it?" Lilly grabbed the phone. "My mom's going to kill me."

After Lilly left, it was a couple of hours before Sarah got home. By the time she did, Hamish had decided not to tell her what had happened. Lilly had said she didn't know how she could explain it to her parents. They would just have to think of something else.

∞

The next day, Hamish walked Lilly and Clothilde home from Junior Rangers. Clothilde jabbered and held onto Hamish's elbow as though he were leading her into dinner and she was in an elegant gown. Her monologue covered the glances between Lilly and Hamish, the ones that gave way to a slight smile when eye contact zapped them.

When they got to the White's house, Lilly told Clothilde she was going to walk some more with Hamish.

"Oh, come on!" wailed Clothilde. "I saw him first!"

"Go inside," Lilly ushered her firmly.

Clothilde leveled a pudgy finger at Hamish. "You better treat her right!"

Hamish bowed like a courtier, and Clothilde cackled as she slammed the door closed.

As they began to walk, Hamish asked, "Where do you want to go?"

"I don't know, just not home. Not yet."

Hamish resisted reaching over to hold her hand as they turned the corner.

A whooping siren made them both jump as a large town-car stopped suddenly beside them. Hamish looked around to see if someone was running. Lily shrank.

A large man built like a concrete block emerged from the driver's side, and for such a large man moved in an easy swift curve around the front of the car to meet them on the blue-stone sidewalk. He flashed a badge and pocketed it. He was suddenly very close to them.

"All right, you two, get in the car."

Hamish started, "What the hell—"

The man's hotdog hand attached itself to the back of Hamish's neck and squeezed, making Hamish's vision darken at the sides. He grabbed Lilly's upper arm, lifting her left half nearly off the ground. As a unit they moved to the car door, and the man pushed them both in, slamming the door after them.

"Hamish," hissed Lilly. "The door—"

But the door he tried was locked, and the man was already in the driver seat. He turned to look at them over the back of the driver's seat, his tie pulling his shirt. He smiled.

"Lilly White," he snorted a guffaw. "I can't get over that. Lilly White. That's so messed up." He turned more comfortably, pulled out a cigarette and lit it with his eyebrows up. The car filled with smoke. "And Hamm-ish"—he pronounced it like the pig meat—"Hamm-ish Taylor. Some seriously fucked up names. But hey, you gotta live with them." He chuckled at his cleverness and dragged again on the cigarette. They realized he was out of breath from his exertions. "Lilly here made a phone call she shouldn't have made. That was really dumb. A dumb-ass move. And then there's this boy, thinking about fucking what doesn't belong to him. Hunh?" He reached over and cuffed Hamish on the head, almost affectionately. "Trying to get a little piece of ass for free, hunh? We're all pretty lucky it turned out I was available to talk with you guys. Otherwise, you might be getting a visit from someone else. I'm the nice guy in all this."

Hamish began to speak, but the man held up a finger.

"No speaking." He looked steadily at them both, his eyes as empty as a salamander's. "No speaking at all. You two are going to go about your little lives just like you always have, and not speak. I really don't want anything to happen to anyone. I'm here to protect you guys. And your families. I mean, Hamm-ish Taylor, it would be so hard to lose two parents in one year. That would suck, wouldn't it? Yeah, that would suck."

A stab of fear Hamish had never experienced before jammed gently into his throat.

"And little miss Lilly White. Yo mama spends a lot of time on public transportation, doesn't she? She's a fine looking woman, yo mama. I'd really hate for anything to happen to her on her way home, you know?"

Lilly had tears starting down her face. Her lips caught them, and she pressed her lips together.

"And that retard sister. I don't know. You're one monkey-crap family, that's all I know."

The man turned even more, massive, a garish rock formation.

"I know you'll do the right thing. You two. I don't want to hear about you again, unless I'm arresting you for drugs." He smiled.

He lipped his cigarette and then punched Hamish precisely in the nose. Blood spurted, as Hamish saw darkness and stars. Lilly screamed and moved to stop the man, who grabbed and twisted her wrist and her scream changed to one of pain. He let her go.

"So that's your first test of imagination. How are you going to explain that to Mommy?" He pulled at Hamish's shirt and wiped blood from Hamish's chin. "You'll think of something, I know you will."

There was a tapping on the front windshield. All three of them looked. A crow was perched on the wiper. He cocked his head and tapped on the windshield again. Another crow landed on the hood with a clunk, slipping on the car paint before settling.

"What the fuck?" The man pressed the horn. The crows lifted off, but not immediately.

"So, kids. Out. Goodbye," said the man, as though they'd just traded addresses and were going to be pen pals.

They got out of the car on either side, and the man drove swiftly down the street and turned towards Flatbush. Hamish was in the middle of the street, and a car beeped at him to get out of the way. Lilly came over, guiding him to the sidewalk. They sat on a stoop.

"You OK?" asked Lilly, examining his nose.

"Yeah." He sniffed in congealed blood and gaggingly swallowed. "God," he breathed. He found himself laughing. "That's a first." He reached for Lilly. "You?"

"First for me, too," she smiled.

"You OK, I mean?"

"Yeah." She stretched out her arms to demonstrate. "No broken bones."

"Well, I don't think the nose is broken, so that's good."

Hamish put his hand on Lilly's knee. She covered his hand with her own and leaned on him.

"What the hell's going on?" she whispered.

"I don't know," said Hamish. "But it's something to do with that place, the prostitute—the brothel—That place, and with that girl—the one I told you was with the man we saw from the roof?—the one crying in the park. I think it's got to be her."

"What was her name?"

"Helena. Helena Padar."

They sat in silence.

Lilly sat up. "But a cop?"

Hamish shrugged. As he did, they realized there was a shimmering all around them, and little scratches and rustlings like gusts in a field of loose paper. Four crows landed on the sidewalk in front of them, and a fifth on the railing. Songbirds and pigeons were crowded into the trees. Hamish looked to the side of the stoop and saw a few rats scuttle behind the garbage containers. A cat was under the car across the street, and another cat—a blond tabby—walked easily up the stoop onto Hamish's lap and began to lick his face, cleaning the remnants of blood.

"Hamish," said Lilly, her eyes wide. "What are you doing?"

Hamish's eyes were closed. He squinted them open. "Uh, there's something I should probably tell you."

All the animals seemed to be moving around them like the summer breeze, not exactly getting closer, but moving in and out like waves, changing places and circling. The cat stopped licking Hamish's chin and after considering him, turned her gaze to Lilly. She stepped onto Lilly's lap and curled up.

"They think about me."

"What are you talking about?"

A crow landed above them on the stoop and hopped onto Hamish's shoulder, flicking Hamish's hair with his beak.

"The animals. They—I can, well, I kind of understand them." Hamish smiled at a pigeon who was on the sidewalk doing a huffy circle dance.

"What are you talking about? You mean, you understand, what? Animals?" Lilly looked at him, her hand instinctively stroking the cat. "Like Dr. Doolittle?"

"Not exactly. They can't understand each other, really. I mean cats don't speak dog, like that." Hamish reached up, smoothing the chest-feathers of the crow on his shoulder, and the crow launched away.

Suddenly Lilly laughed. "You're not kidding, are you?"

Hamish shook his head. "It's good to tell you, finally."

"How long—?"

"Oh, only since I got here. Brooklyn, I mean."

"Like that dog, with the man with epilepsy." Lilly went silent. The city swelled and faded around them, like a distant throbbing. The animals—dozens of them—shifted.

"What does this cat say?" She stroked the tabby.

Hamish smiled. "Nothing right now. She likes you. She calls you 'the one with warmth and light.'"

Lilly caught his eye.

"She's right," he said.

They couldn't look away from each other.

"This is very weird, you know," said Lilly.

"Tell me about it."

Lilly reached for his shoulder and a sparrow landed on her wrist, pecking at her.

"Ow!" She jerked her hand back.

Hamish's eyes followed the retreating sparrow. "I'm sorry! You OK?"

"Yeah."

"He was thinking the danger wasn't over. He didn't get the message, I mean, well, he was like, you know, helping."

They sat. The cat sat up and stretched, her little pink tongue curling up with her yawn.

"What are we going to do now, Hamish?"

"I don't know."

"This is so weird."

CHAPTER 23

They talked on the phone that night, not saying much, but wanting the company of the other. They'd told no one about the cop. Their fear that he could do what he said was real, and that he already knew enough about them to frighten them made them feel helpless. Hamish had told his mother he'd gotten into a fight with some random kids in the park. He persuaded her not to call the police. Lilly's arm ached, but was not visibly injured. Hamish had had to assure all the animals the danger had passed. The cat kept following Lilly, even to her house with Hamish. They tried to be casual about saying goodbye, but the world had changed for both of them. Lilly, understandably, thought maybe he was a little crazy.

∞

Hamish called again the next day, soon after his mother left for work. But this time it was different, a different voice, a different need. Lilly—clearly a nascent Witness, if Hamish had only looked— could hear that he wasn't quite on the planet, that something had gotten into his flesh like a stubborn splinter; he couldn't extract it and he was entertaining different methods of just shoving it through.

His first words were, "They're coming. No, it's coming. Now. Soon, soon, it's—"

"Is it about Helena?" she'd asked.

"No! Oh, jeezus. It's. Something's going on. Something. Maybe I should call my mom." Hamish's voice sounded like he was holding the receiver about a foot from his head, and not really listening.

"Is it your animal thing?"

"Goddammit it's not a thing!" Hamish choked. "It's not a thing," he repeated hoarsely.

"OK, OK. It's not a thing." His loneliness flowed through the phone line. "What do you want from me?"

Silence. Lilly thought he'd hung up.

"Everything," said Hamish quietly. "I need—I want—you, I need you, I think—maybe I'm very scared, please, Lilly."

"Is someone coming after you? The cop? Kuusk?"

"No no no," Hamish was impatient. "No, it's not people."

"So you want me to come over?"

"Yes," he said. "Now, please."

"OK."

"Now." Hamish hung up.

As Lilly left, her mother told her to be back by 7:00. Lilly said she'd call. Her mother told her, "No, you'll be back by seven."

Lilly got to Hamish's house in a record time, her mind creating seventeen different scenarios of how this encounter was going to go down.

"What took you so long?" demanded Hamish as he let her in.

"Hamish, what the hell?" Lilly tried to look at him, but he avoided her, walking to the kitchen in the back of the apartment. He splashed water on his face and let it drip off him, leaning with both hands on the sink.

"I don't know what to do, Lilly."

"What is it you want to do?" She surprised herself with her gentleness.

"I want to move, but not just move, I have to go somewhere. It's just. If I move, I'll go there. I'll go where I'm supposed to be, where I have to. And I don't know where that is."

"Is this drugs?" Lilly tried to keep her voice neutral.

"Are you kidding? How could you think that?" Hamish cried out and hit the cupboard above the sink. "I've just got to move."

"Maybe you should." Lilly sat on the kitchen stool.

Hamish ducked his head in the sink. "They are all calling me!"

"Who? Animals?"

"No! Yes! I don't know. The wind!"

"Maybe you should just move," said Lilly, reaching for him.

Without a second's hesitation, Hamish ran from the apartment. It took Lilly a moment to realize, he had been so sudden. She ran after him, slamming the door.

She ran down into the park. He'd gotten way ahead. Summer held a hint of dying already. She could feel the leaves beginning to loosen their hold, begging to be let go into the breeze. But their green is tenacious, insisting on being in blasting heat a few more weeks before the cold, which is just over the north-western horizon, past the apartment buildings and the Hudson and New Jersey and Canada, begins to gird its loins. That stark white and red-blotched face that was Hamish as he left was dangerous, like he'd seen something or found out something that shouldn't be faced by himself.

Lilly saw him run down towards the bandshell. Small birds seemed to be dive-bombing him.

"Hamish! Will you wait up?" She began to sprint, knowing she was faster than him.

Hamish ran past the empty band shell, footsteps scraping loudly as though the entire world had become an auditorium.

Birds, mostly sparrows, swooping. *He's moving he's moving he's moving. There he goes he's going. Follow everybody follow follow follow follow follow everybody. Up up up up up up up up arooooooooound and BANK and dip. Yes!*

Hamish yelled at them, *Leave me alone!*

Aroooooound!

"Hamish!" She saw him way ahead.

Hamish swung his arms at the birds. *I don't want you!*

Lilly was following him through the trees. He got to the end of the horse trail, and Lilly saw a horse. There are never horses on the horse trail. A young woman with a helmet and those ridiculous riding pants was leading it around by the halter. Lilly could see Hamish slow, looking at the horse, and it gave her a chance to nearly catch up.

Hamish heard the horse say, *You! You stay. Stay a moment.*

I can't, said Hamish.

Stay or I follow.

I can't, said Hamish. *I can't I can't I can't I've got to go now I've got to go.*

The rider pulled on the lead. "Buckets. What are you doing? This way, kiddo. Come on."

Fine! Here we go!

Buckets lurched her lead out of the woman's hand and ran over to the fence toward the playing fields where school teams were winding down their games. The woman screamed, "Buckets!! Buckets, what the hell—" as the horse took flight over the fence, out from under the trees and into the open fields.

Hamish caught up to the horse and held the horse's huge nose to his own tiny forehead.

Will you stay now? asked the horse.

It's not going to be possible for long, said Hamish, still leaning.

More and more birds swirled above and around them, seagulls joining in the high thermals, songbirds flying so low they swept under the horse's tail. Hamish didn't know who was chanting. *The fever's starting in his heart, in his head. He's moving. Soon he'll be moving. The fever will be his moving and moving and moving. Follow? Follow! Follow fever follow fever follow fever and move with the moving. Up up up up WAIT and circle back. Where'd he go? There! There.*

The horse's gaze followed them. *What are they saying?*

You can hear them.

I can't understand them.

They are crazy. Then he admitted, *Something about moving. About a fever.*

Oh. Oh, I see. The horse nuzzled Hamish. *It's you. You've got it strong.*

Hamish reached for the horse. *I don't understand.*

There's something pressing from inside, isn't there?

It's white. Hamish closed his eyes. *There's two of them. And something else. Nothing's where it's supposed to be.*

Lilly could see she and the rider were converging on Hamish and the horse.

Hamish said, *It's so hard and so wrong and I've got to be there.*

Yes, I know. The horse nudged Hamish away. *It's—I can't say. Go.*

Help me. What are they?

You go. Go. Find out. I don't know what they are. Find out. Go.

Lilly saw the horse give Hamish a shove with its nose. Hamish stumbled and ran. Lilly followed, sweating and thirsty.

"Come here, Buckets." The rider caught the bridle. "Come on, girl. Don't scare me like that. Come on."

"Hamish!" called Lilly. "Hamish, wait up!"

Lilly dodged through a late summer baseball game, players cussing her out. She caught up at the Quaker Graveyard fence. Hamish shook the chain-link as though he could tear it apart, the springing sound of the wires muffled by vine leaves.

"Mr. Knox! Get out here!"

Hamish climbed over the fence, dropped to the other side and ran up the hill. Lilly followed muttering, "I'm going to kill that little white boy…"

She found him at a hut in the middle of the graveyard. She touched him from behind and he spun as though to hit her. But she saw him see her face, and he crumpled into tears.

"Lilly! Lilly. How did you—? Oh, God."

"Hamish, it's me."

"Come with me." He took her hand.

"Where?"

"Come now."

He pulled her through a gap in the fence and started running. Lilly had never run so far in the park, over Nethermead, past the Gazebo and the Boathouse. Birds were everywhere, groups landing in trees while others circled and still others suddenly abandoned trees forming clouds of black moving leaves.

Moving he's moving. Fever fever fever it's on him and in him, it's taking him into his fever fever fever.

Hamish stopped, looking up at the dark blizzard. Leave me the hell alone.

Wow! He's talking to us, maybe we can ride with his wind, get on his trail see with his stars because he's off, there he goes he's going into his fever fever fever. I want some—No, me, me!—I want to ride it with him—Here I go!!

Hamish moved again. "They drive me crazy."

"Who?"

"The birds."

"Oh," Lilly looked nervously around at the gatherings.

The birds would not stop. *Come come this way with me I'm with you, you with me, of course you are with me aroooooound NOW and down with him, let's ride his stars his fever fever fever.*

Lilly asked, "They are here for you?"

"I'm not sure. I don't know. I think they just want to be part of it."

"Of what?"

The trees were getting louder and louder with birds, and there was all sorts of crashing around in the bushes at the sides of the trail as the way flattened, and Lilly realized they were almost at the zoo.

"Hamish."

"We can't stop."

They came at it from the back. Lilly could hear the mix of seals honking and the traffic on Flatbush Avenue. Hamish went to the gate and opened it. A sign said in great big letters: AUTHORIZED PERSONNEL ONLY.

"We can't go in there," said Lilly. "Are you crazy?"

"You with me?"

"Damn, Hamish." Lilly tried for tough girl. "You are one strange little dude."

Hamish held the gate for her, and she slipped through.

A guinea hen who had escaped from the farm section screamed, *IT'S HIM! I TOLD YOU! HE'S HERE! HE'S HERE RIGHT NOW!* And ran ahead.

All right, I'm here. Where here? Why here?

As though in a panic, the guinea hen led them. *THIS WAY THIS WAY THIS WAY. FOLLOW FOLLOW FOLLOW.*

They crossed the huge half circle of the zoo. Lilly felt so exposed, like she had a target on the back of her head, and she was waiting for a police-voice to stop her. She could see the seals in the center, lined up at the side of their round tank or on the tall rock all following her and Hamish's progress across the open area. Some birds like spotted chickens scampered out of their way, and then turned to stare. The seals were yelping.

SEAL 1: *That's him.*

SEAL 2: *That's him?*

SEAL 1: *That's what I just said.*

SEAL 2: *Who's she?*

SEAL 3: *Maybe she's his.*

SEAL 2: *She's bigger. Maybe he's hers.*

SEAL 1: *Him? He can't be hers if he's going to Speak.*

SEAL 3: *Maybe they aren't the same.*

SEAL 1: *Don't be stupid. They're exactly the same. Just look at them.*

SEAL 2: *Ask him.*

SEAL 1: *You ask him!*

SEAL 2: *OK. I'll ask him. Hey! Are you going to Speak?*

Hamish mumbled to Lilly, "Don't look around. Just come on." He pulled her across.

SEAL 1: *Hey, you! We're talking to you! You going to Speak? It would be great because we're tired of this, you know. You took your damned time!*

SEAL 4: *Did they bring any fish?*

SEAL 5: *Fish? There's fish?*

Lilly said, "What are we looking for?"

"I think it's just over here."

"What is?"

"I don't know."

"Hamish…"

They stopped at a long building fronting Flatbush. It was unremarkable.

"It's got to be right here. This is where—it's got to be. I know it. I just know it."

"What?"

A sign said, Discovery Center. They walked further. The door into the building said, Classroom. She could feel Hamish deflate, and the hand that held hers loosened as he used it to cover his heart. She felt this boy falling into a grief as profound as anything she'd ever known, and a desperation of her own started to set in. She had no idea what to do.

"There's nothing here." Hamish knelt. "Oh, God. There's nothing. Nothing here. It was so wrong. Everything was wrong. God, it hurts so much. How do I make it stop hurting so much?"

"Hamish— " Lilly knelt beside him.

And then she saw it. A black panther standing under a tree. It came toward them.

Ah, you're here. Bagheera sat.

Lilly was in a dream of fear.

She is yours? Bagheera pretended to be laconic, and stared at Lilly.

She's herself. Hamish had no patience.

She is afraid.

I'm afraid.

She does not submit. The panther curled her lip.

I don't submit.

You are the Speaker. She—

Hamish stood in front of Lilly.

She does not submit! If it could be called yelling, Hamish yelled at the Panther.

The panther turned her gaze to Hamish. She blinked. She looked back at Lilly. Differently.

She does not submit, she repeated.

Hamish's hand started to reach back to Lilly, but he stopped when he felt her fingers. He felt a swelling surround him, as though the world were a balloon inflating around him, but most of the pressure came from his left, and he looked in that direction. It was terrifying. There was whiteness like snow moving in swirls and currents, and an ochre streak staining and fading all about the white. This was what was calling. This was what was so dangerous. This was the source of the pain.

It was an embroilment of confusion. Hamish knew what it was, not knowing how he knew. This was the spot where the polar bears had been shot. This was the spot they had killed the 11-year-old boy. This was the tangled, unresolved left-overs. Hamish knew that animals were all around calling him to heal this rift that came from time to time like the rhythms of epidemics or the cycles of earthquakes. He knew if he did nothing this would dissolve after a while, leaving an uneasiness and tremor in its wake that might be called a haunting. It would stay that way until the swelling, the fever, took hold again, and someone else and all the animals around would feel its wrath and fear and loneliness and longing and helplessness.

But Hamish knew the words because he knew the names, and he could call to them so they would recognize themselves.

So he did. He Spoke.

The male polar bear came first, the one the zookeepers had called Teddy. He looked at Hamish with surprise as Hamish told him the way to go home. An explosion of seagulls curled up into the sky and headed north, escorting for a ways the dorsal electricity of his progress.

Lucy was what they had called the female. Hamish saw her as diminutive compared to the male, but she came to him angry and more powerful than tornados. He had to call out her name three times before she settled into sensing what new thing was happening, before she knew that Hamish had already shown her the way home, and she had only to take it. Assemblies of birds disappeared into the trees and over Brooklyn, and profusions of animals stirred in the bushes, heading back to where they belonged in the wake of Lucy's exit.

What was left? His name was on the tip of Hamish's tongue. His strength was as astonishing as the fulcrum that moves mountains, and his desire was endless, having wrapped itself around each hair follicle of those bears and dove into each corpuscle of their blood with the hungry curiosity of a boy. Hamish could see him, known to the boy's mother sixteen years ago as Juan, sheepish, afraid he'd done something wrong, wanting to run.

Lilly saw Hamish on an edge. The breezes of the late summer evening were capricious and strong, buffeting them and the birds that took off and disappeared. It seemed only the panther was left, watching them. Hamish was stuck, she knew. She reached for his shoulder and the panther hissed into a high yowl, lips stretching back to show teeth and whiskers winging out. Lilly looked at the panther, but she touched Hamish anyway. The panther licked the side of its mouth.

With her touch, Hamish knew. He called out the name of this boy who was so alone and reminded him that home was where he needed to be, and he knew where that was already. He was being waited for. Go. Follow where the path leads, and there you will find it. Home.

The boy was gone.

The air stilled. Hamish sat down on the ground, and flopped backwards, almost hitting Lilly's legs. He started to laugh.

The panther licked his face with her rough tongue twice, and bounded away until they could not see her.

Lilly laughed, too. They laughed a long, long time.

PART 2

THE GIRL

CHAPTER 24

With Fall comes school, and with school comes structure built at a time when children worked the fields and tended the livestock, not when their parents had jobs in big cities and transportation was the biggest challenge of the day. For Hamish, it was a welcome and nerve-wracking reprieve from Speaking and Kuusk and the responsibilities of his nascent skills. It is important to understand where a new-found Speaker spent two thirds of his time. Hamish's new highschool, Herman Melville HS39 for the Gifted and Talented, was three times the size of his school in Plains, all confined in a huge rectangle of brick built nearly a century before. It was all the way on the other side of Brooklyn in Coney Island. Sarah had talked with Mrs. White and Daniel's mom Mrs. Zhao and determined that Hamish was going to take the subway out to the end of the line, and then a packed city bus from there for ten blocks to the big brick school with some fields and a tidal basin in back.

Hamish met Lilly and Daniel at the subway and they went together. It was a Thursday, three days after the storm at the zoo. Lilly and Hamish had walked home from that lightly holding hands through the park, and then letting go as they got on public streets. They'd hugged long and gently at Grand Army Plaza, agreeing to a silence that ached. They called each other the next day, Lilly telling Hamish she'd gotten a scolding for being home after 7:00, but not much more than that. They didn't know what to say. They'd made arrangements to meet at the subway.

Zooming over Brooklyn on the elevated first thing in the morning felt magical to Hamish, watching people moving with hasty deliberation along sidewalks and across streets and in their cars, getting to where their days started. It was as though he were watching the pieces of a huge puzzle fall wondrously into place. When they got to the school, Hamish had to go the central office. Being the newest kid among thousands of new kids did not feel special. It felt like he was that extra thing no one knew what to do with, a bay leaf in the soup. Do you take it out, or throw it back in?

They threw him into homeroom, and launched him into classes. It was a foreign country, and he was clearly the odd infant in a cool universe filled with grown-up children who looked like men and women, all of whom knew more than he. After the whirlwind subsided, he found himself on the street in the mid-afternoon in a river of children, looking for Daniel or Lilly. Steve Mondolfi was also at the school. He'd jumped up and down when he saw Hamish after school, embarrassing Hamish with his goofiness. But he came from a different part of Brooklyn, and ran to get on his school bus. Daniel and Lilly had each found friends they'd not seen for the summer, and were engrossed in reestablishing connections that had been so important months before. Even though the school was in the middle of a Hispanic and black neighborhood with Italians still hanging on, the school was mostly white and Asian. Lilly was walking with three black girls making up one of the smaller cliques, and she merely laughed a "Hey, what's up, Hamish?" when she saw him. He followed in their wake.

On the subway platform he found Daniel. They sat together on the subway, comparing notes on teachers, with Daniel playing the expert on all the personalities. School had changed Daniel, making his laugh louder and wider, showing his braces more, and then suddenly he would close his mouth as though he'd finally remembered to shut the door against the wind. Hamish learned that Daniel had a crush on every girl he met, and the crush lasted for about fifteen minutes after he couldn't see them any more. Then, slack-jawed and craving and harmless as a puppy, he was distracted by the next girl.

Hamish discovered two things in his first week: People love a tragedy, and he loved school. As soon as both students and teachers found out his father had recently died, he became special. He suddenly had an authority about life that few others had, and that everyone acquiesced to. He was subtly inducted into the Dead Dads Club by Steve Mondolfi, but there were few members. Steve and one other boy had lost their fathers in the towers on 9/11, and another girl's father was killed in a car accident while she was in the car. Hamish met her in his biology class when Steve introduced them by saying, "Cindy! Here's Hamish. His dad's dead, like ours. So he knows." And he waggled his eyebrows like Groucho Marx. "You're coming to my bar mitzvah, right?" Steve leaned confidentially to Hamish. "Probably happened with you when your dad kicked the bucket. Everything's late. Ha! I'll be the oldest kid in Brooklyn to have a bar mitzvah. But everyone has to come!"

Cindy looked at Hamish as though he'd confessed to being the product of incest, her face a mixture of repulsion and intrigue and sympathy. She nodded her hello, holding her book bag tight to her chest, and kept walking to her lab table.

It was the teachers who surprised Hamish. Even though he was cautioned against his English teacher (or "Language Arts," as it was called in this school), he found Mrs. Small to be a ferocious defender of the written word. Living up to her name, she was five-foot nothing, and would peer over her glasses at the student she was peppering with questions about what Shakespeare had written 450 years ago. She never asked for raised hands, but searched the room for her next interrogatee. If someone didn't "get it," she perched on the edge of her desk like a tiny Socrates lasering through the student's panoply of emotions at being pinned under her microscope until a little light went on in the student's head creating a miniscule moment of silence before Mrs. Small turned from the class with a whispered, "Good" on her lips.

The unfortunately named Mr. Jones taught Chinese, and was himself an immigrant from Macao. Hamish was coming late to languages at Herman Melville, and he could only choose between Italian and Chinese. He had thought to himself that learning a language could only be a snap, given that he could talk with animals, so he picked the difficult one. Frustratingly, he found Chinese impenetrable, even when he got assistance from Lilly, who wasn't even taking Chinese. But the class was tolerable because Mr. Jones, with his extremely thick

Mandarin accent, kept the students up to date on Chinese current affairs like an addictive gossip columnist.

For some reason Hamish could not explain, he felt most at home in History. Mr. Freeborne looked like a musician with dark skin, long dreds, and beads around his neck. His shoes and pants were always impeccable, and his shirts always had deep maroons or hunter greens in them. His glasses were aviator-like, and made his large eyes even larger. And he told stories. The more crazy the story, the more real something became.

Their subject was "the creation of wealth." They had to start with the Industrial Revolution. Mr. Freeborne read to them from a book: "'The advent of the steam engine and machine-made goods raised the standard of living for everyone. Food became cheaper, more jobs were available, and people were able to travel more easily in search of more productive employment.'" He put down the book. "OK, so let's say it's you, Maria. You're looking for a job."

Maria looked up from her doodles. "I don't need no job."

"No, but you've got to get one because you're 15 and your mom just had another baby and your dad was injured at his work so no one will hire him."

"He gets like workman's comp. I know about that." Maria smirked.

"Workman's comp doesn't happen for 75 years."

"What, we're just going to starve?"

"No, you're going to work. You'll get a dollar a day. You work 12 hours a day, get half an hour for lunch."

"What am I doing?"

"Making cloth. Textile industry. Weaving with big machines."

"Awesome."

Mr. Freeborne casually took out a piece of paper, tore it down in size a bit, took out a Bic lighter, and lit the paper on fire. There were gasps around the class.

"So, what did I just do?" asked Mr. Freeborne as he stamped out the ash on the floor.

"You're just trying to burn the school down."

"But what did I do?"

Shy Natalie put up her hand. "You burnt a piece of paper."

"Good! The obvious. I burnt a piece of paper."

Mr. Freeborne took out his wallet, and a dollar bill. He held up the dollar bill. "This is what Maria gets paid for twelve hours at the mill."

He lit the bill with the Bic lighter. It didn't burn as fast, but it burned, until it was a crisp ash on the floor. The class was silent.

"So, what did I just do?"

No one said anything, until Natalie said quietly, "You burnt a piece of paper."

"I burnt a piece of paper. But it feels different, doesn't it? Because we all believe it's different. Because it's what we call 'money.' We believe in money. We believe in it because it works for all of us and it works for us because we all agree to believe in it."

Mr. Freeborne turned to the front of the classroom. "By the way, what I just did was against the law. I could get six months in jail for burning up money. Now, why do you think that is? Who does that protect?"

Hamish loved Mr. Freeborne.

Twice a week there was chess club at the school, which Mr. Shenouda ran. He would travel all the way across Brooklyn to be with a group of ten or twelve students huddled over vinyl cloth chessboards with green and cream-colored squares. He brought a clutch of plastic chess clocks that he would beg the kids to not destroy as they hit the buttons. He would hold impromptu seminars on particular chess problems that appeared in their games, opening books to show how Kasparov or Anand handled similar situations. He would declare an instant winner if someone forgot to shake hands with courtesy both before and after a game. And after the sessions, Hamish's other education would begin. Kaphiri Shenouda would guide him through the world of being a Speaker.

∞

Kaphiri Shenouda came to being a Keeper late in his life. He was already well into his 30s. He had the instincts and skills of empathy and persuasion, but not yet the spark that turned his demeanor into a force for balance. It was oddly when he left Egypt with his family and he arrived at the airport in the United States that the role fell on him. There was a dispute in the passport line that quickly devolved into a riot. It was crowded and messy and violent. Shenouda found himself lifting his voice just enough towards the principal players in the chaotic room—both customs security officers and men desperate to get their families into the safety of America—and to his own surprise they stopped to listen to him, nodding in recognition, grateful for the moment of respite. One security guard extended a hand to help a man from Yemen off the floor, and the riot was over. Everyone started talking about it was though it was something they had experienced the day before and were slightly embarrassed by.

Thaddeus Knox happened to be at the airport that day. He knew a confluence of events when he saw one, and he made sure to know Shenouda and his family better.

Shenouda discovered early on he couldn't use his skill for violence or anger. He couldn't incite people to do things against their will. He couldn't make them blind to the deeper truths before them. He could allow people to see the present moment. He could move them towards their better nature. He could deflect them from the desire to harm.

But he didn't know much about Speakers. Alicia Markova was the only one he'd spent time with. He'd learned much from her, and from Knox. But as far as tutoring a new Speaker, he was as inexperienced as Hamish.

During the Summer, Hamish would spend an afternoon with Shenouda. Shenouda would try to get Hamish to consciously perform some of the skills he knew many Speakers had, such as the Cry—which summons animals for a purpose – or the Amusement—which created an elaborate game whose only purpose seemed to be play. The deeper skills, the ones connected to migration, mating, or territory, were beyond Shenouda's scope, and at the time they seemed beyond Hamish's growth.

They continued afternoons in the Fall from time to time. Shenouda was convinced that animals would be the best teachers, even though he had no idea what they would teach Hamish. Mostly, Hamish just connected with new groups, new species, new areas. But once they went out to the literal wilds of Brooklyn.

Shenouda had ushered Hamish into his green VW Beetle, and said in a loud voice, "We're going to the ocean!" They drove east from school across Brooklyn, stopping once to get a sandwich and juice for each of them. Hamish was too tired to resist. Along the way, he told Hamish he was taking them to an old airport that now had a small forest on the side, and it opened up to Jamaica Bay.

Mr. Shenouda was an enthusiastic driver. He gestured with his left arm out the window, never cursing other drivers or the traffic, but expressing his joy at the competitive exercise he clearly felt driving to be. If he beat someone skipping ahead a light, he slapped the outside of the door triumphantly. If someone cut him off to slip ahead of him, he would lift both hands into the air and say, "That was beautiful. Well done!" The streets across Brooklyn were full of sporting opportunities.

Suddenly it seemed as though they were out of Brooklyn. They passed a huge mall, and then of all things there was a golf course, and then reeds on either side of the now divided road. Trees took over, and there were no buildings ahead. Mr. Shenouda turned left into a parking lot with a sign that said, Floyd Bennett Field. Mr. Shenouda had not been exaggerating; it was an old airport, but not just a little airstrip. This was huge, with wide runways and airplane hangars in the distance. The fields in between expanses of concrete were flat as banquet tables with volunteer trees exuberantly placed. When they got out of the car and shut the doors, the openness took the thunk of the door closing and spread it out thin and distant, making their ears stretch for sound above the steady wind.

"This, my boy," proclaimed Mr. Shenouda, "is a place to come when the city closes in. The edges here are not so sharp." He breathed deeply, patting his chest. "Come! This way."

He strode north across the airport runways. To Hamish it felt like he was breaking some vague understanding, like not lying down in the middle of the street at night even though no cars were coming. He half expected to turn to see a large military aircraft bearing down about to land on their heads. But he followed, his body letting itself be infected by the containerless sky.

Shenouda led them onto a path off the north runway, plunging away into trees that covered them and quieted the sea breezes. The path curved along, passing an abandoned building, its bricks lichened and its roof partially broken. There was an army truck next to it, its tires flat and its doors windowless. But the path swallowed them away from this, and Shenouda got lost up ahead in a twist of the trail.

Two coyotes appeared in front of Hamish. He turned, and there was a third behind him. The lead male was large and smiled as though he knew a secret. The female was impatient.

Get the hell out of here, she said to Hamish.

Hamish could feel hackles go up, both on himself and the coyotes. *What, is this yours?* He could feel himself scoffing.

Ours, snarled the male.

Hamish felt rather than saw the young male behind him burst towards his legs. He turned and felt his lips retract and his eyes narrow. The coyote stopped.

Hamish said to the three of them, *You don't tell me where I can go. This will all be MINE!*

A vibration went out, like a circle out from a blast site. The coyotes jumped, and the two younger ones fled. The eldest licked his snout.

We'll come back. Watch yourself. He disappeared into the trees.

All his long walk through the trees to find Shenouda, the coyotes pushed the boundaries. It was now a territorial skirmish. Hamish even stepped into fresh coyote scat deposited immediately before he turned around a tree. He had to pee desperately, and found some bushes to screen what he was doing, but he realized he wanted to pee everywhere. As he was relieving himself, a young coyote came and nipped at him, fraying his jeans, and then scampered quickly into hiding.

Hamish found Shenouda, sitting on a log on the low and quiet shore, looking out over Jamaica Bay. He excitedly told him what had happened, what new aggressive power had come out of him and how the coyotes were challenging him. It felt terrific.

Shenouda admonished him. "You have started a war. This is not becoming. You are messing with ownership, and you have no interest in it except ego and mischief. You must stop it, end it. Go. Tend to that now." He turned back to gaze at the water.

Hamish began to object that the coyotes had started it, but Shenouda was suddenly an immobile statue. It was as if he had cut Hamish off completely from his presence, and it made Hamish feel bereft and ashamed.

He ran back into the trees and called out to the coyotes. He could sense them surrounding him, but couldn't see them. He could not understand what prompted him to say what he said, but he cried out,

Brothers! Sisters! I made a mistake. I tried to take what wasn't mine to take. Please allow me passage in your land, and take my promise I will not overstep again.

The lead coyote showed himself. He laughed. *Cool. Come back and play sometime.* The air felt clear.

When Hamish returned to Shenouda, he was still gazing out, but instead of inert substance Hamish could feel him completely there, as though they had just embraced. He walked over sand and pebbles and crunchy dried seaweed to sit by him on the log. The water was still. The only sound was the far off cry of an occasional seagull, and the low hum of the BQE traffic whirling around the borough. Gulls drifted overhead, watching them. Terns hovered over the water, wings fluttering back and forth, and then their beaks extended downwards, the wings folded and the little birds crashed into the water, disappearing for a few seconds before struggling out and flying free of the surface.

"Oh! I always wonder if they will ever come back to the surface," said Mr. Shenouda in mock worry. "I hold my breath until they do."

"I'm sorry," said Hamish.

"No apologies to me, truly. I think you have apologized where you needed to. I, however, am human, and understand the dark temptations of power." He tossed a pebble into the water.

Hamish followed the ripples and saw tiny jets lifting off and landing at Kennedy Airport a couple of miles across the Bay.

"We have one thing in common I know," said Shenouda. "Grief. It is understandable to want power after grief. Especially when you feel all was taken, as you must have felt, must still feel, when your father died."

"Yes."

"My wife," said Shenouda, "she was also taken."

Hamish's face asked the question.

"It was an accident with a plane. She died. And our sons, they died as well. They were on the way to visit her mother, back in Cairo. The flight 990. Just before the new millennium. Just over there—" he gestured vaguely to the southeast "—it disappeared into the ocean. And they were gone. Everyone on the plane was gone. So I was not alone in my grief." He stopped. "No, that's not so. You know better than most, don't you, my boy? That we are alone in our grief, finally, aren't we?" He patted Hamish's back delicately with his hands of bread.

Hamish nodded, as he put his hand on the shoulder of his teacher.

CHAPTER 25

Hamish hadn't worn a tie since his father died, and it felt maudlin, sexy, and responsible all at the same time. Sarah had shined his shoes for him, and they clicked on the floor with a movie-like authority. He looked at himself in the mirror, never sure if this was really what he looked like.

"They're here!" called his mom. "Come on, Hamish. You don't want to hold them up."

Sarah tucked an envelope into his inside pocket.

"You can just ask Steve's mom where to put it. At the bar mitzvahs I went to there's usually a table."

"How much is it?"

"Fifty dollars."

"Fifty dollars? Jeez. Does it have to be that much?"

"Well, if you got bar-mitvahed, you'd be getting that much."

"Why don't I?"

"Oh, God, Hamish. You know. I can't allow—Oh, come on. Get out of here." And Sarah shut the door behind him, the bell inside the door ringing once softly.

∞

As soon as he opened the brownstone door, he heard Ron.

Where are you going?

Hamish glanced up into the tree. The crow hopped, and tilted his head so one eye took him in.

I don't know.
Can I come?
Hamish laughed. *Sure. Just follow this blue thing I'm getting in.*
Sometimes I just don't understand you.
Hamish saw Lilly lowering the window.
Just follow, you crazy bird.
Cool! And Ron took to the air.
"What's so funny?" Lilly asked, leaning out the car window.
Hamish flushed. "I don't know." He motioned up to the crow.
Lilly smiled. "Crazy white boy."
Mrs. White looked sharply at Lilly. "What did you say?"
Hamish defended her. "It's OK."
"No," Mrs. White quashed it. "It is not."
Mrs. White was driving. Lilly was in the front, and her friend Carla sat in the back. Carla was wearing a pink dress that spread across the car seat like foam, and Hamish had to be careful not to sit on it. He felt his thigh contract as though the lace was hot.
"Hamish," asked Mrs. White, making conversation. "Have you been to a bar mitzvah before?"
"No."
"Well, I hope you have a good time."
Lilly turned around and rolled her eyes at Carla and Hamish, making them co-conspirators. Steve Mondolfi had invited everyone he'd ever gone to school with. Lilly had been in sixth grade with him, and Carla hadn't seen him since fourth grade. But everyone accepted the invitation because his father had died in 9/11.
They drove out to Bay Ridge. The Shore Road Temple fronted onto a sweeping panorama of the New York harbor with the Verrazzano Bridge looming pale aqua to the southeast. Well-dressed people with children were coming from all directions, aiming for the double doors of the stuccoed front. Hamish had passed this place once on his wide walks, wondering what was out there, beyond the bridge, out to sea.
They pulled up to the front behind a stretch limousine, and waited for it to unload. The driver had gone around and was opening the door. Heigo Kuusk got out, stooping momentarily as though the sky were

going to bump his head, and then stretching tall. He looked around, shooting his arms out to pull at his shirt cuffs. His cufflinks glittered. He seemed large in every way, even though he was not fat. His face was immobile, like an animal, watching. His suit fell from his shoulders and waist like comfortable water. But, most astonishing, his hair was white as salt. It wasn't short, and it moved with the breeze off the bay, showing no hidden gray or yellowing. Just white.

Kuusk turned to the open door as two young girls and a nine-year-old boy poured out. He suddenly smiled, warming everyone around him. He took his small son's hand as the girls skipped ahead.

"Come on, out you go." Mrs. White felt in a hurry. "I'll pick you up at the other place at seven."

Ron was in a tree across the street. *What the hell's going on?*

I'll tell you later. Hamish was being as subtle as he could.

Got anything for me?

Later!

Anything I should do?

Later!!

"Hamish? Is that...?" Lilly looked startled.

Hamish avoided her eyes, as though making contact would expose them to Kuusk. He just nodded.

But then he looked fully at Lilly standing there in front of the synagogue. Lilly was wearing a dark blue dress with spaghetti straps that moved loosely on her body. Her simple necklace glowed gold against her warm dark skin. Her earrings made her look 17. She'd pulled her hair back, and Hamish realized she was wearing make-up. And then there were her eyes, their liquid pulling him in so he could feel his throat close as he drowned.

∞

Hamish had to find a bathroom. Inside the synagogue, there were helpful signs that led to doors that led to stairs that led to more signs. In the basement, where everything was covered with gleaming thick paint—blue-gray on the floor, cream on the bumpy brick walls, and fudge brown on the ceiling and pipes—Hamish found "Men."

As he peed, men came in and ran water in the sinks. He could see one of them was the white-haired Kuusk, who rubbed his face with cold water.

"Oh, I can't wait to get the smell of Jew out of my nose."

His companion, a balding stocky man, assented, "I know what you mean. But these things don't take too long." The man hawked into the sink and rinsed his spit down. "You helping out?"

"Mondolfi did something for me." Kuusk smiled and patted his face dry. "This is the least I can do."

Kuusk moved to the urinal beside Hamish and glowed at him. "Hey, kid."

Hamish grunted, "Hey," very conscious of his underpants snapping back in place. He quickly dribbled water over his fingertips and left the bathroom.

As people began to find seats for the ceremony, Hamish could see Steve Mondolfi with his family up in the front, waiting to be called on. At chess, Steve mentioned the process only once, saying his rabbi had said something funny about sex, which made him laugh till snot came out his nose but it was too embarrassing to impart in Mr. Shenouda's hearing, and the moment passed. Steve now looked small and important, like a pubescent soldier. He should have had this ceremony two years earlier, but when his father was killed on 9/11, everything, even Steve's growing up, was postponed.

Steve's yarmulke, embroidered by his mother, had slipped backwards slightly and his mother was reapplying its bobby-pin. Hamish saw that Lilly and Carla had found seats in the front rows, but there was no room near them. He was suddenly lost. He knew some of the kids whispering to each other, but none of the adults, and everyone was suddenly a New Yorker and he was not. He turned to find a seat at the back and smashed into the flowing clothes of Kaphiri Shenouda.

"Ah! Hamish Taylor. Someone to sit with. Do you mind?" Mr. Shenouda gestured into a row. "I see Steve there, who graciously invited me to this important event in his life. And you are here. I see Abraham, and there is Daniel. But Pradeep is missing."

"He's not coming."

"I see. Then we must witness this without him."

They sat, and Hamish felt trapped and secure, sure he could smell cumin and woodsmoke emanating from Mr. Shenouda's beard or sleeves. People began to quiet as the rabbi walked to the ark.

Suddenly, there was a harsh and echoing squawk. Two crows had gotten in the open side-windows and were flying around the gallery. People could hear the rough cloth sound of their wings. Their call was sharp, breaking the space like a smashed bottle. Heads craned and turned to catch their looping flight.

Ron spotted Hamish. *There you are!*

You gotta get out of here!

What's going on? What are all these people doing here?

What the hell are you doing inside? And bringing your friend? Do you know how dangerous this is?

Ron's friend was perched on a lighting fixture. *This is crazy. You're a putz.*

Mr. Shenouda looked at Hamish as though he'd found a small fish in his tea. People were moving, men conferring. The rabbi tried to calm people from the bimah. Hamish pretended not to look at Ron, who flew back and forth between chandeliers over his head. The other crow flew down to the podium.

There was a collective gasp as a shoe knocked the crow off the podium onto the stage floor. Mr. Kuusk strode up with one stocking foot and grabbed the bird.

Ron screamed, *He's going to kill him! He's going to kill him. Stop him! Speaker, stop him! Now!*

It was clear to everyone that Kuusk was going to wring the bird's neck. His daughter shrieked, "Daddy! Don't!" And he hesitated.

Hamish didn't plan anything. He whispered, "Excuse me," to Mr. Shenouda and ran up to the stage.

"Excuse me, sir. I can take the bird."

Kuusk's authority was absolute. "I got it."

"I can take care of it for you, sir." Hamish held out his hands.

Kuusk looked at his daughter, and handed the bird over, immediately taking a handkerchief out and wiping his palms. Hamish held the crow close, finding his way off the stage.

The crow was panting, *Am I dead? Am I dead? I think I'm dead.* His tongue was visible, his eyes stuck on Hamish.

You're not dead. You're talking to me.

No I'm not.

Yes, you are. I'm going to take you outside.

You sure I'm not dead?

Damn right I'm sure. Hamish stroked the black feathers and felt the loud landing of Ron on his shoulder. There were a couple of cries from people. Kuusk called out, "If those are your pets, you made a big mistake." There was murmuring all over the congregation, but no one moved.

"They're not pets, sir. I'm just pretty good with animals." Hamish could tell Kuusk had him pegged as a liar. "I'll just get them out."

Hamish hurried up the aisle.

Ron was muttering in his ear, *You wanted me to follow you for this?*

I didn't want you to follow me. You wanted to follow me.

Am I going to be OK? asked the other crow.

Shut up, you nincompoop, said Ron.

Both of you. Enough.

Hamish turned to butt open the door. He could see Lilly was following him. And behind her, Mr. Shenouda had risen.

Come on, guys. Let's get you out of here.

Hamish crossed Shore Road to the tree-covered slope that led down to the waterfront playfields and the parkway. The crow's breath was coming easier to him. Ron flew to a maple with low branches.

Bring him over here.

Hamish tipped the bird onto a branch. His feet held, but he wobbled like a drunk.

Wow, that's amazing. I'm alive. Ha! You. You're the best. Woah.... The crow ducked his head and gripped tighter.

Don't go inside any more. OK?

Sure. Not going inside. Not me.

You, too—what the hell do I call you?

Ron did a short glide to the same branch. *Genius?*

Hamish looked back across the street at the synagogue. There was Lilly. She gave him a short wave. He stood too quickly and the blood flooded out of his head. Behind her, the door opened, and Kaphiri Shenouda looked out. Hamish squatted to keep from fainting. He felt Lilly run across the street and he started to get up again.

"No, keep down. And sit." Lilly guided him.

"It's dirty. My mom—"

"It's OK. Lean forward, head down."

Hamish felt her hand on his back like a tropical ocean. His peripheral vision became floodgates of clarity, and he saw Lilly's knees on the pine needles. He wanted to lean into her. And he did. And she let him.

"I don't know what happened."

"Your brain just didn't have enough blood, and then—vertigo."

Ron called to Hamish from the trees. *She's yours, right? Do we need to watch after her, too?*

Hamish lifted his head. *Yes, you watch after her.*

"There's that crow again." Lilly moved, thinking Hamish was going to get up. "These crows love you. What are they saying?"

Hamish stood slowly. *Wait. What do you mean 'watch after'?*

It's OK. I got it. Ron laughed and flew off, calling to the other crow to follow.

"Hamish?"

"I'm OK."

As they crossed the street back to the synagogue, Hamish could see Mr. Shenouda deliberating with himself, and then go inside.

∞

The ceremony went off without a hitch, energized by the crows. Steve read from the Torah with a kind of panache that made tears of pride leak down his mother's face, clearly missing her husband on this day. He spoke with unusual authority on the need for imagination in our day-to-day affairs, and cited comic-book super heroes as a sly reference, equating them with Joseph and David. He beamed as the rabbi blessed him. Hamish watched a ritual work its magic.

The rabbi announced that the reception was a short walk away at a large catering establishment, and the gathering rose. People glanced at Hamish as they passed him, where he was sitting with Lilly in the back.

Mr. Shenouda approached him, angling over the pew. "Your friend was not injured?"

"My friend is an idiot."

"As so many of us are. Our intentions, however, are inevitably good. Oh, and please do me the favor of coming to visit Madonna soon. She clearly needs conversation, and I am not up to the task." He smiled at Lilly, also. "I'll see you over at the reception."

Lilly leaned over. "Who's Madonna?"

"His parrot. A big, blue parrot."

"You talk to his parrot?"

"She talks to me." He lifted his finger to show her the scar. "And bites."

Lilly giggled, and as Carla approached them, they got up to leave.

Outside, people were stalling in front of the synagogue, waiting for friends to walk over with. But mostly, they were staring across the street and up into the trees.

There were hundreds of crows, almost like a gigantic hive of black bees. A susurration filled the afternoon sky. A moment after Hamish and Lilly came out, all the crows lifted into the air, making a circular cloud over the street. They swirled and banked and called. The air through feathers made a huge hushing sound. They started going up, as though the sky had pulled a plug and the crows were spiraling into the void. Then, inexplicably, they dispersed and were gone.

Lilly turned to Hamish. "So what were they saying?"

"A lot of things." He laughed a deflection. But as he did, he saw Mr. Kuusk, who was holding his son's hand, gazing at Hamish. Kuusk nodded to Hamish as though they had an understanding.

∞

They ended up walking over to the reception with Steve and the cohort from Herman Melville. Hamish was able to ask Steve how he knew Kuusk.

"He was a friend of my father's, did real estate with him or something. He's a money man. Moves money around. Hey, Jack! Lemme see that!" Jack threw Steve a little leather ball meant to be kicked and kept in the air. Steve did his best, whooping at each failure. "Why you want to know? You want him as a new father?" Steve snorted his laughter through his nose. "He's rich enough. – Hey, Hamish! Think fast!" He kicked the little ball at Hamish.

"There're those crows again," said some kid. Hamish gazed with everyone into the trees. There were dozens of black birds calmly gripping branches.

Hamish turned back to Steve. "But what does he do?"

"Kuusk? I don't know. He's like a banker or investor."

"Those are his kids?"

"Yeah. That one girl—wahoo!—she's hot, isn't she? Here!" The ball came Hamish's way again.

Hamish chased it into the street, looking back. There was Lilly with two boys about sixteen on either side of her. They were flirting with her, and Hamish could see she was trying to put a good face on it. He started to move back down the street towards her.

A crow landed on one boy's head, grabbing at his hair and pulling off. Two others attacked the other boy, pecking at him. All three of the kids ducked and ran forward on the sidewalk. Hamish called out to the crows.

Stop! Enough!

Ron swooped down to the wall bordering the sidewalk. *Pretty great, hunh? Got them out of here. Taught them a thing or two.*

What are you doing?

Ron laughed and leapt into the air. *Watching out for her!*

Shit, thought Hamish.

Lilly looked scared, and Hamish didn't know if it was of him, or of the two boys who had run off down the street to the reception. Or just all animals.

∞

The banquet hall was enormous. Mrs. Mondolfi had spent a fortune to make up for the fact that her husband wasn't at his son's bar mitzvah, and a portion of settlement money from his death in the Twin Towers went towards the event. One side was taken up by a buffet that had an ice sculpture of a lion and a Star of David on it, the other side with dessert and liquor. Through doors at the end was another room reserved for kids that had stations of activities and a large round swimming pool filled with plastic balls in primary colors. Children would disappear under the moving surface and pop up someplace else scattering balls in all directions. People landed on round tables, creating small cliques of eaters. Others wandered trying to find somewhere to put their plates and glasses, which turned into a number of isolated, lonely pictures. A large table at the head of the room was reserved for family members and friends, at which Steve spent all of five minutes. This was where Kuusk and his young son sat as though it were their event.

Hamish and Lilly sat at a table, eating some chicken and having a Coke. Lilly asked in a low voice about the crows, if this was all part of the same event as the polar bears.

"No, they're just annoying and curious. They just want to be a part of everything, until they don't."

"Hamish," Lilly looked at him. "Can you teach me?"

"To what?"

"Speak. Like you do."

It was not something he'd ever considered. "I don't think so. I don't think it's a skill. I think it's a trait."

"I would love to have that."

Hamish was suddenly shy. "I think you have something else."

"To be able to talk to a panther."

"Shh!" Hamish touched her arm. "It's really important that not get out."

"Yeah, I know." She shrugged herself closed. "I just mean, it's bizarre. And then—" she chinned in the direction of Kuusk—"him."

Hamish nodded. "I don't think he knows us."

They didn't want to be away from each other, but they didn't talk any more. Even indicating what table they were headed to and whether they wanted soda or juice was done with tilts of the head. Carla found them and chatted about school, Lilly turning gratefully to her. Hamish realized he'd only gotten himself a chicken leg and a spoonful of cheesy potatoes and he was suddenly starving, so he mumbled about getting more and headed to the buffet table.

A boy nudged his way in front of Hamish to look over the food, his blond head coming almost to Hamish's chin. He reached over the table, pulling a morsel of meat off a serving plate with his fingers, chewing it, and reaching back for more. Hamish felt a strong hand on his shoulder turn him around.

"So. It is the crow boy." Kuusk smiled at him, his cheeks creasing as his eyes remained neutral. "How did you manage that with those crows? You saved that one, you know. I would have wrung its neck."

"He was just being curious." Suddenly Hamish was not hungry.

"But you got them to come with you. How did you do that?"

Hamish shrugged. "I guess they trusted me."

"No, seriously," said Kuusk, putting both hands now on Hamish's shoulders and looking down at him. "How did you do that?"

"Dad!" The blond boy squeezed in between them, chin up to his father. With a flash of annoyance, Kuusk's hands came off Hamish and replaced themselves on either side of his son's face. "I'm going to go jump in the balls!"

"First, you are going to meet this young man." Kuusk turned the boy around by the head to face Hamish. "This is Vladimir. Vladimir, this is -- ?" Kuusk waited.

"I'm Hamish." Hamish waved a small wave.

Vladimir took his hand and shook it dutifully, looking down to the right as though there were a spot on the floor he had to clean up later.

"Hamish -- ?" Kuusk smiled again, seeking a surname.

Kuusk's son Vladimir spun away, instantly smashing into Shenouda and getting momentarily lost under his feet, scurrying out the other side and running off towards the kids room with the pool of balls. Shenouda recovered, picking the little guest yarmulke Vladimir dropped off the floor. He handed it to Kuusk saying, "Your son might want this souvenir of today."

Kuusk looked at the folded black silk circle in his hand. "I don't think he'll need any souvenirs."

"Ah," smiled Shenouda, "but we never really know what is important to children, do we?"

Kuusk's eyes etched an outline of Shenouda. "You are that man with the chess shop on Union."

"Fourth Avenue, but yes, I imagine I am that man."

"How is that business?"

"As well as can be expected in these times of war and uncertainty." Butter wouldn't melt in Shenouda's mouth.

"War?"

"Iraq. Sad Afghanistan. War. Unfortunate, don't you think?"

"Those Muslims needed to be taught a lesson," responded Kuusk, "don't you think?"

"Ah, but I always wonder what the lesson is, and who is doing the teaching. I'm sure you've had the same thoughts."

"All I know is I have friends in Bosnia who know a thing or two about teaching lessons to Muslims."

"That must make you very content," said Shenouda, enigmatic.

As though playing a good card, Kuusk asked, "You're Muslim, aren't you?"

"I have that honor," Shenouda bowed.

"I thought so."

"And you?" asked Shenouda. "You aren't anything, are you?"

Kuusk did not have an answer before Shenouda took Kuusk's hanging hand, gripping it warmly and saying, "I learn so much from these encounters. It has been so very interesting." He turned, his hand on Hamish's shoulder, moving him towards the dessert table. "I believe, my young friend, that I saw some baklava over there, and if you have not had it with real crushed pistachios as they made it in the Topkapi Palace centuries ago, as this appears to have, you have not savored the real thing."

Hamish felt lifted by a swift tide and moved through crowds to the other side of the room.

As Shenouda handed Hamish a diamond of baklava on a napkin, he said, "On Monday we can discuss our friend, Mr. Heigo Kuusk. He is an interesting man, in the manner of a facultative kleptoparasite, and deserves study."

"A what?" asked Hamish.

"We'll talk more on Monday. Please, what do you think of the sweet?"

Hamish decided he never wanted a bar mitzvah.

CHAPTER 26

The bell at the top of the door rang as Hamish came into Kaphiri Shenouda's chess shop a couple days after the bar mitzvah. Mr. Shenouda had asked him to come in, and Hamish could see that the enormous Rabbi Adams was sitting at one of the small tables waiting.

"Why don't you take Madonna out of her cage for a moment while I finish up with Mr. Adams," said Shenouda. "But take a care, and don't let Polly get too near her!"

Polly was leaning back in a chair against the wall near the back of the store looking like she was waiting to be booked at a police station. She brightened at Hamish's approach.

"You going to take Madonna out?"

Speaker! Let's go, let's go, let's go!

Yes, O Royal giver of color and sweets.

Listen, you pissing puppy—

Do you want out? Hamish had learned to speak Madonna-speak, and Madonna liked it the way an angry old lady liked being challenged without being beaten.

I will bite off your nose.

My finger was quite enough.

Just remember.

Oh, I remember, said Hamish, as he opened the cage.

Madonna levered herself out of the opening and grabbed bars with her beak and talons to get to the top of the cage where she leaned her body far forward to gaze into Hamish's eyes.

You've been busy.

What do you mean?

Everybody's talking. I hear things.

But you don't understand other birds.

I know when they're talking about you. And everyone's talking about you.

What are they saying?

Something big happened, didn't it? What did you do? Why didn't you come right here? How are you going to learn, you broken lump of dried fish shit?

"Boy, she's pretty talkative, isn't she?" said Polly. "Can I feed her?"

"Just a second," said Hamish.

You see this girl here? Hamish put his hand on Polly's shoulder.

She's barely an egg.

She wants to give you food.

What kind?

You cannot use that to bite her. You will not bite her.

If you tell me what's going on. Then I will not bite her. If she doesn't annoy me.

Even if she's annoying! You cannot bite her.

We'll see.

No! Or no food.

Madonna swayed back and forth, dipping her head, whistling a casual little tune. *OK,* she said.

"OK, you can feed her. Here, she'd like this strawberry."

Polly reached a strawberry slowly up to within Madonna's reach. Madonna nibbled the strawberry, and then drove her upper beak into it and turned away from Polly. She used her foot to turn the fruit and she took out small chunks, relishing its sweetness.

OK, tell me.

Hamish hesitated, wondering for a moment where to begin, even whether he could tell this hyacinth macaw from the Amazon about the storms that led him to the zoo and the polar bears and boy from years ago. And then it started coming out of him.

Hamish found himself telling Madonna about the hallucinatory feeling that overwhelmed him, that made him rush in directions as though he were steel responding to a colossal electro-magnet that went on and off, getting stronger as he got closer. The current of animal life that was swept up in his wake had increased his own speed, like the spinning of a cyclone meeting the ocean. He'd held onto Lilly's hand as a kind of anchor, grounding him in the world of Brooklyn, a place of trees and gates and asphalt pathways. He'd felt no one and nothing could understand. He was shot through with adrenalin and visions, and nothing could be more important than the completion of his task, even if he couldn't tell what the task was. The thousands of birds and Bagheera and even the seals all pointed him towards this incontestable rift in the air. And he knew.

What did you know? asked Madonna, with a low purr.

I knew what needed to be said.

You Spoke.

I Spoke.

And what did you say?

Without thinking, Hamish said, *I Spoke their names. I called to them through the storm they were in. They untwined. They unclenched. The grip loosened. They could hear me then. And I told them the way to go Home.*

Home.

And they went. They were gone. They were done. It was over.

Hamish's hand was on the cage. Madonna walked onto his arm and up to his shoulder. She tickled his ear.

Not bad, hatchling.

Hamish blinked his glazed eyes. Polly was in a chair, watching him. On his other side, Kaphiri Shenouda, sitting on a chess table, was also watching him, a soft smile emanating from under his moustache. Twirling his fingers in his gray beard was Mr. Adams, sitting on a low chair, eyes narrow as he contemplated Hamish. He looked to Shenouda.

"Every time I see it I think I'm witnessing a miracle, but it always seems so normal."

"Yes, that is true," mused Shenouda.

Did you do something bad, kiddo?

I don't think so.

Why are they all on you?

Because I'm talking to you.

Tell them to mind their own pissant business.

This struck Hamish as very funny, and he burst out laughing. Polly walloped his leg. "Shut up. You're weirding me out. What's going on with you?"

"Nothing."

"Hamish and Madonna were talking," said Shenouda to Polly.

"Ha ha," said Polly flatly.

"You can know this, Polly, because of what you told Hamish about your experiences with Mr. Kuusk."

"How did you--?"

"I understand," intervened Mr. Adams to Hamish, "You have crossed paths with Heigo Kuusk recently."

"Uh, yeah," said Hamish cautiously.

"I must tell you, he has been on our radar for a while now."

"Etan, perhaps now is not—" Shenouda tried.

"Yes, now. Regardless of what Thaddeus thinks." Mr. Adams leaned his bulk towards Hamish. Hamish noticed oddly that the bobby pin that held his yarmulke in place on his gray hair had a tiny design on it, and that the yarmulke itself was not plain, but had a swirl of letters through its fabric.

"Here's the thing: You must not take it upon yourself to approach Heigo Kuusk. Polly will back me up on this." He winked at her.

"What makes you think I'm going to approach this guy?" Hamish protested. He figured they couldn't know about Helena.

"Polly has told you about him, and you strike me as the kind of young man who will go out of his way to help even people you don't know." Adams' face was infinitely compassionate.

"Why shouldn't I? There's a lot I could do, right?" Hamish's mind was suddenly planning. "I could at least interrupt what's going on so people have a chance to get away."

"In the first place, he is too dangerous." Adams tone changed to one of patient severity. "In the second, there is already movement afoot to neutralize him and all that he does. And in the third place, if he sets his sights on you, others will also set their sights on you, and that could spell disaster for you. And for your family. So." He patted Hamish's knee. "You study, learn. We'll figure out what direction to move in."

Hamish pretended to be accepting and adult. He was still thinking about Helena. "What are you called?" he asked.

"People call me Rabbi."

"No, I mean all of you. The ones Mr. Knox got together."

"Oh! It's kind of silly, really. Gardeners. We call ourselves Gardeners. If you don't tend a garden, it fades. And this world, with us in it, is a garden. We've taken on the task of tending to it."

Rabbi Adams shook Hamish's hand like a man, embraced Kaphiri Shenouda kissing him on both cheeks, cupped Polly's face with his hand, and left.

CHAPTER 27

Charlie O'Keefe had been Hamish's best friend in Plains. They'd known each other in first grade, and ended up spending every bit of unsupervised time exploring the parks adjacent to the townships nearby as though they were Tarzan's jungles, hacking their way through underbrush, finding vines to swing a few dramatic feet on, suddenly turning into pirates and attacking each other with sticks as swords. Sometimes they went down under Charlie's house in the large crawl space where they set up a shooting range for Charlie's BB gun, cracking bottles and ripping cardboard cutouts. Their favorite was the Christmas light arrangement Charlie had invented, where they would aim at brightly colored bulbs on a string and high-five when one of them exploded.

After Hamish's failed attempt to run away, Sarah and Charlie's mom had arranged for the boys to get together in Plains for a weekend during the school year with the idea that Hamish wouldn't forget his old friends. September came and the boys found themselves being excited and dreading the visit, like jumping off a boulder into a cold river. Hamish took the casino bus from New York City to Mohegan Sun and the racetrack where his father had worked with the horses. Charlie and his mom picked him up in front of the brightly lit gaming rooms as night fell.

"So Mom said we could go to Hawk Falls tomorrow if you want," said Charlie after they had shyly touched each other's shoulders, not sure whether to embrace or shake hands.

"Great!" And Hamish meant it.

Hawk Falls was in Hickory Run State Park, about forty minutes from his Plains house, where Hawk Run, Mud Run and Panther Creek came together, the Pocono mountain water spilling down into the Delaware Water Gap. He had last been there a year earlier, just before his dad couldn't get outside to walk. The hike into the falls wasn't hard, and it was short. His dad used a cane, and Sarah brought liquids and snacks. The water cascading down the layers of rocks was clear, like it always was, and no one was there that day. It was too cold to go in, and the water level was low, so jumping from the cliffs would have been tricky. They had actually had a good time, going to the top of the falls to improvise boats that they'd sent to their certain demise over the edge of the waterfall, and watch them crash on the rocks below.

Hamish and Charlie had been to the park with Charlie's family often in grade school when they would get lost in the streams and return wet and disheveled and happy. They had clambered up the rocks around the falls, edging out Charlie's older sister Abigail's friends and careening off the cliff, arms and legs pumping, and smack into the water, raising red patches on their backs and thighs, emerging from the clear green water spitting for breath and wiping hair from their foreheads. The food Mrs. O'Keefe packed was always deliciously full of fat and sugar. The drive home was always sleepy and soggy.

Hamish slept that night on a sponge mattress on the floor of Charlie's room. They talked in the dark, mostly Charlie catching Hamish up on the dramas of Solomon High. The biggest scandal was Bradley Fox being caught with a baggie of marijuana. He was expelled, but wouldn't tell where he'd gotten it from. His mother showed up at a school board meeting screaming that he'd been framed. She had to be led out by two community minded business leaders who brushed their hands when they got her out on the sidewalk and told her to calm herself down. Her tears meant nothing to them. Bradley was in the car watching his mother's inglorious ejection, his eyes hardening inside his doughy face and his chewed fingernails picking at the zipper of his hoodie.

"Now he just sits in the bleachers all day, watching gym classes. It's weird."

"Does anyone talk to him?" asked Hamish.

"You know Caroline," said Charlie knowingly. "She'll talk like a parrot to anyone. But he just sits there. I've seen her, you know, that—" Charlie batted his eyelashes which Hamish could sense even in the dark "—'See you laytah.'"

They both laughed.

"But, I don't know," ruminated Charlie. "It's kind of sad."

"Yeah."

They rested in the silence.

"You smoke pot?" asked Hamish.

"Uh, well, I, you know," Charlie stammered. Hamish could tell that Charlie was trying to suss him out, to know whether that would be a good thing to have smoked pot.

"I haven't," rescued Hamish.

"Yeah, me neither," breathed Charlie.

Hamish felt small pressures on his legs. It was Charlie's cat, who hadn't been around all evening.

"What's your cat's name again?" asked Hamish.

"Felix." Charlie rolled over to check. "He bothering you?"

"No, he's OK."

"He doesn't usually like people. I can kick him out if you want."

"No, it's OK."

Well, well, well, well, said Felix.

"He sometimes wraps himself around my neck at night, and I can't get to sleep because he's so loud." Charlie's voice took on a sense of ownership.

"He can sleep here if he wants," said Hamish.

You going to sleep here? Hamish asked Felix.

"OK," said Charlie. "Mom's going to wake us early." He rolled over. "Goodnight."

"OK. Goodnight," said Hamish.

This is pretty strange, said Felix. *What brings you here?*

I'm visiting my friend.

The boy?

Yes, the one here with us.

Charlie's voice came out of the dark. "I'm glad you're back."

"Me, too," said Hamish, feeling strange admitting his feelings to Charlie, who he'd known longer than anyone but his mother. "I'm glad to be here, too."

Wait, said the cat. *You've been here before. Right? A very long time ago. But you weren't you. Right?*

Right, I was here a lot a long time ago.

I thought so. But it's like you've been washed. Inside out and washed.

Hamish was exhausted from being back in Plains. *You want to sleep?*

Yes, said Felix. He treaded slowly up the blanket towards Hamish's head, and settled into the crook of his neck. Purring started deep inside Felix's little body. Hamish realized it was a kind of individual song that Felix was singing to himself. It came across to Hamish as opaque and childish; he could only manage translating a kind of sing-song silly rhyme.

Sleeping with the Speaker
I breathe into his head
Cuddling with the Speaker
I heard just what he said

The night is long and quiet
I am warm and dry
The stars are so defiant
There is no harm or cry

Moving through the air
A cat melts out of view
A lingering eye will stare
And find out that it's you

The purring subsided. Felix's ear twitched against the nape of Hamish's neck. Hamish felt the tip of Felix's tail move. The cat was dreaming, and he was telling his dream, as softly as butter melting in the sun. Hamish fell asleep, listening.

∞

Hamish woke from his own sleep to the sandpaper warmth of Felix's tongue on his temple.

What is it? Hamish asked.

I want to show you something.
Now?
Of course. Come.

Felix hopped off the mattress onto the floor and eased around the edge of the door. Hamish checked the steady breathing of Charlie, and followed.

They were going outside into the late September night. Hamish found a pair of boots by the back door that were two sizes too large, and he plunked his feet in.

Come on, come on. Felix impatiently indicated the door.

The cold tasted wet and leafy. Felix trotted down over the lawn to the edge of the woods, and Hamish walked behind, feeling the large boots squish slightly in the dewy grass. The back of his neck chilled, and he had no pockets in which to put his hands, so he wrapped them under his armpits. Felix stopped, staying poised, looking back for a second at Hamish. Hamish didn't move.

Hamish felt it through his feet first, the tiniest rumbling, like a little irregular machine. He realized it was coming from the ground, a vibration so small it could have been a moth trapped in a jar on the other side of the world. Felix shifted his hips, his ears up, his eyes sure and expectant. About two feet in front of the cat, Hamish saw the grass waver in the reflected light of the distant garage, the light that people in rural places leave on all night in the odd hope it will bring safety to their home. A leaf moved, then another. Something was coming out of the ground beneath them.

Felix leapt, front claws out. He flipped, a claw leveraging something out of the ground. It went in an arc and bounced in front of where Felix landed. *HELP!* rang in Hamish's head. It was a mole, about the size of a rat. It was stunned, and just beginning to move when Felix pulled it to him, turning to bite the back of its head. Hamish could feel the small crunch of bone. He could hear the tiny cry of the mole, short and sharp, not even a thought as it died.

Felix released the mole, having to shake his head lightly to wiggle a tooth out of the mole's skull. He licked a moisture of blood off his mouth. As he turned to Hamish, pride emanating from his eyes, Hamish felt a shift, like a puzzle being redesigned, pieces moving all of their own accord and bumping other pieces that turned and fit snugly again but differently, all then settling like dust on a table. The smallest of breezes caught the motes that didn't make it back into the puzzle, and they lifted away into a mysterious hugeness, gently and as remotely noticeable as a door closing down a mile long hallway.

It felt good.

You can have some if you want.

Hamish seriously considered biting into the warm dead mole. He almost felt as though he should, that this was a courtesy, a delicious opportunity that shouldn't be passed by.

You are very generous, but I have eaten. This is yours.

Suit yourself. Felix picked up the loose corpse, his mouth looking stuffed and greedy, and headed off towards the darkness.

Felix suddenly stopped at a high-pitched growl coming from a branch ten feet off the ground. Both Felix and Hamish looked up. Hamish could barely see from the weak garage light a form reclining on a branch suddenly swinging up to all fours. The growl was clear to Hamish:

If you want to die, keep hunting in my neighborhood.

Without a signal, Felix zipped off into the night.

The bobcat—for that is what it was—stretched slightly and cut the bark of the branch with his claws.

And you?

Hamish found himself resenting this bobcat's lack of surprise or even lack of reaction to the Speaker being here in his woods. Perhaps he'd grown too used to the celebrity. Maybe it was the blood-sport of hunting the mole that had tweaked him, maybe it was the challenge to him in a place where he'd known himself as a child, that was part of his proving ground with Charlie as they tramped through the woods being explorers and spies. He and Charlie had killed armies of itinerant knights, hundreds of invading Romans or Nazis, zombies determined to eat them alive, and marauding bears, tigers and pterodactyls caught in the madness of this thickly timbered forest. This was still his place, where he owned the air itself.

Be very careful, kitty-kitty. Hamish felt patience leave him, and felt a field swell and settle in his chest and hips, giving him balance and purpose. His neck throbbed with blood.

The bobcat's tufted ears went up like devil's horns, and then leaned back with the snarl, *I don't care who you are. You are nothing to me.*

Hamish could sense bluffing, and it made him reckless.

Leave before I make you. And I will make you.

The bobcat—Thor, Hamish named him in the moment; a worthy opponent—came to the ground in an elongated streak, stretching down and making no sound. Thor sat, the tip of his tail turning only slightly, saying, *Ah, yes. Ah, yes.*

Hamish became aware of Felix watching them from behind a tree. The mole was gone, left somewhere in the woods. Hamish knew Felix knew he should leave, but he was too curious about the outcome of this strange encounter to tell his legs to move him away.

In the thought, Thor was on Hamish, running up his chest. He weighed as much as five moving gallons of water with spikes. Hamish staggered, throwing his arms out, preventing Thor's claws from grabbing his neck, and Thor flipped over Hamish's head, landing behind him. Hamish could feel the stinging bruise of puncture wounds in his chest. He turned, pinning Thor with his look, and he felt something else rise in him like a wave through a blow-hole. All his peripheral vision sank away, and sparks of electricity spewed through his muscles. His focus on Thor was microscopic and explosive. Birds woke in the trees, calling out and flying to new roosts. Felix, in the disturbed company of rabbits and mice and some wandering bugs, crept behind foliage to shield themselves from Hamish. Thor's limbs were frozen. Hamish told him he was going to die.

Hamish took one step forward, grabbing Thor by the rough thick fur on the sides of his face, and he swung him around in circles, Thor's body out parallel to the ground with centrifugal force, like a Scotsman throwing a hammer. Thor dug a claw into Hamish's forearm, a white-hot screech of pain that made Hamish bellow and with one last lunging turn, he released the cat into the air. Thor couldn't turn fast enough, and he hit a tree-trunk with the side of his body, the thud of broken ribs echoing in Hamish's teeth. Thor wobbled to his feet and weaved away like a drunk into the night.

Hamish's mind began to clear as though a light gold bell had gone off in it. There was sticky dark red on his shirt and he felt a drip off his finger, looking to see his arm glistening with blood. He sat on the grass, spent.

For a few moments, he had no idea where he was. He was triumphant and ready. This was good.

He felt the small warm touch of Felix's tongue licking the blood off his hand and arm. They continued this way for a while, Felix's purring saying, *The Speaker is a hunter, the Speaker is a hunter, the Speaker is a hunter. This is his place, this is his place, this is his place...*

∞

In the bathroom, Hamish laid out band-aids and ointments and wads of toilet paper. He washed off his arm first, the water in the sink turning copper-colored. It smelled muddy and stringent, the sour plastic smell of band-aids mixing with the tangy iron and earth of fresh flesh. Felix stroked Hamish's calves with his body, having made it clear he thought Hamish should leave all the ministrations to his tongue.

Charlie opened the door, blinking against the bright bathroom light.

"Jesus! What happened?"

Hamish had rehearsed this on the short walk back to the house. Keep the story close to the truth.

"I couldn't sleep and I went outside for a little, you know, like we used to do?"

"OK..."

"And—it was so weird—I saw this bobcat in a tree –"

"You're kidding."

"No, I could see it by the garage light. And I was under the branch watching it, and it jumped down on me. I guess I scared it."

"Jesus."

"It just caught me wrong."

"We should wake Mom. You don't think that needs some stitches?"

"No. Really. Just help me here a little."

Charlie poured hydrogen-peroxide over Hamish's arm, pink foam bubbling up from the wounds like a volcano science experiment. He patted it dry with surprising tenderness, daubing ointment and attaching band-aids with precision. He used five of them.

When they took off Hamish's shirt, Charlie breathed out slowly. There was patched blood all over Hamish's chest and nearly a dozen perforations in his pale skin, each oozing a bit of darkness.

"OK," said Charlie. "This hurt?" He applied a wet washcloth, softening the blood where it had dried. Hamish shook his head, trying to ignore the open ache.

When they were done, they were conspirators. They threw the gory t-shirt in the trash burying it under a milk carton and pungent peelings. They crumpled all evidence of red into a plastic bag and trashed that, too. They set an alarm to get up earlier than anyone else so they could replace the bandages that had seeped through, a task that Charlie did in silence and with warm and gentle hands. Hamish realized he was getting to know Charlie for the first time.

As they fell asleep again before dawn, Charlie whispered, "You OK?"

"Yeah," said Hamish. "It's been so strange."

"Yeah," said Charlie. "I'm really sorry about your Dad."

"Yeah," said Hamish. "Yeah. Me, too. Thanks. Me, too."

CHAPTER 28

"You are such a cute boy."

Helena's soft accent hit Hamish's ears like a backhoe. He turned around, the key still in the lock of the street door. He was only just getting back from his bus from Pennsylvania, and the afternoon fall sun was still high and warming in the city. His mom's shift wouldn't end until 10:00. Helena was standing close to his stoop on the sidewalk, one hand delicately playing with the wrought iron spikes that fenced in the garbage pails. She was wearing a dark navy terry-cloth bathrobe over jeans and a t-shirt. Her sock-less shoes were platform—cork or something—and looked ready to slip out from under her on the wet leaves that scattered the blue-stone sidewalk. The pink barrette in her hair was a tangled, childish afterthought.

The smell of her almost made Hamish faint with a desire to be near. He didn't really understand it, even the obvious biology of it. It was the most dangerous feeling he'd ever felt.

Her hand anchored the fence and her other hand brushed his cheek. "You let me in, no?"

"Ah, sure."

As Hamish let her in and they trudged up the stairs, he tingled with panic that his mother might be there, that the large man in the polyester suit would break down their door, that Helena would take off the robe.

When they got inside the apartment, Helena pulled the robe tight around her and flopped on the sofa.

"You have girlfriend?"

Hamish blushed and laughed, "Well..."

"Sure, you have girlfriend. Cute boy like you." Coyly. "What's her name?"

"Lilly. She's Lilly. But we haven't really, you know, decided on anything—"

"Lilly," Helena smiled and wagged her finger at Hamish. "Ah, you want her, don't you? Ehn? Don't you?" She laughed to herself. "Boys. All the same." Helena crossed her arms as though to shut down. "You call her."

"What? Why?"

"I want talk to girl." She stared ahead.

"Uh, OK."

Hamish went into the kitchen to use the phone. When Lilly answered, Hamish felt like whispering.

"She's here!"

"Who?"

"Helena, that—that girl I told you about, from the park, from the roof guys. Kuusk."

"Oh my god."

"Yeah."

"What's she doing? What does she want?"

"I don't know. She just like showed up."

"Well ask her!"

"I can't just—"

Helena wandered into the kitchen and opened the refrigerator. The kitchen was small enough where she brushed against Hamish's hip. She'd taken off the robe. Her t-shirt had a soft-drink logo on the back, and he could see the line of her spinal column through it as she leaned into the open door. His throat was closing.

He managed, "Can you—?"

"Oh!" said Helena turning, "That is Lilly?" She took the phone, the cord trapping Hamish close to her. "Lilly! How are you? What you doing now? You come over, visit? I know this boy would love it, to see you. I need to talk to you....No, everything is perfect. Perrrr-fact!...Just see, just talk with girl, you know. Boys are so silly, yes?...Is OK, I will tell you. No one to talk to in my home, you know?"

Hamish could feel her breathing change, feel her soften, like ice cream.

"How do you know this? You are guessing things, you don't know.... How do you know this about me?" Helena was accusing and scared.

She listened more, and then pushed the phone against Hamish's chest. He could feel her breath on his face as she untangled them from the cord. She grabbed orange juice from the refrigerator and went back to the living room.

"What is it?" Hamish asked, following.

"Nothing. She's coming over."

"Now?"

"I said so." Helena sat down, hugging her robe into her lap. "She's coming over." She sulked like a child. Then, "You have that music?"

"Music?" Hamish squinted.

"The CD I left for you to keep here." Helena's voice was either going to yell or cry.

"Oh, yeah. Yeah. You want it?"

"No," Helena whispered. "You just keep for now."

∞

"I took a car service," Lilly whispered after he'd buzzed her in. "Hamish, she's in real trouble."

"How do you know, you just—"

"She's pregnant."

Hamish felt the weight of that like a sudden mantel being thrown over him, so heavy he didn't even think of struggling to get out.

"Lilly!" cried Helena hearing her. "Awesome! You came. You're here." She stood and turned to meet Lilly. Her smile wiped off her face when she saw Lilly was black. "Oh, this is your girlfriend?" She turned to sit back down.

Hamish looked to Lilly horrified, expecting her to leave on the spot. Lilly glanced at him and comforted him by dismissing Helena's comment with a shake of her head. She mouthed, "Girlfriend?" with her eyebrows raised.

She stood in front of Helena. "So why did you come find Hamish?"

"Oh ho! So you are jealous now, are you?" Helena smiled as though she knew how this would all play out.

"Is it because of the man with the hat?" Lilly's tone was firm; she was trying not to get ugly. "The one Hamish saw you with?"

"I don't care about him." Helena was retreating. Hamish and Lilly could almost see her grow a bit smaller.

"I would be scared of him if I were you."

"You are not me!" Helena held her knees. "I'm not afraid of nobody."

"Oh, I am," said Lilly. "I'm afraid of men who sell girls. Like your friend."

Helena quieted. "It is good to be afraid of them."

The three of them went into a mutual hush, as though they'd just finished a round, and were taking a break. Lilly sat in a chair. Hamish sat on the sofa again. Helena avoided looking at both of them. She seemed to think about getting up, but pulled her feet up under her instead and leaned her head on the back of the couch. Hamish sipped some juice, and looked to Lilly, silently offering her some. She shook her head.

Hamish turned to Helena. "How can we help you, Helena?"

Helena started crying. Not slowly, but all at once, as though tears had been waiting behind the dam of her eyes and had suddenly seen an opening, so they all crowded out like loyal workers leaving the factory all at once at the 5:00 whistle, streaming out in different directions. Snot, that monster goo, dripped out of her nose onto her upper lip, and she felt so gross and exposed that her mouth opened in horror as she tried to push the air back in with her hands. The entire economy of her face crumbled. She couldn't even think of hiding it.

Hamish leapt up to get her tissue. He was gone merely seconds, but Helena was then sobbing in Lilly's lap on the couch, her shoulders shaking like she was building into a seizure. Lilly stroked her back.

"Breathe," said Lilly. "Just breathe." Lilly looked to Hamish, shrugged, an almost disgusted expression on her face. He handed her the tissue, which she offered to Helena at the level of her thigh as Helena's paroxysms subsided. Helena lifted herself up, a string of clear mucus snapping out of her nostril onto Lilly's pant leg. She wiped at Lilly's leg, humiliated.

Hamish got more tissue.

"I am prostitute," said Helena when Hamish came back.

"No you're not," said Hamish, handing her tissue.

"I do sex with men for money." She blew her nose.

"Where's the money?" asked Hamish.

"I don't have it. They have it."

"So you're not a prostitute," reasoned Hamish. "They get the money."

Lilly smoothed Helena's hair out of her face. "Maybe we could try the FBI."

"No!" said Helena in genuine distress. "They will hurt Mama. My little sister, they will get her, use her."

"Who?"

"Heigo Kuusk."

"The man with the white hair," said Hamish.

Helena saw in Hamish the potential for the next betrayal. "How do you know this man?" She was harsh, snarling.

Hamish told Helena about his and Lilly's adventures on the roof, but not about Steve's bar mitzvah, or Polly. As he told her, he realized how absurd it was that he was having this conversation. He wanted to be in a clearing somewhere, scratching Bagheera's ears, drinking cool water, knowing he was invulnerable.

Helena looked at Lilly, her wet eyes wide. "You should not have done this. You would never have gotten out of that house. Never. He cannot see you."

"He didn't," Lilly assured her.

"And no police!" Helena almost barked. "I know police. I met police. He—many times he come to me. Dangerous, like Heigo Kuusk."

"Yeah," said Lilly quietly. "We know police, too."

"Helena," said Hamish. "Let's come up with a plan. We can get help from people, we can maybe get your sister and your mom somewhere."

Helena's hooded eyeballs held the weariness of war. "And how you protect your mother, your sister?" She let it sink in. "No, I don't want them to make my sister into me. She's twelve. She's cute. Heigo Kuusk, he likes her." She stood up. "I find another way."

Lilly stood up, too. "Let us figure something out. And figure out if you want to keep your baby."

Helena, a knife in her voice. "You tell me: how do you know this about me?"

"I guessed, girlfriend. It wasn't hard."

"You a crazy black girl." Helena seemed to want to hit her. "What the fuck you know."

"Hamish," said Lilly. "Maybe you should let Helena and me—"

"No! That boy stays here. You sit down right over there." Helena pointed to a chair.

Hamish realized he'd been standing. He sat. "You're pregnant?"

"I'm pregnant, I'm pregnant, of course I'm pregnant! What you think. I have big stupid men fuck me every day of course I'm getting pregnant." Tears started to come.

Lilly asked hesitantly, "They don't put on, they don't wear—"

"Con-domes? Joke. Just joke. They pay extra, stupid raw dog. Like they own me. They own me. They just own me. I'm nothing to them. Nothing." Helena melted into Lilly's lap, and then just as suddenly pushed up and away. She hurled at Hamish as she went towards the kitchen, "Your mother have booze? Any vodka? White wine?"

Lilly followed her, Hamish getting up after like he was moving through glass. Helena had already found some wine in the refrigerator and poured some into a coffee cup.

"Helena—" Lilly moving to stop her.

"Oh, no. Nothing matter about this. They all want more. This baby just makes them line up and bang harder." She drained the cup and poured some more. She swallowed. Hamish and Lilly could almost see the cool astringent pale liquid pass over her tongue and down her throat in comforting gulps. She breathed, her eyes closed and her nose and upper lip still in the coffee cup as though solace were somewhere at the bottom just out of reach.

"He was nice to me."

"Who?"

"Heigo. Heigo Kuusk. He was my uncle, like that. We all came here to America because of him."

"What about your father?"

"Ha!" She sputtered over the edge of the cup and put it down. "He big joke too. Took us to Kaliningrad, leave us there. Fucking Papa. Fuck him fuck him fuck him. I don't even remember his ugly face. Kaliningrad is so cold, so dark. No one is kind in that whole place, no one. Except Heigo. He take us somewhere warm, give us little money, say he need someone to work at his place in America for a while. So Mama she say she do it, and he says OK, but I must work, too. OK, says Mama. OK. She doesn't know. She's stupid just like everyone. Just like me. We get to America and Heigo and me are in a bedroom. He says he got to show me how to work. It will be fun, he says. He make me take my clothes off, right there. It not so bad. I'm scared I will pee, but not so bad. He does it. Hurts, you know. Hurts like I should screaming. But not so bad. A woman, Odilia—pretty name, no?—she clean me. Like I was a baby, she clean me and wrap me and that was the last time. Heigo and she, they make me learn, and some other man, Danny or something, make me do all these things until I can do all these things. I do all these things." She whispered. "All these things."

Lilly reached for her, but Helena pulled back. She wasn't finished.

"I have abortion then. They take me. They're mad because I can't work for a week. They have people who want me. They want young thirteen-years-old. They pay very very well. I'm a princess." She smiled to herself. "One man, he's very nice to me, brings me presents, some jewelry, you know, necklaces, a diamond earrings, and he's kind. He goes slowly. I think he loved me. But I don't see him now. Now I have men who want me, only me. They can't wait for me. They think I'm very special. Better than the other girls. Everybody wants me."

Helena looked slyly at Hamish through her glistening eyes. "You want me, don't you?" She touched him with a teasing finger.

Hamish felt sick, and knew he did want her, but he didn't know what that meant. He even knew that wanting her wasn't what she'd figured, an ugliness so cruel it brooked no mercies or sympathy. No, his want had something to do with wrapping his arms around her and holding her so she would stop trembling, so her tears would quiet, so he could understand what she was saying.

"Helena, stop that!" snapped Lilly. She grabbed Helena's hand and held it even when Helena tried to pull it away. "Not fair. Not kind. He just wants to help you."

"You jealous, little girlfriend? You afraid his little pee-pee going to end up in the wrong place, hunh, that he want to put it in me and not in you? Hunh?"

Lilly started to cry. "Helena, we're all too young for that. It's like, it's just not time."

"It's time for me."

"No, girl. Really. Not yet."

"Too late. Too late for not yet."

Lilly shook her head, lowering her cheek to the hand she still held, that allowed itself to still be held. Then she looked at Helena.

"Do you want this baby?"

Helena said wistfully, "Do I want this baby?"

"Yes."

She withdrew her hand. "I can't."

"We just have to find a way for you to get out."

"They kill my mother. They take my sister. They will do this. You know."

"Right, Hamish? We just have to find a way."

Hamish nodded, all speech having left him.

"Oh, you are good people," said Helena, tearing a paper towel and blowing her nose. "I'm bad and you're good. You can't help."

"We can. We will."

Helena, as though she'd made a decision, cupped Hamish's face, kissed his cheek, and turned to hug Lilly.

"Maybe you buy me." She laughed. "Maybe you fucking buy me."

She walked to the door, grabbing her robe on the way.

Hamish called after her, "Would that work?"

She laughed out the door.

"Would that work?" he asked Lilly.

Lilly shrugged and looked at him. He saw in that moment how much she'd been holding onto, as though all the secrets of the universe had been stuffed into her head and the angel who had been doing the stuffing had suddenly grabbed her and hissed, "Shhh!" He let himself move slowly into holding her, like a shore hugging a wide, wide bend in the river.

∞

Later that night, Hamish inserted the CD into his mother's computer, which whined and clunked and hummed. He felt so dumb that he had not questioned the Britney Spears label on it. A numbered list came up on the directory, and the first one Hamish clicked on was a spreadsheet that asked for a password. One folder marked FOUR contained maybe a hundred .tiff files. Hamish clicked on one.

It was a photo of a large white man sitting on a bed naked. His hand was on the small breast of a young Asian girl, thirteen, maybe fourteen years old. The quality of the photo was poor, as though it had been taken off a security camera. But the girl's face was clear. A face with no expression. The face of an animal who has replaced fear with a fake death.

Hamish looked at many photos. It made him sick, but he kept on looking. Photo after photo of men and girls. Nothing like any of the pornography Hamish had ever seen. There was no sense of movement or pleasure, no sense of stupidity or illicitness, no sense of comic book or desire. It was only fear and stasis. Death without death. Desperation everywhere.

There were three photos Hamish saw with Helena in them. Her naked body was paler than real; there must have been night-vision equipment with the camera. In one, her eyes glowed like a coyote's eyes on a deserted highway. He wanted to look at her, but he was so clear that to look at her would be a dishonor. He looked. And he didn't.

It was three different men. Their skins were like dead fish bellies. One of them was the cop from Brooklyn.

CHAPTER 29

Hamish felt guilty about hunting with Bagheera at night, but he did it. It was wrong in so many ways. He could understand the cries for help and then stunned silence from squirrels he'd known, rats out on a sojourn, feral cats, loose dogs. Sometimes he thought of Thor. But the satisfying crunch of a broken spine or wet squish of a warm body bit into was somehow both delicious and bad. He knew that Bagheera merely tolerated him, and had taken on the role of a teacher since she clearly felt Hamish was inadequate in every way except in his role as Speaker. He knew that she was always waiting for him to step up to leap at a treed raccoon or cornered mouse. But he always bowed to her grace like a courtier, relieved when she went ahead with the kill. Bagheera could sense another person before Hamish was remotely aware and would smoke herself into the darkness before a lonely figure walking along a pathway scraped the dirt or a drunken couple negotiating their way across the park giggled hollowly yards of night away. She somehow knew that hunting people was fatal, and though she could kill them with a swipe of her paw, they were dangerous beyond anything else in the world.

One night in October after Bagheera was chewing on a little cat and had companionably offered some to Hamish, who felt like an incipient cannibal as he declined, they were in one of the darker parts of the Park above the Lake. Hamish could see the lanterns of the pathways winking through the crisping autumn leaves. It was an oddly warm night for fall, and Hamish left his sweatshirt unzipped as he squatted, leaning back against a tree. Bagheera's chewing was quiet; there was not much effort in pulling apart the cat, one paw hugely on the torso while she stretched off the leg.

Bagheera suddenly hissed a *Stupidities!* and disappeared behind Hamish. Hamish heard someone coming up through the trees off the path. A low voice called out.

"Hamish?"

It was Mr. Knox.

Hamish had tried to find Mr. Knox after the bears, and then had spent days haunting the graveyard after Helena had told him about being pregnant and about Heigo Kuusk. Shenouda had patiently reported he didn't know where he'd gone, and he told him they needed Knox in order to make a decision about Kuusk. Shenouda had tried to call Knox, and even given Hamish a phone number, but it just rang and rang and rang. Email was something Mr. Knox apparently didn't indulge in. So Hamish wasn't feeling cozy about this encounter. Bagheera was much more direct.

"How did you find me?" Hamish shifted his butt on the cold ground.

"Bagheera is often up here. I thought you might be with her." Mr. Knox sat on a rock opposite. Hamish could hear Bagheera scratch her ear in the dark behind his tree. "Kaphiri said you needed to talk."

"That's OK," said Hamish quickly.

"Well, I have to talk with you."

Silence. One nightjar called to another. Traffic ground faintly in the distance. A car horn. Very small, a siren going away. Not quite cold enough to steam the breath.

"I owe you an apology." Mr. Knox took off his hat and leaned his elbows on his knees. "I left you to your own devices just when you were coming into a sense of what has been happening to you. That was unfair of me."

"Where were you?" Hamish cut in.

"Fair question, fair question." Mr. Knox rubbed his hands together. "I was—" he laughed "—I was gardening. Things are moving, and not with a kind of conscious effort that we might understand. There's a tipping of balances that we have some influence on, but cannot control completely. There is not a side to take, necessarily, but sides do form or occur simply because balance is seeking to find itself. And interestingly, balance doesn't have an investment in time, so balance can happen over the course of a split second, or centuries, even eons. The actions of a very few can affect the realities of many, now or years from now. I am dedicated to making the balance right itself in a lifetime—your lifetime—rather than a couple hundred years from now. You are here as a sign that the balance is out, just as my father was a sign. He and others succeeded, I think, because there was a change, a victory, but now we are headed into an even more difficult era where there are not Nazis but people who believe in a system that has had hundreds of years to make itself a part of our innate understanding. And it's killing us. We are killing us. There are species whose evolution is precarious, whose nature must be adapted to the realities of the planet, and we are one of those species. We have to see more clearly."

"Bullshit," said Hamish. The anger he'd been feeling for weeks swelled in him like a boil. He tried leaning back against the tree, but it didn't work so he curled to a squat and moved fallen leaves with his fingers. "I just got it. You are like all those old men in all the stories I thought were so important. You're Gandalf or Dumbledore and you don't really give a shit because you won't get on the front lines with us children. With Helena, who is—I don't know! You say you're trying to make it right but just to make yourself feel better, but you can't, and we—God! I can't believe what suckers we are!—we just have to make up for how you fucked it all up." He threw leaves in the air, scattering the litter over them both. "Oops! We didn't get to it. Oh, well! I mean, shit, you and Shenouda and Adams have known about Kuusk forever, but you've done nothing. You let a fifteen-year-old girl get—screwed—day after day after day, again and again and again and did nothing about it. Nothing!"—his voice cracked high—"And you think I'm just some idiot teenager who can talk with animals, and isn't that cute? He's worried about the little prostitute girl, isn't that cute? He's worried about the rest of his life—of all of our lives—isn't that fucking cute?"

Quiet. Knox breathed in deeply. "Heigo Kuusk is a scary man, isn't he?"

"Yes, he's a very scary man."

"Will you stay away from him?"

"No, I will not."

"I have a way to—?"

"I don't care! I made a promise. Lilly and I made a promise. We've got to find a way to get her out. Are you going to help us or not?"

Mr. Knox sighed. "And what of all the others?"

"What others?"

"The other girls, and women, and people indentured and under threat from him, whose lives get ruined because of what he does."

"I only know Helena. That's who I promised."

Mr. Knox considered. Hamish could see him in the faint city darkness looking off to the north as though asking for help.

"I must please converse with you," said Mr. Knox. "Heigo Kuusk. He will kill anyone who displeases him or betrays him. He would kill that little girl Polly that Kaphiri is so fond of if he knew and took the time to look." Hamish glanced up, remembering Polly's story. "She knows who he is and what he did. He would kill you if he thought it would give him an advantage. He would kill Helena."

"Then why not just kill him?" Hamish had reached the edge of patience.

"Then you are in a hot war. We don't have the resources to do that."

"Isn't Helena in a hot war already?"

"Yes, she is. You're right. I wish she wasn't."

"So I'm supposed to sit around and do nothing?" The night took Hamish's last word and shook it through the trees.

"Hamish," Knox's voice was soft. "I have to go away."

"Where?"

"Iraq."

Sarcasm. "Isn't there a war going on there or something?"

"Yes, that's correct. There is a war going on there."

"You going to stop it?"

Knox sighed. "I'm going to try."

Hamish realized he wasn't kidding.

"I want to ask you something before I go."

"Oh, Jeez." Hamish wanted to choke.

"Come." Knox stood and extended his hand to give Hamish a lift from the ground. "Come with me for a moment."

Hamish stood on his own. Knox turned down the hill west towards the Quaker Graveyard. Hamish heard Bagheera stir in the dark.

Do you need—?

I'm going with this man.

To his home?

You know his home?

Of course. Bagheera purred. *This is a good man. He is not a danger.*

Hamish looked at the receding back of Knox. *Finish your meal. Good night.*

Bagheera had never been dismissed before. She stood still, melting into black rocks and branches, watching the boy walk away.

∞

When they got to the shed, Knox opened the trap door to Underhut and went down without looking to see if Hamish was following. But Hamish went down, too. Knox put on the kettle for tea without asking if Hamish wanted any. He pulled two cups out and plopped in tea bags. He put sugar on the table and a small carton of milk from the fridge. The spoons rang as he tossed them on the wooden surface, the whole silverware drawer clanging as he closed it.

"From many years ago I have friends in Iraq and Persia. They have asked for my help." The water was already boiling. Knox poured it into the cups and pushed one across the table towards Hamish. "The Americans are making a mess of things, and there may be some things we can do. So: I go."

Hamish sat and began to dunk his teabag. "Are you going to fight?"

Knox chuckled. "No. Not in the way you mean. My work is to remind people. To hold memory. Sometimes from a very long time ago." He slurped his tea noisily.

"I don't get it." Hamish was suddenly very tired.

Knox waited while Hamish didn't get it. "Here's what I want to ask of you."

"OK."

"There will be one, maybe two people who will need the refuge of Underhut. You will get a message—here—" Knox took out one of the flip-phones and handed it across the table to Hamish "—someone will call you on this, you will meet this person and bring them here. And you will ask animals to watch. To watch and warn. You can do this, yes?"

"Who's going to come here?"

"This is a sanctuary for those who need respite on their journeys. Maybe a man, or a woman. I don't know. But they deserve a place to rest." Knox was looking at him. "Will you do that for me?"

"Who will call me?"

"Her name is Sandy. She will make sure the people get where they need to go. I asked her to be here, but she's busy, a busy Keeper. She can do things without anyone knowing and then disappear. Remarkable, really."

A harsh voice—man? woman?—came from the makeshift bedroom. "I can hear you!"

Mr. Knox's eyes widened. "Sandy! You are here."

Sandy emerged, a woman somewhere between fifty and seventy. She had on an aquamarine pantsuit, Nikes, large clunky beads and glasses strung around her neck. Her hair, which had seen a permanent last week, was slate gray, and her lips were bright with paint. She yawned.

"You got a cigarette?" she asked Knox.

"I am so grateful to be able to introduce you to Hamish."

"He's the one you were telling me about?" Sandy's deep eyes squinted as though Hamish were difficult to see. Then she sat in a chair and searched her pockets for cigarettes. "Dammit, no butts. And someone coming later tonight."

Knox chuckled. "Yes, he's the one I told you about." He turned to Hamish. "You'll do it?"

Hamish had no choice. "Yes."

"Good. I am grateful. I will give you money for things you might need. There is a list always there on the wallboard. And the keys. Here." He leaned across the table and squeezed the keys into Hamish's hand. "And now I want to tell you what I can about Heigo Kuusk. Listen.

"Heigo comes from an Estonian family that moved to Russia, that small part between Poland and Lithuania that's not connected to the rest of Russia, that has the city of Kaliningrad. Heigo was a bright boy with a fanatical father who thought Stalin was a god and Jews were devils. Heigo even went to the Kant University there. He did quite well study-ing engineering, I gather. But his father was a poor man who wanted to be rich, and his mother was a wealthy woman who had married badly and was bitter about it. He had an older brother who was killed in the

Russian war in Afghanistan, and then it was up to Heigo to make an impression on the world. I think it was an accident that he discovered the slave trade that went though that port, but it made sense to him, and he caught the attention of some powerful people who helped him. He branched out into real estate and shipping and extortions. But his first love is still the sex trade. It doesn't make him as much money as all his other ventures, but he does it anyway. I think it gives him a sense of power he can't get anywhere else. He doesn't mind hurting young girls. And he likes to take pictures so he can have a hold over the men who come."

Knox stopped, making sure Hamish's attention was still with him. "This doesn't shock you, does it?"

Hamish shook his head. But he was lying.

"He is at the top of the pile of men who still get their hands dirty. And he has to please men who don't. His weakness is that he likes to have sex with young girls, and he has a long and very private list of clients who like the same thing."

"But he has a daughter!" said Hamish. "He has two daughters."

"And if someone did to his daughters what he does to girls, he would kill them."

"God." Hamish rested his head in his hands.

"Heigo got obsessed with your girl—"

"She's not my girl," objected Hamish.

"Alright," Knox calmed. "She is his niece, I have found out. Through marriage, I think. He has a number of young girls from Vietnam and Thailand, but he's good with girls from the Baltic. That's where his connection is strongest."

They held their tea.

"I will be dealing with some of the people who Heigo answers to."

"In Iraq?"

"Yes, I'm afraid so. There and elsewhere." Knox leaned forward. "Heigo is a parasite. He is expert at getting into someone's life and then staying there until they are depleted, sucked dry. Once he is in, he is like those intestinal worms, or those worms that get in through your feet. He will never leave until you die."

"Then we have to get her out!" Hamish insisted again.

"Yes," said Knox. "But we have to wait a bit. If you pull a parasite out too violently, it kills the host. And then there's another problem." Knox hesitated.

"What?"

"You." Knox held his eyes. "You are important. I haven't been able to determine what it is that you are here for, what the issue is that brings your talents out into manifestation. But I do know there are reasons. It was true for my father, it has been true for other Speakers with whom I have been acquainted. Heigo knows about Speakers, and he now knows something about you and your interest in Helena. So you are in danger if you pursue this course. You are too important to risk on this."

"I am more important than Helena?"

"In the grand scheme of things, it would seem so." Knox settled back.

"And how does Kuusk know about Speakers?"

"He figured it out once, in Kaliningrad. He killed him. Heigo Kuusk has skills, just as you and Kaphiri do. He is like teflon, like ice. You must be wary."

Hamish sat thinking blank and furious thoughts. Light flashed in his mind's eye like siren strobes. Lilly was there, her eyes soft on him, that wistful smile playing at her mouth. And Mr. White, whose dark face carried judgment. His dad, retreating voicelessly into a bedroom after a long day, and Hamish looking down at the cartoon they'd drawn to scare his mother when she got home. And the notes they wrote in place of talking:

Gotta love a wake-up call.

What's a wake-up call?

A call that wakes you up!!! And here I thought you were the smartest kid in the world…

I am!

I know. So wake up!!

But it's time for bed. Mom's coming home.

You're right. Bed. You. Now. Love.

Night.

The tea in the Underhut had become cool, like fresh air.

"Helena's important. Just as important."

"OK," said Knox.

"And I promised."

"All right. Just please don't do anything until I get back."

Hamish barely nodded. He didn't want to lie too much.

They both noticed Sandy snoring gently in her chair. The spirits of the Underhut were quiet tonight, as though they'd accepted him and had decided to leave him to himself.

CHAPTER 30

All fall in Prospect Park there had been shifts, the feeling that there was something to do, or something that had been forgotten, or something that was on the tip of the tongue, that caused Hamish a curious anxiety, but it was also akin to pleasure, like dancing. Every animal he met had a piece of it. Squirrels were a stereotype. Their summer generosity of offering him acorns every time they saw him was gone. Now they were jealous and secretive, except for the young one Hamish called Hamster who holed up near the Picnic House. Hamster thought everyone was being crazy, and kept trying to enlist Hamish in finding his passion: apple cores. Since he was convinced that apple cores came in all weathers and all seasons, he didn't see why there was all this fuss about storing stuff. He was constantly scolded by other squirrels, but like the grasshopper in the fable, he just laughed.

It was warmer in New York than the woods of Pennsylvania, but the activity was furious. In Brooklyn, and in the city flyway, it was busy as rush hour.

The birds at the lake had conversations among themselves. They would include Hamish if he inserted himself, but they knew he wasn't coming with them, so in the middle of a thought, a goose or a duck would turn to him and say, *Well, we're off.* The contingent would scoot along the water, wings grabbing the air again and again until their feet no longer hit the surface and they tucked up like little airplanes lifting landing gear, angling once to get their bearings, and then fading over the trees.

There was one pair of Canada geese who Hamish knew was staying. A few times Hamish was with them as their eyes followed another group heading out. The male watched for a minute.

Nope. Just not feeling it.

I know, his mate would rejoin. *Let's go to the other side.*

They would fly formation across the lake to the island, and ski to a stop on the water.

Hamish soon realized there was a kind of hierarchy between those who wintered in shelter and those who had to brave the wind, those who went south and those who stayed. Then there were the long-distance geese, who came through town like a motorcycle gang from northern Canada on their way to Georgia or South Carolina. They were tough and disrespectful of boundaries, bullying their way onto the lake, crash landing into the rest stop and making a racket as they gulped as much food as they could, letting their wiry exhaustion turn into small feather-losing fights, and then the following dusk allowing the call of a few of them to lift the flock off again into the sky, the V forming before the sun set over New Jersey, and the night becoming quiet with distant cars and fading sirens.

School tunneled into the darker months, the end of October hitting the high-school student body like a plague of sloth and forgetfulness. Hamish couldn't remember when his tests were, so when he failed a number he was astonished and hid it from his mother. He'd thought his time of battling school like he did in Pennsylvania – as though it were a jackhammer just outside his window – was over. He'd been so stunned that year by his father's operations with hopes raised and hopes dashed and secrets and bravado that he couldn't face his classmates, who were living their lives as though they didn't matter. The trouble he caused simply by not showing up made his mother so furious she couldn't speak to him, instead screaming at him "Why are you like this?" Like what? he'd thought. I'm not like anything at all.

Later that same night, after she'd seen Henry in the hospital, she came home and got into Hamish's bed, pillowing his head on her chest.

"I'm so sorry I yelled at you," she kissed the top of his hair. "I'll do better. You do better. We'll take care of each other."

∞

Knox's phone rang in Hamish's pocket. At first he didn't know where the sound was coming from, but the phone also quivered slightly on his thigh. He reached in and pulled open the phone. He impressed all the students at his lunch table.

"Hamish?" the smoky voice said. "Sandy. Honey, listen. You're going to Grand Central Station."

"Now?"

"Now, kid. Gotta step up."

"Uh, OK." Hamish's brain geared up, thinking how he was going to escape Herman Melville School and get into Manhattan.

"You're a smart kid. You'll figure it out." He could hear Sandy inhale on her cigarette. "So at exactly 2:07 you're going to see a man walk over to the information booth under the clock in the center of the station. You know what I'm talking about?"

"Uh hunh."

"Good. He'll be wearing a green shirt. That's all I got for ya, a green shirt."

"A green shirt."

"You go up to him and greet him like he was your uncle, like you're expecting him, like you are so glad to see him, and that you can't wait to get him home. Got it?"

"OK. My uncle."

"And then you get in a cab — not the subway, get a cab. You take him to the Park, and then you walk him to Underhut. And you make sure he's watched, got it?"

"Yeah, Mr. Knox told me."

"Get him some food. He's a Speaker, Hamish. That's why it's gotta be you, darling. He's been doing it for longer than you, but, you know. Wrong people found him, shit hit the fan — same old story. Take care of him. I gotta go." She hung up.

Hamish's mind raced as the subway sped through the tunnels into Manhattan. Another Speaker. He was relieved he'd prepped Underhut, stocked the fridge, made sure the sheets were clean. Hamish's visits to the Quaker Cemetery were accompanied by a small crowd who were celebrity hounds, thinking Hamish had come to live with them. Bagheera, for one, couldn't understand why Hamish didn't just stay in the park with plenty to eat, and already independent of his mother. The dogs in their evening walks pulled owners to the fence of the graveyard, calling out to Hamish in what to the owners seemed like a happy frenzy. Raccoons congregated outside the hut in the hopes of a game. The fox was always looking for something to filch, and would harangue Hamish for his lack of provision.

The most interesting network Hamish met was the rats. Their curiosity was unstoppable. They were everywhere and knew everything. After hours of interpretation, Hamish could find out where there was construction on the BQE or where Bagheera had eaten last night, if any animals were born at the Bronx Zoo or what time Delmonico's closed in Gramercy. The one who decided he owned Hamish and who Hamish met while he was cleaning up the Underhut, Hamish named Aesop. The second time they met, Hamish was bringing laundry back; someone completely unannounced had spent the night and then disappeared before Hamish returned in the afternoon. How he got in without keys was a mystery. Only a note on the small kitchen table in the Underhut was in evidence: 'Thank you for shelter. Not unrewarded. Mislov.' Next to the note was a small stack of $20 bills. Hamish counted it. Two thousand dollars. He found a piece of aluminum foil, wrapped the stack, and put it in the freezer.

Aesop was on top of the refrigerator. *What's that?*

Nothing you can eat. How did you get up there?

On the back. Easy. Sure you checked it out for eating? Maybe I should take a look.

No eating it!

OK, OK, just asking. What's that? What you got?

Hamish took a box of tic-tacs out of his pocket. *This?*

Yeah.

Come on. Hamish scooped the rat up and put him on the table. Then he lay a tic-tac down like a tiny egg. Aesop sniffed it.

This is no good.

Why not?

There's nothing to eat here.

Hamish laughed.

∞

At 2:07 Hamish saw a man with a deep olive green wool shirt and a shoulder bag walk over to the booth with the clock on top. He was diminutive, with dark Semitic features – he could be from anywhere from Cyprus to Tehran. Hamish took a deep breath and moved forward, spreading his arms and forcing himself to smile. The man saw him, glanced around, and stepped into Hamish's awkward embrace, which the man took control of like he would take control with a younger relative and formalized it by kissing each of Hamish's cheeks.

"So good to see you again!" said Hamish expansively. He didn't know where this acting for an audience came from.

The man smiled and nodded. Hamish ushered him out of Grand Central to the side where taxis lined up. They got in a cab – it was Hamish's first time—and Hamish called out, "Grand Army Plaza."

"Manhattan or Brooklyn?" asked the Nigerian driver.

"Brooklyn, Brooklyn." Hamish turned to the man. "My name's Hamish, Hamish Taylor."

The young man looked blank. "No English."

Hamish's heart fell. He touched his own chest. "Hamish." He raised his eyebrows, gesturing for a response. The man's eyes lit with understanding.

"Iskander Aria," he said, touching his own chest.

Hamish pointed at him. "Iraq? Israel?"

Iskander made a face and shook his head. "Iran."

He looked out the back window of the cab. His foot was jiggling. He looked forward again through the front windshield and leaned his head towards the Nigerian cabbie. He said something, and the cabbie shook his head. Iskander fell back into the seat. Hamish tapped him and shrugged, indicating, What's going on?

Iskander, talking in Arabic or Persian, pointed out the back window, pointed to himself in a dramatic way, and made it clear that someone was following him. He then made it clear he wanted Hamish to be ready to jump out at a stoplight. Hamish looked behind them. There was a black town car that changed lanes on 2nd Avenue when they did.

Hamish leaned to the sliding plexi opening. "Excuse me. Someone is following us, and we would rather not meet them. Let me pay you now."

The Nigerian driver smiled hugely. "No problem no problem. You getting out when I say, OK?"

"OK." Hamish handed him a $20 bill and waved away the idea of change.

The driver went a couple more blocks and turned left. Half way down the block was a garbage truck blocking the entire street and Hamish's heart fell. But Iskander smiled, and reached through to pat the driver on the shoulder. It had been the driver's plan. Iskander tapped Hamish and they got out, walking swiftly to the other side of the garbage truck. The town car was stuck two cars behind them. As they headed around the truck, Hamish saw one man in a suit get out of the town car to follow.

Iskander went a few yards and then took Hamish by the shoulders, asking him something. Hamish shook his head, wishing he could understand. Iskander stepped back and lifted his head. Hamish himself, as though he were an animal, heard the call—unmistakable, clear, compelling as a bugle reveille. He knew he could resist, but he knew most animals could not.

Pigeons flocked out of the trees and over the edges of the buildings. They flapped in crowds up the street. Rats—maybe four dozen—swarmed out of doorways and openings and garbage containers. There were three cats and one lone dog trotting up from the East River. They kept a bubble of a couple of yards around Iskander and Hamish until the man following them came in sight, and then they broke formation, hurling themselves in the man's direction. He threw up his arms, protecting his eyes from pigeons' claws and wings. He kicked out as rats tried to get up his legs. He shouted as a cat's claws sunk into his thigh. He turned and ran as the dog growled him backwards off the street.

"How did you do that?" shouted Hamish.

Iskander shouted something back, beckoning Hamish on down the street. They hailed another cab going uptown. Then they ditched that and found one to take them down the East Side to Brooklyn. Iskander, looking out the back window often, laughed in relief and triumph, grabbing Hamish's leg and shaking it.

∞

As they crossed Prospect Park, Ron found them, landing on Hamish's shoulder.

Who's this putz?

To both Ron and Hamish's surprise, Iskander answered, *This putz traveled a very long way just to watch you preen your very black feathers, a sight I wouldn't have missed for all the wind in the world.* His sarcasm was unmistakable, and to Hamish's senses, very thickly accented.

Two of you, hunh? Ron's talons squeezed Hamish's shoulder, pricking through his shirt.

And you will watch after him, said Hamish.

No more than for a friend, warned Iskander.

Yeah? Ron wiped his beak on Hamish's hair. *OK.* He took off.

Iskander and Hamish looked at each other. Iskander said something in Persian. Hamish said only, "Come on," and gestured him towards Underhut.

∞

Iskander was hesitant to go down the stairs under the rug, but he did. Down in the kitchen, Hamish put on a kettle for tea, thinking hospitality was the best way to go. Aesop appeared on top of the refrigerator.

Who is this new creature, and why does he smell of so much eggplant and gas and anxiety?

I am pleased to meet you, as well, said Iskander.

Nice! Aesop waddled to the edge of the refrigerator top to get a closer look.

"Would you like some tea?" asked Hamish, forgetting.

Iskander looked blank.

You don't understand each other? The rat was pleased with himself. *Fascinating.*

No, said Hamish. *I know it's strange.*

Talk through me! said Aesop happily, always glad to be the center of attention.

How do we talk through you? they both understood Iskander to say.

You're doing it!

The humans looked at each other. Iskander gave it a try, looking at Hamish but speaking to the rat. *How is a boy a Speaker?*

How is this man new in a new place and people are already trying to kill him? retorted Hamish.

Iskander smiled. *Let us begin again.*

It was awkward that they couldn't talk clearly and directly to each other. It was as though they each spoke a distant dialect of Aesop's language when they heard the other. Aesop could understand them both perfectly. So Aesop was the center of the dialogue.

With Aesop as an eager intermediary, Hamish discovered that Iskander Aria had been a Speaker for three years. The first time it happened, as with Hamish, it had come on suddenly. It was during an execution. As part of his role in the Guardians of the Revolution, he and his fellows were called awake in the middle of the night and rushed in vans to the large prison in Mashhad, the city his unit was in charge of. In a walled cement courtyard they had a small construction crane and a blue rope with a noose hanging down. Iskander and his fellows ringed the courtyard at attention. The commander chewed on sunflower seeds, spitting the husks into the shadows created by the bright klieg lights. The prisoner was pushed off his stool, and Iskander watched him strangle, legs kicking for some seconds.

A shot—a crack, really, amplified in the courtyard—interrupted the prisoner's death struggles. The commander had fired his sidearm at a rat who'd been picking at the commander's discarded sunflower shells. The rat skidded a few bloody feet. Iskander heard a flurry of exclamations:

Out! Hide! They're hunting. Go! He's gone. Nothing there. Go!

And differently, above him:

Not here, nothing here! Up up up arooooound swoop over the top.

Iskander felt himself calling up to the sparrows fleeing out of the courtyard: *Who are you? Where are you going?*

A rat skittered between his legs. Iskander turned and felt his face, body, nostrils, throat morph: *What is happening to me? Stop! Stop!*

The rat did, looking at Iskander, sniffing in the chaos. One of Iskander's fellow guards strode forward and kicked the rat. It flew a few meters, rolled, and ran. The man turned and pointed at Iskander.

"Djinn! He is possessed!"

Others had noticed his strange behavior and sounds, too. They grabbed Iskander and held him as he protested his innocence in all things, but still hearing the other-worldly conversation of birds. The speed of his life only increased, even as he sat in a small room bright with fluorescent light and no windows. A doctor came in and asked him two questions: "Where are your wife and child?" and "What did the animals say?"

The doctor—a Keeper—got him in the next few hours in a car to be whisked away to some kind of safety. As they were waiting for documents, the doctor had brought a parakeet into the office. The parakeet sat on the doctor's shoulder, her light blue chest and white head puffing and bobbing. She was very excited to meet Iskander. In an overwhelm of emotions, he understood the bird and found that he was a Speaker, that this was a time he was needed—for what exactly he couldn't understand—and that he had to protect himself. She also wanted to ask him questions about how she could get some really good mango.

The Guardians of the Revolution and MOIS, the intelligence agency, would be relentless in looking for him, the doctor told him. His wife and child would be hidden, but would have to stay where they were. Iskander was going to an enclave in the Caspian forest, closer to Tehran but still rural and remote. This was where his training would begin.

"Training for what?" asked Iskander.

"For whatever you are meant to do," replied the doctor.

∞

This guy is amazing, editorialized Aesop to Hamish. *You should go with him.*

The woman said to watch over him, said Hamish, *not go with him.*

What woman? said Iskander, concerned.

A Keeper, here. "Sandy," Hamish said in English.

Your Keeper?

Hamish pondered Shenouda. *No, my Keeper is new also. He's never taught anyone before.*

Iskander's face was full of questions. *So is it true what I've heard, that they don't have any more in America? Except you, a boy?*

Hamish knew Iskander would be leaving him soon, and it made him feel more lonely than he had in a long time. *It's just me.*

For the next hour, with Aesop scurrying back and forth on the little table and occasionally demanding food for his "exhausting work of explicating all these stories," Hamish listened to Iskander tell him some of the things that were possible for a Speaker, and to stories of Speaker lore he'd been exposed to. But Hamish more wanted to know about how Iskander had been able to summon animals to his aid with the MOIS agents following them. He called it The Cry, and explained the mechanism for expressing it, but also warned Hamish to never do it unless he meant it and was prepared for animals – whatever animals heard – to do their worst. When Iskander had tried it for the first time in Golostan near the Caspian Sea, wolves, leopards, and red deer with huge dangerous antlers came ready to kill anyone near him.

The most perilous skill Iskander told Hamish about was The Arrest. He could call an animal – even a human animal – into a state of paralyzing fear. It would not kill them unless their heart was fragile, but it would immobilize them for a brief time. Some predators were able to do this with prey. After Iskander told him how, Hamish realized he'd done it unwittingly with Thor, the bobcat in the Pennsylvania forest. But he didn't know if he could do it willingly. He felt like he was a good card player being told how to do a high dive.

Mostly, Hamish wanted to know about why he was here, what his "famed" purpose might be. Iskander explained that he was still looking for his greater one, although he thought his had something to do with the regime in Iran and their use of religion to create law. Perhaps it was the exploitation of religion for destructive purposes in general. This, he said, took everyone's attention away from what was important, which is how we are a real part of this world. So he worked to that end, patiently keeping his attention on what he could do to keep us honest animals. And then the government found out about his activities. Iskander discovered they knew about Speakers and did not want them to exist.

Have you ever Spoken? I mean like, you know, with dead things? Or done that Going In thing? asked Hamish.

Iskander had not Spoken, although he knew about it, and he felt the tide of energy that occurred where the residue of trauma remained.

I have, said Hamish. *I did it.*

No! Iskander was astonished. *This is a very ancient skill I have been told. Few do it now, or are called upon to do it. You must tell me.*

So Hamish told him the story of the polar bears and Juan. Iskander was a little awestruck, and warned Hamish of the dangers ahead if he was called upon to Speak an adult. *My teacher told me it can kill the Speaker. They hold on, and they hold on to you.*

Aesop was delighted, crying out, *That was you who stopped them! Oh, thank you! That was such a mess over there for so long.*

And this Going In? asked Iskander. *I was not aware anyone could anymore. My teacher said it was a forgotten skill.*

Alicia told me you have to be invited. She invited me. And an elephant did.

Iskander was silent until he finally said, *In one so young, this is a sign of something greater to come. I will look forward to that.*

Hamish showed Iskander where the food was, the bed, and assured him he'd be back early in the morning before school to check on what he needed. He hoped that Sandy would call.

As he left, he realized that there were a dozen crows in every tree. He felt animals in the bushes. Pigeons walked on the grass and song birds flitted over the hut. Ron clattered down, adjusting his wings as he strutted on the ground.

Pretty good, hunh? Watching out for him.

Couldn't be better. Keep it going. I'll be back in the morning.

∞

In the morning, no one was there. Even Aesop had gone somewhere else. There was a note in Arabic script, which Hamish pocketed to show to Mr. Shenouda. A pigeon said they'd all tried to follow "the other Speaker" out of the park, but it was deep night and he'd told them to leave him alone. The last the pigeon heard, only one cat kept up the pursuit.

Hamish had to wait through the whole school day before he talked to Mr. Shenouda at chess. Mr. Shenouda took him aside and quickly said in a low voice, "Rabbi Adams just contacted me. They found him. They're helping him to get back to his home."

"Why aren't you teaching me?" Hamish's voice was angry.

"Hamish, my dear boy—"

"Iskander said he went through a whole training. That his Keeper—his Keeper—trained him for months in some forest near an ocean so at least he knew what he could do. So he wasn't so fucking alone."

"Hamish—"

"Are you my Keeper?" Hamish demanded, looking him in the eye.

Mr. Shenouda sighed and looked back at Hamish with moisture beginning in his dark eyes. "I am now. Yes."

He extended his hand, as though they'd played a match. Hamish looked at the hand—solid, fleshy, distinct and deep lines, the nails cared for with a few straight ridges, a gold band with symbols on it that Hamish had never really paid attention to. The ring that had wed Kaphiri Shenouda to his now dead wife. Hamish grasped the hand.

Shenouda said, "I am glad you were able to talk with Mr. Aria."

Hamish took out the note and handed it to Mr. Shenouda.

He chuckled. "It is a thank you note. It is a line or two from Rumi. You will come to know Rumi, I hope."

"What's it say?"

"'Be grateful for whoever comes / because each has been sent / as a guide from beyond.' As you, Hamish, have been sent to me. Iskander." Shenouda squeezed Hamish's shoulder.

"Why," asked Hamish, "if you all know about him and can do all these things to help him, why can't you guys use your powers to help Helena? Why can't you use all that amazing stuff you guys can do to stop Heigo Kuusk?"

"It is an excellent question, my boy, an excellent question. Here's what I can tell you as of now." He leaned until their heads were practically touching. "Mr. Kuusk is connected to a financial empire that is using him and many people all over the world to increase their hold on things that you and I imagine are more free than they are. If we move on Mr. Kuusk and his hobby – because let us be clear, the unfortunate enterprise poor Helena is caught up in is only a smidgen of what he is involved in. But it is his pathological passion. However, if we eliminate him from the board, the others know to aim their weaponry in lethal directions. And they will not hesitate. To be skilled in destruction and mistrust is to be more quickly effective than using the skills of creation and love."

"It doesn't help Helena."

"No. You are entirely correct. It does not."

"And she's not just 'poor Helena.'"

"No, you are right. My phraseology is unforgivably pompous."

"Why can't you just teach me what to do and I'll do it?"

"Hamish Taylor," Shenouda sat so his gaze was up at Hamish, "you are a human being, not a superhero or a god. You have a remarkable gift, and we will, I trust, discover more and more of that gift together. We are not here to fix but to guide, to—"

Steve Mondolfi interrupted them, claiming the first game with Hamish.

So Hamish discovered what it was like to be of service without ever knowing the result. He never saw Iskander Aria again.

CHAPTER 31

The next morning, Ralph the sparrow found Hamish on his way to the subway before school. Landing on his head, he started an exploratory picking of Hamish's hair. A Park Slope mom with her $300 stroller called out in disgust, "Don't let that thing on you! It's carrying things!"

"It's all right, Ma'am," replied Hamish, picking up his pace.

"Really, you shouldn't—" hating being called Ma'am.

But Hamish was out of range.

Nothing for me, Speaker?

Maybe, teased Hamish, pulling his hand out of his pocket into the cold December day. Ralph saw the bread in his hand, and flitted down to hammer it apart.

This is good! cocking an eye at Hamish every pass at the bread.

I'm glad you like it.

Better than pigeon leavings, at least.

Great.

Hold on. Ralph flew off in a little angry ballet with another sparrow who was approaching. In a second he was back, gripping Hamish's thumb.

Hamish said, *You could let someone else have some.*

Ralph glared. *You brought this for someone else?*

For you, for you!

I thought so. He jabbed, grabbed, and tore. *Why do you let one of yours wander away every day? Is she doing something for you?*

Who?

The wet face one. She's yours, right? I got that right, right? I told every-one, so that better be right or I have a lot to do. She's hurt, wounded, something broken, I don't know but she's not well, maybe sick, but not that, broken, snapped. This is good, spearing a chunk, *I'm going to take some with me.*

Wait! Hamish stopped Ralph from glancing off his hand. *Where is she? Do you know?*

She's over there by the flower pool, where the robins nest.

Hamish put it together; the Vale of Cashmere, the nearly abandoned gardens near the Flatbush side. *Go find her, then find me, then find her, then find me!*

Speaker's crazy again.

Not crazy. Now go, go!

Hamish ran towards the subway to head off Lilly. She was down on the platform of the 7th Ave. station talking with Carla. The screech of the train entered the station and people prepared themselves. Hamish came so close to her ear his mouth touched her as he yelled, "Helena!" Lilly looked at him, shrugged at Carla, and they ran out of the station up Flatbush. Hamish's lip burned.

Ralph hovered in front of Hamish's face briefly as they crossed Grand Army Plaza, dutifully telling him where Helena was. He flew between her and Hamish ten times before they got there. They found her walking in circles around one of the old fountains. She was in sweatpants and a hoodie pulled down over her face, puffed with a sweater underneath. Her pink sneakers shined like misplaced tropical flowers in the late fall colorlessness.

Lilly put a hand on Hamish. "Hamish, she's not—I mean, something happened that—"

Helena saw them and strode over like an avenging angel and began to hit Hamish.

"You! Fucking! You! You didn't! Nothing! Why didn't you! Nothing! Get away from me! Get away! You boy! You stupid, stupid boy! And your stupid black girlfriend! Go fuck yourselves! Go! Go! Go!" Tears and snot and cheeks streaked with red.

Hamish hardly lifted a hand to protect himself. Lilly moved to catch her arms.

The sparrows started to dive, dozens of them, hitting her head, zooming in like a swarm of locusts, but with purpose. Helena screamed and flailed, batting the air, hitting Lilly by chance on the side of the head, knocking her sideways, running to the other side of the dead fountain, the sparrows snatching at her hair after her hoodie fell away.

Hamish called out from somewhere yards behind the back of his heart. Everything stopped in mid-motion. The sparrows went silent and found a branch, looking around as though nothing had happened. Lilly turned to Hamish, her head clear. Helena crumpled to the ground, ready suddenly to sleep. The quiet infected even the trees and the cold grass.

Hamish lifted his face and the sparrows lifted as one from their branches, dipping down then up and away east. The only sound was Helena beginning to cry to herself.

"She's not pregnant anymore," said Lilly, coming to Hamish. "She's been hurt."

They went to her and sat in a small triangle on the ground.

Lilly whispered, "I'm sorry about the baby."

"Oh, it does not matter," moaned Helena. "No babies should come into this shit world. Better they should be dead, garbage. Not here. This shit world." She wiped her nose. "It's good. No one here."

They sat quietly.

"Can't you come with us now?" asked Hamish.

Helena smiled. "You good boy. You so good you forget. They use my sister, they use my mother. Your mother. Black Lilly mother. I am a cow. They milk me like cow, own me like cow, kill me like cow."

Hamish ventured, "Is it true we could buy you? I didn't know you were serious."

Lilly looked at him like he'd proposed lopping off her foot. Helena laughed high and hysterically.

"So I be your cow?" She giggled, wiggling her fingers off her breasts.

"No, you said something before."

"Achkt!" she spat. "Some man want me all to himself. Heigo said fifty thousand dollars, he do it. That man, he disappear, never come back. I was glad because he like to slap a little." Wistful. "Fifty thousand dollars, U.S. Doesn't seem like so much for a person, no?"

The plan was coming to Hamish. "What if we get fifty thousand dollars. We could buy you, and then you'd be free."

"Hamish!" Lilly.

Cynical squint. "Where you get fifty thousand dollars? Mommy's nursey nursey, she don't have nothing. You got rich grandpa?"

"Say we got it. How do I talk with Kuusk?"

"Who say I want to be your cow?"

Hamish wrinkled with disgust. "Not mine. You'd be yours. Your own."

"I owe you fifty thousand dollars."

"No! You just be done, do what you want, go to school. I don't know."

"I don't owe you nothing?"

"No."

Helena looked at Lilly and back at Hamish, suggestively, "Nothing?"

"No!"

Helena smiled at the impossibility of it all.

"How do I talk with Kuusk about this?"

"You crazy. He eat you for breakfast."

"How do I do it?"

"You mean it?"

"Yes."

"Give me paper. I write it for you."

Hamish got a notebook and pen out of his book-bag. Helena hunched, writing slowly in her best penmanship. She handed it to him, her face suddenly glowing and child-like.

"You do this today?"

Hamish choked. "Uh, well, maybe, but maybe tomorrow. I have to find money. Soon."

Helena was already thinking about the possibilities. "I get my mother and sister out of New York, Florida, where it's sunny, not dark like home, and nobody knows us, we get jobs there, no paying for ugly things, you know Florida?"

Hamish shrugged, about to tell her.

"Or California. We go, I could do modeling, Los Angeles. You think I make a good model in Los Angeles?"

Hamish tried to say yes.

"I think so. Maybe that better than Florida. It's farther away, yes? From New York and all this, yes?"

"Yes," said Hamish.

"Then maybe I send that fucking CD to CIA! Serve them fucking assholes—" Her giddiness slammed into today. "Oh! What time? Oh, doesn't matter, I have to go. You find me later? You talk with Heigo, make deal, find me later?"

"Yes," said Hamish.

His pen still in her hand, she skipped away, jumping as she went to grab a twig from a low hanging branch, snapping it off and throwing it away.

"Oh, Hamish," said Lilly. "What are we going to do?"

Hamish felt like crying.

∞

"We've got to call the police," Hamish turned to Lilly.

"If we do…"

"Maybe we should tell your dad."

"Oh, no." Lilly shook her head emphatically. "He would play this exactly by the book."

"But they aren't going to get our families," said Hamish.

"Are you willing to risk it?"

That stopped them both.

"We've got to at least find out where she's going. Come on."

They ran towards the direction Helena had gone, towards Flatbush.

What you hunting, Speaker? It was Ron, who separated himself from five or six other crows who circled around. *You got things riled up. It's exciting!*

I'm not hunting.

Sure you are!

"Oh, no," said Lilly.

They saw across Flatbush Fallon in his hat approach Helena. He took her by the shoulders, telling her something in her face. A black town car pulled up alongside, and Fallon shoved the girl inside, slamming the door. The town car glided towards the library.

"Don't look," hissed Lilly.

But Hamish couldn't help himself. He thought he could see a white haired man in the back seat with Helena. Hamish looked back where Fallon was. Fallon was being picked up by another car, and he stared at Hamish and Lilly over the roof of the car as he got in. Fallon mouthed some words, which Hamish couldn't understand. But he knew what was meant.

You're right, Hamish called to Ron. *I'm hunting. I need help.*

Woo-hoo! I knew it. Ron swooped down and landed on the sidewalk.

"Oh my God," said Lilly. "What's going on?"

Hamish addressed all the crows. *That thing that moves there, hard and black. Follow it. Circle back to tell me where to go. It is faster than me, and I must find it again.*

Ron hopped up and down. *You going to kill it? Can we have some?*

I'm going to find it. Please. Go. Keep it in sight.

"Hamish," said Lilly, turning him around. "What are you doing? You're acting all weird."

Hamish looked Lilly in the eye. "I'm telling the crows to follow the car so we can find out where they go."

"You're telling the crows," Lilly repeated, even now finding it hard to believe.

The first crow had circled back. *Straight and around, towards your nest!*

Thank you! Hamish yelled to Lilly as he ran across the park towards his own building, intending to get his bicycle. "Come on!"

Their lungs burned. Hamish got his bicycle out of the basement and gave his keys to Lilly.

"Can you wait for me upstairs?"

"Shit." But Lilly nodded yes.

∞

The crows circled back to tell Hamish where the car was, and then headed out again in pursuit. They started competing to tell Hamish the movements of the car, so a couple of times Hamish thought the car had turned twice when it hadn't. There was no chance to teach them well this new form of hunting, but they loved the game, and speculated loudly about what treats were in store for them after allowing Hamish his portion.

Ron glided by Hamish's head. *It stopped. The people got out.*
Where are they?

There! Ron suddenly veered right.

Hamish looked down the new street and saw them walking away from him. He stopped behind the cars parked on the street. Ron landed on top.

Now what? You move in? How you going to do it?

They are going to go inside.

Then you better do it now, Speaker.

I'm not going to kill them, said Hamish looking around. *I'm going to find them. I need someone small to watch.*

Hamish peeked over the car, and saw Heigo Kuusk leading Helena by the upper arm to a place called Prospect Park Banquet Hall. Fallon and two men dressed all in polyester followed.

Hamish closed his eyes, and thought of Aesop. He knew from Iskander and even Shenouda there were ways of calling, but he'd only tried a few. He felt a swelling in his nose, like he was having an attack of hay fever on top of the beginnings of a cold, and then suddenly cool air came into his sinuses. He could see under a hedge by the wrought-iron fence the curious nose of a rat. He called him over, and quickly dubbed him Spencer in his mind.

What are you bringing all these crows here for? He scooted quickly under the car over to Hamish. *They are trouble. Only trouble.*

They have helped me, and I would be very grateful if you would help me.

I've got no time. Things to do. He started waddling fast.

Hamish grabbed his tail and held him upside down. He concentrated on him. *Not help the Speaker? I think you can spare a moment.*

You don't play fair! You don't have a tail.

Hamish let him down. *You see that one with white hair?*

Good for nests! Very good for nests.

Can you get in there? Indicating the Banquet Hall.

Spencer looked offended. *Of course.*

Find out where they take the young one, the girl.

Ahhh! Spencer looked knowing.

Hamish gave up. *Yes, she's mine. I want her back. So go, and don't get hurt.*

Back soon. And no more upside down! Spencer squeezed under the fence out of sight.

You know, said Ron, landing on Hamish's shoulder. *We can do anything a rat can do.*

Except, squinted Hamish, *go where he's going.*

Ron and the other crows laughed themselves into the trees, creating a noisy spectator gallery. Hamish walked gingerly down the sidewalk, leaving his bike on the ground.

∞

He's there, on the left, with others. Spencer was nervous. He sniffed Hamish's sleeve for crumbs.

You OK? Hamish tried to catch Spencer's eyes.

Cat. Inside.

You OK? Did the cat see you?

Yeah, but I got out. She's a killer.

OK. You saw them. The one with white hair?

I like the white hair. Now he's got a tooth.

Hamish went slowly. *A tooth?*

In his hand.

A silver tooth?

In his hand. Is he going to eat her?

Hamish felt sick.

Spencer shied away. *You are dangerous.*

I'm OK. I wish I had something for you.

They're not going to believe this at home. Spencer did his quick rat waddle into the bushes and was gone.

∞

The Prospect Park Banquet Hall was neither near Prospect Park, nor a hall. It was near the expressway which came careening off the BQE before screeching to a halt at the beginning of Ocean Parkway, one of the green-belts envisioned by Olmstead and Vaux, Prospect Park's designers. The Hall was nestled in between some modernized brownstones, with gingko trees out front, peeling bark, and forged iron gates. The white and gold double doors opened onto a carpeted shoebox of a foyer, and

then more double doors like those on high-school gym classes into a
drop-ceiling, Chihuahua-colored wall-to-wall, rolling circle table room
that seemed to make the stage at the end, with its miniscule dance floor
and lonely microphone, a couple miles distant.

Hamish crossed the open area towards a door to the left of the stage.
He could hear his mind shrieking at him as though he were a lunatic
child, "What the hell are you doing?! Go call the cops. Get away from
here. You stupid freaking idiot, what the hell are you doing?"

He peeked through the little window down a short hallway. No one.
He went through. One of the doors off the hallway was labeled in chocolate brown with white lettering, MANAGEMENT. Hamish pressed
his ear to the door. Nothing. He slowly opened the door. It was a small
office area, with a desk, some file cabinets, a table with a Mr. Coffee on
top, calendars on the walls, a little Russian icon in a place of honor. And
a cat sitting in the middle of the desk.

Who the hell are you? she demanded.

Hello, cat.

I haven't seen you before.

They call me The Speaker.

The cat's ears narrowed, and she stood, her tail upright.

I don't believe in you.

And yet here I am.

You are not talking to me! With a hiss that was reptilian. *I am not
understanding you!*

There is a girl here.

There is my man here who will destroy you.

I came to see the girl.

Follow me and get destroyed!

The cat jumped down and trotted to the slightly open door at the back
of the room. Hamish could hear voices from there.

"What the hell is that cat up to now?"

"Want me to check?" Fallon's voice.

"Oh, there she is. Come on, come here, kitty kitty."

Hamish knew it was Heigo Kuusk's voice. He walked quietly around
until he found he could see a mirror on the side of the room which
showed him most everything through the narrow opening.

Helena Padar was there in a chair. Fallon and the two polyester men were there behind her. Heigo Kuusk was leaning forward in his chair, a lock of white hair dangling over his forehead, his concentration on the point of his knife spinning in a slow sharp circle creating a pinhole in the wood under his large and oddly balletic fingers.

The cat on Heigo Kuusk's desk faced the mirror, and her back arched as Kuusk ran his fleshy hand over her head and down her spine. The cat turned to look where she knew Hamish was.

He's so much better than you. See?

Hamish kept his mind quiet.

Kuusk stood behind his chair, cleaning his nails with his knife. "Helena, my dear child. Disappointment doesn't begin to tell the story."

Helena Padar's young face could not have looked younger had she been five instead of fifteen, even with miles of make-up tweaking her little features.

"He set me up. You gotta—"

"I don't 'gotta'."

Helena was crying, her face streaking with colors, her hair mouse-colored spaghetti.

"I need you to understand something. Because, now, I think you don't understand." Kuusk came around the desk. "You know that money you owe me?"

"Yes, Mr. Kuusk."

"Who's going to pay me that money if you don't?"

"I don't know, Mr. Kuusk. I will pay you."

"But you were talking to—"

"He was talking to me!"

Kuusk's fleshy hand moved so suddenly it seemed to appear in a different place. Hamish only registered it because of the crack of the hand on her face and the jolted cry of surprise from Helena.

"I'm talking." He lay the knife down on the desk.

"Yes, Mr. Kuusk."

"I don't want to have to find him. His family."

Interesting. He's going to kill her. Are you watching?

The cat's look of smugness was as out of place for Hamish as a needle in an eyeball. His breathing was short; he felt like he was choking on his inability to do anything.

"Your mother. She's going to have to pay. You remember your mother. Sweet old mother. I got all of you out of Kaliningrad. So you could come and get the American money."

"I will pay you."

"Of course there's your little sister. I hear she's getting to be an attractive little girl."

"Please, Mr. Kuusk. Please, I didn't mean—"

"Shhh." Heigo Kuusk picked up the cat and stroked it. "I just want you to know what will happen."

And Hamish knew. He tried to warn her. He spoke as loudly as he dared: *Get out of there. Now! Now!* But the cat realized what was happening only too late.

Kuusk's hand closed around the back of the cat's neck, and he swiftly slammed the cat into the girl's lap. The cat's front claws dug into Helena's thighs as her back feet tried to find some purchase on Kuusk's arms to force him to let her go. The cat's choking and hissing scream mixed with the girl's as the girl tried to back away from this bizarre strangulation. But Kuusk's other hand grabbed Helena's hair and made her watch, even as screams came slower and lower from her and the cat. The cat's body suddenly froze with a whip-squeeze from Kuusk. Kuusk lifted it, plucking the claws from Helena's blood-pricked skin, and held the now gently twitching carcass of fur in her face. Then he threw the cat against the wall, just missing Fallon's head. It sounded wet when it hit, and sandy on the floor.

Fallon looked at the little body, jerked his head to one of the boys, and turned back with new appreciation in his eyes.

Hamish was silent, shocked for a cat who despised him.

Heigo Kuusk cradled Helena's young face in his hand. "You will not talk with anyone again. We will call you 'The Quiet One.' The men will like that, I think. Yes. The Quiet One."

Then he kissed her, slowly, on the mouth. Hamish felt it from where he was, as though slimy slugs were firmly imprisoning his face also.

Abruptly, Kuusk pulled away, cuffing her cheek with gentle possession. He turned to Fallon.

"I need a kitten."

CHAPTER 32

When Hamish knocked on the door of the English Tudor house in Queens, his entire peripheral vision was taken up by the knowledge of Lilly standing behind him, and the blood throbbed at the edges of his eyes. The leaves had turned early this year, and a soggy brown took up the edges of everything. He wanted to whip around to instruct Lilly in the embarrassments of his cousins, in the way they plowed through a world of privilege and entitlement that left him drained, and that he could find no excuse for being part of that world. He wanted Lilly not to think the less of him by this crushingly humiliating association.

Drew, his littlest cousin, opened the door.

"Who's that?" he asked accusingly.

"That's my friend Lilly." Hamish was on the edge of patience. "Let us in, OK?"

"OK, OK," Drew ushered them in as though offended at the hasty interruption of his placid schedule.

"Where's Sam?"

"Upstairs."

Lilly stuck out her hand. "I'm glad to meet you."

Drew screwed up his face with the force of logic. "You haven't met me yet."

"Shake my hand, and it'll happen."

Drew shook her hand with two up-and-down swipes.

"Good." Lilly raised her eyebrows at Hamish and they took the stairs two at a time.

As they went by Drew's room, the guinea-pig screamed, *I know you're there! Carrots! You bring me carrots!*

Soon.

Lilly saw. "Who—?

"Drew's stupid guinea-pig."

They climbed up to the top floor.

Samantha was lying on the pillows among the instruments and electronics and plastic toys, thumbs pushing on a little screen. "Hamish!" She leapt up and hugged Hamish tight.

"Samantha, this is Lilly, who I told you about."

Sam smiled wide. "Awesome." And she hugged Lilly as well. Lilly looked at Hamish for clues.

Sam cut right to the chase. "So how much do you need and what's it for?"

They sat down, as though beginning a poker game, seeing if they were actually going to call each other, or if bluffing was a part of this circle.

"I don't want to shock you, or anything." Hamish was suddenly completely uncertain of his whole plan. The phone conversations with Lilly, his surety in his cousin's ability to be persuaded, the legends of his aunt's personal wealth, all seemed child-like and absurdly naïve, like anyone who proclaims an intention to save the world and then actually tries. Hamish found himself pitying himself for the vastness of his foolish ignorance of the workings of the world. He had seen awful things. Animals had surprised him with things more uncaring than he could have imagined. He had experienced the scent of human depravity and the violence it visited upon itself, and he knew now that a full inhalation would cause him to lose his senses.

"Oh, come on, out with it. A couple thousand? You, like, broke something and you don't want your mom to know?" Sam's eyes narrowed. "Wait, are you in trouble?" She turned to Lilly. "Is he in trouble?" Her face gasped. "Did he get a girl in trouble?" She blushed burgundy. "Did he get you in trouble?"

"No." Hamish was quick, even as Lilly was shaking her head in protest. "Nothing like that." He went quieter. "Sam—"

"So, what?"

Deep breath. "We have to buy someone."

"Buy someone what?"

"Buy someone."

Samantha's face went blank. The edges of her mouth tried to curl up, but couldn't. She looked at each of them in turn, as though she was watching them age a hundred years in seconds and she couldn't do anything about it.

"What?"

Lilly leaned forward, and Samantha leaned to hear her. They looked like intimates, frozen in a painting of the Annunciation.

"Samantha, there's this girl we know. Her name is Helena Padar. She's, uh, she's. A prostitute."

"You want to buy a prostitute."

"No," protested Hamish, "we want to buy Helena so she can stop being a prostitute."

"Why doesn't she just stop?"

Lilly, "It doesn't work like that."

"Or just go to the police?"

Lilly and Hamish looked to each other for help. Lilly took it on.

"Helena's been basically, well, since she was 13. She's been a kind of slave since she was 13."

"She's 13?"

"When she was 13."

Hamish interrupted. "She's been there for almost three years. She's still there. We have to get her out."

Samantha couldn't believe how dumb they were. "Why aren't you guys going to the police? Or the FBI? Somebody!"

Hamish and Lilly looked at each other.

Hamish told her, "We tried that."

Lilly bowed her head. "Yeah, we didn't get very far."

"What do you mean, 'didn't get very far'? What the hell is that?" Samantha was angry now.

Hamish stuttered. But Samantha herself saved him.

"They threatened you. They threatened you, didn't they? Oh my god, they threatened everyone, didn't they? Your mom?" To Lilly. "Your mom?"

"Look," said Lilly. "It's not really about what they'll do. No. Scratch that. It is. But. We just—We just want to help Helena."

"How could you possibly know her?"

Lilly touched Samantha's knee. "Hamish knew her. He'd seen she was in some kind of trouble, and he got to know her a bit. And then I met her. Helena, she's really smart, she's really got something going on. She— Well, it's almost like you have to think it's you."

Hamish said, "Sam,—God! It's just—She's."

"What, you got the hots for this girl?"

"Sam!" Hamish wailed. He appealed to Lilly for help.

"You guys are so weird." Sam shook her head.

"See," Lilly continued, "Helena was scared into having sex with this guy, and then he acted like he owned her, and after a while he really did own her as far as she could see. She couldn't get back to her mom, and he'd said her mom didn't want her anymore now that she'd had sex, but her mom owed him money for getting them to America. And he needed her to have sex with someone else because she owed him now, not just her mom. That changed into she had to pay her mother's debt. So that happened for about a year—"

"A year?" Samantha said.

"Yeah. And then, because she was so pretty, he decided to train her, to move her up in the corporation, so to speak. There's a high-class house, a place where men come, and they pay a lot of money for time and security and very young pretty girls. The girls are all convinced they can never leave, and that the only one who will protect them is Kuusk."

"Kuusk?"

"That's the name of the boss. The man."

Samantha hugged David's guitar to her chest. "And you know this guy?"

Hamish and Lilly looked at each other. Hamish said, "He knows us."

Lilly continued. "We're all kids here, really. I mean, I know you're older than us, but you're still only, what, 17?" Samantha nodded. "Yeah, we're still kids. But we remember, you remember, when you were 12, 13. You remember what happened to your body, how electric and full and itchy and ugly and beautiful you felt all the time. And a lot of it was good, and you could have crushes on some boys and have your heart broken—we can still do that—" Lilly half glanced at Hamish, "But think, I mean imagine, really imagine, some man who's older than your father, and who you have to trust but are afraid of because he can hurt you, and he gets you to take off all your clothes, and you see him naked, too. And you can't really believe this is happening, you know, like it can't be real, you're a kid, a little girl. Just a little girl. And men aren't even supposed to notice you like that. And then there's this man who's not got any clothes on who's making you lie down and moving you around, and then—you know and you don't know what he's doing, it's so painful. His hand is over your mouth so you don't scream, even though a scream comes out, and it's hard to breathe, also because he's heavy, real heavy, and you can't believe how much it hurts."

The attic room was quiet, late morning winter sun striking the sloping ceiling, glinting on the electronics and instruments, shining up into the children's faces.

"That is so disgusting," muttered Samantha.

"That is Helena. Your life is over—you know, the life you thought you were going to have—is over even though you can't even believe what happened happened. It's like a stain in the mirror that you have to use every morning, and you see it, and you're reminded of how that stain got there every time, even though you keep on living and using the mirror and fixing your hair and putting on some make-up. It's always there."

"Shit."

"I'm just telling what happened. These women begin to like take care of her, like their niece or something—not too nice, not too rough, and they kind of treat you like a grown-up woman. These women teach you things about sex and women and men, and in a way they make you feel powerful. They make you like it. They bring men in and they watch and they tell you what to say and do, and sometimes they make you watch, and every once in a while, they hit you suddenly, out of no where, just to make sure you are paying attention to the fact that they can do anything. Anything to you at all."

Samantha tried to look at Lilly, like she was trying to be brave.

"It's the worst thing in the world," said Lilly.

For Hamish, it was a nightmare he'd no idea he'd stepped into. "How do you know—I mean, it's so, it's not, she didn't say anything."

"Not to you. To me." Lilly's voice went small. "To me."

"God," said Samantha, trying to take it in.

"She got pregnant when she was like 13—Hamish heard her in this part—and they took her to have an abortion, but she can't even really remember that. And then she just got pregnant again, like a couple months ago, and that's after when we started, you know, like seeing her sometimes. But she said, she knew, the men thought she was especially pretty then. The men wanted her. And she wanted her baby, but they didn't let that happen."

Samantha turned to Hamish. "She asked you. She asked you for help."

Hamish nodded, and gestured. "It's because they have her little sister and her mother. They all owe money. And she's afraid they'll start her sister on, you know. So we're trying to help her."

The three of them sat in silence, each wondering what was next, like people do when they are young and daring and are about to jump off a cliff down to water, and they're pretty sure they'll be OK—everyone else who jumped was—but there's a chance this time something could go wrong.

"How much?" Samantha asked.

"Fifty thousand dollars," said Hamish.

"Oh my god."

"I know it's a lot to—"

Samantha waved him away, smiling to keep from crying.

"I'll pay you back. I will."

"We're going to have to get Drew. He's the one who can do the computer stuff to get at the money."

Lilly stopped Sam from getting up. "Are you really sure?"

Samantha said, "Look. I just met you, and you don't know me. But I trust Hamish, and for some reason I trust you, and I hate my mom sometimes, but one thing she says that makes it so I don't hate her all the time is she says, If you can do something and you don't, you're as bad as Hitler. So it sounds like this is what I can do."

She turned to the stairway, yelling, "Drew!" But she was cut off short by Drew popping up his head.

"I'm right here."

"Oh my god. You little creep. Did you just hear everything? Were you eavesdropping?"

Hamish ran over and pulled him up into the attic. "You can't say anything. People's lives are depending on it. Please."

Drew twisted. "I'm not going to say anything. Jeez."

"Promise?"

"I promise." Drew settled his shirt. "So what do you need on the computer?"

"I thought you were listening," Samantha's sarcasm trying to jab holes in her kid brother's forehead.

"Money. I got that. But what you want me to do?"

"We have to get into grandmother's estate and put money in my trust, and then transfer out of there into my account."

Drew thought, like he was working on a small puzzle. "OK."

Samantha watched him work on the computer while Lilly and Hamish went down to the kitchen to get them all some nachos.

∞

Lilly took over in the kitchen. Hamish sat on a stool and they didn't say anything as Lilly found a bag of chips, grated some cheese over them and stuck them in the broiler. Every time she came near him, Hamish felt the heat off her body, felt her movement as ripples in water. He tried not to stare at the back of her neck as she leaned to get things. When she turned to ask him something, he had to straighten up and ask, "What?"

"Can you see if there's salsa up there?" she asked, pointing to a cupboard.

Hamish found some and put it on the counter.

Lilly rested after she unscrewed the lid. "Do you think we're doing the right thing? I mean, getting your cousin involved and all? Taking their money?"

"If you want to know the truth, it feels awful. But I don't know what else to do. You know, like it's war, and you have to do awful things."

"True. I just wish there was someone we could tell." She looked in the fridge for sour cream.

"Well, I've been trying to tell Mr. Knox. He told me if I needed him he'd help, but he's nowhere." Hamish broke a tortilla chip on the marbletop.

"What about the chess teacher?"

"No, not Kaphiri. He's—He's been through too much already."

Lilly plopped a spoon in the sour cream container. "Well then, we just have to remember we're protecting our family." He could see her dark skin blush as she looked at him quickly. "I mean, our families, the people we love."

"And us," said Hamish, astonished at himself. "We're protecting us."

Lilly smiled with a small nod.

Drew and Samantha came pounding down the stairs.

Drew pulled himself up on a stool. "Wow, cool! It's not Cheez Whiz."

Samantha said, "You love Cheez Whiz."

"No, you love Cheez Whiz. You just think I love it." Drew tucked into the nachos, spreading salsa and sour cream everywhere.

Samantha leaned on the counter. "So we got it all done, I think. We just have to go to the bank tomorrow and act cool."

"I got it all done," said Drew with his mouth crunching.

"Yes, you got it all done."

"Thanks, Drew," said Hamish. "It's really important what you did."

Lilly put her hand on Drew's shoulder to give it a small squeeze. Drew looked at her hand, she hesitated, he shrugged, and she smiled, patting him.

They all ate.

Drew spoke up. "So a person costs $50,000?"

The three older kids looked at each other, wondering who should answer.

Hamish said, "This person costs $50,000. And the safety of two other people. Well, a lot of other people."

"So other people cost less? Or more?"

Samantha was annoyed. "People don't 'cost' anything."

"But you're buying someone. And she costs $50,000."

Samantha wiped her hair out of her face. "That's not what I mean."

Drew looked around. "When you buy her, do you own her then?"

"Nobody owns anybody," Samantha was getting frustrated.

Lilly pulled her stool to the counter. "Look. We have to do something bad, so we can do something good. We have to give a bad guy money so he will let this girl go. You heard. She cannot survive there, and we're the only ones who can get her out."

Drew turned his head nonchalantly back to the nachos. "OK."

They finished eating, making plans for meeting at the bank the next morning. Lilly and Hamish got their jackets, and Samantha once again hugged them like they were going to another country for years.

Hamish called back as they opened the front door, "Oh, Drew. Take your guinea pig a carrot. I promised him."

∞

Hamish got out the crumpled paper Helena's number and touched it on the keypad. The sudden cranking of the refrigerator startled him, and his heart slowed with the steadying of the fridge's fan. The phone rang three times before she answered.

"Yes, hello?"

"Hello, Helena?"

"Who is this? Who?"

"It's Hamish." He suddenly thought maybe she'd completely forgotten him, that he was such a minor character in her life that she couldn't place him at all. "From the park."

"You shouldn't—" Her voice was replaced by a man's.

"I think you called the wrong number. I think you've been told this is the wrong number. Little fuck-wad." The line went blank.

Hamish's body felt like he'd just broken a bone.

∞

Then there was the message on Hamish's phone machine.

"Hamish?" It was Helena, her voice not quite whispering. "Hamish? Pick up? Pick up? You not there? Where are you? I cannot find you now, so you have to. They going to go after my sister. You have to do what you said. You have to. No more time. I can't take it. You said. You said. I need to go now. I—" And that was the end.

CHAPTER 33

As Hamish punched Kuusk's numbers on the payphone pad, he thought to himself, Why do we say dial? What does that have to do with putting numbers into a phone? Steve had gone into his dead father's study, searching for Kuusk's contact information. He never told Hamish what else he found, but he was sober as he had handed him the phone number.

The metal pads of the numbers on the pay phone always seemed a little greasy, and the receiver antique, like something from a movie. Hamish hunched away from the chaos of the coffee shop, fried food and rings from doors and cash registers. He put his left index finger in his ear.

"Sasha Imports," answered a female voice.

"Uh, hi."

"Sasha Imports, can I help you?" Annoyed now, ready to hang up.

"Uh, yes. Is Mr. Kuusk there? Can I speak to him, please?"

A pause. "Just a moment, please." The empty phone space of hold.

As Hamish waited, he realized he needed to pee.

Another female voice came on, but her voice was crisper, not a native speaker. "Can I help you?"

"Mr. Kuusk, please?"

"May I ask what this is in reference to?"

"Uh, tell him. I guess tell him, it's about Helena."

"Helena?"

"Yes."

"Hold, please."

The coffee shop was warm. There were regulars coming in for orders that seemed already made and waiting, as though there were a mystical connection between the customers and the shop, a transaction of infinite fluidity that moved everyone through their day until the shop closed down and the customers went home to bed. Hamish heard someone yell, "Whiskey down!" and thought he was in a different place from the one he'd entered. Someone edged by him to get to the restroom. He pressed himself to the phone, afraid of hitting the keys and cutting off the call.

A man's voice. "From where are you calling?" Accent, polished. Hamish thought it must be Kuusk.

"Uh, from a pay phone."

"OK. What?"

Here goes. "I thought. I want to. I want to buy out Helena's contract."

Laughter. "Contract?"

"Uh, yeah. She said $50,000."

"Who the fuck is this?"

Here, Hamish decided to have chutzpah. "I think you know."

More laughter. "And your balls haven't even dropped." The voice chuckled, as at a favored student doing something wonderfully unexpected. "Take this number down and call in two hours." He said the number quickly with staccato precision. "Got that?"

"Yes, sir." Scribbling on the wall next to the pay phone.

The line went dead. There was a tinkling of coin in the pay phone.

He had two hours to wait. He decided to go over to the chess shop since he knew a couple of the boys would be there. This was all going to work out. He turned into the rest room, realizing he still needed to pee.

∞

Abraham was the only one there. Hamish didn't see him very often because he was over at Brooklyn Tech, a year ahead of everyone. He didn't like hanging out with younger kids, but the team at Brooklyn Tech was not challenging to him, and Shenouda gave him private attention. He was turning into a brilliant player. Hamish had once seen him in Washington Square take down seven players in the course of an hour and a half, and pocket some pretty good money. He made Hamish jealous.

When people saw him, they looked at him like he was famous. He had a stoic coolness bordering on hostility that Hamish wanted but could never master. Then, when he smiled, you melted as though you'd broken out of some fortress into a clear meadow.

Hamish flung his bag on a chair. "Where's Mr. Shenouda?"

"Said he'd be back in a while." Abraham set up pieces. Madonna seemed to be asleep.

"You wanna play?"

"Why not."

Abraham held out his fists. Hamish tapped the left; it was a black pawn. Abraham spun the board around. He held out his hand, and they shook.

"Go." Pawn to Queen four, and hit the clock.

They played rapidly, the clicking of the clock when they hit it an irregular metronome. Hamish found himself in a place of calm attention, matching the trades Abraham offered with a kind of authority he rarely knew. They came down to an endgame that blundered into a stalemate, each left with only a king. Abraham stuck out his hand again.

"That was more like a tango than a game."

Hamish giggled at the idea of them dancing.

Abraham let go of Hamish's hand slowly. "Hey, man, are you in trouble?"

Hamish felt blood leave his face. He felt exposed in a flashlight beam.

"You know no one mess with my chess brothers."

"I'm OK. Just—" Hamish couldn't get anything else out. They held the silence. Abraham's face was still a question.

The door rang as Shenouda came back. Rabbi Adams was with him, and they bundled into the chess shop exuding cold from their clothing. Polly shadowed them through the door. Abraham and Hamish leaned apart, and Madonna woke, suddenly screeching from under her cage cover, *Speaker! Speaker! You squeamish little mud worm, get over here and get me some fruit!*

Hamish knew Shenouda and Adams were watching him as he went to the back and found the bowl at the side of the cage that always had something in it. A bit of drying pineapple.

This sucks, said Madonna, shaking her head until the pineapple fell apart. *Too big, you crawling idiot.*

You're in a great mood.

You woke me up.

Not me. The guy who feeds you.

That fat alligator... Madonna settled into her fruit.

"Polly, why don't you play Abraham? I must confer with Hamish here." Shenouda turned to Abraham. "Let me put off our lesson for the length of a game. Do you mind?"

Abraham pierced a look at Hamish. One eyebrow told Hamish he wasn't done. Abraham went to the back of the shop with Polly and cornered a table.

Shenouda gestured Hamish over. They sat at one of the small, crowded chess tables. Mr. Adams leaned over to Hamish.

"Hello, young man."

Hamish nodded.

"Kaphiri tells me your teachings are going well. I think you are discovering things about yourself that you didn't know before, aren't you?"

Hamish shrugged. "It hasn't been much so far." He felt like a brat.

"I think you want to move against Mr. Kuusk because he has his hooks in you with some kind of temptation. Am I right?"

"I said I wouldn't."

"But that's not the same thing, is it?"

Hamish tried to turn the tables. "Where is Mr. Knox?"

Shenouda and Adams looked at each other.

"He said he was going to Iraq to stop a war. Now that's moving against something. It's been like a couple months and nothing. Is he OK? Is he coming back?"

Shenouda looked embarrassed. "Ah, my boy. The ways of Thaddeus Knox are mysterious, to say the least. We have it on fairly good authority that he is well, that he is fine, but beyond that we can only pray for his success and wellbeing. He has been watched over by some force for many years now, and we can only trust that that watchfulness continues with the strength and love it has shown him for many a year, for his very long life, and we ourselves must continue to send him our best thoughts, confident in his enterprises and sure of his adventures."

"You're doing it," said Hamish.

"I'm doing—?" Shenouda, innocent.

"You're doing that thing where you make someone relax. Like you, you know, hypnotize or something."

"Ah." Shenouda looked at his lap. "I see."

"Kaphiri, I think we must address this young man in a different way."

Shenouda was grim when he lifted his face. "Certainly, Etan. Right you are."

"Hamish," began Rabbi Adams. "We—"

"Oh God!" Hamish stood. "What time is it?"

"I don't know, I—"

"Shit." Hamish knocked over a chair as he grabbed his jacket and bag and left the shop without zipping up.

∞

When he got back to the coffee shop he still had ten minutes left. He let his breathing slow. There was someone at the pay phone, but she was just hanging up and pulling on her coat. He took over the wall cubicle, tapping his quarters on the top of the phone box as he waited. The dialing was awkward, Hamish sure of hitting a wrong digit.

"Hamish." It was the white voice.

"Yes, sir."

"So. Talk to me."

"OK. Uh, see, I. I thought that, you know, since Helena, well. I mean, I could get, I think I can get, $50,000, and that we could, you know, agree on. That Helena could not, uh, like work for you anymore." That didn't go so well.

"You come talk to me. Tomorrow. 9:00." The voice brooked no refusal.

"But school—"

"You know where, I think, yes? Oh, and Hamish." The voice was smoother now, lotion on chapped skin. "You have a friend looking out after you at the counter."

"What do you mean?"

"Look."

Hamish realized he meant here, and he scanned the lunch counter. There was one of the polyester men sipping a cup of coffee.

"Tomorrow." The phone went silent.

When Hamish hung up, he could feel the man at the counter turn to him, his thighs spread to the sides of the stool, his coat hunching off his back. The man smiled.

∞

"So here is the boy who is in love with Helena." Heigo Kuusk clicked the cigarette case he was holding closed and slipped it in his pocket. He leaned back in his chair behind the desk. "It would be cheaper to just have an hour with her, you know. One thousand dollars. And you don't have a limpet for the rest of your life."

Hamish felt nauseous. Fallon was on one side of the office, near the door. Hamish could still feel Fallon's hands squeezing him slowly all over as he searched him before he was allowed into the office, even sticking his hand down Hamish's pants to fumble around his genitals, a charming smile on his face. The window behind Kuusk looked out on the New York Harbor, the Statue of Liberty in the distance, watching green over orange and blue container ships all facing the same direction like patient geese. Loading and building cranes dotted the horizon, dinosaurs dominating the jungle below, Manhattan like the distant Emerald City off to the northeast.

Kuusk's blue suit gave him a youthful air, as though he were a young professional fearlessly at the top of his game. The white hair lent him a dramatic, alien look. His pink skin revealed some jowls and neck wattle sinking away from his bones. But his clear blue eyes were movie-star bright and amused.

"You risk so much," he purred in impeccable English. "For love?"

Hamish saw Ron land on a roof outside the window.

"You have an empire," said Hamish impulsively. "Why do you care what happens to this one person?"

Kuusk laughed one laugh. "She is special, isn't she?" He pulled the cigarette case out of his breast pocket. It was silver, catching light. He withdrew a cigarette and tapped it on the closed case. The lighting of the cigarette was delicate, even intimate, as he luxuriated in the first inhale. "She was my cousin's daughter, so I have a special feeling for her."

"Was?"

"My cousin is, alas, no more." Kuusk grimaced through the smoke.

Hamish tried to remember the psychotic lion. "I'm going to get the money."

"Good. I like that. To the point." He flicked ash. "Fifty thousand dollars and you can buy out her contract." He almost leered.

"And you leave Helena's mother and sister alone?" Hamish challenged.

"Oh, I did not say that. We have no bargain about that. They owe me separately, and their debt is not paid. Besides, Helena's mother is a very good worker."

"She--?"

"Of course she is. What did you think?" Kuusk sniggered.

"How much?" asked Hamish quietly.

Kuusk considered. "You are a good boy. I like the way you do business. So I will do you a favor. Seventy-five, you can have it all. Everything you want. Everything! Use your imagination. I have done business with your uncle. You can do business with your uncle. You see? Everything is good. How does that sound?"

Hamish found himself thinking that it sounded very good, like he was getting the better of the deal, even though the ghost of a thought that Uncle Colin and this deal-making man in front of him were compatriots shadowed his reverie. Two people for twenty five thousand dollars, where before it had been one for fifty. Surely Kuusk was right, if he could get fifty, he could get seventy-five.

Another crow landed next to Ron, a third behind them. It was comforting that he had forces behind him, even if he didn't know what they could do for him.

Kuusk was laying out Hamish's plan as though he'd thought it all through himself first.

"After you have the money, you use this number"—he gave him a little card—"and call. You leave a message that it's done. Just that: that it's done. Then I will tell you where to come." Kuusk chuckled, forming a joke. "Because you are so in love, I will give you until the day before Thanksgiving." He laughed. "Thanksgiving. My favorite American holiday. Here." He took a ten-dollar bill out of his pocket and handed it across the desk, folded, like Hamish was a stripper. "Buy her a turkey."

Hamish took the money. "Do you want my phone number?"

"Oh, I have everything," said Kuusk in a low voice.

Hamish thought to himself, this is brilliant. Clean as in a movie; it will all work out. Helena and her family will be in Los Angeles by the end of the month.

Suddenly there was a pincer on the back of his neck, shooting pain through his skull and jaw, cutting off his breath. Fallon had a large hand on him, the other grabbing his hair. One of the crows screamed and flew at the window. Hamish felt her wing crack as she slammed into the glass, and felt the awkward tumble to the ground. Hamish knew she would die soon on the cold pavement. The surge of surprise and anger that welled from inside Hamish compacted like a sphere inside him, and exploded out to burn Fallon's hands with a shock that left them both breathless—Iskander's lessons. Kuusk lunged across the desk, grabbing Hamish's cheeks in one of his puffy hands, paralyzing him with a certain knowledge that this man was in charge and Hamish's only way to life was through his eyes. Iskander had nothing on this man. Kuusk dragged him towards him, until Hamish was nearly embracing his body.

Kuusk's voice was even, casual. "A missing white boy—that is something the police pay attention to. But a missing nurse, someone who's been overworked, who's in a new city, whose husband recently died, who has a difficult son—well, there are very good reasons she might disappear."

The puckering of Hamish's mouth under Kuusk's hand-grip made him start to drool. In an instant Hamish's mind was crystal clear. Kuusk was working him. Not the violence, the threats, the charm, but in the way Shenouda might work him. The intention penetrated Hamish at first—with Shenouda it would be like colorful ink soaking into paper, but with Kuusk it was like a pointed shovel stabbing earth – but then that energy hit a hard and deep interior in Hamish, slipping off and having no effect except what a glare of light has on a dark room.

Kuusk pushed him away and wiped his hand on Hamish's shirt.

"Now," said Kuusk. "We have a deal. You have a job to do, Speaker. Go do it."

The word stabbed Hamish's brain. Kuusk knew everything and everyone. No hiding. What was he that he could know even the word, Speaker?

As if in answer, Kuusk's voice a gutter, he said, "You think no one knows about your kind? I can smell you." He sniffed his newly wiped hand. "I got rid of one of you animal talkers once." He smiled. "1989. Kaliningrad. Tried to call the dogs." Laughing. "Literally tried to call the dogs. It was very ugly, I think. But you're like all the rest. You will do what I ask and you will like it." He turned dismissively. "Now go."

Hamish would get the money and follow instructions. But his mind spun like a swarm of starlings in spring. No way out but through.

∞

The crow was already dead in the grit when Hamish got there. Ron scooped onto a sign above him.

That was amazing. You Speakered him! Just waiting to take down the other, faking him out, hunh? I didn't know you could be so clever, but now I get it. You're not so dumb as you act.

Hamish held the still warm black corpse. *She's dead.*

Oh, yeah. Couldn't hold herself back. Where we going now?

Hamish vomited, dropping the bird off to his side. The acid got in his nose and he sneezed hard, making Ron lift from his perch. He felt like poison was coming out of him, rushing out, and that exhaustion and pure rest would follow. He had to get home.

CHAPTER 34

The day before the exchange had dragged endlessly. Steve called him to come over, but Hamish made an excuse. He had called Samantha to tell her it was now $75,000, thinking she would drop the whole thing. But she didn't blink. Her voice was faint as she intoned, "In for a penny, in for a pound."

The night was even longer. It reminded him of the night of his father's funeral. But then, every long night reminded him of that night. He had walked out of their house on the edge of Plains, not caring if his mother tried to stop him, out under the black spring sky. It was cold and humid, the kind of air that makes you want to take off your sweater because you're sweating, and then have to put it right back on because you're chilly. The darkness pulsed. He wondered now if the animals knew about him then; there were animals in the shadows. A coyote as a turning flash in the light from the porch, he thought, and a nighthawk calling high and sweet. He went into the barn where Henry's last patients were still waiting to go to other vets. A horse and her colt who had picked up a lung infection, a prize ram who butted the side of his pen out of frustration, and a llama someone had decided was still going to give them great wool after its skin disease was treated. The colt didn't get up, but the mare took the couple of steps to the gate and nuzzled Hamish's shirt, looking for sugar. She'd not stopped as she usually did after finding nothing. Instead, she smelled his ear with her huge hot nose, and rubbed his cheek with her muzzle. It made him laugh, and he scratched her forehead and slapped her neck. He had slept there that night, piling crusty quilted blankets on himself in an empty pen. Sarah had found him there in the morning, and had gone back into the house to bring him cocoa to have when he woke.

Tonight, Sarah watched TV until 9:00, and then went to bed. She had a shift starting early in the morning. Just as she came in to say goodnight, the phone rang and it was Lilly.

Sarah kissed Hamish's forehead just as he said, "Hello."

"Don't stay up too late. School tomorrow."

Hamish palmed the receiver, waiting for her to go. "OK."

"I'll be gone before you get up."

"OK."

"Love you."

"You, too." And Hamish turned to the phone.

Lilly said, "Your mom?"

"Yeah."

"My mom's been asking things. Like she knows something's up."

"Sarah's in her own world."

"Are you OK?"

"Yeah." Hamish wanted help, wanted to be held, wanted to yell and cry, wanted to run down streets, wanted to be stopped, wanted to be given a warm bath, wanted to be told Yes, wanted to be sure, wanted to hug something fiercely, wanted to sing off mountainsides, wanted to dive off buildings, wanted to sink, wanted to sleep.

He said, "You?"

"I'm OK."

They held the phone silence for a long time.

Hamish said, "I'm going to try to find Mr. Knox."

"Now?"

"Yeah."

"Shh—OK." Lilly paused. "You want help?"

"No. I'll have some help."

"Right," said Lilly. "I keep forgetting." She was silent for a minute. "I'm scared for you, Hamish."

"I'm scared for us both. I mean, what happens if we lose the money, or don't get there on time, or—I don't know—a thousand things could go wrong. What if Helena changes her mind?"

"She won't. She's really strong."

"We just don't have any back-up plan."

"We'll have to trust."

"You can't trust a hyena."

"What do you mean?"

Hamish was embarrassed, trying to think how he could tell Lilly of the knowledge he dove into during his encounter with the lioness. "It's just something I heard."

Lilly laughed. "You'll have to tell me that story sometime."

They fell into silence again, full of desire to speak their hearts and having no words to speak.

"Are you really going to go tonight?"

"Yeah. Mom's gone to bed. I can get out OK."

"Should I come?"

"No. No, you sleep, so at least one of us is fresh tomorrow."

"Will you call me? For anything? I'll keep the phone right here."

"OK. Yeah. Otherwise, I'll see you at the bank."

"OK."

They didn't want to hang up.

"I gotta go," said Hamish, breaking it. "Sleep."

"OK. Good night."

∞

It was cold and sluggish. Hamish went into the park at the Litchfield Villa, that only had a few safety lights on. The little masked raccoon family must be waking up in the basement, ready to come out and to raid the garbage cans. The hawk's nest on the other side of the drive was still empty. An owl slipped secretively over Hamish's shoulder, his wings almost brushing Hamish's cheek, and he landed on a bush, turning his head backwards as he settled his feathers.

Cold for hunting, he remarked to Hamish politely.

Looking, said Hamish..

For?

The man who looks after the forest. He gave you a mouse in the snow.

I have not seen him. He is gone.

I want to find where he has gone.

The owl blinked. *You are near something. I thought you were not dangerous.* *I'm not!*

You will have to move. Soon. It's on you.

I have to find the man. I must go. Hamish left the owl and began to slug across Long Meadow. He heard the owl behind him.

Go quietly. It is upon you.

Hamish remembered Mr. Knox telling him that he had to listen to what the animals told him, that they knew things he could not until he experienced them. But he was fed up with Mr. Knox, and his mysterious pablum and his wiry oldness and his leaving Hamish to fend for himself. Shenouda's teachings were narrative. Hamish just wanted someone to take over, to tell him what to do. He was in a lake that was too large and too deep and he was too tired. He couldn't reach the shore by himself.

The lampposts were Dickensian in the misty night air, creating auras of amber and sodium light, pools of brightness on the strip of dark walkway between glowings of fallen leaves. Hamish went straight across towards the playing fields and the hill with the graveyard beyond. Beyond the light, Hamish knew he was being followed. He turned, and at first he couldn't see her, but then she moved towards him. Bagheera.

Hamish began. *I'm looking for the man who lives on that hill.* He pointed. *His scent is old.*

I have to see. He turned away from Bagheera, and she trotted to walk beside him.

Ears.

He scratched her ears as they walked.

Will you hunt tonight? Hamish asked conversationally.

Yes.

No people, please.

No people.

They got to the hill, and started up between the trees.

Bagheera went ahead suddenly, jumping lightly onto a rock so her eye was the same level as Hamish's. *Stop.*

Hamish stopped. It was difficult to see anything, much less a black panther's face, in this darkness.

The passion is coming on you, isn't it?

What?

You said the birds called it a fever.

Hamish's heart was growing fuller by the minute, enough to break his ribs and bounce over the trees.

I don't know. I can't tell.

Bagheera put her face very close to Hamish's, smelling his breath and his eyes.

Soon.

How do I stop it? I can't have it now. I can't.

It comes when it comes.

I've got to find the man.

Hamish brushed past Bagheera, and did not see her again that night. He circled the Quaker Graveyard until he came to the small gate and used the key Knox had given him to get through. He picked his way past a few headstones until he came to the hut. There was no light on inside. His note was gone from the door, which gave him a moment's hope. He knocked on the door, and even called out Mr. Knox's name. But there were only cold breezes among the branches. No moon, no stars.

He had paper and pen in his jacket pocket, and he wrote a last simple note: 'Where are you?—H.' He left it in the crack of the door.

∞

When Hamish stopped by Lilly's place to pick her up on the way to the bank, every follicle felt itchy. He'd hardly slept. He'd spent an hour trying to figure out how big $75,000 was, and he finally decided his regular school backpack could handle it. His was slung empty over his shoulder as he met Lilly at Grand Army Plaza. She was stunned at his transformation. He looked as though he'd lived the last twelve hours digging himself out of a grave.

A block from the bank where they'd agreed to meet, they saw Samantha. She was dressed in a dark blue tailored business suit with a blouse that had a spilling cream silk bow. Her hair was up, and she had grownup makeup on under her black-rimmed glasses. Her nails were a subdued red, and her heels were a good three inches tall. She had a very large cream leather handbag. She looked 28 years old.

Both the girls laughed at Hamish as he stared, wordless.

Samantha turned around. "Got to look the part."

Lilly looked at them both. "You ready?"

"Uh," hesitated Samantha. "I did something." She turned to look over her shoulder.

It was David, walking up to them, favoring his prosthetic leg.

"You didn't!" The whole plan seemed to crumble in that moment.

"Wait, listen," started Samantha.

"Oh, god," Hamish turned away from her.

"Hamish," said David loud enough to cut through, "I know Heigo Kuusk."

Hamish looked for another betrayal, searching David's face.

"He's the one who paid for my leg. He's the one I have to write to every year. He's the one who tries to get everyone's nuts in a vise."

"What do you mean?"

"About a year, maybe more, after my leg, he took a walk with me. He kept telling me stories. He had plans for me. He'd done me a favor. So I owed him a favor. He was nice—very nice—but it wasn't right. One time he had me deliver something to a fancy building mid-town, one that had all this incredible security, sensors, that sort of thing. He had me take it inside my leg."

"When was this?"

"A couple years ago. I never told anyone. Except Sam, last night, when she mentioned Kuusk, and that he's the guy you're giving this money to."

"We don't have a choice, David."

"I know. I know how Kuusk doesn't give choices. It's terrifying how he does that. That's why I want to come with you as much as I can."

"She told you everything? What we're doing?"

"Yep. I'll get the cab. Samantha honey," David turned and gave Samantha a kiss, "we'll be right here waiting."

She went through the revolving doors.

∞

The cab driver was playing tinny dancehall music on the radio that pounded the car. David had to use sign language asking him to turn it down, so he plugged in earphones. David got in the front seat, Lilly in the back, and Hamish went to the pay phone on the corner to make the call.

"It's done."

The payphone rang a few seconds later.

A voice Hamish didn't recognize. "Pete's Tavern, Flatbush, just off Grand Army Plaza. It'll be closed, but knock. By yourself. Two hours."

When Hamish got back in the cab, he felt a stab in his ribs, as though he had a side-ache from running wrong. There was an awful clatter in his ears.

"Can you turn that down?"

Lilly and David looked at each other.

"Hamish," Lilly pointed.

The cab driver was nodding his head to his music, eyes closed and ear phones firmly in place.

"Ohhh." Hamish put his head down. "Where is she?"

It took over twenty minutes, but Samantha finally came out as though she were being chased. She flopped into the cab.

"It didn't work. I couldn't get it. They don't let you take out more than ten thousand dollars a day." She was in tears. "What kind of stupid law is that?"

"Shit!" Hamish slapped the ceiling of the cab.

"It's OK," said David, "we'll figure it out."

"I'm so sorry," pleaded Samantha. "I was sure Drew had gotten it right. He did get it right. We just didn't know about this, this rule. It's some terrorist rule, like for after 9/11."

Lilly said almost to herself, "What are we going to do?"

Without having any idea what he was going to do, Hamish said into her ear, "Take the cab around the corner and wait." He'd remembered Alicia, and he thought, It's not the end of the world, but it could be the end of the girl. He got out, grabbing his backpack. David followed.

He went to the front of the bank. He was thinking of the money and for no reason he felt powerful, as though he had an army behind him. He looked at the building, willing it to surrender. And then out of nowhere he began to feel as though he were sinking. He was the center, a column of liquid that had suddenly descended on the spot, and the liquid spread and splashed in all directions around him with the speed of sound. The first to come at him were small birds, the last hangers-on of the fall, sparrows and chickadees and flycatchers. They made a swoosh out of their hundreds and Hamish opened the door beside the revolving doors. They charged in like speeding smoke.

Screams came from inside the bank. The first person to exit smashed the revolving door off its track, leaving the doors open. Into the gaping hole rushed more birds, larger birds, going from robins to starlings to blue jays to pigeons to crows. People battled their way out the side doors as dogs and squirrels and raccoons, some coyotes and cats and even two skunks charged in underneath the current of birds. On the lowest level came rats and mice, streaming into the building as though the Pied Piper of Hamlin were urging them on.

Inside the bank at the center of the Collecting – for that is what we call it – was a confettied maelstrom of living creatures. Hamish's clothes tugged at his body as he went in, his hair ruffling in the tremendous wind. But no one bumped him, no one careened into his head, no one stepped on his feet. He could barely see the bank counter where damage seemed to be occurring, and then an explosion of wings and fur that was fatal to no one, but cleared a space. It was mostly dogs and crows who dove into that space. A terrier was the first out, a neat packet of bills in its jaws. He came and dropped it at Hamish's feet. He was followed by a chocolate lab, and then a crow with a packet in its talons. Hamish had envisioned each one. Stack after stack of bills, mostly with $1000 printed on the paper band, piled up at Hamish's feet amid the swirling. Hamish stuffed them into his backpack until he knew he had enough. He turned to leave, surrounded by a cloud of animalia that stayed with him out the door and seemed to expand on the street covering Hamish's traverse to the corner.

David followed him backwards, looking back at the bank to see if anyone knew it was them.

Once Hamish's hand touched the cab, he felt himself release. The animals shot off in all directions, suddenly confused and disorganized as though a torrent's flow had been cut off. He got in the cab. David leapt in the front.

Lilly took one look at his face. "Grand Army Plaza in Brooklyn," she instructed the cab driver.

"Plaza Hotel? Plaza Hotel?" asked the cabbie, lifting his earphone from one ear.

"No, Brooklyn. Brooklyn. Grand Army Plaza in Brooklyn."

"OK OK." He pulled out. "What the bloody hell was that thing, eh man?"

"I don't know," responded Lilly loudly. "It's New York."

Samantha hissed at him so the driver wouldn't hear, "What did you do?"

Hamish sighed. He was bereft, like Alicia said he would be after a Collecting. "I got the money."

"You fucking robbed a bank?" Sam pressed over Lilly to get in Hamish's face.

"I'm trying to save this girl's life."

Samantha could barely contain herself. "What the hell was that? Where did those animals suddenly come from?"

"I'll tell you. Just give me a minute."

"What kind of freak are you?" Sam was trembling.

"Sam," said David in the front, "There's something going on that we don't understand yet. Your cousin is something we don't understand yet. He'll tell us."

Lilly reached her arms around Sam and held her, hugging her fear out. She breathed with her until they had the same breath and the light-headedness of shock lifted. She held her all the way to Grand Army Plaza as Hamish whispered to David and Sam the story of becoming a Speaker, while the cab driver nodded his head to his music.

∞

When they got to Grand Army Plaza, they got out and Hamish turned to Samantha and David. The traffic was loud and fast around the circle. The archway towered behind them, the bronze horses galloping towards the park under the victorious guidance of winged angels.

Hamish said, "You can't go with us, you know."

"Let me just go down to the tavern with you. I'll stay on the other side of the street," insisted David.

"No, there's something I have to check first. We've got time."

"What?" said Lilly, "what's going on?" But she probably knew even then.

"There's something – somewhere, there's someone I have to talk to." Hamish shouldered the backpack and started walking into the park.

Lilly pleaded with David and Samantha. "Don't follow. I know your world just changed – mine's changing, too – but we have to trust him."

"Go," urged David, "go. We'll be OK."

Samantha nodded to Lilly to go. "He's a fucking asshole, but take care of him."

Lilly ran to catch up.

CHAPTER 35

They crossed the park to the Quaker Graveyard. It seemed like it took forever. Hamish was sure Knox would have come back, would have gotten his message, would have been there to help him. The gate was locked, but Hamish still had his key. On the other side, they were met by the fox.

What the hell?

Where's the man? Hamish tried to get the fox to stay with him.

You aren't supposed to be here.

Where am I supposed to be?

You can tell. It's time to hide or move. And the fox ran off through the naked trees.

Lilly asked, "What's happening?"

"I don't know." Hamish looked for hints from the trees, but no one was around, even though the air buzzed with energy like before a curtain goes up, or a storm starts. "Something's wrong. We're—I'm supposed to be someplace else." Hamish felt something between panic and intoxication. "We shouldn't have come here. We've got to move."

Lilly was in a foreign country where she didn't speak the language. "Where?"

"I'll show you. By the beach."

"I thought we had to go to Kuusk? The tavern, it's the other way."

"No, I'm sorry. We've got to go out to Helena's mom's."

"Her mom? What the hell are you telling me?"

"It's like the first time. Like the bears. Like Juan. But worse. Way worse. We gotta go. Now." Hamish felt his blood beginning to boil in his veins, and he exhaled bullets. He held Lilly's eyes for a second, and then grabbed her in an embrace so hard he felt he would cry. Lilly's hand on his head made him pull away, but he held onto her hand, and they started running.

As they headed across the park to get to the subway, the birds appeared. A murmuration swept out of the trees into the air above them, loud and raucous and chaotic as an organized dust storm, thousands upon thousands of starlings black and green-metallic, occasional flashes of their bright yellow bills, spinning in a cloud, pulsing up and flattening down towards the ground and heading like a fat spear into a whirlpool of jagged specks. They got close to Hamish and Lilly's heads, clamorous and exhilarating.

Time to move move move go around there and there up Speaker up on the wind touch your neighbor's wing tip miss miss twisting open to the ground and up up up you know where we're going we're going to it to it to it here it pulls and pulls open wings dodge the air and around that and that and that it's you you you Speaker you move you go where it pulls it pulls you pulls you let it speak to you Speaker we follow follow the turn and twist of air breeze wind we are making the wind to blow you on and on and there.

Hamish said again and again, *I'm going, I'm going, I'm going,* as they ran up the hill along the wooded path. The leafless trees crackled. Dogs were barking everywhere in the park sounding hollow in the cold. Lilly could see some feral cats looking around the bottom of tree trunks, a couple of raccoons were in the crux of branches. Her lungs were burning. She wanted to keep holding onto Hamish's hand, but she couldn't as they took stone stairs up to the very top, where they would descend to cross by the lake and to the Church Avenue subway stop.

She banged into Hamish's back, starting to say, "Sorry," when she saw ahead the black panther she had seen months ago in the zoo parking lot. Hamish put his hand out, as though stopping a child in a car from a sudden stop.

Hamish said, *Where am I going?*

Bagheera blinked. *You know where. You don't know why.*

It feels like—Hamish was quaking. *It feels like the polar bears.*

Because it is.

Why?

Something has crossed. Imprinted already. It is very strong. A woman. Like that one. Bagheera cocked her head towards Lilly. *Why do you destroy these things?*

I don't.

No. You don't. Others of your kind.

I can't do this, not now.

The panther walked slowly up to Hamish until she was just in front of him. She sat. Hamish wanted to scream. He shook his head.

Bagheera screamed for him, a sound he'd never heard, really. It reminded him of the lion proclaiming ownership in one roar. It woke him up. It said to him:

Death is here always. I will bring it, but I don't have to. It cannot stop. It is moving towards the sunrise. It's moved already.

Then Bagheera opened her mouth and bit down on his hand leaving pointed bruises. She released him.

Now go.

Bagheera melted away just as a group of dogs came barreling up the path. Birds of all kinds lifted from the trees overhead.

Hamish yelled at the dogs, *Follow if you must, but do not get in my way!*

They hollered back, *OK, I'm coming. I got here first. I know the way, which way are we going? I'll follow, I can follow anything.*

One mutt that looked like a bedraggled Benji-dog stood expectantly. *I will journey with you. You don't want to stop me, do you?*

Hamish shrugged. *OK.*

As they moved off the hill, Lilly said, "What was that?"

Hamish took Lilly's hand again as they walked fast down the path. It felt like he needed protection from what was coming, and that he needed to protect her.

"Bagheera talks in bumper stickers. It's so aggravating. She says something has, I don't know, crossed. Female."

"Does she mean, died?"

It was hard for Hamish to get the words out. "I think so." His side-ache was killing him.

"You mean Helena's dead?"

"Yes."

"He killed her?"

"Yes."

"That's what's going on with you, isn't it?" It fell into place for Lilly. "It's her. It's Helena."

"Kuusk lied. He's probably got Fallon waiting for us so he can take the money and probably kill us." He shook his head, blinking away tears. "What was I thinking? You can't buy a person." Hamish put it together and blocked it at the same time. "We have to move. We have something important to do."

They ran to the subway, dogs and birds following, and people watching them, drawn by the spectacle. As they passed the lake, the cold water erupted with the take-off of ducks and geese. Seagulls circled.

Hamish heard Ron over his head. *You're in a hurry. Very demanding today.*

Nearly crying, Hamish said, *Of course I'm in a hurry.*

Ron glided lower. *Still with that one. She yours yet?*

Yes!

Thought so.

Leave me alone!

Ron laughed. *I'll see you there.* And he flapped up into the open sky with three or four other crows, and headed southeast.

As they got on the subway, Lilly said quietly, "Our world is very strange."

Hamish could see tears on her cheeks, which he reached to wipe away. He nodded, not knowing what to say.

Out the window all the way to Brighton Beach they could see hundreds of birds following the train. Lilly caught a glimpse of the Benji-dog running on the streets, keeping the train in sight, its tongue small and pink and hanging out the side. She expected him to die of exhaustion.

When they got out of the train at Brighton Beach, the air was electric. Each movement inside their jackets generated little bursts of static. It was much colder than it had been in the park. A moist, brittle wind blew towards the ocean. The roof of the open elevated subway platform was covered with seagulls, their white feathers being blown every which way.

Hamish saw them and whispered, "Oh, God."

There he is! They lifted off like a million warplanes off a carrier, beginning a spiral above the tracks. *I told you he'd come.*

The dog met them at the bottom of the stairs. His pawprints were bloody, but he didn't seem to notice. *I know where.*

Hamish touched the dog's head. *You are amazing.*

Ron was overhead with his crows. *It's bright, Speaker, it's very very bright. You gotta see this. I gotta see this.*

The dog led the way, trotting a few blocks away from the beach, across Neptune Avenue, and to a small brick house with a white metal awning. Hamish was suddenly aware of the money in his backpack. He found himself thinking of the glowing ash of Mr. Freeborne's dollar bill on the classroom floor. He wondered where his faith had flown off to.

Wow, Speaker! This is fantastic! Ron swept down and landed with a rocking motion on Hamish's shoulder. *This is just fantastic! Are you going to move it?*

"Where are we going?" asked Lilly.

Hamish pointed. Sparrows, buntings, chickadees, starlings, jays, pigeons, crows, green parrots, terns, seagulls covered the little brick house and the trees around it. Lilly could see a faint nimbus on the leaf-covered stairs.

Hamish could see it as Helena.

Ron pushed off Hamish's shoulder. *Do your stuff, Speaker! Oh, this is so good!*

They crossed the street to the house. Helena --- something that once had been Helena --- regarded Hamish. It was the first furious swell of the tide that would repeat at chaotic intervals for the rest of time unless Hamish could respond to its parabolas and storms in just the right way. She was new, so she was not holding tight. But she was grown, so her strength was tremendous.

"I'm sorry," Hamish yelled over the din of birds.

Hamish heard her say, "I want to go home. I don't know where it is."

In a dozen different languages of a dozen different species, Hamish looked up and said, *She must go home. Show her the way to go.*

The dog shouted, *This way, this way!*

The birds lifted off their perches, calling to each other and to Hamish.

Hamish walked backwards, leading the not-Helena on, towards the beach, watching her all the way. He was pulling her as he walked, he one end of the rope, she the other, but she was anchored to the streets and the buildings and the sky so with each step, Hamish felt his own being was disintegrating and he didn't know how he could hold out. He was reciting names under his breath, lists and endless lists of names, full names, each so close to Helena's as to mock perfection, but each a hair's breadth or a leaf's shadow different, recited to bring her on, to entice her, to keep her attention. There was so much coming from her Hamish could barely keep his eyes on her without squinting, like looking into gusts of ash or flame. When he could see her, she looked curious and sad and undone

Lilly could see nothing but chaos, but she walked slowly beside it because company seemed important. She held the strap of the backpack Hamish wore and was able to guide him around little obstacles – a bottle, a curb. Cars stopped for them as though by previous arrangement. People walking saw them and looked elsewhere as though seeing someone unwillingly naked. When they finally got to the damp frigid sand on the shore, Hamish turned and walked directly into the water, hardly feeling the stabbing cold numbness on his legs. A seal bobbed up its head.

Hamish gestured to the east. He looked at back at Helena and Spoke. Her full endless name. She was huge and nothing, like the eye of a cyclone. She was frail and full, like fertile earth. She was power and tenderness, like a mother's love. As she went by him, he heard a whisper, "My sister."

She passed over the ocean, gulls leading and terns in her wake.

The small waves were freezing on Hamish's legs. He felt a warm hand on his arm. Lilly was there, helping him out of the water, onto the land. And the dog was there, too, awaiting the next adventure.

From above, Ron called down, *It's not stuck, Speaker. You got it to move. Amazing. Wow, that was good.* Every bird whirling in the crowded sky seemed to take up the cry, a chorus coming to the finale of the concert.

But it was too late. The money was useless. Hamish's plans and efforts and all he had put everyone through were useless. The god in him was useless. Helena Padar had died anyway, alone and very far from home.

PART 3

DADS

CHAPTER 36

Hamish told me once he had seen a photograph of the "Valley of Death" in the Crimea, where six hundred galloping soldiers of the Light Brigade were mowed down as they attacked guns with their swords and spurs. It was a nearly barren landscape with some cannon balls lying around looking like black pebbles, and a gentle upward slope with a road scratched out. It was unimaginable that the bloody violence of a brief and hopeless battle had taken place in a scene of such inconsequential desolation. It wasn't even, as Tennyson had so urgently described, a proper valley.

That was Hamish's world now.

Uncle Colin had gotten the story out of Samantha after the bank called him. She told him everything, except how Hamish robbed the bank after she couldn't get the money out. That whirlwind of animals was, she said, the strangest thing she'd seen in her life. But she did tell him what the money was supposed to be for.

Everyone was blinded by rage and fear. Uncle Colin and Aunt Cammy shut their door to Hamish and Sarah. David disappeared except to see Samantha away from her home. Mrs. White kept asking questions that no one would answer. Lilly was confined to her house, and Mrs. White wouldn't leave her alone. Sarah was stunned into a kind of silence Hamish had seen in her soon after Henry died, only this silence reeked of betrayal and disappointment. Words stuck in Hamish's throat when Sarah tried to asked him what he could have been thinking. He could only see Kuusk's steady, charming face telling him his mother would die.

Hamish knew there were dozens of behind-the-scenes conversations he wasn't privy to, with Shenouda, with the Whites, with his grandparents, even his counselor at Herman Melville. He heard tears and high voices on the phone. He knew Aunt Shirley was coming, a pitch by his mother to break through his wall. Still no word from Mr. Knox.

Kaphiri called me, also, but I was in Myanmar at the time and couldn't get out. It took me a number of months before I was able to get to America, to my eternal regret. One note of joy came out of it all, that the little dog that followed them to Coney Island came back with them, and was passed onto Kaphiri's household, where he became a favorite of Polly's. They are inseparable.

Hamish felt like he was going to die. Exhaustion crept from his pores, tying him down so it was difficult to even move. He thought he had the flu until he remembered reading in Alicia Markova's journals about after her first time experiencing a Collecting in 1962, how she couldn't even get out of bed. Speaking had been a final blow. He felt like sadness had taken up residence in his bones.

Lilly had called Samantha to tell her the money had been useless. Samantha came and got the backpack from Lilly and, wearing an overcoat and a hat with her hair stuffed up in it, she crammed the money into the bank's overnight deposit slot. The security cameras didn't give a picture of the person who picked up the money out of the swirl of animals and left with it, nor the person who returned it late at night, but between having tracked down the cabbie and Samantha's attempted withdrawal, all the authorities were poised when Uncle Colin called the FBI.

Samantha, I have come to realize, is a planner. Her conversation with her father was calculated to put herself and Hamish in the best possible light. She was clear with him about their motives, clear about the threat and therefore their reasoning behind their secrecy. She and Hamish and Lilly might have gone about it wrong, but they were trying to save a young woman's life, and wasn't that what her parents had raised her to want to do? She did not mention David's participation. He had troubles enough of his own.

When Kuusk's name came out of his daughter Samantha's mouth, and it made Colin Taylor uneasy. He'd served Kuusk's interest in three real estate deals without knowing anything about him and feeling like he was doing the best work of his life. But Kuusk hung on, showing up at events, open houses, even a party at Colin's house once. When Kuusk paid for David's leg, Colin kept the cement feeling in his stomach to himself. But in his interview with the FBI, when they invited him pleasantly to their offices in Manhattan, Colin told them everything he could about Kuusk. He felt he was protecting his family by opening up to the authorities. They would protect him and his. He'd done nothing wrong. His family deserved peace and prosperity.

They grilled Colin about the real estate deals, so that he began to suspect he was a suspect. He gave them all the paperwork without them getting a court order. But they were mostly interested in things not on paper, who he had been with, who he talked to on the phone, getting Colin to wrack his brains to remember even the most subtle things wrong. They seemed to want to know if there was a connection between Hamish and Kuusk. But as he tried to recall, it seemed like he couldn't even remember Kuusk's face, as though the memories of him had a coating on them that made everything slip away.

The FBI had had Kuusk on their radar for a number of years but, like Thaddeus Knox, they had made no moves. Two agents came to visit Hamish and Sarah. They introduced themselves as Special Agent Packer and Special Agent Thomas, a salt and pepper team that dressed exactly the same and were exactly the same height, although Packer, the salt, was portly and probably 45, and Thomas, the pepper, was thin, an ascetic 35.

"Well, son," said Packer, sighing onto the couch and slapping a little notebook on the coffee table in front. "Let's see what you can tell us."

Hamish was silent.

"And there's the little matter of a bank robbery. You happen to know anything about that?"

"Is any money missing?" said Hamish being a smartass.

"Not anymore, now that you mention it," said Packer.

"My son did not rob a bank."

Hamish put a hand on his mother's arm. "If I talk with you, can you protect my mother?"

"Has Mr. Kuusk threatened you? Your mom?" Packer leaned forward.

"I didn't say that," Hamish put on his best lawyer. "I asked if I talk with you, can you protect my mom."

"From what, son?"

Hamish winced at being called "son". "I don't know, traffic accidents, muggings, slipping on the sidewalk, alien invasion—I don't know!"

"We gotta know where this stuff is coming from, kid."

Agent Thomas leaned from where he'd perched on the arm of the sofa. "You working for Kuusk?"

"What?" Hamish was taken aback.

"You get a cut of the money? That what it is? Or maybe you get girls to sign up with him, is that it?" Thomas laughed loud and slapped Packer's shoulder. "You 'member that kid—what was his name?—Jolly!, that's right, Jolly—he was, well, he was probably a year older than you, but he was running girls, had a stable of 5 or 6—you 'member that? Fat ass kid." He laughed in memory, then was suddenly serious. "You helping Kuusk?"

"No!"

"You get a little fuck every once in a while for helping Kuusk?"

"Excuse me!" Sarah interposed herself in between the agents and Hamish. "You can get the hell out of here! Now!"

Thomas squinted at her. "We're not done—"

"Oh, you're done." She pointed at the door.

Thomas still leaned over. "You did, didn't you? Felt great, hunh?"

"No!" Hamish yelled. His vision was contracting, and he knew he had to breathe. He saw a mouse out of the corner of his eye running along the baseboard to behind a planter in the corner. "I was trying to buy Helena."

"Who's Helena, your girlfriend?"

"No! She's a girl Kuusk has—Who works—Who is, who was working for Kuusk."

"Someone you wanted for yourself?"

"This has got to stop!" screamed Sarah.

Silence. Hamish put up his hand.

"It's OK, Mom. It's OK."

"OK," said Packer, adjusting himself on the couch. "So you said this girl was working for Kuusk. Where is she now? Did you buy her?"

Hamish hung his head. "She's dead."

"She's dead?" Packer tried to see Hamish's face by twisting his head parrot-like. "How do you know she's dead?"

Hamish had nothing. "I just know."

"And you were going to buy her."

Hamish looked up, his voice stronger and sadder. "I didn't buy her because she was already dead."

Sarah came to him. "Oh, honey." She looked at the men. "No more. Not until he has a lawyer. No more."

The agents exchanged glances and surrendered. It was odd to Sarah that as Thomas passed Hamish on the way out, he put his hand on Hamish's shoulder and said in a low voice, "Good job."

They could both hear the hum of the refrigerator at the other end of the apartment after the agents left. Quiet traffic noises came from outside, a gurgle erupted through the radiator pipes. They scarcely breathed so as not to interrupt the peace. Sarah then let herself sit next to Hamish and put her arm around him. He was stiff, but he didn't shrug her off. She left her arm there lightly. She reached to brush his hair with her other hand.

"Who was Helena?"

"A whore." It wasn't bitterness in his voice exactly, but loss of faith.

Sarah found herself so shocked by the word she nearly froze. But her hand on her son's hair had a mind of its own, and continued to smooth across his head. She gently urged him on. "What was she like?"

"Oh, I don't know. Like. Like any girl, I suppose."

Sarah tried to smile. "Did she make you laugh?"

"No." Hamish stared straight at the floor, his head moving slightly to the movement of his mother's hand. "She gave me hope."

∞

A couple of days went by when Aunt Shirley arrived in the morning after a nearly twenty-four hours of canceled flights and missed connections. Sarah still wasn't allowing Hamish to go to school, and Aunt Shirley, bleary and wired, took Hamish out for a walk in Prospect Park. She was ten years younger than Sarah, but that day she looked like Hamish's older sister. Her hair was loose and she wore a long dress and strings of beads. She tried to elicit something—anything—from her nephew, but he seemed more interested in staring around at the cold earth. They walked in silence. Hamish was distressed that pigeons and squirrels seemed to brush by him, like passersby on Fifth Avenue.

Even the dogs off leash in the Great Meadow barely gave him the time of day. He could understand them, but they didn't seem to care. Aunt Shirley and he walked up the hill beyond the graveyard, and Hamish realized he was looking for signs of Bagheera. So he closed himself down and said they should go back.

Sarah had already left for the hospital when they got back. The sisters weren't close, in fact they often fought, but they also showed up for the other no matter what. Aunt Shirley made herself some tea and Hamish closed himself in his room. He drew scribbles on a drawing pad that turned into faces and imaginary animals, trees and cityscapes, long roads going nowhere and monsters emerging from darkening lines. He found his box and opened it to look at his father's mute pad. His own handwriting had changed in the past couple of years. He found a page where his father had gotten him to develop a signature, and "Hamish Taylor" was written over and over again, the "y" with a flowing tail, in some the bar of the "H" and the "T" the same stroke through the names. He realized he didn't think of a signature now at all, and whenever he wrote his name, it was just like all his other handwriting, half printed and half awkward curls. He had printed more than used cursive in the mute pad so his father could read it. His father printed because he could sometimes only get one letter out at a time, and his use of words was spare.

Water
How much will you pay me?
$1000000.
Cool. I'll bring your checkbook.
Haha.
You want the water?
IOU.
I suppose it will have to do.

And then a simple drawing of a glass of water that his father had "X-ed" out. Hamish remembered that he had to hold the glass for Henry, water spilling a little out the sides of his dry lips and Hamish saying, "Oops," as he used his own sleeve to catch the dribbles.

Shirley knocked on the door. "Hey, kiddo. You OK? Can I come in?"

"It's OK." Hamish didn't look at her as she slowly opened the bedroom door.

She sat on the end of the bed. "You gonna tell me what's going on?"

Hamish shook his head.

"Because you're afraid of people getting hurt?"

"People will get hurt."

"That puts you in an impossible place, doesn't it?"

Hamish threw himself back on his pillow, but Shirley could see him about to open. She waited.

"You know, it was a stupid idea."

"What?"

"Buying Helena. I don't know how I could have been so stupid. It's not like I've never seen a movie or anything."

Shirley waited more.

"She was something, I don't know what it was—Lilly could tell you, I think she could, yeah. Sandy said she was everything. Just like everything is everything."

Shirley put her hand on Hamish's ankle. "You lost me."

"It sounded good when she said it. 'Destroy a soul, destroy an entire world. Save a life, save a world entire.' Fuck. I fucked up." Hamish's fingers played with the edge of his shirt.

"How do you know? Maybe she's OK."

"I saw it! I saw—It was what was left, no, I mean, you know, like—the spirit, like the shadow. The essence, like if you distill it all down, the whole ocean, into one drop, all of it—That was what she was. Everyone could feel it. They all came. They all followed me. But she didn't know the way, you know, she was lost. And I don't know why, but I know the way—When I'm—when I see it, when she needs it, when they need it—I know and I can tell them the way, just point and Speak the right name and there they go and then they know and they go—they go—They go home."

Shirley could see Hamish's eyes shining.

"That's some heavy shit you got going on, my friend, and I have no idea what you're talking about." She squeezed Hamish's ankle. "But we got to get this guy off your back. Off everyone's back."

"How?" Hamish sat up, asking. "Really: how? Even the FBI has been trying—for years!—and they can't get him. Nothing sticks. Like he's charmed, like he's got witchcraft on his side or something."

"Well," smiled Shirley. "We've got your mom, and we've got me. Right?"

∞

It was one of those broad-daylight muggings, only a couple blocks from the apartment. Two guys took Aunt Shirley's purse and the beads from around her neck that ended up scattered on the sidewalk. One of the first kicks blew out her knee before the men ran off when some pedestrian yelled for help. Hamish met his mom after she called him from Methodist Hospital a few blocks away. Entering the hospital room was like going through a hostile force field. Shirley's cheeks were covered in sidewalk burns and her encased leg was hanging out of the covers. It was whisper quiet, just hissings and very small, very regular beeps.

Sarah got up and hugged Hamish. "She's going to be OK."

Aunt Shirley turned towards him. The eyelid Hamish could see was swollen like an over-ripe peach whose peel had been smushed.

"Hey, boyfriend. It's not as bad as it looks." Shirley managed a smile. "I'll probably fall asleep looking at you. The drugs in this joint are fantastic."

Hamish touched Shirley's hand, and turned to his mother. "What am I going to do, Mom? What am I supposed to do?"

He went to leave and ran into a man in a rumpled suit.

"Hey! Sorry! We just came to see if she was awake." The man pulled a badge out of his pocket.

Hamish heard the "we" and looked towards the door. As though on cue, the detective who had forced Hamish and Lilly into his car came in, smiling. He even winked at Hamish, wickedly confident in Hamish's discretion.

The first detective looked over Sarah's head. "No change, hunh?"

"Did you find the men?" Sarah's anxiety was physical.

"You are—?"

"Her sister. Did you find the men?"

"That's a pair of sisters I'd like to know," he turned to Hamish's detective and laughed at his own cuteness.

"Did you find them!"

"Sorry, lady," giggling and turning back. "No, but we got someone who described them, two black guys, maybe early 20s, one with a green parka. We're looking around the neighborhood."

"Great." Her sarcasm got her past the men as she prepared to leave with Hamish.

Hamish's detective said in an oddly querulous voice, "That description bring anyone to mind?"

"You just described half the men in Brooklyn."

Hamish wouldn't leave his aunt alone with those policemen.

∞

Saba Weg, Hamish's grandfather, arrived at the apartment from Florida while Packer and Thomas from the FBI were back with more questions. The introductions were brief. Sarah and her father hadn't even embraced before Saba Weg launched into them with what the hell were they thinking, why hadn't they locked this guy Kuusk up, what are they going to do to keep his family safe—although it was a little late for that now, wasn't it?—get out there and do something! He looked like an old Doberman spoiling for a fight.

He turned to Sarah. "Take me to her, OK?"

"Yeah," said Sarah.

"We're not done," said Thomas, playing the rough cop again.

"Come on, Hamish," said Sarah, "get a coat. We're going to see Shirley."

"Mrs. Taylor!" Agent Packer leaned back in the couch as though he intended to watch a football game on TV. "Look at it from our perspective for a second. Do me the favor, for a second. You got this guy, Heigo Kuusk, really bad apple stuff, organized, lots of connections, his own band of operators, his own protection racket, into smuggling, real estate fraud, extortion and almost as a side line this prostitution thing—little girls. It's pretty good money, but nowhere near the money he gets from his other operations. He gets these girls, like really young, barely into puberty—I don't know how he does it. He brings them to this country somehow. And then there's no streetwalker stuff. This is fancy hotels, rented apartments—classy. But we can't find him even when we've found him, we can't make anything stick to him because he's got a talent for making people very afraid." Agent Packer then beamed at Hamish. "And then we got this boy. A person who's had real conversations with him, who's got some real good information on him locked somewhere in his noggin, right there." He tapped the air as if tapping Hamish's head. "We just need his help—your help—before this Heigo Kuusk character leaves the country."

Saba Weg said, "You haven't even arrested him yet? After what he did to my daughter?"

"See, that's the thing," shrugged Packer. "There's nothing to connect him. And we can't find him. He's smoke."

"He's going to end up back in Estonia, or in Russia, Hamish," said Agent Thomas, looking at him evenly. "Is that what you want?"

Hamish got to his feet. "We gotta go."

"The thing is," said Thomas, "I just can't get over all this animal stuff. I mean, people are saying some pretty out-there things that happened at the bank. And the security footage—" he whistled "—I've never seen so many animals in one place. Can't see anything else. What's up with that, kid?"

Bitterness erupted. "Figure it out."

Sarah pulled him. "Come on, get your coat."

CHAPTER 37

Besides school, chess was the only place Hamish was allowed to go. Sarah would drop him off only if she knew Shenouda was there. Sometimes instead of chess, Sarah brought Hamish to her hospital with her and sat him in the lounge on whatever floor she was working on. He would fall asleep on the vinyl sofa, drool lubricating his cheek in ways that woke him.

Shenouda was quiet with Hamish, playing games that matched both Hamish's skill and mood. On the second day, he asked, "You did your best to save her, yes?"

"Who?" Hamish didn't look up from the board.

"Helena. The one who died."

Hamish moved a piece. Shenouda shook his head and moved it back because it was a lousy move.

"I was an asshole. I should have just left it alone." He moved another piece, not caring. "She'd be like alive if I'd just left it alone."

"The Qur'an reminds us that we cannot not act in the way of Allah. But it is our intention that brings us in alignment with Him. He knows the movement of our hearts, always. I think your heart is good, Hamish Taylor. And you are part of the good that is written."

Madonna screamed from her cage.

"What is she saying?" Shenouda had been holding onto his curiosity.

Hamish laughed a bit, glad at least she was trying to get his attention. "She's got a filthy mouth. She just wants to be let out so she can lecture me."

Shenouda was enthusiastic. "Of course she does! Let her out! Translate for me!"

So Hamish did. As she climbed up on top of the cage, she said, *So what is that old butt mite trying to make you do? He's been puking purple crap at you all day.*

"I don't think I should tell you, I mean, it's hard to—"

"What is she saying?" demanded Shenouda.

"OK, she called you a bad name and wants to know if you're making me do something I don't want."

Hey! she squawked. *You're done with him!*

He helps me.

More than I do, you shit squirt?

No one could possibly help me more than you do, you blue turd with a wimpy beak and a voice like a dying fish.

Yahooo! You're learning, beetle bait. You're Speaking a lot these days.

What do you know?

I hear things. The green parrots chatter.

You can understand them?

Of course! What do you think, I'm an idiot? Some big thing in the east, everyone came. It's going to happen again, right?

Hamish was taken off guard. *I don't know.*

You should know, you're the fucking Speaker.

"I must ask," interceded Shenouda. "What is she saying?"

Tell that ball of grease to stuff his limbs in his mouth and eat them!

Shush a moment!

Hamish turned to Shenouda. "She seems to think there will be something that will, I don't know, like—uh, like be like when it happened with Helena. Like Speaking with Helena. But she could be full of shit. I mean I can barely carry on a conversation, much less stuff like that. It's like Alicia told me, that Collecting took it out of me."

"Ah," Shenouda contemplated the tale Hamish had told him, out of some book of spirits or Arabian nights. "And how does Madonna know this—this thing?"

"They sense something, I don't know, like vibrations or energy fields, like when a volcano's about to erupt, a lot of the animals know something big is about to happen."

"And you are the volcano?" Shenouda's huge eyebrows met in a querying frown.

"I guess so."

The door to the shop tinkled, and in came Thaddeus Knox, bringing with him a waft of cold air. He had on his duster, as usual, his hat, but he was walking with a cane, polished ebony and curved into his right hand.

Shenouda spread his arms. "Thaddeus! What an unexpected pleasure." He spilled a chair in his haste to embrace his friend. Mr. Knox held him close for a long moment. Kaphiri Shenouda then stood him at arm's length. "Ah, the leg. The pain is lessened?"

Mr. Knox nodded, and then turned to Hamish.

Hamish attacked him.

It was a kind of fury he'd never known before, and never knew he had. It overcame his exhaustion like an explosion. His tunnel vision was sudden, his heart swelled and his lungs filled. Then from his groin and his throat a surge of electricity wove out and through his arms and hands, and he crashed onto Knox's chest, hammering and hammering. He was screaming at him. It all seemed to splash away from Knox, like milk. Hamish was screaming, "Where were you? Where the hell were you? We needed you, we needed you fucking here. Where the hell did you go that was so fucking important? Helena died. She died. You weren't there and she died. And my mother's sister, you fucking—My mother's only sister, she may never ever be all right, because—Fuck! I should get inside there and squeeze your fucking heart, just reach in—stop your lungs!"

Knox's chest absorbed the violence, which even Shenouda off to the side could feel as pain inflicted from some source that he couldn't place, like a stab from inside the breast bone. But nothing penetrated Knox; he was an inert substance. Madonna shrieked and shrieked, waving her wings so much she nearly lifted the cage.

Stop, Speaker! Stop! Stop! Stop! You're hurting. You're hurting everything! Stop it. Speaker!

Hamish stopped, mid-breath. Exhaling a sob, he fell forward onto Thaddeus Knox, who held him tight and close. He soon lowered him into a chair, handing him a perfectly white handkerchief.

Shit, Speaker. Madonna wiped her beak on the cage. *You are one scary animal.*

"Where the fuck were you?" Hamish blew his nose.

"Iraq."

"How was the war?"

"Not so good."

"How'd you get hurt?"

"Shot." Knox rubbed his face, saying philosophically as though quoting, "Spring is the time for battles, after the winter retreats."

That quieted Hamish. He wiped his nose more. He had no ideas; his mind was blank as paper.

Speaker, you going crazy?

"Shut up, Madonna," Hamish said.

"Is she being rude?" inquired Shenouda as he handed both Hamish and Knox cups of water.

"No, she's just being—nothing." Hamish made sure she was attentive. *I must talk with these men.*

OK, Speaker, no problem. Madonna made as much clattering sound as she could as she leveraged herself back into the cage and cracked sunflower seeds.

"Thank you for looking after Underhut," said Knox. "Sandy tells me nothing was ever wanted, and about everything that happened with Iskander Aria."

"You're welcome." Hamish wanted no debts.

"You'll be glad to know he's back in Iran."

"It's where he wanted to be. With his family." Hamish commented.

"The people for whom Kuusk is a soldier, they are the ones who wanted him found."

Hamish laughed. "Are they the ones who shot you, too?"

Mr. Knox sat, glad to be off his leg. "Yes. And so. This was them."

"Hamish, my dear boy," said Kaphiri Shenouda, folding his hands on his chest. "What you have just done, what you did here, directed at your friend, Thaddeus Knox, that was what we call The Arrest, was it not?"

Hamish looked at him, already realizing what he was going to say. He nodded.

"And that Arrest was not in your control, am I correct? What I mean to say is, it was not something you chose to summon, rather something that came upon you. Yes?"

Again Hamish nodded.

"And I'm sure you could feel it, that it did not effect Thaddeus in the way you felt it should, that it was more – how shall I say? – splashing against him and falling away. Is it not so?"

"Yes."

"Yes," affirmed Shenouda. "And that is because of Thaddeus' skills as a Witness, did you know? He can choose not to be affected."

"I didn't know," said Hamish.

"Yes," continued Shenouda, "but if he hadn't been a Witness—and this is the part that is important to comprehend—Thaddeus Knox would this minute in this place be dead. You would have killed him."

Hamish felt thunder in his ears. "Killed him?"

"Yes. His heart would have stopped—it would have arrested—because the power you bring to this is uncommonly strong." Shenouda squatted in front of Hamish to look up in his face. "The destruction you can bring is a phenomenon. So when you feel this rise in you, you must look at it well. You must practice what Abraham so kindly calls my 'Shenouda Shit.'"

"Breathe three times."

"Yes, breathe." Shenouda placed his hands on Hamish's shoulders. "You will do that?"

"I will do that," said Hamish. He meant it.

"Now," commanded Shenouda.

Hamish looked at him to check if he was serious. He was. They both breathed in slowly and deeply looking at each other until there was no more room, and then let the air out easily, completely. They did it again. And then a third time.

The air was clear.

Hamish turned to Mr. Knox. "I'm sorry," he said. "I don't feel so good."

Mr. Knox bowed. "We both have apologies to make. I have been unsuccessful in my venture to stop the people for whom Heigo Kuusk is a kind of sergeant at arms, and therefore have been unsuccessful at stopping Kuusk's enterprises."

"We have been unsuccessful," chimed Mr. Shenouda, generously.

Mr. Knox nodded. "We have. And now we are at a juncture where some advocate punishment and retribution—Mr. Adams is in that camp.

And some are suggesting we have a chance, suddenly and with surprise, at a whole array of victories if we practice a peculiar patience. This is very much because of you."

"Me?"

"Hamish, my dear," spoke Kaphiri Shenouda amiably, "you and I have talked about Speakers and what they can do—especially in times gone by. And we've talked about how busy Speakers are around the world— Iskander is a supreme example, as is Nadine, the Speaker who helped Thaddeus here out of Afghanistan. But something they had is time. They had the time to grow. Look at me."

Hamish did. Shenouda's smile was captivating.

"We have talked – have we not?—about your wish to be taller."

"Oh," scoffed Hamish.

"You will be, you certainly will. However, nothing but time will allow that process to unfold. You may eat and exercise and stretch to your heart's content, but still only time will deliver tallness. Only with time will you grow."

"You want me to back off Kuusk." Hamish was bitter.

"You have to give your talents a chance to come into ripeness. It is like a singing voice, like muscles, like wisdom, like sex. They all take an annoying amount of time." Shenouda chuckled. "I'm still working on some myself."

Hamish was not going to fall for his humor.

Mr. Knox reached out for help from Shenouda to rise from his chair. "Hamish, there are a number of people all over the world working to end the scourge of Heigo Kuusk. Give them a chance to do their work. Mr. Smith, on the other side of the world, thinks that with the connections that have come to light between Heigo Kuusk and some members of your family, your family is safe. You can take some comfort in that. Mr. Smith is rarely wrong about these things. We will be asking for your help. Wait." Mr. Knox was unsteady on his feet. He leaned heavily on his cane. "I am tired. Please wait."

Strangely, he leaned to kiss Hamish's cheek. At first Hamish pulled back, but then he realized what this was.

"Go home," said Mr. Shenouda. "I will see you the day after tomorrow. We have class."

On his way home, Hamish was able to find a crow who got interested in him. He started him, and every crow in New York, on a quest to find the white-haired man.

I only wish he'd not been quite so young or quite so strong. I wish what he did hadn't led to me entering his story the way I had to. I wish he hadn't had to visit death quite so much in that first year of being a Speaker.

Hamish finally thought of the CD that Helena had given him.

∞

After a week in Methodist Hospital, Aunt Shirley was able to hobble on crutches. Saba Weg rented them an apartment off Craigslist for a couple of weeks. Hamish was on his way to visit them when he saw Samantha coming up 9th Street towards him. Hamish just stood still, wondering what the hell his cousin could possibly want with him.

Samantha's breath was a wisp of steam as she stopped in front of Hamish and sighed, looking around as though she'd just had a thought. "We got to come up with a plan."

"What the hell are you talking about?" Hamish was annoyed past caring.

Samantha looked at him. "Everyone you know and love is in danger. Everyone I know and love is in danger. The people who should do something can't. So it's on us. I think you've been doing this by yourself for a while. Lilly some, but mostly you. Now you're not by yourself."

Hamish could already feel the thrill of relaxing into action, like a runner starting a serious race.

"OK," said Hamish.

"You're going to tell me everything." Not a question.

"You going to tell your dad?" retorted Hamish.

"The only person I'll tell is David, if we need him."

"What do you want to do?" Hamish looked at her reddish hair, and her faced slightly puffed with cold. He saw lines already beside her young eyes.

"I want us to stop Kuusk from ever bothering or threatening any of us ever again. Or anyone. Good enough for you?" She dared him.

Hamish realized for the first time how grateful he was to have a cousin. "Good enough. Then I have to show you something."

Hamish showed Samantha the CD with the photos. Hamish didn't feel embarrassment as they looked through a few of the stark images of naked girls and pudgy men. He could feel rage build in Samantha until she said that she'd seen enough. They still couldn't get into the spreadsheets, but Samantha said this was something David could handle. They copied the CD, and Samantha took it away like it was a nuclear key.

CHAPTER 38

The time between Thanksgiving and Christmas always seemed absurd to Hamish, full of useless attention grabbers and vacant anticipation, tests that were rushed and parties that other people seemed to be involved in, school projects that had been procrastinated and the intention of planning without actually doing it, the anxiety of cold coming and the retreat of the sun. And now it was dangerous.

He kept on thinking about Alicia Markova telling him he was dangerous, but that was OK. When Kaphiri Shenouda told him she had finally succumbed to pneumonia, Hamish wasn't surprised. She was, after all, 94. The loss he felt was akin to losing the right to visit a country he loved ever again.

Hamish talked with Lilly almost every day, but never anything of substance on the phone because they were convinced their phones were tapped. Twice as they walked on 7th Avenue in Park Slope to find a coffee shop to sit in together, they knew they were being followed. Once it was a man in a navy parka who had a curly wire coming down from his ear to under his collar. Lilly noticed him as she glanced across the street at Union. Another time it was a twitchy man with gloves and a sports coat over a thick sweater. They decided the first was FBI, the second was Kuusk's. Both times Hamish tried to get birds to swarm them, but the birds wouldn't listen, or would get bored before they even started. The length of time it took to cure his depletion from the Collecting and then Speaking was disturbing.

After a late November snow, blue jays invaded and Hamish learned they were the lovely, petty thugs of the park. If there were such a thing as waiting lines, they would butt to the front. If it were a restaurant, they would steal the tips. If a baby were to be left unattended, they would do their best to eat it. Squirrels, bats, feral cats, even raccoons were busy or sleeping. It was a spooky kind of vanishing. Any life in the park that was in evidence was singular, a spot speeding across the vacant grass or through bare trees. Hamish was mystified that Bagheera had escaped detection all these winters.

At school kids talked about their Christmas plans. Hamish learned to keep his mouth shut that he was going to visit his grandparents in Florida. Other kids didn't want to know he was getting out of the cold and dark prison of New York. He told Lilly, and she sighed in exasperation.

"Everyone's going. We just got my aunt and uncle coming up from Atlanta. The house is going to be like a hotel."

Hamish reached in his pocket and took out a small wrapped box. "This is for you."

Lilly was embarrassed. "I didn't get you anything!"

"That's OK."

"Should I open it?"

"Sure."

Lilly slipped the ribbon off and tore the paper. In the box, lying on white cotton, was a little silver pendant with an opal. Hamish had scrounged and saved and gone to The Clay Pot on 7th Avenue, determined to get the prettiest thing he could afford. The girl at the counter smilingly pointed him to this, and it seemed at the time wonderful. Now as he looked at her looking at it, he thought it small and pathetic. But then he saw her face change, and she turned to him, lunging into a tight hug.

"It's awesome. Awesome."

She gave it to him to put on her neck, and he leaned close to fasten the clasp. She smelled like open fields, like sun. He kissed the back of her neck. She turned her lips into his, and her warmth melted his heart.

∞

On Hamish's way home, Fallon stepped out onto the sidewalk nearby the park. Hamish felt his vision collapse in from the sides. Fallon was dressed neatly, as always, shoes polished within an inch of their lives and his leather jacket supple and dark as silk. His fedora was the branding of his vanity. He beckoned Hamish to him. There were two other men in polyester, one approaching from the street, and one from behind Hamish. The low wall bordering the park was on his right. Hamish stood still.

"Hamish. That's a faggot name. Your mother hate you?" In three strides Fallon was within touching distance. Hamish could smell aftershave and ashtrays. "But you got balls, don't you kid? I tell you to do something and you just don't do it. That takes balls." Fallon laughed and ruffled Hamish's hair, ending with a punctuating cuff to his cheek. "Or maybe you're just stupid." He peered at him. "You stupid?" Fallon clamped Hamish's upper arm. "We're walking." He lifted one side of Hamish, steering him onto the pathway into the park, then up the berm in between trees.

Hamish was racing inside. The phrase "don't get in the car, don't get in the car" sped through his head, repeating and repeating. He chuckled. There was no car.

"What you laughing about, faggot?" He slapped the back of Hamish's head.

"Nothing," mumbled Hamish.

"Listen," said Fallon, sounding reasonable. "My friend's disappointed. You know him? You know him. He's so disappointed. You playing detective, hunh? You sure you not playing detective? Wants you dead. Well, not dead. But to stop. Shut up and stop. For all time. You know silence? What it is? Really truly is? I can teach you."

The fear was new. Felt like foam. Sharp foam growing. Closing off ears. Darkness around eyes. Throat deeply clogged. Numbing of knees. Where's my voice?

Seagulls are uninterested. Too far away. Dog walking along. He's already gone. Any pigeons around?

Fallon's knife was out. It was oddly short. Like a tooth.

Not even cats. Or rats. Hamish could usually see them watching.

"An ancient technique. Kind of messy. But very effective. Tongues are surprising. How they bleed." Fallon smiled quietly. "I can fuck you up."

More dark, coming from where? The darkness became a pinhole. Everything Iskander had told him made sense. Hamish felt like someone had thrown a switch, like he was both hammer and anvil, and the slam of metal on metal sent a wave out in all directions. The wind was knocked out of him from inside, and he gasped in air.

"Ow! Shit!" Fallon touched his own chest. "What the hell was that?"

Hamish more sensed than saw rats and squirrels and chipmunks running over the ground, around trees, to claim pieces of Fallon's legs. Sparrows, chickadees, woodpeckers, blue jays, wrens, even the red flash of cardinals clustered in the air around Fallon and the two men, spinning them, the men's arms swatting chunks of breeze like falling off the last stair. Above crows flapped, and above them glided gulls.

"What the fuck!" yelled Fallon. "Where are you, you little shit!"

Hamish was running. He crossed the wide street, a car slamming on its brakes and leaning on the horn, as Hamish ran downhill towards 7th Avenue where people would be. His lungs hurt, and he tried to not go in a straight line to throw them off. There was a hardware store. There would be men in there. If he screamed for help, they would help. He could hide behind a row of tools, he could be about to buy something. The door tinkled. The air was new and useful smelling, the fluorescent light bright and unstartling. He walked to the back and pretended to look at paint.

But it had worked.

CHAPTER 39

On the airplane down to Florida for Christmas vacation, Hamish had to sit by himself. The flight was crowded and Sarah had waited too long to get the tickets. He was in an aisle seat towards the back of the plane, sitting next to a very tall man who, when he fell asleep, let his elbow fall into Hamish's side, his slight snore punctuating the engine's drone. The line for the bathrooms brushed Hamish's shoulder every time it progressed, people's bodies looming. As one person came out and back up the aisle, he lurched and fell, catching his fall on Hamish's armrest and tray table. The man smiled an apology, and Hamish grinned forgiveness. The man patted Hamish's head strangely and walked up the aisle. Then Hamish saw them – two photographs – in his lap.

One was his grandparents' house in Cape Canaveral. In almost child-like lines on the photo, someone had drawn a fire consuming the house.

In the other was Helena, smiling and young, her arm draped lovingly over the shoulder of a younger girl about Polly's age. The girl was skinny, wearing shorts, her hand rising as though about to say hello to the photographer.

Someone had scraped out her eyes in the photo so they were only white paper spots. Written in black Sharpie across the bottom was: "Shhh."

Hamish felt a fear for Helena's younger sister that paralyzed the back of his throat. He looked around for help, to see the man who fell. But there was nothing.

∞

The Christmas vacation in Florida started badly. Aunt Shirley wanted to burn the Christmas tree. She said Jews should never uphold killer traditions. Bubbe and Saba Weg looked weary. Aunt Shirley, still in her cast, edged into confrontations with Sarah like they were girls again. Hamish wanted to retreat. He would go on walks on the beach, but was sure he was being followed. He got some seagulls to ward off a man Hamish thought was carrying a rifle, but he was simply a beachcomber with an old metal detector sweeping the sand. Hamish talked Shirley into taking him up to Merritt Island to go kayaking. The others said Shirley shouldn't go because of the cast, but she loved the idea.

Hamish strapped the kayaks that were in the garage to the top of the car—proudly and defiantly remembering all the knots that held his father's canoe up to Maine—and they drove north on I-95 up to Indian River, adjacent to the Kennedy Space Center. Hamish could see a couple of the towers in the distance.

Shirley had a plastic bag for her foot. They scooted into their seats, and scooped the water back with the paddles, wavelets making baby slaps on the fiberglass. It was a perfect if hot day, not quite eighty degrees, only a small breeze, and clouds tumbling overhead to block the sun when it got too strong on the back of their necks.

Hamish felt strong and grownup being on the water with his aunt. They headed north, their arms filled with the generosity of gliding speed. Their hips rocked with the dip and pull of the paddle. Hamish could hear the urgency of gulls over the water, but couldn't make out their destinations or purpose. It was a relief to be away from the chatter of life, on the silky quiet of the lagoon.

Shirley called to Hamish, "What's up between you and your mom?"

"Nothing," Hamish called back. "What do you mean?"

Shirley paddled up so they were even. "She doesn't know who you are these days."

"So?"

"I'm just thinking about stuff you said back at Thanksgiving, when all that shit went down. Before I got mugged."

Hamish stopped paddling and glided. "Aunt Lee-Lee, I am so sorry about that."

"Hey, not your fault. I just—"

With a thump and the sharp clatter of nails on the deck of the kayak, a gull landed, waving her wings to keep her balance, her pinions just whipping by Hamish's face.

Hey, you want to come help? Really fresh. You just need to get the others away, maybe help it die. We'll let you have first dibs.

Hamish had nearly jumped out of his skin, thinking Kuusk's minions were attacking him, and he desperately tried to play it cool. *How the hell did you find me?*

"Whoa!" yelled Shirley. "You OK?"

The seagull screamed in Hamish's face. *Now! Come on!*

She pushed off into the air, rocking the boat, and Hamish watched her trajectory. She went west, and there was a cluster of birds above some small froth in the water.

"Let's check it out," said Hamish, turning his boat.

It took them almost five minutes to get to the birds. There were a couple of humps in the water, and some splashes that sent the gulls and terns into the air, like a large rock being thrown from underneath. Shirley realized what they were. "It's manatees!"

As Hamish approached the froth, he could see the shapes of a few manatees under the white in the green clarity of the water. They were fat cigars or small blimps bending underwater, their large tails fanning them into close circles surrounding a young calf that had gashes on its back. He had clearly been sliced by the rotors of a boat's motor. The gulls and the terns were hoping for a quick death, and screamed at Hamish to hasten the process.

Hamish's kayak bumped a manatee. She turned to look at Hamish, her eyes small on either side of her long, sad face and her whiskers. Even at that distance and through that water, Hamish saw the change in her eyes. She flipped her tail and charged his boat. He felt suddenly jolted as though he'd run aground on rock, and the balance tipped too much. He turned over, hearing Shirley crying out to him. The warm water was full of sensation, and he wiggled himself out of the kayak and came up to the surface. Shirley was coming towards him. Hamish felt the manatee glide under him and move him towards the calf. He could feel the manatee speaking.

He's hurt that hurt that breaks and breath is hard, Oh, breathing takes so much effort. No pain, some pain, he'll go away from you, he's a baby, he doesn't know you, but here you are, he might bite, no, he won't, he'll go away, don't let her stop moving, I'll help him keep moving and breathing, you fix the break.

The manatee's communication was a full-body experience, squeals and clicks in the ears, and other sounds as though through the pores.

Shirley cried out in a hiss, "Be as quiet as you can!"

"I'm OK, Shirley, I'm OK."

"No, stay still."

"I'm OK."

The singing started. It was a chorus of the six manatees in a loose circle. Hamish could feel the sound through his skin. It was a message of comfort, a carol without words. The calf struggled less, and let himself be bobbed on the surface by an adult. As Hamish came close, he could see the terrified eye of the baby, and as he turned away, he saw the cuts on his back leaking blood, the skin and flesh opened like a sliced cake. He could see down to the white bone.

Suddenly, the manatees went still. Even the young one, wounded as he was, held himself in place with a slight scooping of his flippers. Hamish knew. There was a crocodile coming.

The lack of movement made Shirley crazy, crazier than the sloshing before.

"Hamish? You OK? What's going on?"

"Aunt Lee-lee," Hamish said, treading water. "This is going to get weird."

"Come on," said Shirley, pushing Hamish's kayak towards him. "Get back in the boat."

"There's something I have to do."

"Just get in the boat."

Hamish felt himself joining the circle around the wounded one, facing the direction of the shore. The water was only about eight feet deep, and clear as a bottle. On the top, about fifty feet away, Hamish could see bumps that were not the ruffling of wind on the surface of the water. The manatees were like a bunch of boom-boxes, each pulse of communication shook the bones.

Move away. Deeper water. Start the circle. Stop him, Speaker. Circle.

"Hamish! Listen to me!"

"Would you please just wait?"

Hamish reached towards the first manatee. He named her Florence, although he couldn't at the moment think of why. With his arms around her as she moved in the circle, he said,

You know this. Hold your child. Keep him clean. Keep him with air.

The manatee's long face and whiskered eyes peered at Hamish. In that moment, between the baby manatee's slashed back, Shirley's panicked concern, and the crocodile's looming presence, Hamish felt for the first time in his life what a completely open heart was.

Is he safe? the manatee asked.

I will talk with the crocodile.

You can do that. It was a remembering, not a question. *We will sing for you.*

Hamish didn't say more. He swam towards Shirley, who was about to break the circle of manatees. He grabbed the point of the kayak and held the rope handle.

Shirley was furious. "Get in the goddam kayak. You're freaking me out."

"Shirley—"

"Get in the boat!"

"There's something I have to do first."

"What the hell are you talking about? Get in the boat now."

Hamish lost patience. "There's a crocodile that might want to eat that child and I've got to tell him he can't. I made a promise. Otherwise, it would be none of my business."

"Ooo, boy," Shirley laughed an angry laugh. "Hamish, come on. Just get in the kayak. It'll be OK."

"Oh, damn," Hamish hung his head towards the water. "Here we go." He looked up, and called to a passing tern.

Can you come down here, please? Near me?

The tern angled sharply and scooped air to plop in the water beside Hamish.

Hey, Speaker. What you need?

"What are you doing?" asked a bewildered Shirley.

Will you give this to that woman? Hamish fished into his trunks pocket and pulled out the set of keys to his grandparents' house.

She's too dumb to get it herself? You can't go to her? The tern looked at Shirley. *She doesn't know where she's going.*

She needs help. Hamish proffered the keys.

Sheesh. OK.

The tern lifted over to Hamish's hand and snatched the keys, holding the ring in his beak. His wings beating rapidly, he jolted over to Shirley and hovered just in front of her head. He dropped the keys in her lap.

That good?

"What the hell—" said Shirley.

Perfect, said Hamish. *Good fishing!*

Good fishing to you, Speaker!

Shirley was frozen, her one hand clutching the keys, the other hand barely keeping hold of the paddle. She stared at Hamish.

"Hamish, talk to me. Tell me what's going on."

"You've got to promise—"

"I can't promise anything until I know what's going on!"

"OK, OK," Hamish tried to speak calmly from the water. "We've only got a minute. I have to talk to that crocodile—you see him over there?" as Hamish pointed behind him, in the direction Shirley was facing. "The manatees are scared he wants to get the wounded baby manatee, and I gave a promise that I would tell him he couldn't."

Shirley laughed. "How can I believe any of this? You know what you're saying?"

"I'm saying I can understand them. And they can understand me. And that's what you have to promise not to tell."

"Look, I don't know how you did that trick, but you've got to get back in the boat. Hamish, are you listening to me?"

Hamish looked away, down into the water. There was a moving stillness he felt in his ankles and calves that affected the beat of his heart.

"I've got to go, Lee-Lee. This is important."

Hamish started swimming breaststroke towards the crocodile, and he knew he was being watched. He knew they'd all been mistaken. This was a female. And she knew who he was. He felt an explosion of contact in his chest and throat.

Speaker!

Here I am.

What is it that brought you here?
I promised the manatees you'd leave them alone.
But what brought you here, now?
I don't understand.
Something brought you here, to life, now.
Oh. I don't know yet. I am trying to find out.

The crocodile was silent, and Hamish thought of Captain Hook's crocodile with a ticking clock, because it felt like she was pondering. He named her Tinkerbelle in that moment.

Come, said the crocodile.

"Hamish!" Aunt Shirley was nearly shrieking with fear.

Careful of the one on top of the water, said Hamish. *She is frightened.*

The crocodile stopped and just floated. *You must come.*

You will let me hold you and you will take me with you?

If you must.

You understand I am not food?

Alright.

Then I will come.

Hamish turned to Shirley. "Here's how it's got to work. I'm going to get a ride with Tinkerbelle—"

"Tinkerbelle?"

"The crocodile. That's what I call her."

"Tinkerbelle?! You crazy little—"

"She's got something she wants me to see, and it will keep her away from the manatees. You follow, or go alongside. But be careful not to spook her. She's very cautious."

"Hamish, just get back in the kayak. Come on."

"Aunt Lee-Lee," said Hamish, near tears that couldn't be seen on his wet face, but calm, "if you're ever going to trust me about anything, trust me about this, now."

He swam out towards the shore and the crocodile. As he approached, he felt her as a wall of stone, like something inert but with spirit, something extremely old but still active in its original purpose. She turned to receive him on her back, where he held her shoulders as her arms relaxed under her, and her long tail and lower half of her body started to undulate back and forth. The rough-smooth hardness and pliability of her skin was foreign, the slickness of algae on her back against his stomach was odd, her silence as they slipped through the water was primordial.

Hamish glanced back to see Aunt Shirley towing Hamish's kayak and following the crocodile's trail.

They approached the beach, which had shrubs and small trees nearly to the water. Hamish rolled off Tinkerbelle and got to his feet. Tinkerbelle rose onto her legs and started her waddle into the plants. Hamish followed, brushing through the branches that cut him and slapped at his skin. He finally surrendered to crawl after the crocodile.

Aunt Shirley grounded the kayak and called, "I can't follow you! Wait!" She indicated her leg cast.

"I'll just be a minute," Hamish called back.

It was a path in the sand, worn by the passage of the crocodile. Under a thicket a kind of bowl was scooped out. Hamish stopped, realizing they had come to the crocodile's nest.

Tinkerbelle curled around the far side of the nest. *They are all dead.*

She scraped at the sand, and Hamish could see eggs and small crocodiles drying in the heat.

They keep coming too early. Again and again. The heat makes them come too early, the cold dark kills them.

Hamish turned to Tinkerbelle. *Why am I here?*

Tinkerbelle looked at him like he was stupid. *You are here. You must fix this.*

Your babies cannot come back to life.

You must make it so the world doesn't kill my next babies.

How?

The world is changing like when the fire started in the sky, and everything was ocean. We went in the water, deep and far. It was lonely. It was death. But you are here. Which means you will help. That's what you do.

Hamish felt ashamed, for no reason he could determine other than the fact that he was a kid who had no idea how to talk to his family, much less save the crocodile from extinction.

How long have you been here? Hamish asked.

I am here. I am. Tinkerbelle seemed slightly bemused, but also baffled at the question, as though it didn't quite make sense.

Hamish made his way back to the water where Aunt Shirley had gone from fury to weeping.

"What is going on?" she whispered as though not to draw attention.

"Her babies are all dead. They all die." Hamish stepped into his kayak. "She wants me to make it so her babies live next time."

"How are you supposed to do that?"

"I don't know. Change the world."

∞

They coasted on the way back. The wind was behind them. They sweat, but the breeze took away weakness. The water seemed cooler than before.

There was no sign of the manatees, or the birds who had been waiting for a meal.

Aunt Shirley broke the silence above the rhythm of their paddle strokes.

"You going to tell me what's going on?"

"OK." Hamish hesitated. "But I don't know where the beginning is."

"Work backwards."

Hamish told Aunt Shirley what the crocodile had said, and what the manatees had said, and what the gulls had wanted from him. He told her about the squirrel falling from the tree, and Ron, and the rat, and the dogs in the park. He told her about Lilly. He told her about being The Speaker.

"So like the Speaker of the House in congress?" joked Shirley.

"No," said Hamish. "It's like being able to say something that needs to be said when it needs to be said in a way those who need to hear it hear it."

"Whoa. Say that again in different words."

Hamish told Shirley about the polar bears and the boy. About his own feelings of being swept into a running current he couldn't understand but knew he had to ride. About tearing through Prospect Park, with hundreds of birds and animals sweeping into his wake. About Lilly coming with him, witnessing it all. About the tornado that was two bears and Juan mixed and caught and pulsing. About calling out to each of them, pulling attention to the direction home.

"You are certainly in the middle of something."

Hamish was silent. He knew he wasn't telling about Helena, or Bagheera, or Mr. Knox, or Kaphiri Shenouda's teachings. He didn't want these things to be taken away from him. They felt like his responsibilities, his children.

"So let me get this straight. You can understand all these animals, and they can understand you if you want them to, and you somehow got this sense you had to go to this place in Brooklyn where years ago a couple of polar bears killed a boy and they were all stuck together and you said the magic words that freed them up, or freed their spirits or whatever up, to move on to where they had to go, like ghosts in a ghost story with a happy ending. And above it all, they seem to know who you are automatically. Is that what you're telling me?"

"Sounds stupid, doesn't it?" said Hamish. He was mistaking bewilderment for sarcasm, and wanted to get away. "But that's just about it."

"And now a crocodile is asking for your help in saving the world?"

"Yeah, you got it. But don't worry about it. It'll be OK. Just—you can't tell mom. She can't know about this yet. Too much has happened." Hamish paddled hard to get ahead and away, a small bow-wave forming which his paddle sliced through with each stroke.

"Hamish, she's got to know. This is important." cried Shirley after him.

They paddled for nearly an hour to get back to the landing. On the way, a dolphin surfaced near Hamish's boat.

Hey, you wanna play?

Hamish ignored him.

I said, you wanna play?

Hamish looked at him. The dolphin's eye opened Hamish's heart, and he couldn't stand it. Tears welled, and Hamish stifled a sob.

Hey, sorry, man. Another time, another time. Smooth waters, kiddo.

And he disappeared under the water.

In the car on I-95, Shirley tried to ask questions, tried to persuade him to tell his mother what was going on. Hamish pled exhaustion, promised answers and pretended to sleep. Hamish determined more and more to let no one know. He would have to be like Batman or Buffy the Vampire Slayer, keeping his true self hidden from a world that couldn't handle it. Even with proof in front of them, people couldn't see a truth they had no faith in. People preferred to live with lies that made them comfortable rather than realities that seemed impossible and made them have to reassess everything. Hamish knew it was like if aliens came, but they were not like anything anyone had ever imagined, not even in the most strange sci-fi fiction, people would not believe it until they had had time to learn a whole new way of thinking, and even then they would have to want to. It was like someone getting stuck in a room, and not trying the door because they didn't understand the concept of a door. It would have to be discovered by accident. So maybe I'm the accident, thought Hamish. Maybe Lilly is the only one who will ever understand the truth.

Hamish told everyone he'd gotten too much sun and was going to bed.

Aunt Shirley knocked on the door and cracked it slowly open.

"Hamish?"

"What."

"Can I show you something?"

"Oh, God." Hamish turned away from the slice of light coming in the door.

"Let me show you one thing, and I'll never mention it again if you don't want."

Hamish sat up. "OK. Show me. What?"

"Come see it on Saba's computer."

"God…" Hamish threw off the sheet and followed Aunt Shirley down the hall to Saba's study. Saba had gotten a huge Dell computer the year before for his "research." He liked to think of himself as still involved in science, since he'd spent his life before retirement as a biologist working mostly for the Department of the Interior in Washington.

Aunt Shirley patted the chair next to her. Hamish sat. Shirley pointed to the computer screen. On it was a map.

"So what?" Hamish was annoyed, feeling like he was being treated like a young student.

"This is Florida about fifty million years ago."

"So?"

"Look. This whole part, where we were today. That was ocean. And here. Look. They think this was where an asteroid hit the earth." She pointed to a part of the Yucatán in Mexico that was outlined in white on the map. "It killed everything. It was one of the mass extinctions, the end of the dinosaurs. It was so hot there is still glass from the impact."

"Why are you telling me this?"

"You remember what you said the crocodile was telling you? The sky was on fire, and this was all ocean?"

"So you believe me now?"

"Wait. Listen to what I'm saying." Shirley lowered her voice. "Some people think the Aborigines in Australia have an ancestral memory of a land bridge between Australia and Borneo that sunk forty thousand years ago. They've somehow kept the memory of that alive, through their stories, or traditions or something. And the crocodile was one of the only dinosaurs to survive the mass extinction, and to remain pretty much they way they were 65 million years ago. What if they remember, somehow, like the Aborigines do? What if Tinkerbelle remembers, and thinks it's happening again?"

Hamish looked at the map on the screen. "And wants me to fix it?"

Shirley touched Hamish's knee. "I don't know. I guess. She wants you to fix it."

Suddenly, Hamish knew. The clarity and the immensity. The long view. A remarkable vision, really, for one so young. And I am beginning to think, only possible in one so young.

∞

That last night the sisters got into a fight. When love is deep and distance is great, sometimes the bridge is aggression. Even Hamish could see that Shirley was desperate to tell Sarah, his mother, about what had happened, but she couldn't find a way to break her promise. She started accusing Sarah of taking cover in a hospital, hiding in other people's problems.

"So you're saving the world again up in New York?"

Sarah's fork stopped in its travels around the plate. "What do you mean, saving the world?"

"You know, you're working with dying children now. I just don't know how you keep from getting overwhelmed by the hopelessness of it all."

"Lee-Lee, what are you talking about?"

"Girls," interjected Bubbe, their mother.

"Mother, I'm interested." Shirley had addressed her mother formally ever since anyone could remember.

"But maybe Sarah wants a vacation from that," said Bubbe, touching Shirley's shoulder with her hand that looked skeletal to Hamish, covered by ropey veins and parchment skin.

"We're her family, Mother. We need to know what she's doing. Just like she needs to know what we're doing."

Sarah placed her hands on the table. "You don't call for a year at a time, you hole up on a plot of land somewhere in the Northwest with a guy your family has never met—"

"We met him," volunteered Bubbe.

Sarah glared. "You pontificate on astro-physics and 'we're all one on the subatomic level' and organic living, and you expect me to tell you intimate details of people you've never met and have no interest in?"

Shirley looked back at her older sister levelly, her smile aggressive. "Yes."

"Girls," said Bubbe wistfully. "We were doing so well, don't you think? Can't we just let our visit end on a good note? For the boy?"

"Mama," said Sarah. "You know she does this because she's still mad."

"I'm not mad," said Shirley.

"Sure you are. You still think I should have left with you when you were sixteen to that crazy place in the Southwest so I could help live in some fantasy in the desert. Or that Mom and Dad didn't give you enough money to do exactly what you wanted before you even got out of high school."

"Oh, you've got it all figured out," Shirley gestured dramatically.

"You want to know what I've been doing? I go spend my nights away from my son to sit in the emergency room with a 16-year-old girl as she has a baby and most of the time she's alone and she's not healthy because they wait for me to sit with the ones with HIV because that's what I do, or they're crazy because someone's been using them and then they've been left, all promises broken, and I sit with them as they do the hardest thing they've ever done in their lives. They have a baby. And then I also leave them." Sarah choked.

"Mom, it's OK," said Hamish rising.

"I also leave them," she continued, almost to herself, "because my journey is with the child, the perfect child, the perfectly damaged child. And they fill rooms, these children. And they grow, and you love them, and one thing after another happens to them, in their brain, in their blood, like cancers that we thought we understood but we don't, really, and Henry is with me every step of the way because he knows cancer, knows it like you know a lover, a really intimate, horrible lover, and he's sorry but he helps me when these children die. And they die. And I can't do anything about that, Lee-Lee." She looked at her sister.

"I'm sorry, sweet—" started Shirley.

"But I can help the ones who are going to live. And let them know—" Sarah looked at Hamish "—I let them know they are loved. We do a good job. We really do. But it's a plague, a huge living chaotic plague. We hide how we treat people, and I come in the back door and help clean up the mess."

Sarah looked around the table, until she got to her mother. "I'm sorry, Mama. I'm sorry, Hamish." She put her hand gently on his jaw as she got up and left the room.

Saba Weg said to Shirley, "You should be proud of your sister."

"I am, Daddy. I am." She followed Sarah.

"Oh, Hamish!" exclaimed Saba. "You never know what's going to happen when family gets together, do you?"

But Hamish was elsewhere. For many people, there is a moment when the parent they thought they knew becomes something else. They become at once diminished and infinite because they become human. Hamish for the first time understood the immensity of his mother's life outside of him. It made him feel guilty for dismissing her. And made him understand his love for her was active, was real.

∞

Saba Weg called Hamish to the phone after everyone it seemed had retreated to their various rooms. It was Samantha.

"Hey, Mishmash. How's Florida?" She sounded extra cheery.

"OK. How's New York?"

"You know, the usual. Just giving you a little holiday phone call, our house to yours. Since you couldn't be here to do anything with us."

"OK." At first Hamish was mystified.

"Oh, David and I went to see that movie. The one you told us about? I can't even remember the name of it, but we stayed for the whole thing, even though it was terrible. Every little bit, terrible. I'm going to have to talk to you about that when you get back."

Hamish got it. "OK. I'm sorry you didn't like it. But I'm glad you saw it."

"Well, I'm going to make you go over it when you get back."

"OK."

"And I'm going to introduce you to other movies. Other kinds of movies." Samantha would not make a great spy, but she was doing fine.

"OK. Everything else OK up there?"

"Easy breezy."

They hung up after a bit. David had somehow broken into the spreadsheet on the CD. The information was dangerous.

There were closed discussions all night that Hamish was not invited to. He decided to go walk along the beach. The sand was warm in the dark, and the hushed sound of waves filling and emptying the night followed him, like the moon follows a speeding car, silhouetting electric wires swooping up and down in long curves beside the road. Otherwise, there was quiet. His paranoia about someone watching was in reprieve. If he turned towards the land, some streetlights glared, or lights clustered around condos hiding elderly inmates. He was too far away to see the towers of the space center, but every time he looked he wished he'd see the flare of a rocket on the top of a column of smoke arcing into the sky and out into space.

A dog was coming along the beach towards him. He was large, a complete mutt, but he had a collar that jingled as he walked. He saw Hamish and huffed.

Hey, Speaker.

Hey, yourself.

The dog trotted on, as though they saw each other every day. But then he stopped, barking back at Hamish.

Hey, I got one for you.

OK.

Chasing your tail can be an act of love. He was giving Hamish a koan.

What—?

Pretty good, hunh?

The dog turned and walked on into the night.

CHAPTER 40

All the way back to Brooklyn, Hamish and his mother didn't talk, except for the courtesies of acquaintances traveling together. Hamish kept thinking how quickly Helena was being forgotten, a tenuous gathering of dust on an unused shelf. Brooklyn, cold as it was, was a relief. His room felt like his room, and his feet guided him places without his having to guess. He ached for Lilly.

School was a comfort. The craziness of the hallways between classes was surrendering to a river, the peace of the hallways while class was in session was pausing on the bank. Watching teachers act as though this thing they were talking about was really important, as though this small drop they were putting in the vast bucket of chaos of life that all these teenagers brought into the building was going to make a difference. Hamish didn't mind seeing that drop as it got diluted until it was unrecognizable, colorless and odorless in the sea of jackets and book-bags, scuffling shoes and hairstyles, pockets and purses and moving lips. He knew it was still there.

Lunch was always with the same people in the same place—Steve and Daniel and a couple other boys from chess, a guy named Frederick from Mr. Freeborne's class—who all gathered in a corner of the library. They whacked each other and made stupid jokes and avoided talking about girls. Hamish paid attention in class, did his homework, volunteered answers, had some good ideas, and a tentative, itchy normalcy descended on his life. Sarah's schedule had ironed out for the new year, and he could depend on seeing her. They ate dinner three evenings a week, ordering pizza on Wednesdays.

Hamish and Lilly met at her place because her father did not like them alone at Hamish's place, where there'd been so much plotting. They kissed on Lilly's bed, wet kisses that felt important and immanent. Their chests wanted to open to the other. They were in some kind of agreement about not having sex, as though they were in a country where that wasn't what people did. For that, you would have to get a passport and travel a long way, and that was a journey neither of them wanted to take on. Touching was fine.

∞

The end of Christmas break also brought the return of Special Agents Packer and Taylor and their questioning. They didn't get anywhere. But the next morning as Hamish walked to the subway, a man caught up with him, gripping Hamish's elbow and walking him faster down the sidewalk. It was the cement-block detective. He smiled, not even looking at Hamish.

"So, kid, I have great confidence in you and your nigger girlfriend, you know? I have great confidence you both know how to keep your mouths shut. I have such great confidence in the two of you that I'm going to let you grow up to have little mixed breed mutts, and continue with your happy little lives, so long as you always remember me. You're going to remember me, right?"

Hamish didn't respond. The detective shook his body with one hand.

"Right?"

"Right."

"Good." He stopped them on the sidewalk and cupped Hamish's face in his hands. "Remember." He patted Hamish's cheek and went back the way he'd come, pulling out a cigarette to smoke.

∞

Mrs. White was accosted on her way home. Her neighborhood had always felt safe, and she walked there all times of day and night. But on this night, a man with an Eastern European accent quietly asked for her purse while preventing her from moving forward on the sidewalk. She handed it to him, sensible to his threat. Then he said, "I won't be asking for your wedding ring. I know how much your family treasures such things."

That night, after the police had gone, Lilly heard her mother telling Lilly's father again how peculiar it had struck her, that this nearly polite purse snatcher had mentioned her family.

Lilly knew why.

∞

Hamish took the train to Queens. It felt like it had been years since he was at his cousins' house, but the ban had been lifted. There were perverse signs of too-early Spring peeking out in the square across the street, and the spreading trees over the sidewalks.

Samantha led him to her room. Drew wanted in, too, but Samantha shooed him away. Hamish challenged him with a puzzle about his guinea pig, that if he put a small carrot in his pocket and snapped his fingers three times, the guinea pig would find it. He told the guinea pig about the game, too.

Samantha had an Apple PowerBook. A grid came up on the screen that was the spreadsheet.

"This is what I figure," said Samantha. "Names," she said, pointing. "Dates. Amounts, I think. And then these numbers: It's code. Not computer code or anything, just '15' means one thing, and '14' means another. And here's the key."

She brought up another small spreadsheet. It was surprisingly simple. Each number had a single word attached to it, like "Services" or "Insurance." One was "Elimination." Attached to some of the entries were half-hidden commentary, mostly with names, as though multiple people were involved.

And there were photograph files, each associated with a name. Samantha opened one of a man about fifty years old naked on top of a Cambodian girl who couldn't have been more than fourteen. She closed the file.

"You OK?"

Hamish nodded his head.

Samantha took the CD out of the computer. "I'll hide this. It will be insurance."

"Against what?"

"We're going to lure him out. With this. And when he comes to get it, we'll have the FBI waiting." Samantha smiled as though she were reciting a favorite recipe.

"He would kill us first. Besides, how can we even find him?"

"Oh, I'm sure they can find him."

Hamish listened to Samantha's whole plan. It was simply that she would take the CD to the FBI and offer her and Hamish's services as bait in getting Kuusk out in the open. In exchange for the CD, Kuusk would let their families lives in peace. It sounded pretty sensible. Hamish wasn't going to do any of it.

Before Hamish's father had died, they had watched a documentary together on lions and hyenas. One hyena had been harassing and teasing the pride for weeks, but no lion wasted the energy in more than chasing him a few yards. One day the camera was on the second in command, a lion with a very full and dark mane. The lion raised his head, his eyes lasering in on something across the veldt. Suddenly, he rose, moving so fast his mane flattened. He whizzed by gazelles, zebras, flamingos, buffalo—all whom rose in his wake. He ran faster and faster until he was a blur on the film. And then he slammed into the hyena, snapping its spine as they both rolled. With his jaw around the back of the hyena's neck, he crushed it on the ground. Then he walked away, calmly, as though he'd rid himself of a tick.

Hamish was going to be that lion.

CHAPTER 41

There was no refuge except Lilly's room. Underhut was not his, the park was everyone's, the apartment had been invaded, school was school. Even the library at lunch had become a kind of nerd circus. Bagheera was patient with him, but was not a great conversationalist. When he was over at Steve's or Daniel's, they generally played video games or did homework, but he couldn't talk with them anyway. When Steve turned his computer at them to show naked bodies with fake breasts bouncing, Steve laughing his high-pitched laugh, Hamish found himself telling them he had an appointment elsewhere. He still had a difficult time telling Lilly about the animals he'd become acquainted with, as though he were betraying confidences. He tried telling her about the family drama in Florida, but he felt it wasn't coming out right. The something more he wanted brought loneliness with it.

Thaddeus Knox took Hamish on some walks, telling him war stories to let him see the extent of his network's efforts. They did not involve actually apprehending Kuusk. But since Florida and the beach at Coney Island, Hamish had only two goals in mind. One was only a vague plan that he knew he had to have patience with. The other was a project that would last the rest of his life.

Kaphiri Shenouda did his best to guide Hamish into exploring his talents, but since Hamish was his first new Speaker, he didn't quite understand the intricacies of animal energy. He persuaded Hamish to take him to the Bronx Zoo, to introduce him to a wider range of beast. The subway ride there was longer and more crowded than Hamish's journey in the summer because everyone was covered with layers of clothes, and the cold seemed to slow down the trains in inexplicable ways, wafts of freeze spilling in the pneumatic doors at each station. There were not many people at the zoo, and Hamish detoured Mr. Shenouda around the lions to get to the elephant pavilion.

The cavernous room was cold, and every breath clouded briefly in front of Hamish's face. Mr. Shenouda kept a respectful distance. Pigeons floated around Hamish, one landing on his shoulder unsteadily.

Hey, Speaker. What gives? You traveling? Come to see us? Social call? What'd you bring? I know you got something. He tried to demonstrate his knowledge and prowess by puffing out on Hamish's jacket, but he fell off and landed on the floor. *Whoa! Come on, what you got?*

Hamish threw the seed that was in his pocket around the floor, and a small flood of gray birds came angling clumsily down. Some sparrows also hopped in between them as though the floor was theirs and theirs alone until a person took a step and up they flew to the rafters and outside.

The elephant was watching him with clear expectations.

I brought you something. Hamish reached into his other pocket and broke open a large bag of salted peanuts. He extended a handful.

The elephant snuffled his palm with the end of her trunk, the peanuts disappeared, and she inserted them delicately into her mouth.

More?

Of course.

I'm so glad you remembered.

They spent the next few minutes simply doing peanuts in silence.

Your child? inquired Hamish.

They have him in another place.

Is he well?

He is well. She took another number of nuts. *You are different.*

Yes. Much has happened.

You have a friend.

Happy pushed Hamish aside with her trunk and reached out for Mr. Shenouda to come forward. He raised his eyebrows and did. She ruffled his hair with the end of her trunk and smelled him.

This one you can trust.

Hamish smiled at his teacher. "She says I can trust you."

"Please tell her," said Shenouda, bowing slightly, "it is an honor to hear that."

May I ask a question about what you would do if you were me?

Happy shook her head, both laughter and confusion. *I don't know what you mean.*

I mean, if a bad person hurt one of your children, what would you do? Do you have children?

No! I'm too young.

No you're not.

It's this. Hamish tried to think of what he was trying to ask. *There is a person who killed my friend. That person will hurt my mother and other people if I try to do anything. What would you do if you were me?*

Stop him. I don't understand why this is a question.

He might kill me.

Oh. The elephant considered. *Then you must surprise him and destroy him. Or get everyone and go away. But he must be stopped. You must stop him.*

I don't know how yet.

Happy ruffled his hair with her trunk. It felt clumsy and companionable. *You'll figure it out.*

Great. Hamish thought wearily about everyone's faith in him, and it exhausted him. *So should I go see the lions?*

Why not? Father lion is dead.

Wait. How do you know this?

I know the sounds. You still think elephants don't know things. That we're silly.

No, I—

Don't worry. I think you are silly, too! The elephant lifted Hamish's chin with the delicate tip of her trunk. *I think you know what you are going to do. So do it.*

∞

The lions were inside because of the winter weather. The air was gamey, pungent in the moist cold. Hamish hesitated to go in, and he peeked around to see if they were paying any attention. Shenouda again followed him at a slight distance. The large cubicles were covered with thick plexiglas, so Hamish wondered if he could even understand or make himself understood. There were vents in the white tiled tops and sides. Maybe this would help. Or maybe they wouldn't remember him at all.

As soon as Hamish stepped forward, the old lioness was immediately on her feet, pinning him with her focus.

Hamish looked away. *I submit.*

The old lioness was silent and continued to stare at him. The younger lioness came into the pen and saw him. He was so relieved. He could see scars, but she walked well. She called out a small roar.

Well I'll be damned. It's the mole who thinks he rules the world. She licked her lips as though fantasizing his taste.

The old lioness clearly said, *He submits.*

Does he? Hunh. Can we kill him anyway?

He's not a hyena.

You can't trust him any more than one. The younger lioness was not having it.

Speaker! said the elder. *Why are you here?*

Hamish knew what he had to say. *Merely to honor you and yours.* He still kept his gaze askance.

And you submit?

I do.

Come here.

I am unable to. For this truth, Hamish was immensely relieved.

What are you here to change?

That's what he was here for: To change.

I think I must do as your mate did.

Go then. Make it good.

Yes, mother.

Hamish left without looking back. Kaphiri Shenouda tried in all the ways he knew how to penetrate the mind of the fifteen year old that was Hamish, but Hamish was beginning to settle, like a cat settles before it leaps.

∞

Samantha was waiting for Hamish and Lilly as they came up the stairs from the subway after school, the train's wheels screeching away underground. She looked around her, full of the paranoia that had been Hamish's constant companion for weeks. She steered them into the park, where Hamish had to announce to the residents that he was to be left alone. One starving squirrel who had woken from his winter rest too early screamed that Hamish was hiding food. Hamish threw him some of the bread he now always carried in his jacket.

Samantha got them into a huddle just before they exited the short tunnel onto the great lawn. "The FBI's not going to do anything with us. They were very excited about the CD, but they don't want us involved."

"So it's a total bust," said Hamish with anger.

"I said why aren't you arresting him? And they said they have to find him first, and they said the CD would help. I guess they know the people on it and can start asking them."

"And that gives him a chance to dig a deeper hole. They all just wait until it's perfect, and meanwhile the bad guys are getting away with murder."

Lilly took Hamish's hand.

"I've got some ideas," Hamish let slip.

Samantha played the responsible one. "You going to let us in on it?"

"Sure," Hamish lied. "As soon as it's perfect."

∞

In English, when crows gather, it is appropriately called "a murder of crows." They are a murderous bunch. Like most birds, they haven't got an ounce of sentimentality, but they have more curiosity than any other creature except perhaps dolphins. Crows would fly in to report on Kuusk sightings, arriving in front of Hamish from even Staten Island or Westchester to tell him a white-haired man had gone from here to there.

Ron and his immediate bunch thought they had him. Ron got Hamish to meet them on the roof of Hamish's apartment building because there were too many crows who wanted in on the revelations, who had something to contribute. When Hamish came up the ladder, there were rustling black birds everywhere, clutching antennae, lining wires, hopping up to low walls, latecomers swooping in from the park. Ron was in the center of the roost on the top of the neighbor's exit doorframe, acting as a kind of MC. Members of the flock had been following every man they'd seen with Kuusk, and they'd followed this linking puzzle out to Bay Ridge. He'd already sent scouts out to the most promising locations, and they would be returning within minutes.

What makes you the boss? complained a crow.

You're so dumb you couldn't find a dead horse in a desert, retorted Ron.

He's right! A few laughed.

You clodhopper, I'll show you! hopping into the air a few inches.

Hey, folks, Hamish interrupted.

Everyone began talking at once, explaining how they and they alone knew the secret of Kuusk's disappearance. Then the scouts came back as darkness approached, and all attention turned to their story.

They'd found him, holed up in a house in Bay Ridge overlooking the harbor. Voices cried out they should immediately set out to scare him, and the sound of their wings as they prepared to take off was echoed by the strengthening wind coming in from the west. Hamish tried to convince those impulsive ones to wait.

A couple crows called out, *Everyone should get the hell out of here. Everything's going to stop for a while. It's going to be rough.*

What? asked Hamish, misunderstanding.

That!

Hamish turned to look, and was touched on the face by the first flakes. It began to snow.

∞

It was light at first, and pretty. White sparkles poured out the bottom of every streetlight, angling to the ground, and the edges of everything softened. It was surprising how quickly white filled in the cracks of the darkness. The black became blacker, and the snow in the sky made the night a gray-orange above the blurry trees and buildings. At first it didn't feel all that cold because the snow made it seem like a holiday. But the temperature fell, and Hamish entertained the idea of pulling his hat over his ears before they numbed completely. But fashion won out.

Even in the short while Hamish was out, the snow accumulated. The streets were white, and car tires started making parallel trails. Flakes filled the air, caught briefly by the cones of headlights widening up and down the streets. The sound of cars was a quiet rumble, like someone rolling rocks in a muffled drum, starting as distant echoes, then climaxing and receding in fuzzy red taillights. The smell of cold snow was sharp, hardening the sinuses. The few people who were out held their heads down, nearly bumping into street signs and forgetting to pause at disappearing curbs.

When Hamish got back there was a phone message from Sarah.

"Hamish, darling, look. I'm stuck here. The F train is down, and there are people pouring into the hospital tonight. Everyone's so frustrated. I mean, it's almost Spring, right? They've asked me to stay on, so can you give me a call? Call the nurses station, you know, the number's on the fridge. Let me know everything's OK. I love you. TV dinner's in the freezer, you know. I love you. Make sure you call. OK. Oh! Happy Valentine's Day. OK. Bye bye."

Hamish called and left a message at the nurse's station. On TV there were reporters in red or blue parkas with fake fur lining the hoods, squinting against side-blown snow, telling people how bad it was outside. There were clips of cars' tires whining to get out of drifts, and intersections with street lights and white outs. Schools were announcing closings even the night before, nearly unheard of in New York City. Hamish could see the names of schools crawl across the bottom of the screen. Herman Melville was one of them, and Hamish breathed a sigh of relief.

He was about to call Lilly or Daniel, but he held off. He remembered Bagheera last time he'd seen her. Thin. Slightly vicious. Winter was a difficult time for food.

After he threw away the empty TV dinner tray, he decided to call Daniel. They talked about going sledding in the park the next day and how awesome it was going to be. They talked about making a snow fort with walls seven feet tall and so thick you could walk on top of them. They talked of tunneling under the drifts from fort to fort. They talked of moving to the park for a few days, holed up in igloos disguised to blend into the landscape, and using just one candle to warm the entire space. They talked of the quiet and the cold of the night, and the blinding snows of the arctic and high mountain passes they would cross some day. They hung up full of plans that could never be fulfilled, but somehow knowing that the plan was the important thing here, not the execution.

As he lay in bed, he could hear the winds wiggle the glass in the window frames, and the small thumping made it seem as though the world was a train chugging through time. A dog barked outside.

I'll find you! I'll find you and eat out your eyeballs! Delicious, and chomping chomping your feet, your little tiny feet. Where the hell did you go? Get the hell back here!

Hamish sat up and went to the window in the living room. Snow was coming down at an angle, ghosting everything. Light diffused into darkness. The street was a runway of white into gray with no traffic. Parked cars were even now disappearing under cushions of snow, black punctuation marks at rear-view mirrors and wheel-wells. The park across the street melted into shadow pricked with flakes changing focus under street lamps and under trees.

Hamish saw him across the street, running in an angular circle in the falling snow, biting the air, squatting as though to pee and snapping his jaws at something behind him, running a short distance, jolted by the mis-wired electricity of his brain.

I saw you! You left over there. Don't hit me! I'll kill you, I will, I can do it, I'll rip you apart. Where's supper? Isn't it time yet? Ow! That hurts. You smell like you've been somewhere. Where did you go? Dammit! Leave me alone!

Hamish suddenly knew: this dog is a gift.

He dressed for snowshoeing, his woolen hat now low over his ears. As he left his building, he had to squint to keep the stinging flakes out of his eyes. His cheeks burned cold already. He ducked his head and crossed the street.

He was a mutt who had some German shepherd and Rottweiler in him. He saw Hamish and turned in a circle, growling and whining. He was bigger than Hamish wanted, but he was here. And he was crazy.

I will kill you! Who the hell are you? Get away! Go! I—

No, said Hamish. *You won't kill me.*

The dog's ears went up. *What the—*

You will follow me.

Without looking, Hamish broke ground through drifts towards the center of the park. The dog slunk behind, grumbling about dinner and killing and being alone, but not questioning. Once the dog began to lunge at Hamish. He couldn't help himself. But he had announced it to the night and Hamish turned on him, telling him to quiet down and follow like a good puppy.

They went slowly, down through the gorge and across Nethermead, to get to the bridge over the easement into the lake. Even the water was white and flat. Hamish's feet were beginning to feel the cold, and his lungs felt hard from freezing air. He knew the dog was weaker, his body temperature lowering, his feet covered in packing snow as he walked behind. Everything around was rounded shapes, the only straight lines being the shafts of light from the lamps that marked the walkways.

Hamish led the dog onto the bridge. In the middle of the bridge, Hamish turned to the dog.

This is where we stop.

Dinner?

Yes. Now sit down and wait.

My butt is cold.

Sit!

Hamish leaned over the railing, calling out into the night.

I am here.

They both waited. There were millions of sounds in the quiet and snowy darkness, each miniscule crystalline structure crashing into the ground with something less than absolute silence. The world was soft as a bed of razors. A thousand movements jumped in their peripheral vision, spirits playing hide-and-seek with consciousness, but both he and the dog narrowed their eyes against the stinging.

Bagheera appeared at the far end of the bridge, coming into focus through the snow.

Hamish stayed at the railing.

This is for you.

The dog lifted himself, beginning his rant. But it ended with a squeak as Bagheera hit him like a torpedo. In the snow, the only sound Hamish heard was the crunch and crack of bone breaking as Bagheera bit down on the back of the dog's head. His body was silent as it was whipped to the ground. There was only the slightest quivering as Bagheera held him down, making sure of his death.

She looked up.

Do you need—? She indicated the corpse.

No, said Hamish. *This is your kill. The winter is hard.*

Bagheera licked her mouth. Hamish could not see the blood in the dark.

This is a kindness of you. I will not forget.

Bagheera gripped the dog and started to drag him off the bridge. Hamish watched for only a moment before he realized he was being rude. He turned and broke through the snow the other way.

∞

At home Hamish was in the mood to stir up trouble. He had invaded his mother's pockets way back at Thanksgiving and found the cards the detectives at the hospital had handed her when they visited Shirley after the mugging. One of them had been the detective who worked for Kuusk. Each card looked identical, except for the name, the phone and the email. But Hamish was sure he'd heard the 'good' detective call him Tony. And one of the cards was for Detective Tony Manzini. Hamish recovered the card from its hiding place—a copy of "A Farewell to Arms" on his bookshelf. Hamish found the photo of Tony on the bed with Helena and used his mother's computer to email it to the other detective.

It made him feel dirty and terrific. It was a mistake.

CHAPTER 42

It took me two days to get to Brooklyn after Hamish found the body. The heat wave had hit just after the snow ended, and within a week only small piles of greasy slush were left. Hamish had gone to the Underhut after school not to look for Thaddeus, but to consult with Aesop. He'd unlocked the door to the hut, instantly seen the rug pulled back and the trap door open, and the sole of a shoe at the top of the stairs leading down. The shoe was still on Thaddeus' foot. Hamish knew in the moment he was dead. He went down the stairs and gently eased the man's body to the floor as though he might harm him. The bullet hole in his forehead seemed like makeup, but Hamish could smell it, and knew it as real.

He made his first call to Kaphiri Shenouda, using the cell phone Thaddeus had left with him. Of course Kaphiri called Etan Adams which set into motion a series of communications, including to me in Mumbai. But within fifteen minutes Kaphiri was there at Underhut.

He found Hamish sitting on the floor near Thaddeus' body, as though he didn't want to leave him lonely. Aesop was curled on Hamish's shoulder and Hamish absently stroked Aesop's tail.

"I killed him, Mr. Shenouda. I killed him." His face searched Kaphiri's.

"No."

"As sure as if I pulled the trigger. I sent that photo. How stupid could I be? How stupid? How—?"

Kaphiri lifted the boy and embraced him. He held him a long time.

Sandy came and walked with Hamish slowly through the park towards

Hamish's home. Kaphiri stayed at the Quaker Graveyard to call police, and to keep Hamish anonymous.

"You don't have to babysit me," said Hamish without rancor.

"Oh, honey," sighed Sandy. "I'm not. I need the company, you know, kid? Someone who knows what's going on. You do, and believe me, there aren't many of us. Kaphiri will take care of things, and it's better I ain't there. I'd just start blubbering." He could hear the catch in her voice. She reached into her handbag and pulled out a cigarette, stopping so she could light up. "That's better," she exhaled. "You OK?"

Hamish nodded.

"Well, hell, I'm not," she laughed. "He was a know-it-all old man but I loved him. And now I'm sure that Mr. Smith is going to show up, and he's cranky as shit."

"Who's Mr. Smith?"

"Oh, you'll meet him."

Him is me. I was coming to bury my friend, to find out what had happened to him.

Sandy took another drag. "Your mom home? She know about all this stuff?"

Hamish shook his head.

"You mind if I stay with you a while?"

Hamish shrugged, thinking he must have things to do, but he couldn't think what any of those things were. It was as though his father had died again.

∞

Lilly recognized him from his hat. It was the same hat he'd been wearing as she had watched him bundle Helena into a car in the fall, that he'd worn in the car as it smoothed by her and Hamish, his face white and turning at them. Lilly's house arrest had been lifted after Christmas, but the snow storm had interfered with really stretching her legs. So on this day, as Hamish was approaching the Underhut, Lilly had gotten off the subway a stop early where another friend of hers always got off. She had wanted to walk across the park to clear her head.

The path she'd taken was roughly parallel to Flatbush Avenue and took her by the zoo. The mysterious, nearly physical crescendo within that whirlwind of life that had happened with Hamish at the end of the summer reverberated in her memory, which is where her mind was when Fallon grabbed her upper arm from behind, saying, "Fancy meeting you here!"

Lilly took a breath to scream. Fallon laid a finger on her mouth and said, "A sound and I will snap your neck and no one will find you except the cockroaches." He smiled as a kind of grimace and raised his eyebrows. "Capiche?"

He pulled her along, and the woods on the side of the park swallowed them until Lilly could see nothing of people, only hear cars gunning by on the avenue to the east. When he stopped he leaned her against a tree, putting arms on either side of her and moving in close. She could smell cigarettes and old aftershave and remnants of lunch. He came so close she could feel the sandpaper of his chin on her temple.

"It seems your boyfriend is trying to fuck with us. He needs to get the message," he tilted Lilly's head up with his hand, "and I want you to give it to him."

His smile made her nearly faint.

"But we're going to have some fun first."

He smashed his mouth on hers, and she could suddenly feel his tongue like a huge worm trying to get inside. She twisted her face and hit and hit and hit, gasping that it had worked, pulling in air as he fell away from her.

Her ears cleared into a cacophony of crows.

She could see only ten feet away the black panther that had sunk its claws into Fallon's back to pull him off of her—that's what had worked—and she stayed for a second with her spine against the tree. She could see Fallon trying to turn on the ground, and she could see the panther calmly, with one paw on the side of Fallon's face and the other on his chest, dive down into his neck as though hitting down with her teeth. Fallon's legs came up at weird angles, and Lilly could feel his throat open and his neck crack. The panther looked at her without letting go of the neck of the warmly limp man.

Lilly turned and ran. Crows—dozens and dozens of crows—followed her, as though tag-teaming from tree to tree, and then when she got out of the park even landing on sidewalks and fences and dumpsters in front of her, looking in all directions, calling to each other in a staccato chorus, letting her pass—her lungs sharp and her face streaked with tears—and then jumping in the air with their black jagged wings making puffing sounds again to take on new positions further along her path home.

CHAPTER 43

Sarah took a cab home from the hospital after Mrs. White called to make sure Hamish was alright, and to tell Sarah about the attack on Lilly. Sarah became crazy with fear. Simply imagining Lilly in that situation sent her into a kind of paralysis. She wanted to take away that knowledge from Hamish, wanted to go back to Plains, or perhaps somewhere completely different—New Zealand, maybe. Nursing could take her anywhere. She began to create plans that she would announce to Hamish, and he would come whether he wanted to or not. He was only 15 and had no say in the matter. She was not going to lose him, too.

When she barreled through the door of the apartment, she saw a middle-aged lady sitting on her sofa in a lavender pantsuit and with rhinestones on her glasses watching the local news on TV. Hamish was on the phone, his voice shaky and raised.

"Are you sure?" Sarah heard Hamish say. "Are you sure?"

The lady stood up and stuck out her hand. "Mrs. Taylor? Sandy."

Sarah nodded, letting her hand get taken.

"Boy's been through a lot today."

"What's going on?" said Sarah.

Then Sarah heard her son say into the phone, "I love you." He hung up. He turned to his mother. "Lilly's OK."

Sarah did what she could never imagine herself doing. She took Hamish's shirtfront in her fists and she shook him violently. "What the hell is going on with you? What is happening? What are you doing? What is it that is happening with you?" When she felt Sandy's hands on her shoulders she tried to shake her off, but found herself instead whipping around to look into those strange glasses with those deep moist eyes behind them, and hearing Sandy's voice say, "You're right, something is happening with him, something he's going to tell you about now, because you deserve to know, and he's going to tell you. Hamish?"

He started, "Mom?" He blew out through puffed lips. "Mom, there's stuff going on that you don't know about." Hamish didn't really have a plan for this part. "I've got to, like, tell you."

∞

He told her.

She began by thinking her son had gone crazy, that he was in the middle of a psychotic episode brought on by the stress of his father's death, the attempted rape of his friend, the move to Brooklyn, his aunt's attack, this monster Heigo Kuusk threatening everyone, all cathected in the story he'd created about him having some kind of superpower to help his friend, and he'd somehow persuaded this stranger in the pantsuit to back him up. Talking with animals and secret groups—the perfect setting for a paranoiac with grandiose delusions. She was scared into being calm, as though trying gently to guide Hamish away from a precipice without breaking his concentration.

When he asked her to go outside with him across the street to the park, she went, all her antennae up. The pantsuit followed like a specter. When a crow landed on Hamish's shoulder, she wasn't sure she was seeing correctly, her focus was so strong on her son. When the crow left, a small brown bird took its place for a second before nipping Hamish's ear and flitting off. She followed that one for a moment with her eyes. The squirrel who ran up Hamish's back surprised her. It rubbed its nose on Hamish's neck as though scratching, put its little hands at its mouth, paused looking directly into Sarah's eyes, and scurried down and away. All the time Hamish was talking to her and she wasn't listening, only catching words and phrases like "they don't understand each other, really" and "there's someone you've got to meet, she's the coolest, but she's a little scary."

I liked Sarah tremendously when I met her. Our conversations are among the most interesting and normal I've ever had. She's the first mother of a Speaker who's been important to their education.

"Hamish," she said looking around. "What's going on?"

"Come on," Hamish gestured her across the park to the graveyard. "I have to check on someone. She's been through a lot today."

Inside the fence, she saw and heard her son making strange gestures and sounds. If she hadn't been paying acute attention she wouldn't even know they were coming from him. Then, out from some bushes, she saw a large black animal approach, its shoulders rolling, its green-amber eyes looking around as though there were no cares in this world. She knew it was a panther, but she couldn't get herself to admit it.

"Hamish..."

"Mom," said Hamish as the panther sat next to him and purred deeply as Hamish scratched its head. "This is Bagheera. And I am a Speaker."

As she gazed down into Bagheera's clear eyes, she said, "You'll have to tell me all this again."

And he did.

"Damn," said Sandy, her gravelly voice breaking the air, "this big-ass cat makes me nervous, I gotta admit."

It was difficult for Sarah to look away from the panther, but she glanced at Hamish. "Can I touch her?"

Hamish asked, and then said, "She likes her ears scratched."

So Sarah scratched the ears of a loose black panther in the middle of Prospect Park in the city of Brooklyn, New York, in the 21st century.

∞

Sandy guided Sarah, who was in a kind of shock, away towards the apartment to let Hamish deal with the panther. Hamish wanted to know from Bagheera what had happened with Fallon. When he asked her, she would not tell him, like she wasn't interested in the past and it was a waste of her time and his to try to reconstruct the events of even a few hours ago.

You saved my friend's life. I want to do something for you.

You do for me. Bagheera leaned into his scratching hand. *And she's not your friend. She is yours.* She licked his hand as though cleaning the last dregs of filth from it. *I wish you could smell things.*

Hamish knelt, throwing his arms around her neck and pulling her close. She let him.

CHAPTER 44

Aesop the rat had agreed to help him as Hamish had started on his plan.

It hadn't taken long to get Aesop accustomed to the idea of placing a piece of paper exactly right, given Aesop's expertise with nesting. Finding the right place to put the paper in the house Kuusk was staying in took a combined ingenuity. They bicycled to the house in Bay Ridge, and Hamish waited nearly half an hour for Aesop to come back out. From across the street, Hamish finally saw Aesop running along the building until he got behind a drainpipe. Hamish went along a dead-looking bordering hedge and let him walk onto his hand.

Did you find the room?

I met this great rat, she's a lot of fun. She says Hi, by the way. Knew just where it was, has that smell of tobacco, you know? Burned, ashes. Hard to get in, but she knew a way through the walls, would have taken forever without her. That thing his head goes on? Wow, can you get me one of those? I could get a couple of families in there. Can you get this thing off me now?

Hamish had fashioned a tiny carrier for the paper and it had hunched up towards Aesop's head.

Oh, yeah, of course. Hamish unclipped things. *And the paper? In place? Black marking side up?*

Yeah, yeah. What do you think, I'm a dog?

You are the best rat in the world. Hamish kissed his head, and Aesop took no notice.

Can we get something to eat now?
Yeah, but we've got to move.

∞

Hamish dialed from a payphone.

"Sasha Imports." The same woman's voice from before Christmas.

"Hello," Hamish tried to keep his voice low. "Can you please give Mr. Kuusk a message?"

"Mr. Kuusk is out of the office."

"Just give him this message. Look under his pillow. If he wants the rest of the items, answer this phone in an hour. OK?"

"Sir, I don't understand. Mr. Kuusk is out of the office—"

"Tell him. Answer the phone in an hour." Hamish hung up, breathless. It felt exhilarating.

Under Kuusk's pillow, out in Bay Ridge, Aesop had put a note: Brad Finneman / Sharpovah / 150499 / 19(Elimination) / 10000 / √.

Just one in a long list.

∞

When Kuusk got on the phone, Hamish could feel him working very hard, his powers of manipulation oozing through the phoneline and making Hamish feel sticky and hopeless, even though Kuusk's tone was easy as a warm day.

"Hello, Hamish. Very interesting trick getting into my room like that." He lowered his voice to a cello note, and Hamish felt it trying to get traction on his brain. "Rats. It makes sense, you and rats."

"Good friends to have. Real ones."

"Ooo, you're a tough guy now." Kuusk chuckled. "Your friends in the FBI will be disappointed that I'm not at the phone I'm calling from."

"I don't have any friends in the FBI."

"I hear they visit you often enough." Silence on the phone. "What did you do to my boy?"

"I did nothing," said Hamish. "My friends did."

"I would like to meet these friends of yours." The oily smile in Kuusk's voice felt contaminating.

"No, you wouldn't."

Kuusk waited.

"OK," said Hamish, making his pitch. "You want this back, you have to leave everyone I know, everyone I love, everyone I even come in contact with—you have to leave everybody alone. Like never interfere in their lives, never let anyone else do it or anything like harm them or anything. And this includes Helena's sister and mother."

"Ah, well, you don't know them, do you?" Kuusk was pleasant. "I don't think you've even had contact with them."

"Whatever. They are on the list. OK?"

"You are a very thorough young man. I admire that."

"Do you want this back or not?"

"But you stole from me! How can I bargain with someone who stole from me?"

Hamish had not counted on Kuusk saying no. "I'll just take it to my friends in the FBI."

"You have already taken it to your friends in the FBI."

This threw Hamish. Everything seemed contingent on his having enough bait.

Kuusk paused for drama. "How will it feel to be the last one?"

"What do you mean?"

"After all those who, as you say, you know and love are gone, how will you feel being the last one?" Kuusk laughed shortly. "I was so happy to be rid of that old man with the silly hat."

Despair gave way to anger, and anger morphed into craft, which changed something in Hamish. He felt his heart slow down even though it should have been pumping furiously. His head started to lift, as though raising his neck. His hand opened so that only his palm was pressing on the receiver. His eyes were wide. His voice was high as a baby's begging to be picked up.

"Oh, Mr. Kuusk. Please don't hurt anyone, please. Just come get the CD. Just come and leave us all alone. I'll wait for you at the Gazebo in Prospect Park, the one in Nethermead. No one's ever there. Please, please, Mr. Kuusk. Just come and take it and then we never have to see or hear from each other ever again. OK? OK? I'll be there. I can be there tomorrow. I can be there—I'll skip school. Please Mr. Kuusk, 9:00? Is 9:00 OK? Cause then my mom'll be gone and no one will know what's going on, and I'll be there. OK, Mr. Kuusk?"

"You're a funny boy, for an animal talker."

"I'm begging, now, Mr. Kuusk. Thank you thank you. I'll be there at 9:00. I'll be there."

He hung up. Hamish had seen mothers misdirect hunters from their children by playing the victim. The hunters lost all sense of judgment, and ran after the most tempting and present target. Hamish had the strangest confidence that his broken wing routine had sunk its hooks into Heigo Kuusk. And that Kuusk wanted to kill him himself.

∞

The park. It seemed now to Hamish that everything came back to the park. Olmstead's masterpiece, farms and tenements turned into a playground for anyone who cared to come and play. Trees echoing lost forests and rocks ghosting their mountainous ancestors and even water finding its own level in ponds now full of life and possibility. Spring was in the air almost as music, full and deep. As Hamish came in from the Southwest corner, no horse was there to greet him. He saw early sparrows and tenacious pigeons stir away from him. A dog far away across the baseball fields barked, *Speaker! Speaker! Run from yourself! Run!* His head was clear, and he knew they couldn't see as he could, couldn't know he was the danger and the balm. He knew that at this moment Bagheera was up on the hill in a tree watching his progress. He knew that she would continue to watch, but that he was on his own. She had looked after Lilly—adopted her, which is why Fallon's broken body was left to mystify park personnel and police. But he was on his own. And he was fine with that.

He felt the heat emanate from his body and face as he took the trail over to Nethermead. Surely Heigo Kuusk would not disappoint. He would be there, ready to seduce his way into another life and also be completely prepared to destroy that young life in front of him. Hamish felt the now symbolic CD in his pocket. Hamish knew he was the wild card, the unfinished business, the thing Kuusk couldn't leave without resolving. But Hamish didn't care. He was wildly sure he could obliterate Kuusk from the planet and grind his dust into the mud. He trusted in his own powers. Thousands of animals could tear Kuusk apart.

The grayness of the morning cooled his palms as he came to the entrance of the field at Nethermead. He wiped an itch on his nose, and felt his whole body through that scratch. It suddenly occurred to him: he was going to die. Heigo Kuusk was going to pull out a gun and shoot him without even speaking and walk calmly out of the park. Now he was the deer on the edge of the meadow, leaning out to smell and sense for hunters. His own electricity had warned all sentient creatures away. No one was there.

In the dingy yellow gazebo across the field was that shock of white hair. Why didn't he have a cell phone? Why didn't he just turn and find some way to tell the FBI Kuusk was here? Hamish looked more. Yes, there was a goon sitting on a bench near the oak, another leaning against a lamppost near the bridge over to the Boathouse. A bee passed near his ear and took a sharp left as though it had hit a window in response to Hamish's field. Hamish followed the bee with his eye, this beautiful impossible bee, as she wended her way back to the hive up under the rocks of the roadway bridge. And he knew. They were all girls. It would be right for them to do it.

Walking nearer to the rocks, he saw bees landing like on a crowded aircraft carrier, and hopping for a second before taking off, quickly finding the line and speeding away. Hamish sat down near the entrance and listened.

Yellow. Angle. Picture. Time. Short short short. Accident. Crawl. Yellow bright. Long point light. Speed. Now now. Tighter. Tight. Leave. Wait. Angle angle trajectory speed short longer. Ah. Where where? Good. So good.

Hamish left himself. Thousands of voices acted as one woven pulsing entity, and Hamish sang to it. He couldn't even tell what part of him did it. He felt like he was at the window of the most alluring woman in the world, and he was serenading her with songs of adventure and change. Change that must come, or all would be lost. Change that everyone would gather for, or no one would live. Change that was more important than staying at home tending the children and making honey. And for sweet sweet food.

They started coming out. There was anger in the voices, and power and generation. The queen took off and they balled around her, spinning in the air.

Hamish sang, *White like a nest. Long not so long. Sheltered yellow, not yellow. Eater and killer. White white movement moving slow. Warm, inside-of-nest warm. Eater and killer, eater of eggs. A promise of peace, from the Speaker. Through many many not so many some trees stop yellow not yellow white stop the white stop it. It.*

The swarm was amazingly fast and direct. Hamish ran to follow them. He saw Kuusk swatting away a couple of bees from his face, but then suddenly he was covered. He screamed through his hands, an awful sound like strangling and broken bones. Hamish could see Kuusk catch a glimpse of him through the bees before he turned to try signaling to his men, but the signal got lost in the flailing, and they were already on their way in any case. It was as though someone had dropped a living blanket over his head. Even hitting them, crushing legions of them to his scalp, had no effect. The red of the stings sprang out of buzzing fingers, and the little corpses of bees littered his clothes. He was swelling visibly, scraping in breath to scream and screaming out nothing but poisonous incapacity and furious surprise. His men kept their distance as his body squirmed on the floor of the gazebo, jerking in spasms of shock. The men looked at Hamish, then at each other, turned in opposite directions, and walked away as though they had appointments.

The bees circled up into the air. Their voices were exhausted and keening, a city after a war. They circled Hamish.

Speaker speaker speak no more. Speak no speak no speak no speak no more here or here or here or here. No directions, no more union, we am other where, nothing here, nothing here, nothing nothing nothing. The eggs must still be safe. Speak to somewhere else.

Hamish said, as best he could, *I promise.*

No. Just no more.

And he was ashamed.

Hamish climbed the stairs of the gazebo. The yellow paint of its low walls and its deco columns—the markers for the bees—contrasted with the gray of the floor, and last-year's leaves plastered around. Kuusk was still breathing, but barely. His puffed face was red, so blown up that his eyes were nearly closed. But Hamish could see the glint of an eyeball, and Kuusk's torso turned, one hand beginning to reach out. Hamish took a small step away. Kuusk tried to say something.

"What?" asked Hamish.

Barely whispered, "I'll kill you." This made Kuusk laugh, an ugly little shake of his neck.

"No," said Hamish, "you won't."

He took another step back, leaned against the half wall of the gazebo, and watched Kuusk die.

CHAPTER 45

It was Mr. White, Lily's father, who got Hamish out of questioning at the police station. It was nearly dinnertime. The police had arrived even as Kuusk took his last breath. Lilly had called the FBI, and eventually talked with Special Agent Thomas. They'd finally been able to put a phone tap on Sasha Imports, and after Hamish's call had put together some pieces. They'd ended up in the park, thinking they were going to watch an exchange. They were late.

Hamish was too stunned to move away or protest any innocence. Hamish had been bundled into the back of a police car in the park and made to stay there for almost two hours while other cops came, park rangers, the medical examiner's office with men in paper booties and purple plastic gloves. Hamish could see Kuusk's body loaded into an ambulance from a stretcher. A different cop would poke his head in every 15 minutes or so. Mostly they stood in a small circle with crossed arms, one telling a story and the others pretending to listen and laugh. Both agents Packer and Thomas arrived, sliding into the car with him. They asked him questions, but he just looked out the window at the gazebo, wondering where the bees had gone. A detective—Hamish knew he was a detective because he said so—came and took Hamish to a different car and they drove to the precinct office.

The cars smelled sour, the precinct office smelled sour and dirty with lemon cleaner misting through. The day never got more than iron colored, and lights were on, all of them feeling weakened by the sky sucking away the light. The detective steered Hamish by the elbow to a small room with a vinyl-covered table and a two-way mirror. After getting his mother's phone numbers, he told him to wait and he shut the door. Hamish needed to pee, and he felt vaguely nauseous, like he might be getting the flu, or he might have been hit over the head with a piece of wood. The overhead fluorescents were harsh, flickering just enough to annoy and disconcert. He had to knock on the door for a few minutes before someone came and let him use the bathroom, then bringing him back for interrogation. At least that's what Hamish thought it was, because the room had a little label on it saying that it was the interrogation room.

"How did you know Heigo Kuusk?" The detective had loosened his tie and taken off his jacket, putting it on the back of his chair. The buttons of his white shirt pulled at his shirtfront over his stomach as he sat. Packer and Thomas stood behind him.

"I. I don't know."

"You knew him, right?"

"Uh."

"The dead man. In the park. Where you were. You knew him."

"Yes."

"So what happened?"

"Excuse me?" Hamish couldn't believe the question, like someone asking why it was day.

"What happened?"

"Bees."

"He died because of bees?"

"He died because of bees."

Hamish started to cry. Not huge sobs, but a steady stream of tears and snot that would not stop, coming down his face and dripping off his chin. He didn't even lift a hand to wipe. He was too old for this, but he just breathed through his open mouth, and cried.

"Oh, kid. Shit. Kid, I'm sorry. I wasn't thinking. Damn. Let me get you something." He'd stood and was leaning across the table, putting his hand on Hamish's shoulder. The detective's sudden warmth made the tears come faster.

Packer stepped forward. "That's not how this works. That kid—" But Thomas put a restraining hand on his partner. Packer shrugged and left it.

"You a Britney Spears fan?" the detective almost snickered. He was holding the CD that they'd taken from Hamish when they searched him. It had a Britney Spears label on it.

"Look at it," said Hamish.

The detective shrugged. There was a laptop there, and the detective put the CD in and started to look.

"Ah, shit. Holy shit."

Packer smiled, "You kept a copy."

Kindly, the detective asked, "Kid, where did you get this? Where did you get all this?"

"There's one of Tony in there, you know," said Hamish quietly.

"Tony?" the detective was defensive.

"Tony Manzini. Number 244."

The detective got flummoxed as he looked for the TIFF file number. He opened it. The three men leaned in, and leaned back. Three different voices whispered, "Shit."

Packer tried to intervene but the detective brushed him away, saying, "We got some real skin in this game now. Stay the fuck away. This is one of ours. We have to play this absolutely right."

The detective moved to help Hamish up, but Hamish stopped him. He dug into his pocket and pulled out Helena's mother's address out in Coney Island. He gave it to the detective.

"Helena's sister. Her mother. Please. I promised."

"Taking care of it, kid, taking care of it. Promise."

The detective gently guided him through a small maze of halls and rooms till Hamish was face to face with Mr. White. Without pause, Hamish leaned against him, letting his cheek fall into Mr. White's shoulder. Mr. White held him until his breath slowed.

"Come," he said. "Your mom's going to meet us at home. Your home. She's had a hard time getting here, but she's on her way home." He looked at Hamish until Hamish looked back. "You OK to go home?"

Hamish nodded. Hamish could feel embarrassment leave him like an annoying leaf blower suddenly going quiet. He was with someone who was going to include him in the next decision. He was with someone who knew what he was doing.

∞

Sarah had been weeping, it was obvious, even though she put on a fresh face for Hamish as soon as he came through the door. She held him close and firm, but the car ride with Mr. White had shifted Hamish's allegiances, and Mr. White was now the one who was his advocate. He'd seen him be firm and authoritative at the police station, calmly weaving quickly through the suspicious bureaucracy and making genial promises that carried the weight of threats. He wouldn't let anyone talk with Hamish any more, and he declared himself responsible. He stated that "no one would want to see a child who'd been subjected to such a trauma abused in such a fashion by even well-intentioned officers of the law." Hamish thought he was brilliant.

Hamish pulled away from Sarah as Mr. White told her what had happened at the police station, and what he understood had happened. He was also clear about what was going to happen now. That Hamish would have to go answer questions about the evidence he'd given the detective and the FBI agents, and what he knew about Heigo Kuusk. It would have to be in the next two days; that was a deal Mr. White had made. And always, with police, have a lawyer.

"I will be with him if he wishes, but my law degree is rather dusty. I have a friend who would be interested in this case, a Mr. Adams."

"A rabbi?" asked Hamish.

"Yes, he's also a rabbi." Mr. White kept his surprise to himself. "How do you know him?"

"Chess," said Hamish weakly.

"Chess," repeated Mr. White. "You know, someday you should tell me about all this."

"Do I have to?"

"Hamish!" whispered Sarah.

"It would be a courtesy," said Mr. White. He sat on the coffee table in front of Hamish on the sofa. "And now you're going to tell me honestly if Lilly is in any more danger."

"No, not any more."

"You know this for sure?"

"Kuusk was the only danger left for any of us. And now that the police have that stuff...." Hamish drifted off, suddenly not sure of anything.

"Who else is there?" Mr. White leaned forward. Hamish realized he would do anything for this man.

"There was a cop who came here. He threatened to, like, hurt Mom and you and Mrs. White. There are some men I've seen, but never talked to. I know there's others who've kept the girls."

"The girls?" asked Sarah.

Mr. White filled her in, "It seems this man Kuusk ran a child prostitution organization."

"All kinds," said Hamish. "There's the one down the block. But I think they've left."

"Did you tell the police about that?"

"It's in the CD."

Mr. White turned to Sarah. "I think you two should spend the next couple of nights at our house. What do you think, Hamish? An awkward sleep-over?"

"Uh, I guess—"

Sarah interjected, "Paul, I don't think—"

"If they are going to do something, it will be now. We're better off together. At least tonight. Humor me."

∞

This was the moment Kaphiri Shenouda, leading me, rang the doorbell. He calmed everyone and made them feel full of purpose and protection. He introduced me, his voice spreading ease and good will like it always does.

"Hamish, this is Mr. Smith."

I know Hamish saw a small elderly man from Northern India with a gray beard and horn-rimmed glasses. I am always cold, so I wear a silk scarf. My hand was tiny in the boy's.

"You knew Alicia," said Hamish.

"For many years," I said. "One of the great people of the earth."

Paul White shook himself out of Shenouda's gentle grip. "Clearly, there is much going on that is not being said. But I think we need to get Hamish and his mother to someplace safe where they can rest."

"I couldn't agree more," I said. "And you and I must converse about your amazing daughter."

"What do you know about my daughter?"

"Only what I know from my friend here. But we suspect she is a young combination of a Keeper and a Witness. I will explain —"

Kaphiri, thankfully, interrupted me. I do tend to take over when I shouldn't. But I was able to take Hamish to the side when Kaphiri extended his farewells to the others. I was able to look him in his face, and I was able to witness for him.

"You have killed a human being. It is yours. It will not be taken away, but it will not define you. I see you, Hamish Taylor." I shook his hand. "You and I—our collaboration will begin."

∞

It was after late by they time they got to the White's. Mr. Shenouda and I left them to it. Mrs. White embraced each of them, and took everyone into the kitchen where there was tea. She gave a cup to Hamish and said to him, "Go find Lilly. I think she's in her room. I'm sure she wants to know you're OK."

Hamish went upstairs, balancing his tea and his heart. The poster on her door made a quiet cracking sound when he knocked. Lilly opened the door as though she'd been standing behind it. She'd been crying; her eyes glistened. She took his tea, put it down, and then held him, an embrace he returned fully, melting into her. She led him over to the bed where she lay him down and held his head on her chest. Her smell was so soft and green, deep as trees and quenching as easy spring rain. He was conscious that his cheek was on her breast, and it felt as honorable and sure as a promise. He thought he had never been safer. He fell asleep.

It was dark when he woke. He was by himself in Lilly's room, lying in his clothes, his shoes off, a coverlet over him. There was rustling at the window, and a pigeon saying defensively, *I'm here, got this covered, this one's mine, no need for anyone. I said I got it! I'm the one who's here. Stupid idiot, can't see I've got this...*"

Hamish opened the shade. There were four pigeons on the sill. He opened the window.

Speaker's here. Speaker's here.

Two pigeons took off into the trees outside the window, trees that had been growing on this block for the last hundred years until their branches nearly caressed the brownstones with old lovers' hands. On one of the branches directly outside the window sat an owl. Hamish realized with a shock it was the same owl he'd met the first night, after the squirrel cascaded out of the tree in the park and the world changed.

He spoke to the owl. *Am I a danger?*

Always, Speaker. Always.

Why are you here?

You are a danger that is good.

I don't understand.

Yes, you do. Otherwise, everyone wouldn't be here.

Hamish leaned further out the window. Dogs pattered around the sidewalks and the pale street, cats took up residence on cars and stoops, rats paused in the gutters and along railings, a raccoon held court on top of a garbage can. Every budding branch of every tree held a bird of some kind, most half asleep, and rocking gently. In the crux of a tree branch, Hamish saw Bagheera lounging, the sodium streetlight catching the tip of her tail flicking like a caterpillar metronome.

What are you doing? said Hamish. *You can't be here. It's not safe.*

It is where your female lives.

Yes. It felt enormously good admitting it, even if only to a panther.

Is she safe?

I think so.

Are you safe?

For now.

That is not what it smells like. It smells like you are calling all these creatures.

I'm not calling anybody.

It is the Speaker's call. Your call.

There was suddenly a river of dogs rushing left. They went charging up the street, to cries of *Is that one? You got him? I got him this side! Who the hell are you? What the hell are you doing here? I'll get him! Get out of here!!*

The hellhound barking made a few lights go on in houses, and some poor man headed back up the street the other way.

Bagheera said, *Ah, there is your man.*

Down on the street Hamish could see me walking. I often can't sleep, and I just wanted to check. The animals know to ignore me when necessary. I gave him a little salute and walked on into the night.

I'm going to take a look around, said Bagheera. *I know what they smell like.*

How do you know that? asked Hamish.

Their smell was on the one who didn't kill your female.

Hamish knew Bagheera meant Fallon. He wanted to thank her.

What do you say when someone does you a service?

Bagheera looked blank. *Nothing.*

But what do you do?

Another service. Bagheera licked her lip before descending. *Sometimes I wonder how you could be such a child.* She fell with a soft metallic thud to the top of a car, and then disappeared in shadow.

CODA

Sarah fingered her coffee cup. She hadn't gotten dressed yet because her shift didn't start for another three hours. She wasn't drinking her coffee.

"What, mom?"

"I thought maybe you and I could go, and. We could go and, maybe go to Hickory Run, you know. The falls." She still wasn't looking up.

"You want to go to Hawk Falls?" Hamish sat at the table.

"I thought we could take your father's ashes to Hawk Falls." Sarah looked up at her son, defensive and pleading.

Hamish took a long time. "That's a good idea. Just you and me?"

"Just you and me." Sarah smiled at her son, grateful. "And we can go into Plains for dinner at the Downs. Gabrielle said she'd treat us."

"Cool," said Hamish.

Gabrielle was the cook at the Rustic Kitchen, an Italian place at the casino attached to the racetrack where Henry had often looked after horses. She'd become a friend of the family when Henry had taken care of her fat old bulldog named Miss Piggy. About twice a year she would feed the family at her restaurant.

"Mom?"

"Hm?"

"There's one thing we got to do."

∞

Very early the next morning Sarah stopped the car in the cul-de-sac of Nethermead, down from the Quaker Graveyard. Hamish opened the back door, standing by it like a hotel doorman. A black panther glided to his side, then sniffed the door and the back seat. She looked at Hamish, and leaped lightly in as though steel weighed nothing at all. Sarah kept her expression as neutral as possible. When the car started, Bagheera braced herself as though in an earthquake. She derived no comfort from whatever Hamish was telling her.

The drive was two and a half hours of shedding skins, all the while feeling the raw new skin rubbing underneath, painful and eager for the open air. Bagheera licked air out the window, staving off the awful nightmare of carsickness. The box with Henry's ashes was in between Hamish's feet. As though as a courtesy, they didn't talk or play the radio. Sarah had made a conscious decision not to tell Henry's brother Colin about the ashes, or any of the other possible friends or relatives. They would explain it to Colin and Cammy when they saw them for Sunday dinner in a couple of weeks. Sarah had said laughing to Hamish that she didn't know how she'd explain it, but she could always pull out the "widow card."

Hamish had laughed along. "What's the 'widow card'?"

"No one questions the actions of a grieving widow. You can get away with murder." Sarah leaned back in the driver's seat to reach for her cardboard coffee cup with her right hand, straight-arming the steering wheel with her left.

Hamish was mischievous. "Are you getting away with murder?"

Sarah sipped her coffee. "No. Just grieving."

"Yeah," said Hamish. "Me, too."

"Yeah," she had toasted him with her coffee. "You, too."

They dove under the Hudson River in the Holland Tunnel, picked up I-80 heading west across New Jersey farmland. They passed signs for places like Waterloo Lakes and Shades of Death Road and Hope. The landscape shifted into the sudden valleys glaciers had carved ten thousand years previous, and the interstate shifted with it, narrowing along the Delaware River and then bridging the Gap. Hamish kept hoping Bagheera would sleep, but she didn't move from her panting position at the window.

Pennsylvania felt like the quiet after the white noise has been turned off. There were stupid, ugly signs just like everywhere, little strip malls and chain businesses offering the same offerings as everywhere else. But they were Hamish's old clothes: they fit pretty much and were comfortable. And finally they were off the interstate, speeding through the country, trees heavy with green on either side of the two-lane highway, glimpses of ponds or farms through clusters of vine-covered trunks and branches. The wind coming through the car window had numbed Hamish's forearm with its constant humid buffeting, and he leaned his head down on his arm and let the air play jet-engine backwash in his hair.

Sarah turned off the highway. It was an old blacktop road that eventually ended and went on as two ruts with grass between them. They bumped slowly, and Bagheera started going from one window to another, sensing she was about to get out of the moving cage.

Sarah came to a stop, and Hamish turned. *Same thing. You've got to stay away from people.*

I've learned, youngster.

Don't go too far, OK?

Let me out.

OK. Hamish was about to open his own door.

I won't be watching for you any more.

I know.

Hamish opened the door and as he stepped out, Bagheera slipped between the front seats and out, running straight into the trees, gone in seconds. Hamish felt he'd been hit. He couldn't get his breath right.

"Hey. Is that OK?" Sarah had no idea.

"It's gotta be." Hamish leaned on the door and looked at the empty forest.

"That was intense." Sarah's voice was small inside the car.

"It was OK." Hamish got back in the car and shut the door too hard. "Let's just go."

∞

Dinner passed like an airplane flight. It felt disembodied to be eating at the casino without his father, but he had shrimp scampi, as usual, and

Gabrielle came out in her whites, as usual, smiling and hugging. During dinner, Sarah told Hamish how glad she was they had come, just the two of them. Hamish told her, "Me, too." He was relieved when Gabrielle came and stole Sarah away to the bar for a few minutes. Hamish went towards the track to see the horses.

Ed, the man who knew Henry best, was overjoyed to see Hamish, and asked after his mother. A mare leaned her head out of her stall and looked at Hamish.

"Well, you look good. Grown," Ed said. "I didn't know what to do when my daddy passed."

What are you doing here? inquired the mare, a little nervous.

"Hey, man," said Ed. "Let me show you something. This just happened." He stood to lead Hamish down the line of stalls.

Hamish touched the mare's nose by way of saying, *You're wonderful.*

They stopped a few stalls down. A horse had just given birth. The foal had not yet stood, and was wet and confused as though she couldn't quite remember her cue. A vet wearing a headlamp sat on a stool and took off his gloves.

"Everyone's in good shape, Ed. You should give Mr. Reese a call and tell him. I'm just going to wait a second til she gets up." The vet tilted the stool back against the wall after a little nod to Hamish. The three of them watched the foal.

Hamish heard the mare. *Tell me I'm not seeing things.*

No, he said.

Whew. Because it's been a long day.

I can only imagine, said Hamish. *Congratulations. She's beautiful.*

She is, isn't she? The mare lowered her head and licked her daughter's body a couple of times. The mare hesitated. *You're here. Is something wrong?*

No. Nothing's wrong. In fact, it seems that everything's good.

The foal began to struggle to get her feet under her. Her hind end went up first, wobbling, and then she extended her front feet. She slanted precariously towards her mother, and then jiggled her legs a bit.

"She's up," said the vet.

She's up, said Hamish. *I wish you well.*

And you, Speaker. Bring sugar.

When I can.

Hamish said to Ed, "Thanks so much. I gotta go."

"That's pretty incredible, huh?" said Ed, nodding towards the newest horse in the world.

"You don't even know. Thanks."

"You take care of yourself. Give my regards to your mom."

When Hamish turned away, he saw that every horse in the stable had its head out the stall door, and the double line of horse heads watched Hamish as he walked the length of the hall.

∞

Next day mid-morning they parked by the side of the road in a turn-off that had a trailhead leading into the park. They put Henry's box in a backpack with their supplies, and Hamish shouldered it without asking whether he could. Hamish leading, they went down through thick rhododendrons, purple flowers exposing themselves like toddlers in dress-up. Hamish ignored birds as they had their arguments over trees, or notified each other of delicious stumps. He heard the yip of a coyote calling to his mate to get the kids, but he ignored that, too, plunging ahead with missionary zeal. Creek sounds came in and out of the groves as they hugged the hill down to Hawk Run. The footbridge made a hollow reverberation as they stepped onto it making it seem untethered to the earth. Winding through a last tunnel of perpetual rhododendrons, they came to the falls.

It was odd that no one was there on this spring day. The water was still cold from the rains of last night, and the woods were damp as the rocky leaf-molds released their morning moisture. The falls got louder as they approached. The water played clear-green and stone-colored away from the white bubbles at the base, jiggling the edges of the pool.

Hamish and his mother sat and watched the water cascading down twenty-five feet over broken cliffs, watching the rhythms of the falling columns as they widened and whitened and bounced and careened and disappeared into the foamy gathering of themselves. The sound seemed constant, but subtle bass tracks kept trying to emerge, or the sound of someone way down a hall dropping large wooden containers and hesitating and doing it again at intriguingly regular intervals. An occasional breeze would bring cool droplets across their faces, reminding them that what they were watching was real.

"Where do you think we should scatter the ashes?" asked Sarah, finally looking around.

Hamish looked, too. "How about there?" He pointed to where water spilled out of the pond. "It goes from there to the Atlantic Ocean."

Sarah smiled. "Good call. Henry would like that."

Because that's what he told me, thought Hamish. Henry had stood right at this spot, leaning on his aluminum cane, and told Hamish that every drop of water coming down Hawk Falls, if it didn't go into the sky, would some day end up in the Atlantic Ocean. Hamish thought then his father looked like he would like to follow that course, even as he turned to get back to his stale bed. And Hamish had hated him for wanting to leave.

Hamish opened the backpack and handed his mother the box. It was a black plastic box smaller than a shoebox. It had a printed label, and Hamish could see his father's name, "Taylor, Henry L.," and the date. The top, which Sarah removed, came off like Tupperware, and inside was a plastic bag with a twist-tie. Inside the bag was what was left of Hamish's father.

Hamish couldn't understand how, even burned, this was all that was left. It seemed so puny and unrelated, as though they had simply bought some ashes at a gardening center. What happened to his bones, his teeth, his heart? Even ground up, how could his spine fit in this black box? His skull alone was bigger than this, and his whole body couldn't fit inside his skull.

Sarah put the box on the ground and reached inside, pulling out a handful of gray and grainy stuff. Puffs of powder lifted out, glowing in the soft sun. She walked over to the small spillway over the rocks, where the clean water swelled to the next level down. She stood there, holding her husband in her hand. Hamish was surprised when she spoke.

"Henry, I made many mistakes in my life. You know that. But marrying you was not a mistake, and having Hamish with you was not a mistake, and celebrating life with you was never a mistake." She looked over to the white and noisy falls. "I want to thank you for being in my life, for being in Hamish's life, for living your life. I'm so mad at you I could just scream, for getting sick, for not getting well, for dying on us and leaving us to fend for ourselves. I'll get over it, but I'm still mad." She smiled to herself even as tears were coming down her cheeks. "I love you, and I wish you god-speed on your next journey." She let the ash pour out of her hand like salt into the water and watched the water take it away downstream. "Goodbye, Henry. Goodbye."

Sarah dusted off her hands and offered the box to Hamish.

"You want to say anything?"

Hamish was stumped. He didn't know what he had envisioned for this moment, but it wasn't this. His brain was empty. He knew something should happen now, but he had no idea what that was, if he was supposed to act, or someone was supposed to act on him.

Sarah put the box in his hands. "You can think about it. I've got to pee." She rinsed her hands of dust, and walked into the trees.

Hamish looked down into the stuff in the box. It was white and gray and black and some red-earth particles. He wondered if that was burned blood. He stirred it with a finger. Grit and sand and fine, fine dust. It seemed more like pulverized cement than something that's been through fire. He suddenly didn't want to be there, but back in Brooklyn on the roof looking out at the city. He didn't want this in his hands.

He looked up and there, about twenty feet away, was a large black bear who had just noticed him as well.

Damn, said the bear.

Damn, said Hamish.

The bear caught himself in the act of turning away and lifted himself up.

Hamish said, *I'm very sorry to be disturbing you. We will be gone soon.*

The bear sat and held his paws like a tired boxer. He sniffed the air.

There's another of you. A female.

My mother.

What are you hanging around with your mother for?

That brought a smile to Hamish's face. *It's different.*

The bear sniffed more, as though finding currents in the breezes. *What's that other smell, like burn but not?*

That's my father.

The bear put his paws on the ground. *I don't understand.*

Hamish felt his face flush. *I don't either.*

The bear looked around like an old man at a bus stop. Hamish waited respectfully.

Hunh. The bear licked his nose. *So you can understand everybody?*

I can understand what someone says.

Hunh. The bear looked around as though making sure he didn't get overheard. *Maybe you can tell me.*

What?

What are those birds saying?

Hamish listened. It was song birds, a number of different kinds, all proclaiming and grandstanding and finding and announcing. But one was doing something Hamish couldn't quite figure out. It sounded like *sky* and *wind* and *more*, but Hamish couldn't really make it out. He saw the culprit, a small bird on a tree limb down the creek. He called to it, *Hey, what are you saying?*

The tiny bird dipped through the air and landed on a bramble near Hamish. He had a little black mask and a yellow throat, and if Hamish had him in his hand and closed his fist, the bird would disappear without getting hurt.

Speaker! Perfect! This is perfect!

Hamish laughed. *This bear wants to know what you are saying. I want to know what you are saying.*

What I am saying? I'm singing! Wow, I thought you were supposed to know everything. Ha! It's an incredible day, we're all alive, no hunters around, plenty to eat. Oh! It feels so good! Sing it, Speaker! Sing it! The yellowthroat flew to Hamish's shoulder, loud and tuneful.

Hamish laughed more. *It does feel good.*

The bird disappeared from his shoulder, calling behind him, *I got to go tell everyone you're here!*

The bear shifted. *What's it saying?*

Hamish thought how to tell him. *He's playing. He's having a good time, and he's playing with life. He's drunk with honey and he's got to tell the world.*

The bear turned over a rock absently. *Such a little thing.* The bear came to attention, muscles moving differently. *Your mother. Fare well, Speaker.* The bear melted behind trees.

Sarah got back, her eyes clear. "You decided?"

"Yup." Hamish took out a handful of cinders and threw it downstream. "Goodbye, Dad!" The grit fell into the water and on the rocks, sounding like rain. The dust drifted away, sun stabbing it solid. Hamish threw another handful. "Goodbye, goodbye, goodbye! I love you I love you I love you! Flow freely down to the sea, just like you said you would. Come back and see us sometime!" He threw another handful.

Sarah took some more from the box in Hamish's hand and threw it. "Come back and see us sometime!"

They kept throwing until it was all gone.

"We love you we love you we love you."

"Come back and see us. Sometime."

Acknowledgments

How many people have contributed to this book in one way or another is beyond measure, from authors past to strangers I've met in parks.

Karen Karbo and the Writers of Renown, you saw me through the finish line, and I'm eternally grateful.

Natalie Serber and the Portland crowd, thank you for embracing me so quickly.

Martha Frankel and her group in Woodstock gave me incredibly valuable lessons.

I thank Jeffrey Davis and all the Tracking Wonder people, who saw me through early days.

To Arthur Goldwag for his unwavering confidence. I am blessed.

Rick Commandich, Will Nixon, Suzanne Kingsbury, Melea Seward, Steph Argy, and Alec Boehm—champions all. Thank you.

To Kai and Lucia, such gratitude for your patience and love and support.

And first and last, my wife, Megan. Thank you.

About the Author

Peter Wallace is the author of two novels and numerous short stories. As a theater director, he has directed and taught all over the country. He was Chair of the Theater Program of Eugene Lang College of New School University in New York for many years. He has also taught and directed at a number of other universities and theater schools, such as Princeton, Yale, and Trinity Rep. Through the Institute of Writing and Thinking, he taught writing practices in Myanmar, Turkey, and Russia, and has also been on the Language and Thinking faculty at Bard. He has written and sold screenplays, written and produced plays. He got his MFA in Directing at Yale School of Drama. He has been a fisherman, a motorcycle bum, a profligate interfaith minister, a sculptor and a bodywork therapist. He now lives in the Pacific Northwest, writing and teaching.

CPSIA information can be obtained
at www.ICGtesting.com
Printed in the USA
FSHW021716061220
76517FS